98.2

HENLEY J. ALEXANDRE

This is a work of fiction. Names, characters, businesses, places, events, locales, and incidents are either the products of the author's imagination or used in a fictitious manner.

ISBN (Print): 978-1-09835-193-9
ISBN (eBook): 978-1-09835-194-6

For all those affected by the COVID-19 pandemic, an event that will undoubtedly shape the way that we treat each other, consider the poor and excluded, and exist in the world.

Special thanks to my dear friend, Elizabeth Nigro, without whom I would have never had the courage to put pen to paper, and to my friends Jordan Conerty, Becky McGrath, and Marina Templin for helping guide this process.

CONTENTS

YEAR ELEVEN

"98.2," declared a calm, robotic voice as the scanners passed over her body. Emily looked up at the room's corner speaker, awaiting further confirmation. "Vitals normal," the voice stated in the same monotonous tone that Emily had grown accustomed to over the years. The light above the doorway changed from blue to green, and the glass doors slid open in front of her. Her ears popped as the bodily sensation of altered air pressure washed over her. Emily stepped out of the entrance examination scanner and walked into the foyer of Walter Reed High School.

She paused for a moment to stare beyond the rows of wash stations and down the long white corridor, sparse with the students who had been granted in-school permissions for the new year.

Year 11, she thought, *Here. We. Go.*

She took a deep breath and peeled off her raincoat, a common ritual for someone who had grown up in the Pacific Northwest. Eden, Washington, was a middle-sized city with roughly twenty thousand residents. Mostly families, the city was divided into eighty different housing clusters across forty square miles. Eden had a similar feel to Seattle, but it was less densely populated. Eden wasn't a shipping hub or a major trade port. It was known mostly for its professional athletics and its ties to the digital education industry. In Eden, you were either trying to make it as a professional gamer or you worked for EduView, a digital learning platform that focused on home and remote education.

Slinging her raincoat over her arm, Emily turned left and walked toward a wash station labeled, "Station E6," just as she had during Years 9 and 10. While she wasn't assigned to any individual station, every student had their tendencies, and Emily embraced consistency and the practice of a routine. Her in-school ritual always began with a sharp left turn coming out of the entrance examination scanner and a quick, fifteen-step march to Station E6 in the left-side wash bank.

Emily kept her head down as she passed the two in-school officers standing in the foyer. Above them, a large painting of the city crest towered over the entryway. A green shield, adorned with filigree, hung over the students as they passed into school premises. She glanced ahead and made eye contact with her best friend, Fae Dotterman, whose lips turned up as she waved excitedly in salutation. Just as Emily could be found marching toward Station E6, Fae's routine was a right turn out of the scanner and a predictable march toward Station E13. Every week, the same.

An awkward sort of girl, Fae was taller and lankier than her peers with a stride that often made her look unbalanced. Her high-waisted jeans accentuated her length as her long strides led her across the entryway. Brown, frizzy hair, left even curlier by the rain, draped down her back, as she turned away from Emily and stepped into her wash station.

Fae was known around school for her contagious smile and her penchant for word play. She was an entertainer above all things and often embraced the spotlight, leaning in with all her quirk and charm. Emily had known Fae her entire life. Their parents had moved into the same housing cluster, and their families had remained close as their children had gotten older. In many ways, Emily looked up to Fae. Fae was always unapologetically herself; a courage and attitude

Emily often longed to emulate—except for those times when Fae found herself getting into trouble.

Emily stepped into Station E6 and kicked the rainwater off of her boots. She opened her tablet bag and removed the bright-blue wallet that her mother had given her the previous day.

"Your favorite color!" her mother had exclaimed, as Emily peeled open the vacuum seal wrapped around the gift. "I thought it would be a nice way to start Year 11."

"Thanks, Mom. It's beautiful." Emily had replied.

"The actions of one...," her mother invited.

"Carry the safety of us all," Emily replied cheerfully, as her mother joined in unison.

Emily looked down at the gift in her hand and smiled. She removed her ID card and placed the wallet gently on the station table next to a cylindrical tube that ran into the ground. She held her ID card beneath the station's barcode reader and the same monotonous voice from the entrance examination scanner called out, "Emily Chang, Year 11. Welcome to Walter Reed High School." A rush of air and the sharp whoosh of the cylinder brought her assigned day-kit up the cylindrical tube. Emily reached into the tube and took her day-kit in hand. Her eyes opened wide as she opened the day-kit and removed its contents.

Green. Of course I got green. Emily thought as she examined her shoe slips and the day-kit essentials.

While most of the shoe slips at Walter Reed were a standard-issue white, a limited collection of bright-green slips had remained in circulation from a previous year. The school had a brief moment back in 2069 where they thought that they could raise school spirit by issuing all-green day-kits. Green wipes, green hand sanitizer, and, of course, green shoe slips. After many complaints, most of the green day-kits had been recycled or repurposed. But, every so often, an unlucky student found themselves wearing a remnant from the all-green era of Walter Reed High School on their feet. A less-than-ideal way to start Year 11, Emily exhaled audibly and shook her head in disbelief as she pulled the shoe slips over her still-wet rain boots.

Turning toward the station sink, she washed her hands as the machine displayed a bright-red timer that counted down from twenty. The rush of water welcomed Emily back to in-school, as her excitement rose. She was back for another year. Emily hummed along with the soft, elevator-style melodies that accompanied the countdown. Upon the melody's completion, she exited Station E6 and caught up with Fae who was now standing with a group of students outside the wash bank area.

"Em!" Fae called out excitedly. "How was your winter season? Everyone stay fit?"

"Winter was good!" Emily exclaimed. "The Chang household was proper fit, no issues! What about you guys?"

"Not too bad," Fae explained, "Dad caught a seasonal, but he was only in isolation for eight days. Nothing too serious...."

Fae's eyes traced the nervous look on Emily's face and she slowly looked down toward the floor, halting abruptly upon reaching Emily's feet and bright-green shoe slips.

"Oh dear. Green, huh?" Fae remarked with a kind, apologetic half-smile.

"Don't get me started," Emily spouted in frustration, as she rolled her eyes. "Where is your first class?"

Fae pulled back the tan fold on her tablet bag, revealing her day-kit and small chrome tablet. She took the tablet in hand and began swiping between windows on an already open web browser. Arriving at a scheduling app, she announced, "Haystead's Reading

Comp, Room 223. What about you?"

"Same!" Emily chirped quickly, breathing a sigh of relief.

Emily had memorized her schedule the week before in preparation for Year 11. Fae and the other girls often teased Emily for her meticulous nature, but Emily didn't know any other way to exist in the world. She was a meticulous sort of person. Seeking a redemptive quality to the bright-green hue that had colored the beginning of her morning, Emily was grateful to have a friend in the first class with her. The girls waved goodbye to the group of students, and began their walk down to Professor Haystead's classroom.

Hyper aware of her appearance and the echo of snickers that followed her bright-green shoe slips down the hallway, Emily lowered her gaze and clutched her tablet bag tightly to her chest. Tensing up, she turned to her friend and whispered, "Urrgh, why do they have to stare? I hate Year 11 already."

"Don't worry, Emily. Everything will be fine," Fae exclaimed matter-of-factly, now displaying a sly, mischievous grin.

"NO. DON'T DO IT!" pleaded Emily in anticipation of Fae's theatrics.

Inhaling deeply, Fae proceeded to belt the lyrics of their favorite pop song at the top of her lungs. The ruckus could be heard the entire length of the hallway. Everyone looked up to observe the grand performance, as Fae sang, skipped, and danced across the tile flooring. She sang louder and louder as the two continued toward Professor Haystead's classroom. Laughter and applause thundered, as students took out their tablets and began to take pictures and videos of the display.

Emily buried her face in her elbow, bright red from embarrassment. All the while, she was quietly grateful for Fae having, once again, proved to be unapologetically herself. Amidst the circus of it all no one seemed to notice the color of Emily's shoe slips and, in that moment, Emily ceased to care.

"Ms. Dotterman!" a booming voice said sternly behind them, "That is quite enough of that."

Turning abruptly to locate the source of the admonishing voice, the two girls looked up at a towering figure of a woman dressed in a black dress and a medical white coat. Emily and Fae shank back into their spines and cowered at the looming and intimidating presence of the woman. Her high ponytail, strong cheekbones, and thick-framed glasses hinted at a carefully curated aesthetic that demanded their attention and respect. The medical white coat that hung neatly over her broad shoulders displayed prominently, "E. Blackwell, M.D., Ph.D."

"Dean Blackwell!" Fae managed to sputter, "Apologies. We're just very excited to be back at Walter Reed."

The woman looked down at the girls in displeasure. "Recall, Ms. Dotterman, that this space is for education and there is little room for your mischief and disruptions." she said sharply. Dean Blackwell confidently continued, standing up straight and looking down the bright white hallway, "The actions of one."

"Carry the safety of us all. Yes, Dean Blackwell," the girls acknowledged apologetically.

Dean Blackwell marched away in the other direction as Emily and Fae slowly turned to look at one another. As their disciplinarian quickly moved out of earshot, they performed a poor, high-pitched imitation of Dean Blackwell's voice, waving their fingers mockingly, "Ms. Dotterman, Ms. Dotterman. That is Quite. Enough. Of That."

The girls chuckled as they continued down the hallway and entered Room 223. Emily glanced around the room, frantically searching for her assigned learning booth. The booths, fixed heavily to the floor in rows, stood five and a half feet tall with tinted glass paneling on all sides. She stood on her tiptoes to get a better look at the second and third rows, craning her neck and searching for a booth displaying her last name and identification number on its external monitor.

"I'll see you after class!" Fae said, as she located her booth in the back corner and darted off in its direction.

Emily nodded, quietly envying Fae's height, and continued to scan the room.

Chang - 662123, she read on a digital display near the middle of the room. Stepping around the first row of booths, she quickly made her way to her assigned seat. She entered the booth, pulled her day-kit out of her tablet bag, and removed two sanitary wipes from the pack. She began to wipe down her chair, desk, the tinted side and front panels, and her tablet. She discarded the wipes in the empty disposal bin outside her booth and settled attentively into her seat, tablet in hand. Emily turned on the device and placed it in the tablet stand affixed to the desk in front of her. Immediately, a timer appeared on the tablet screen that counted down to the start of class.

1:26, 1:25, 1:24, 1:23 ....

Emily looked around the room to identify her peers. The tinted side and front panels on the booths obscured the views of the students' faces, but certain features could still be made out through the glass.

Sandy-blond hair, glasses, red tablet bag, she noted, as she identified her friend Patrice in the back of the room. Going booth to booth, Emily silently named the remaining members of her first class until she came to the front row. Her eyes drifted to a patch of dark hair in front of her. Seeing only the back of his head, Emily failed to identify the boy seated in the booth in front of her.

Who is that? She wondered, noticing a battered, black tablet bag resting neatly on his desk.

As the display timer reached 0:00, a window appeared in the middle of Emily's tablet screen. A young man, nearing thirty, was sitting casually at a white desk with a stack of actual, bound books resting prominently to his right.

Books? Emily thought. *How curious.*

The dated nature of his cravat and glasses were too reminiscent of a lost era. He looked like a character out of an old movie. The man straightened his cravat and cleared his throat.

"Good morning, students," he announced with gusto.

"Good morning, Professor." Emily replied loudly, accompanied by her peers.

The man continued, "I hope you all had an enjoyable and healthy winter season. My name is Jamie Haystead, and I will be your Year 11 Reading Comprehension instructor. As many of you know, our primary concern for this year is your Aptitude Exams. These exams will undoubtedly shape your future in important ways, but we will have time to discuss those. For now, please open link seven and ...." Professor Haystead paused for a moment and scanned the tablet in the middle of his desk, looking to cold call an unfamiliar name on the attendance sheet. He continued, "... Mr. McDaniels, can you please diagram the third sentence for the class."

The dark-haired boy in front of Emily responded dismissively, "Yeah, sure."

Emily's eyes opened wide, gawking at the tone of disinterest in the boy's voice.

"Excuse me, Mr. McDaniels. Would you mind speaking up?" Professor Haystead called back.

"Yes, sir. I would love to diagram the sentence," the boy

said, sarcastically.

Several students stifled their laughter. Emily looked down at her tablet as the boy began to diagram the sentence, his edits appearing on everyone's devices in the room in real time. She watched carefully, as the red markings circled the different parts of speech and drew lines between the related clauses. The boy executed the task to perfection, completing the effort by drawing a big red smiley face in the tablet margin.

"Very good, Mr. McDaniels. Perhaps without the attitude next time," Professor Haystead said approvingly, as if the boy had earned their instructor's respect. The boy slouched back into his chair and began spinning his tablet pen around his thumb.

"As Mr. McDaniels so eloquently demonstrated, diagramming sentences quickly will be essential to moving on in this class. While the exercise may seem rudimentary, the fundamentals of reading comprehension rely on understanding how the different parts of speech are working together in any given sentence ...."

As Professor Haystead continued his introductory lecture, Emily's mind fixated on their upcoming Aptitude Exams. For most students, Year 11 began the Age of Responsibility. Upon turning sixteen, young people were called on to take on a more active role in the community and perform essential tasks for familial obligations. Not only did this grant them certain communal permissions and extended freedom of mobility, but it was also the year that their Aptitude Exams would organize them into career categories. Based on your highest scored categories and the community's needs, you would be set on a career trajectory for Year 12.

"Studying for these exams will be the most important part of Year 11," her father had explained. "As much as our personal and romantic lives are decided by our housing clusters, our professional lives are largely determined by the Aptitude Exams in Years 11 and 12. Trust the aptitude process and do your best. They're nothing to worry about, but they aren't to be taken lightly either."

She replayed her father's words in her head repeatedly until the end-of-class tone chimed. Staring blankly at the front of her booth, anxiety began to swell in her chest as she imagined the variety of career paths that her future might hold. Emily lost herself to her imagination and worry as Professor Haystead carried on about reading strategies and sentence structure. At the sound of the chime, Emily began to gather her things.

"Remember to examine the worksite at home and complete Reading Exercises 1.1 through 2.6 for next week," shouted Professor Haystead as the students packed away their tablets. "Focus on diagramming the sentences, and call Mr. McDaniels if you're having any trouble! I'll see you all for in-school again next week!"

Exercises 1.1 to 2.6 in a single week!? Looks like I'm locking myself in my room, Emily thought.

Emily exhaled audibly as she stood up, pulling two more disinfecting wipes from her day-kit. She wiped down her booth slowly and methodically, in the same fashion and order of operations as when she had arrived. Chair. Desk. Tinted front and side panels. Tablet.

Holding the now-dirty wipes in her hand, she scanned the back corner of the room for Fae. Her eyes honed in on the mess of frizzy brown hair rising above the paneling of a back-corner booth. Placing her day-kit and tablet back in her tablet bag, Emily turned to discard her used wipes in the disposal bin. She lofted them from a short distance and smiled proudly as the wipes fell neatly into their intended destination. She pulled her tablet bag over her shoulder in satisfaction and strode to meet Fae at the door.

A voice called out from behind her, "Kobe."

"Excuse me?" she asked, turning toward the source of the unfamiliar word. It came from the patch of dark hair at the front of the room—Mr. McDaniels.

Emily examined the boy, now standing before her, more closely. She followed the waves of his messy-neat, dark hair down to the contours of his face. His facial features were oddly familiar, but she couldn't place it. Soft brown freckles spread neatly under his eyes, fading as they stretched toward his mouth. His dark-wash, denim button-down lay wrinkled over a tight black T-shirt. He stood at roughly Emily's height with a thin frame and a long torso. Focusing on the familiarity of his face, Emily stared at him intensely.

"Kobe," he repeated in the same calm tone. Displaying a casual smile as he shifted his weight and leaned against the booth.

"I heard you," Emily responded. "What is a Kobe?"

With a quiet chuckle, the boy explained, "I'm sorry, it's an old saying for when you throw something away. The wipes ... you threw them in the bin."

"Oh." She replied. "Thanks. I've never heard that .... Have we met before?"

"No, I'm Cayden," he explained as he started toward the door. "The new kid, I suppose. Maybe I'll see you around though."

The boy waved over his shoulder as he strode away from her. Emily fixated on the perplexing familiarity of his face as her eyes followed him out the door. Furling her brow, she racked her brain for a previous encounter or meeting that they had had. As she stood puzzled, nothing came to mind.

"You okay?" Fae approached. "You look like someone just tried to touch your face."

Emily shook her head from side to side, freeing her mind from its fixation. "Yeah, sorry," she explained, "I just had a weird interaction with the guy in the booth in front of me."

"Mr. McDaniels? Weird how?" Fae inquired with a suspicious tone.

"Oh, it was nothing. Never mind. He said 'Kobe'. Do you know what that is?" Emily asked.

Fae shrugged her shoulders and changed the subject. The girls reviewed their schedules and went their separate ways for their second classes. The rest of the day went by as most first days do. New booths, new professors, new homework. Emily welcomed all of the usual things. She was happy to be back at Walter Reed High School and was already excited to return the following week.

But, as the day carried on, Emily had difficulty shaking the sense of familiarity that washed over her during her encounter with Cayden. Between that and the added pressure of Year 11's Aptitude Exams, Emily struggled to focus through the rest of her classes. Emily was usually so attentive and focused. Something was off about the first day of Year 11.

Nerves, she thought. *It's just nerves.*

As the exit tone chimed for the Year 11 students at 14:00, Emily headed toward the departure examination area on the opposite side of school. As she wandered through the hallways, she tried to shake off the stress of the school day and began to plan her evening walk home. Monday walks were particularly special to Emily's family and even more so now that she had entered the Age of Responsibility.

As Emily planned her evening responsibilities on her way to the departure examination area, she spotted Fae and their friend Marshall walking up ahead of her. She lengthened her pace and stride to catch up with them. At sixteen years old, 6'6" Marshall was hard to miss. Few students at Walter Reed shared Marshall's athletic build and even fewer his height.

"Marshall Kunitz! I swear, you get bigger every time I see you!" called out Emily, as she caught up to the group from the rear.

Emily looked up at Marshall's broad shoulders in awe. He had grown so much over their winter break. His family was one of the few in their housing cluster that could afford a complete, home gym, and he often talked about the luxuries of having a second space in their housing unit dedicated to their family's fitness. Emily's family boasted a stationary bike and treadmill, but the communal nature of weightlifting and group workouts in Marshall's family always made Emily uneasy. Everyone touching everything, sweating everywhere.

Startled by the abruptness of her approach, Marshall jumped at the sound of his name. He turned, raising his hands wide in an attack-pose, and replied, "You be careful, Em! You keep sneaking up on me like that and I'm going to have to start picking you up in these hallways."

"You wouldn't dare!" Emily replied, as she and Fae evaded Marshall's faux lunges. Taunting their playmate, Fae made inviting gestures in his direction as if to say, *Come and get me!*

Laughing, the three of them pranced playfully around the hallways as they proceeded toward the departure area. With each faux lunge, Marshall inched closer and closer to the girls, sometimes coming within a foot's length of physical contact. As the game continued down the hallway, the departure scanners came into view. Emily straightened her posture as they grew closer, and abandoned the playful banter as Marshall lunged for her one last time. A thunderous voice brought the group to an immediate halt, and a rush of nervous energy came over them.

"Four feet!" shouted an in-school officer at the group, having witnessed Marshall's final lunge.

Gripping his rifle tightly, the officer took three large, booming steps toward the group. The bulk of his all-white body armor and dark-gray facemask added heft to his already intimidating presence. With each boot step, the ground seemed to shake more intensely than the one that came before it. The officer brought himself to a stop with a final stomp of his boot, just in front of the group.

A still fear fell swiftly over the group. Their game was over just as quickly as it had begun. Marshall and Emily froze in place, as they had been instructed to do by their parents so many times before. Now statues, they exchanged sideways glances without moving their heads as if to express a concern for and solidarity with one another. Fae stood quietly to the side, as the officer seemed to be addressing only Emily and Marshall.

Both Emily and Marshall had been stopped by officers before, but no amount of exposure normalizes the paralyzing feeling of an officer's gaze and interest, especially in a public context like school. There are some things, for certain people, that never quite feel normal.

Fae spoke up on behalf of her friends, leveraging the officer's apparent lack of interest in her, "I'm sorry, sir. We were just playing around. Marshall wasn't actually going to break distancing."

The officer slowly directed his eyes at Fae, and she took a step back, retreating behind her words. She knew better than to address an officer directly. Officers were an untouchable force and to question them required a great deal of privilege and confidence. Protecting and serving the health and wellness of the community, the officers answered to The Council alone. Fae's words carried little weight in this moment.

The officer returned his attention to Emily and Marshall. "This isn't a game," he lectured them. "In-school is a privilege, not a right. Now head toward departure and maintain your distance."

Loosening his grip on his rifle, the liaison officer gestured toward the placard on the wall with his gun. Their eyes followed the length of the rifle barrel across the room and up the wall.

The group read the bold writing on the placard aloud in unison, "The actions of one carry the safety of us all."

Upon hearing their recitation, the officer strutted confidently back to his post. He performed an about-face and stared back at Emily, Fae, and Marshall. He nodded his head in the direction of the departure area and repositioned his rifle neatly across the front of his bulletproof vest.

The group sauntered off in a quiet shame, still shaken from the encounter. As they entered the departure area, Fae broke the bleak silence that had come over them. She forced a cheery smile and exclaimed, "Wash up, friends! I'll see you guys for the walk home!"

Following her lead, Marshall replied cheerfully, "Sounds good! I've got to be home by 15:30 though. The Vax are streaming live tonight and my mom wants to tune in and relive her glory days—3 v. 3, no respawns, best of 7. 'The real stuff,' as she calls it."

"I didn't know your mom used to be a professional gamer!" replied Fae, as Marshall nodded in confirmation. "That's so fit!"

"She ran point for the 2055 team that lost in the semifinals," Marshall explained. "That's how she met my dad. He was an engineer doing server maintenance during the playoffs."

Emily's mind began to drift. She didn't care for the International Gaming League or for the celebrity of professional gaming. Growing up, her family didn't make a ritual out of watching streams or playing online against their friends in recreational leagues. Her mother was a quiet fan, but she only watched on late nights after everyone had gone to sleep and she was up working. It was an obsession that didn't really appeal to Emily, despite her having grown up in such close proximity to the industry.

"Sorry guys! I'm walking the other direction tonight," explained Emily. "Monday is our pharmacy day. I'm going to see Doc Abrams on my way home to pick up our ...."

"That guy is so creepy." Fae interrupted. "He's always wheezing all over everything and his voice is so raspy."

Marshall turned to Emily, "Are you sixteen already, Em? Welcome to the Age of Responsibility! Where 'freedom of mobility' really just means running errands for everyone .... Abrams is cool though. I heard he's a survivor."

Although Emily had never met the man, few people spoke well of Doc Abrams. He had a mysterious reputation, like most of the survivors in the community. There were so few survivors left that they existed as either myth or legend, and very rarely did any of them talk about the past. Emily nervously dreaded her trip to the pharmacy. Once a member of the community reached the Age of Responsibility, they were tasked with their family's weekly trips to the grocer and pharmacy. Young people were encouraged to learn basic pharmacology during this time and to ask questions, but this would require her to talk to Doc Abrams.

"You guys have fun walking without me! I'll see you on Vid later!" said Emily as she darted toward the wash bank. She waltzed into Station D6 and placed her ID card once again under the machine's barcode reader.

"Emily Chang, Year 11," announced the familiar monotonous voice. "Please proceed with your departure routine."

Emily removed her shoe slips hastily and placed them in her day-kit. She placed the day-kit back in the cylindrical tube from whence it came and waved her hand over the motion sensor. With a rush, the day-kit shot down the tube to be washed, sanitized, and put back into rotation for the following week. Emily said a quiet prayer that next week would bring a standard-issue pair of shoe slips and not those hideous green things. The sink displayed a bright-red timer that counted down from twenty as Emily thoroughly washed her hands and wrists. With another wave of Emily's hand over the motion sensor, a new, thirty-second countdown began, and she washed her face to close out her day.

Emily sighed deeply when the timer hit zero. With water still dripping down her cheeks, she spoke softly to the machine, "Reverse camera, please." A camera lens slid open above the monitor and Emily's reflection appeared on display. She stared deeply into the mirror image, tracing the outline of her face and cheekbones.

You're fine. You look like you and that means you exist differently in the world. Emily thought to herself, as she replayed the encounter with the in-school officer in her head.

She dried her face delicately with a paper towel. The machine timed out and the screen went dark. With a sigh, Emily discarded the paper towel in the bin. She pulled her tablet bag over her shoulder and stepped out of Station D6 and into the departure area.

Across the way, in the other wash bank, Cayden McDaniels emerged from Station D16, still looking down and packing up his tablet bag. Emily stared through the array of students scattered through the foyer, in the hopes of getting a closer look at his face. The familiarity still lingered. She repositioned her gaze in order to look beyond a gathering of students standing near the queue. Leaning to her left, Emily maneuvered around a tallish, red-haired girl to improve her view point.

Cayden was next in line for the departure scanner and stepped up for his turn. At that moment, his dark hair swung in her direction. He looked over his shoulder and his eyes rose to meet Emily's curious gaze. Cayden smiled and chuckled, having caught Emily leaning awkwardly around the group to watch him from afar. He turned back and stepped into the departure scanner, casually pulling his tablet bag over his head as he disappeared from view.

Embarrassed, Emily walked toward the departure scanner in disbelief and waited patiently for her turn to leave. Fae stood nearby in a separate queue and waved to gain Emily's attention. Having witnessed Emily's exchange with Cayden, Fae raised her eyebrows accusingly in Emily's direction. Without words, Emily knew that look.

"He looks familiar, that's all!" Emily called out; a bright-red coloring having overtaken her face.

"Whatever you say, Em!" Fae taunted, nodding toward Emily and indicating that it was her turn to use the departure scanner.

Scoffing, Emily turned and stepped up into the scanner. She waved back to her friend as the doors closed behind her and she felt the air pressure change again. Centering herself in the room, the scanner passed over Emily's body as she silently reflected on her long, first day of Year 11. So much the same, so much different.

The monotonous voice announced, "98.2. Vitals normal."

The blue light turned to green and the doors slid open in front of her. She took a long, deep breath of fresh air and, stepping out of the scanner, felt the warmth of the sun rush over her. She turned her face toward the sky to feel its embrace even deeper, spreading her arms wide as its warm comfort melted away the stresses of her day. Emily lowered her gaze to the sidewalk and pulled a light-blue facemask over her nose and mouth, tucking its straps behind her ears.

She spoke softly into the mask as she took her first steps down the sidewalk, "Year 11. Here. We. Go."

VIRAL

"**98.2, The Remedy,**" announced a sultry smooth, charismatic voice. "Coming at you with the top eight at eight, every morning."

A loud, rhythmic flow erupted from the car speakers, as the latest hip-hop sensation was being featured prominently in the morning radio's top eight songs. The driver-side door made a clicking sound as the low tones of the bass vibrations shook the car. Sam reached out with his long, narrow fingers, quickly turning the volume down as the passenger-side door swung open.

"Sorry, Mouse," he apologized. "I was really jamming out before I picked you up."

Mouse, a broad-shouldered boy dressed in a navy tracksuit stepped into the car through the passenger door. He adjusted his backwards cap and settled into the passenger seat. "No worries," he replied.

Mouse casually tossed his lacrosse stick and a loosely packed duffle bag in the back seat. The words, "St. Agatha University," were stitched prominently across the middle of the bag's front zipper pocket. The writing sat above the university coat of arms—two serpents set back to back on a filigree shield. Mouse buckled his seatbelt and toyed with a rubber lacrosse ball, rolling it around his palm with a comfort and ease only developed through years of playing the game.

Turning to Sam, Mouse asked suspiciously, "Does anyone even listen to the radio anymore?"

Mouse's coarse hands reached for the auxiliary cord beneath the dashboard. He took his phone casually in hand and, adjusting the sleeves of his tracksuit, plugged it into the car speakers. He quickly changed the music and sang along to a dated pop song as Sam's white sedan pulled out of the long driveway and started south down Wisconsin Avenue.

After driving for a few blocks, Sam leaned back and stretched his arm over the center console, resting it neatly on the shoulder of the passenger seat.

His hair is getting long, Sam thought to himself as he twisted a lock of Mouse's flowing, blonde hair around his finger.

Mouse smiled softly and his cheeks rounded under his eyes. Sam's eyes set on the sun-kissed freckles that usually only graced Mouse's face during the summer. "You look tan," he said softly.

Mouse had just returned from a holiday trip to the Bahamas with his parents. An only child, it wasn't unusual for Mouse's parents to dote on him with extravagance. He reached up and took Sam's hand in his own, settling their interlocking fingers gently on the center console.

"So, are you ready to go back?" Mouse asked, staring downhill as they crossed the border from Maryland into Washington, D.C.

"Absolutely!" Sam replied excitedly. "Just one more semester until graduation. St. Agatha University Class of 2020 and then right back here for med school!"

Releasing Mouse's hand, Sam slapped the blue St. Agatha University lanyard hanging prominently from the car's rearview mirror. A proud grin came across Sam's face as he reflected on his acceptance to St. Agatha's Medical School. He had been working toward this for his entire life. He originally applied to St. Agatha because of its distinguished Pre-Med Biology program, but he never thought it would be possible for him to stay there for graduate school. While he was open to a number of possibilities, it was no secret that St. Agatha was his top choice.

"Sounds like you've got it all figured out, then," Mouse replied, tapping his fingers on the dashboard, drumming along with the music. "You might just end up being a D.C. lifer."

Sam rolled his eyes and shook his head, dismissing Mouse's snarky comment. They both knew it was Sam's plan to return to Seattle after graduation. Mouse picked up Sam's half-full, iced coffee sitting in the cupholder between them. He took a large sip and casually slapped the St. Agatha University lanyard, sharing in Sam's pride and excitement for the coming graduation ceremonies and the start of medical school.

As they drew nearer to campus, the car came to a slow crawl. Masses of navy-clad, university students crossed the street in front of them. A freshman girl, wearing a St. Agatha sweatshirt, jumped playfully on the back of the boy in front of her. The boy stumbled across the street, spilling his coffee in laughter as the girl rode him along the crosswalk. The familiar sets of row houses and coffee shops were overflowing with students. Long queues and crowds of people lined the sidewalks of the St. Agatha University neighborhood, meaning one thing. School was back.

Students from all over the world came to St. Agatha. The university boasted top-tier academics and historically competitive athletics, known specifically for its lacrosse program. As the students all returned from their winter break, they joyously greeted and embraced one another throughout the neighborhood. The university brochures all read, "Family and Faith in Community."

This hardly ever felt like a homecoming for Mouse. Having grown up in Bethesda, Maryland, the university was a stone's throw away from his parents' house. He had lived up the street from St. Agatha his entire life. Going home for winter break had been as simple as driving over to the grocery store.

Mouse was well-traveled, as his family came from old East Coast money. But, beyond his affinity for designer clothes and his prowess on the lacrosse field, you would have never known of his affluent background. There was a quiet, humble charisma about Mouse that was hard to describe. Everyone on campus knew who he was. Everyone liked him well enough; however, it would be difficult to say that he had any close friends outside of the lacrosse team. Other than the time he spent with Sam's group of friends, Mouse mostly kept to himself. When he wasn't on the practice field or in the gym, Mouse spent most of his time drawing in the library.

As they pulled up to campus, Sam weaved his car between the careless wanderings of the returning students and parallel parked, semi-successfully, near the front gates. He unbuckled his seatbelt and grabbed his iced coffee from the cup holder. He stepped out of the car carefully, his long, skinny legs finding their footing as he slowly stood up awkwardly from the driver seat.

Sam was quietly self-conscious about his car. It was a gift from his parents, given to him for his sixteenth birthday. He recalled standing, blindfolded, in the summer heat of his parent's driveway back in Seattle. Sweating with anticipation, he anxiously awaited permission to remove the blindfold and restore his sight. As he pulled the covering down, with a hasty yank of fabric, he stood in front of a used, compact white sedan. Excitedly, he hugged his parents and rushed to run his fingers along the hood of the car and place his hands on the warm leather of the steering wheel. Sam was 5'8" at the time and the car was a perfect size; but, by his high school graduation, he had grown to a lanky, 6'3". He reluctantly embraced the teasing of his high school friends, as they so lovingly described his birthday gift as a "clown car." Swinging the car door shut behind him, he looked up at the clock tower on the original campus building.

Main Hall, he thought. *How did four years go by so quickly?*

He took a deep breath, realizing only in this moment that he was returning to campus for the last time as an undergraduate student. Still staring at the clock tower, he began to replay his favorite college moments in his head. Getting lost during orientation. Overstuffing the washer-dryer in his dorm. Late night chats with Professor Bueller. His first party. The hungover breakfast in the dining hall that followed. His first lacrosse game. Winning the junior biology award. Meeting Mouse.

As he stood, frozen beneath the majesty of the old clock tower, Sam spotted a hefty object hurling through the air in his direction out of the corner of his eye. Stumbling back, he reached out his arms to catch the weight of his now distinguishable backpack. He clumsily received the bag in his chest and regained his balance, looking back at Mouse with a stern expression of disapproval.

Laughing, Mouse asked bluntly, "You done over there?"

Sam pulled the backpack straps over his shoulders and replied sharply, "Yeah, I'm done." Relaxing his tone, he continued, "Can't a guy get a little sentimental? It is my last semester, after all."

Mouse walked around the car and, colliding gently into Sam's hip, casually put his arm around Sam's shoulder. "Yeah. You can get a little sentimental," Mouse teased. "Just don't embarrass me out here. I've got a reputation to maintain. Some of us still have another year left!"

Sam leaned into Mouse's shoulder, as they matched one another stride for stride through the campus front gates. They crossed into the quad and walked past the statue of St. Agatha that welcomed students to the campus grounds.

As they made their way through the barren winter of the campus gardens, a voice shouted out to them from a distance, "MOUSE! LETS GOOOOO!" A chorus of shouting voices and cheers followed, disrupting the quiet peace of the boys' return.

A group of tall, athletic boys stood in the middle of the quad, now waving aggressively at Mouse to join them. Leading the chorus of shouting voices were two particularly muscular twins, yelling loudly at the front of the group. Sam recognized them immediately.

Marvin and Jay Bantz were the captains of the lacrosse team. Their short brown hair sat neatly beneath matching baseball caps. While their personalities were quite distinct, the two were identical in looks. Their only visual tell was their facial hair, as Jay often wore a moustache and Marvin a beard. The twins' Midwest pride was on full display, as they were the only two people on campus wearing T-shirts outside in late January.

Marvin and Jay were Mouse's closest friends on the team. Although the twins had grown up in Wisconsin, where lacrosse wasn't particularly popular, the two had attended every major lacrosse camp in the country—including several in Maryland. Mouse had first met them in high school, at a three-week camp for rising stars in the sport. Loud and full of energy, the twins were a magnetic force in the St. Agatha University social scene. Mouse added a quiet calm to their chaotic existence and, somehow, their friendship seemed to work.

Waving their arms in the air, the twins continued to beckon Mouse to join them. "Come on, Mouse!" they yelled. A slow clap and uniform chant bellowed in the group. "Mouse. Mouse. Mouse. Mouse."

"Go," Sam said sharply, pushing Mouse in their direction. "I'll see you later."

The two exchanged smiles as Mouse hoisted his duffle bag tightly over his shoulder and ran off to join the group. Lacrosse stick in hand, Mouse fielded a pass from one of his teammates from across the quad and returned the whizzing rubber ball back toward the group. As Mouse joined them, the team cheered and yelled. The group hurled lacrosse balls to one another as they ran off toward the practice fields.

The team faded off into the distance and Sam turned to make his way down the south campus path. He wrapped his scarf tightly around his neck and pulled his knit hat down over his ears. Walking toward the senior apartments, he took note of the small detailing on the old campus buildings. He had never noticed the intricacies of the stone carvings on the doorways and in the window wells. He soaked in all of the little details, noticing newness in the spaces that he had walked countless times before.

Sam reveled in the sport of tracing the lines of buildings—up every handrail, through every window, across every park bench. He tried hard to see everything with fresh eyes, gratitude and appreciation swelling as he breathed deep and took in the red brick buildings and ornately carved stone intricacies of the window wells. He took a long, scenic route toward his campus apartment. Caught up in the sentimentality of his last semester, he took unnecessary turns and stopped in unusual places while traveling toward his room.

Sam looped around the side of his apartment building, wandering past his usual entrance in search of more newness. He found himself at the auxiliary entrance of the senior apartments. His apartment was on the other side of the building, but he welcomed the change in routine as the auxiliary entrance also led past the student lounge. Although he rarely spent time in the building's common areas, Sam liked the idea of passing the lounge in the hopes of finding his friends there and recapping their winter break adventures.

Reaching into his pocket, Sam removed a brown leather wallet and pulled out his Student ID card. His cold hands, stiff from the winter air, fumbled the ID card clumsily as he attempted to swipe it through the card reader and gain access to the building. The ID card fell hard to the ground and landed face up on the sidewalk amidst the dirt and snow. Sam let out a sigh of frustration and bent down to pick up the card from the wet, freshly salted sidewalk.

Rising, he wiped his ID card on his pant leg. Cupping his hands to his mouth, he exhaled a breath of warm air into his tightening grip. The sensation brought feeling back to his fingers. He gripped the card tightly and swiped it through the card reader once more. The light on the card reader turned from blue to green and the door clicked open in front of him.

He stepped into the warmth of the building and, inhaling deeply through his nose, embraced the musty smell of campus housing. He walked down the long corridor and, as he approached the student lounge, heard the chattering of familiar voices echoing down the hallway.

"Eight ball, side pocket," declared a voice confidently.

Sam turned the corner to see a petite, dark-haired girl bending over a pool table, preparing to take her next shot. The girl, dressed in denim overalls and a black, long sleeve shirt, widened her stance and stared down the length of her pool stick. As she drew the stick back with her left hand, she glanced up to make eye contact with Sam as he stood casually in the doorway.

With a crack of her pool stick, the cue ball rolled gracefully across the table and gently kissed the eight ball. A group of boys stood silently to the side of the table, watching as the eight-ball rolled slowly toward the side pocket.

Before the ball even fell, the girl called out, "Pay up, fellas."

The eight-ball dropped with a thud into the bottom of the side pocket netting. A chorus of defeated groans filled the student lounge as the boys reached for their wallets. Collecting a five-dollar bill from each of the boys, the girl turned toward Sam with a smile.

"Hey there, handsome! How was your winter break?" she asked excitedly, as she wrapped her arms around Sam's neck and kissed him on the cheek.

"It was good, Maisie. I went back to Seattle, hung out with my family," he replied, as they separated from their embrace. "How about yours? Did you do anything fun?"

"Oh, it was pretty casual. I was up in Rochester with my mom," Maisie explained, as she picked up a drink from the table and turned toward the lounge seating area. "Come on, sit with me!"

Maisie walked with a confident elegance. She was one of Sam's first friends on campus. Strong-willed and stubborn, most of their peers found Maisie abrasive and off-putting. These were also often the people who knew Maisie the least. Her boldness was Sam's favorite thing about her. She was unapologetically herself, and rarely did anything that she didn't want to do. In the simplest of terms, Maisie was a badass.

She crossed the lounge in front of several students to find an empty couch near the television. She jumped into the cavernous couch cushions, stained from years of parties in the student lounge, and invited Sam to join her with a slap of her hand on the seat beside her. Sam sat down and Maisie leaned against him, resting her head on his shoulder.

"Did the lacrosse boys take Mouse with them already?" Maisie asked, already knowing the answer to her question.

"Jay and Marvin were practically waiting for us at the gates," Sam explained, as he turned his head toward the television.

"Those boys," Maisie replied, rolling her eyes.

Sam's mouth opened slightly as the words, "BREAKING," spanned across the bottom of the television. Students gathered around, as the reruns of old cartoons were quickly replaced by an empty news desk. The interruption of usual programming hinted at a startling severity in coverage. A news anchor quickly stepped onto the screen with a stack of papers in hand and straightened his tie and suit coat. The anchor sat down behind the desk with hair half-done and tie still off center, and he began to read from the prompter.

"This just in, death tolls rise significantly in East and Southeast Asia today. Hospitals in China have reached critical mass as the spread of a new virus shows no sign of ceasing. Early indications are that the virus holds a 6% fatality rate, significantly higher than the flu or the common cold. The thousands of people who have traveled to and from China in the past six weeks are being asked to please alert the Center for Disease Control through their website reporting mechanism and to self-isolate until further notice," the news anchor announced.

A boy spoke up nervously from behind the couch, "My grandparents just came back from China last week. They were there for the holiday ...." Taking out his phone the boy walked toward the back of the lounge, frantically pacing the width of the room.

"A virus?" Maisie whispered. "Seriously?"

Sam stood up quietly from the couch and whispered a brief goodbye to Maisie, who was still staring intensely at the screen. He sifted through the groups of students huddled around the television and stepped out into the hallway. His chest swelled with concern and uncertainty. Only still finishing his pre-med biology degree, Sam knew very little about the situation that was unfolding before him. He was vaguely familiar with the history of viral outbreaks in the United States and some of the global health crises that had occurred during his lifetime, but none of it could have prepared him for what was coming.

6%, he thought nervously. *A 6% fatality rate seems really high.*

He racked his brain for a reasonable scientific explanation.

Well, if the outbreak is contained to only China, there probably aren't enough cases to say what the true fatality rate of the virus is. I bet there are tons of cases that are unreported and that would totally offset the numbers.

Sam continued to theorize about the high fatality rate and the spread of the virus as he walked down the hall and entered the front entrance foyer. A student worker sat quietly at the front desk, leaning back in her chair with her feet kicked up casually. Walking past her, Sam smiled and nodded in salutation.

She removed her headphones and called out to him with an unnecessary degree of cheeriness, "Hey Sam! Did you have a good break?"

Slowing his pace, he turned to the girl and searched frantically for her name.

She's a sophomore, he thought quickly. *Hangs out with that one kid who is always wearing jean shorts. Brittany? Becca?*

Quickly giving up, Sam replied with a smile, "Hey ... there. Yeah, I did. Thanks!"

She smiled wide and returned her headphones to her ears. She was always so nice to him, so nice to everyone. Guilt set in, as he walked away and tried to recall her name once more. Sam continued out the front entrance foyer and turned right down the long corridor, finally arriving at the elevator. Reaching out, he pushed the "Up" button with his pointer finger curled neatly into itself, exposing only his knuckle to the button's surface.

Sam tapped his foot impatiently as he waited for the elevator, staring at his phone in anticipation. He opened his news app to find headlines featuring, "Viral Outbreak! Pandemic! Chinese Crisis!" in abundance. Sam took a deep breath, in through his nose and out through his mouth, as his anxiety creeped in. He quickly closed the news app and began to scroll through old photos of his family on his phone, attempting to distract himself.

The elevator arrived and, as the ding of arrival sounded, Sam eagerly approached the parting metal doors. Just as he stepped up, a tall boy carrying a stack of books was exiting the elevator at the exact same time. Noticing the heft of the books, Sam quickly stepped to the side in an apologetic fashion. The boy acknowledged the gesture with a simple nod of his head and lightly brushed shoulders with Sam, as he stepped out in the corridor.

Sam's eyes followed the boy briefly down the hallway, checking to see if he needed assistance with the stack of books. Deciding on the boy's independence and perhaps downplaying the weighted tower of books in his hands, Sam stepped into the elevator and pressed the button, "5," again with the knuckle of his curled pointer finger. The elevator rose toward the fifth floor as Sam adjusted his backpack, eager to be relieved of its burden. He trotted down the hallway, already removing his keys from his pocket, toward the warm comforts of his apartment.

He arrived quickly at the door to his apartment, Unit 5F. Inserting his keys and unlocking the heavy wooden door, Sam paused to listen for the sound of video games or the chatter of conversation.

Silence, he thought, breathing a sigh of relief. *Robbie must not be back yet.*

Sam pushed open the door and tossed his keys onto the table in the kitchenette. Can-shaped rings tattered the table's once oak-stained surface. As he crossed the living room, he noticed a scattering of empty cans on the floor. Sam bent down among the bristle of the old campus carpeting and potato chip crumbs, and picked the cans up off the ground. He tossed them in the recycling bin with a shameful pride, taking partial responsibility for the state of the place.

I should probably vacuum... Sam thought, as he scanned the room for any empty cans still scattered about. *Or, at least Robbie should.*

Sam entered his room and tossed his backpack and jacket in the corner. He crashed onto his bed with the full weight of his body. The firm cushion of the blue college mattress welcomed Sam to his university home with a harsh yet intimate familiarity. Rolling onto his back, he looked up at the ceiling and folded his hands neatly across his chest. He kicked his shoes off one at a time and discarded them to the floor toward a disorganized pile of shoes near his desk.

His eyes began to wander around the room, soaking in that satisfied feeling of being surrounded by his own things. He settled his gaze on a single photo, taped up on the wall alongside a scattering of Sam's favorite college memories. He and Mouse were standing prominently in the middle of the group, covered in mud and smiling. This particular memory was taken from last year's St. Agatha Mud Run, a tradition where students run through a three-mile obstacle course that included climbing, crawling, and treading through an assortment of mud-covered challenges. No one emerged unscathed. At the end of the race, Maisie had gathered their closest friends and made them pose for a photo, the mud caking dry on their skin as they stood in the springtime sun.

Laying back, Sam focused on the three lines of mud on his face in the photo, where Mouse had so confidently brushed his cheek before kissing him for the very first time at the finish line. Sam pressed his hands to his face, retracing the lines where Mouse's fingers had been on that day. He closed his eyes and sank into the nostalgic comforts of the memory.

"Honey! I'm home!" shouted a voice from the living room. The door slammed shut with a loud thud that shook Sam's bed. Sam sat up, mourning the loss of peace and quiet, and shifted to the edge of the bed. A thunder of footsteps barreled toward him as a short, stout boy came flying through the door and tackled him back onto his back.

"What's up, buddy?" yelled the boy as he wrestled Sam into a headlock.

"Would you get off of me, you big oaf!" Sam yelled, laughing as he struggled loose of the headlock grip. "When did you get back?"

Jumping off the bed, the boy stepped over Sam's shoes and wandered over to the mini-fridge under Sam's desk. Bending over, he pulled two cans of beer from the fridge and leaned back against the wall. He tossed Sam a beer and cracked his open excitedly.

"I got back a few hours ago. My mom drove me back. She was all like, 'Robbie Eamon, your grades better improve this semester. God help me if you don't graduate on time,'" the boy mimicked in a perfect imitation of his mother.

Robbie's impersonations were famous on campus. He could do any number of famous actors and cartoon characters, making him a comedic sensation at every party. A true class clown, Robbie could make anyone laugh. The previous year, Robbie had even earned a feature at a comedy club in Adams Morgan. The opportunity solidified not only his passion but also his talent. The whole room was in stitches by the end of his routine, begging for more.

"Have you seen all this virus stuff?" Robbie quickly asked. "It's crazy over there. I even read that there was a confirmed case in France this morning. Sacrebleu!"

Sam chuckled, rolling his eyes in disbelief at Robbie's tone-deaf attempt at a French accent. Robbie pulled the chair out from Sam's desk and, turning it backward, sat down. He took a long sip of beer and exhaled audibly in satisfaction.

"Did you just get back? What's Mouse up to?" Robbie asked.

"We got back this morning," Sam replied. "Mouse is doing some lacrosse thing, but I think we're meeting up later. Is anything going on tonight?"

Sam already knew what Robbie was going to suggest. Robbie went to the same bar every night. Sometimes to study. Sometimes to drink. Sometimes both. The Rue wasn't a particularly impressive bar, but it was an institution of St. Agatha University. Down a long flight of stairs, the bar was mostly underground. The decor was that of an old stone cellar, dark and damp, with tight booths stacked on top of one another. The claustrophobic layout forced patrons to practically sit in each other's laps as they enjoyed their drinks.

"The Rue is open!" Robbie exclaimed predictably; eyes wide at the prospect of returning to his favorite bar.

"Urrgh, The Rue? Again?" groaned Sam. "Surprise, surprise. Known 'Rue Rat,' Robbie Eamon wants to go to The Rue five minutes after arriving on campus!"

"You're damn right I do!" shouted Robbie, proudly embracing the term "Rue Rat" as a badge of honor. "Let me unpack and eat something, and we can walk over there!"

Sam nodded reluctantly. Robbie quickly finished his beer and strode out into the living room. "Good to see you, Sammy!" he called out over his shoulder, swinging the bedroom door closed behind him.

Sam laid back down on his bed and reopened the news app on his phone. Scrolling ferociously in search of a non-virus-related headline, Sam settled on a video interview with a billionaire investor discussing emerging industries to watch. The woman spoke confidently about her fascination with professional sports. A part-owner of two major league sports teams, she talked about the reliable gains associated with investing in entertainment.

"I got into sports because of my children. I came home one day and they were fixed in front of the TV watching Kobe Bryant face down a defender," the woman explained. "Pretty soon, I was buying them jerseys, tickets to the playoffs, and, of course, video games. Watching their fascination inspired me to do more research about the industry. If I had to guess what's next, video games."

Sam half-listened as the woman carried on about sports economics and her investment strategies, his eyes growing heavy. He set his phone down and folded his hands neatly across his chest. As he succumbed to the overwhelming exhaustion of his return, Sam closed his eyes and drifted off to sleep.

DEEP BREATHING

Emily adjusted her facemask and typed the pharmacy address into the navigation app on her tablet. A blue line appeared on her screen, illuminating the route through the city in front of her. A series of simple turns down recognizable streets, she quickly memorized the route and excitedly trotted away from Walter Reed High School.

Emily drifted toward the sidewalk's edge and jumped up onto the raised curbing that lined the pathway's outer border. Standing tall above the ground, Emily walked heel to toe, placing one foot in front of the other as she traversed the narrow balance beam of the elevated surface. She stretched her arms wide to maintain her balance and wobbled from side to side playfully, intoxicated with the nostalgia of the youthful game.

She looked up ahead from the raised curbing and spotted two young children on the opposite side of the street. She watched as they jumped up and down on the sidewalk's edge, laughing and challenging one another to leap up and back down again. Their gleeful cheers carried on the light breeze in Emily's direction. Hearing the childish laughter, a rush of discomfort and embarrassment came over her. Emily had played this game many times before, but the stark juxtaposition between the youthful play of her balancing act and the Age of Responsibility gave her sudden pause.

Grow up, she commanded herself. *You're sixteen.*

Emily shamefully jumped down from the platform, returning to the sidewalk with the stomp of a two-footed landing. She straightened her jacket and removed a pack of sanitary wipes from her tablet bag. She wiped her hands thoroughly and trotted toward a public trash can situated on a nearby corner. Waving her hand in front of the can's motion sensor, she tossed the wipe into the depths of the opening bin and stepped back in haste. She clenched her fists tightly. Recoiling from the garbage can, she marched down the sidewalk toward downtown.

A medley of street signs and turns finally led Emily to Foxx Avenue. As she rounded the corner, the pharmacy came into view at the end of the block. She removed her tablet from the tablet bag and checked the time, *15:00.* Emily hastily stuffed her tablet back into its resting place and picked up her pace toward the pharmacy in the distance.

Her strides lengthened and her arms swung wildly at her sides, as she began to power walk down the way. Emily looked up and saw two elderly women walking toward her, carrying large grocery bags. The women, with added bulk of the grocery bags at their sides, took up the entirety of the six-foot width of the sidewalk.

Emily, being visibly younger than the women, knew well what social courtesy demanded of her in this moment. It was customary, and perhaps even the law, for young people to yield the sidewalk to their elders and step into the nearest secure space available to them. As Emily scanned the rows of storefronts that lined her side of the sidewalk, she noticed a recessed entryway with a sign that read, "Closed for Deep Cleaning." She quickly ducked into the recession and bowed her head, covering her face and facemask with the elbow of her jacket sleeve.

The women smiled kindly as they passed her in the doorway.

"Thank you, dear," said the nearest of the two, nodding her head in approval.

As the women gained distance from Emily, she stepped out of the storefront's recessed entryway and hurried down the sidewalk. She arrived at the entrance to the pharmacy and stepped confidently onto the black doormat that sat in front of the doors. Looking up at a small camera in the corner, Emily waved nervously. She had never been inside the pharmacy before but she had always been curious about what went on inside the important building in the heart of downtown Eden.

"Now, when you enter, make sure you ask for the essentials and remind the pharmacist that you need Ted's inhalers," her father had instructed. "Don't worry about your first day. Just ask for help."

She carefully considered her father's words as she stood before the pharmacy entrance. The camera moved slightly and zoomed in on her face. As Emily rested her waving hand gently at her side, the automatic doors parted open before her. She stepped in and turned left, identifying and walking toward the wash station. Emily pulled up the sleeves of her rain jacket and gestured at the sink, triggering a rush of water and soap from the protruding spout. Emily washed her hands aggressively, scrubbing hard and fast against the short cut of her fingernails. Being in new spaces always made Emily feel uneasy. But being clean always brought her comfort. She counted down from twenty in her head, noting the absence of a digital display timer like the ones at school.

She stepped away from the sink and looked out into the store. Emily stood in awe of the abundance of vitamins and medicines that filled the pharmacy. Her hands dried quickly as she wandered the wide aisles of the pharmacy, taking note of the variety of vitamins, medicines, sprays, and bandages that lined its shelves. Fascinated, she wandered aimlessly throughout the store and gawked at the varying sizes and overwhelming volume of treatments available to the community. She carried herself from aisle to aisle, abandoning all sense of time in the store's majesty. She paced up and down each aisle slowly, caught up in the small detailing on each bottle and stopped to read the paragraphs of alien words that made up their ingredients.

After a long while, she finally stopped in front of a section of vitamins that was labeled overhead as, "Essential Vitamins." Remembering the task at hand, Emily took her tablet in hand and opened a list of items that her father had shared with her. She matched the items on the list with the corresponding bottles on the shelves. She identified eight bottles on the shelf that were included in the list and called to the glass booth at the front of the pharmacy.

"Excuse me, sir. Can you please open this case for me?' she inquired, as she stepped back into view and pointed to the case in front of her.

"The essentials case, young lady?" questioned the elderly man in a white medical in the front booth of the store.

"Yes, sir, and a few other cases if you don't mind. My younger brother, Ted, also uses a respiratory aid," Emily responded.

The man stood up from his chair and waved his foot in front of a floor sensor inside the glass booth. The booth door slid open and the man stepped out with a slight limp that favored his left side. He raised a small black object to his mouth and sucked hard on an inhaler. The medicinal spray released audibly into his mouth as he breathed deep. Filling his lungs, he let out a loud, performative exhale.

"You mean like this one?" he asked with a charming smile.

Chuckling, Emily nodded in confirmation. The man waddled over and stopped in front of the essentials shelf. He gestured to Emily's tablet with a slight nod. She held the device out in plain view, raising it higher and nearer to the man's face as he adjusted his glasses and squinted at the tablet screen. He grasped the ID card hanging around his neck in his hand and held it out, drawing tight the tattered, navy necklace from which it hung. He leaned forward and waved the ID card over a black sensor on the shelf. The glass casing clicked open and exposed the overwhelming, colorful abundance of essential vitamins. The man's eyes scanned the case quickly, grabbing bottle after bottle from their memorized locations with ease. Having gathered all of the bottles on Emily's list, he closed the casing and waddled back toward his booth at the front of the pharmacy.

"Excuse me, sir. The respiratory aid," Emily reminded, holding out her tablet as it displayed the required prescription paperwork for Ted's inhaler.

"Ah, yes. Of course," the man responded, turning back to her and directing her toward the back of the pharmacy.

The man opened another case and proceeded to ask several follow-up questions about Ted's age and condition. Emily answered his inquiries confidently as she had taken care to memorize the details of her brother's diagnosis. It was imperative that she understand well the unique medical needs of her younger brother, especially as she entered the Age of Responsibility. The previous week, and many times before, her parents had sat her down at the dinner table and explained the nuances of Ted's health condition to her. He wasn't contagious, but he would require the use of a respiratory aid for most of his life.

Ted had been a baby when he was diagnosed. Emily was six years old, watching as her younger brother wrestled with excessive coughing and difficulty breathing in his crib. Emily's parents were deeply concerned, and Ted spent several weeks in hospitalized isolation. Some of Emily's earliest memories were sitting down with her parents in front of the television and talking with doctors over Vid, a video conferencing app, about her brother's condition.

After months of rigorous testing, it was determined that Ted's condition couldn't be passed to other people. But his symptoms were reminiscent of a historically dangerous and very contagious virus, explaining their extra caution. Emily's parents never expanded on why this particular set of symptoms gave the doctors such pause, but the fear in their eyes spoke volumes. They cried the morning that Ted came home from isolation and Emily knew the depth and severity of their love for her younger brother. He was her best friend and her number one fan.

"A respiratory aid? At eleven years old? Very curious," the elderly man said somberly, taking another puff of his inhaler as he opened the second case. "I'm terribly sorry."

"Thank you, sir," she replied. "You're Dr. Abrams, right?"

"Doc Abrams is fine," he said, wheezing and coughing violently into his sleeve as he attempted to elevate the pitch of his voice in introducing himself. Finding his composure, he continued, "A pleasure to meet you... Miss?"

"Emily, sir," she politely replied. "Emily Chang, and likewise."

Smiling, Doc Abrams pulled a two-pack of inhalers down from the shelf and returned toward the comforts of his glass booth. Emily gave him distance, as he limped slowly up ahead of her. He turned back to look at her, now roughly eight feet behind her, and rolled his eyes. Emily knew better than to walk closely behind or even stand in close proximity to an elder member of the community. It would be rude and, regarded by many as, unsafe.

"You just going to stand there all day?" he asked sharply back at her. "Come along, don't worry about all that nonsense."

Emily nervously caught up behind him, startled and put off by his disregard for the courtesy of her distancing. Doc Abrams waved his foot in front of the sensor of his booth and the door slid open. He stepped inside and set the essential vitamins and inhalers down on the rear table in the booth. He sat down slowly in a swivel chair as the sliding door drew closed behind him. One by one, he picked up the items and cleaned them thoroughly with a sanitary wipe before setting them down in front of Emily. Once he set them down, she picked them up slowly and placed them in a mesh, yellow bag.

"What is your family ID, Miss Emily," asked Doc Abrams, stifling a cough and covering his mouth.

Emily recoiled nervously as he coughed. She replied, drawing closed the mesh bag of vitamins and inhalers, "Chang - 662123."

"Okay, Emily. You're all set, get home safely now," he said, entering the numbers into his tablet. Doc Abrams leaned back in his chair and began to place his personal effects in a tablet bag, preparing to drive home for the day. Doc Abrams continued, "The actions of one."

"Thank you, sir. Carry the safety of us all," Emily said as she turned toward the pharmacy's rear exit.

She stepped up to the exit sink and washed her hands thoroughly. She attempted to count down from twenty in her head, but Emily found herself being interrupted by her own thoughts.

20, 19, 18, 17, 16…. What a strange man, she thought to herself. *I was just trying to be nice.*

Emily had never been made to feel guilty about keeping appropriate distances, especially for community elders. If anything, she prided herself on her social awareness and her over-caution in this regard.

The sink ceased pumping out water and soap, and Emily stepped up to the black mat in front of the exit. The sliding doors opened before her and she stepped outside, returning to the warm comforts of the sunny afternoon. Looking down the street, Emily noticed the red hue of the streetlights and raised her brow.

Peculiar, she thought. *The lights don't usually turn to red until curfew...*

She quickly reached for her tablet in a desperate plea for the time, hoping against hope that there was an error in the street lighting. There was never an error in the street lighting.

16:15! she gasped. A heavy panic filled her chest as she quickly pulled her facemask over her head. *How was I in there for over an hour!?* she asked herself in frustration.

Emily secured her tablet bag at her side and drew its single strap tight around her shoulder, running off in the direction of her housing cluster with a furious vigor. She looked frantically down the cascading lines of street lamps that bordered the sidewalk. One lamp every fifty feet, Emily raced against the deepening of their red coloring as the lamps closed in on the bright, bold red that signified the end of the day and the beginning of the daily housing lockdown. She had never been late for curfew, and she was in no hurry to start.

Emily cursed into her facemask as she approached Housing Cluster B1, the nearest building to downtown. Her eyes traced the windows of the building from top to bottom as she sprinted down the sidewalk, barreling toward her housing cluster. It was in moments like this that Emily longed to live closer to downtown. HC-B1 was conveniently located next to the pharmacy, grocery, and the high school. While no one was permitted to enter a housing cluster without a corresponding residence card, the sight over her classmates' living spaces over Vid confirmed the rumors about the layout and prestige of the housing clusters. HC-B1 was for rich people.

While the housing assignments within each letter group were supposed to be random, determined after a couple claimed cohabitation rights and expressed a desire to bring up children, there was a communal suspicion around the influence of the city's elite over the housing lottery system. More often than not, reputable families were placed higher alphabetically and the tiers of wealth and influence spiraled outward numerically from there.

Emily's panic intensified, as she stared through the lighted windows of HC-B1 and into the homes of the building's residents. A man watching television. A woman reading in a lounge chair. Children running circles around their living room. Everyone was safely at home…. Everyone, except for Emily.

As the red hue deepened further, she spotted her building a few blocks up ahead. A lighted sign read, "HC-F5," above the large concrete columns that marked the building's entryway. She slowed her sprint to a light jog and attempted to catch her breath as she loosened her tablet bag and brought it around to her front. She arrived at the building gasping for air, hunched over with her hands on her knees. She pulled back the flap on her tablet bag and pulled out her Council-issued ID card and quickly held it under the scanner.

The blue light on the scanner turned quickly to green and Emily breathed a sigh of relief. She pulled her tablet out of her tablet bag and checked the time. *16:43.*

2 minutes to spare, Emily thought. *That was a close one!*

The sliding doors parted in front of her and she stepped inside HC-F5. Emily turned to look back at the long road, reflecting on the twenty-eight-minute victory she had so narrowly championed over the city-wide curfew. As she stared back at the sliding doors, now closing behind her, Emily saw two all-white clad figures standing like watchtowers outside. Her triumphant posture quickly melted into a puddle of nerves and fear. Two patrol officers stood there menacingly, displaying their disapproval at Emily's close-call. They stared intensely back at her, judging and clutching their guns. They shook their heads and continued down the street, resuming their patrol of the housing cluster neighborhoods. Although Emily had barely made it inside before the street lamps reached their full crimson red color, she had in fact made it, and there was nothing the patrol officers could do.

Emily's nerves began to calm as the bright fluorescent lighting of the HC-F5 lobby welcomed her home. She washed her hands vigorously of the outside and the remaining stresses of her close-call at the entryway sink. Emily made her way down the white walls of the hallway to the elevator bank. She turned casually and nodded in the direction of the front-desk attendant as she walked by. He stood up from his chair and nodded politely back at her.

"Good evening, Miss Emily," he said. "Close-call tonight."

"Thanks, Tommy," she replied, slowing her pace slightly and peeling her facemask off of her face casually. "I lost track of time at the pharmacy."

Tommy smiled softly as he sat back in his chair. He waved his hands beneath a sensor behind his desk and lathered a clear, sanitizing gel in his palms, waving goodbye as Emily passed his desk.

Emily resumed a comfortable pace and waltzed casually through the fluorescence of the hallway. As she reached the elevator bank, she stepped up to a scanner situated in front of five wide sets of elevator doors. She leaned down, positioning her face over the voice box and spoke clearly, "Emily Chang, Household - 662123." She opened her eyes wide as a ray of bright-red light scanned her face up, down, left, and right, confirming her identity and checking her vitals.

"98.2, Vitals normal. Welcome home, Emily Chang," the voice box called back to her.

The leftmost elevator doors opened immediately and Emily darted in their direction. She stepped in eagerly and waited as the elevator doors closed and the elevator whizzed up and over toward her family's housing unit. The elevator came to a slow halt and eased into a resting position upon arrival. The doors swung open and revealed a small, all-white room with a shower and small row of four lockers. She stepped into the room and set her belongings neatly on the floor beside the lockers.

She removed her clothes and, balling them up, tossed the worn clothes and her boots into an open chute in the corner. An echo of clanking metal resounded as her boots banged against the chute's walls, finally ceasing as they reached the bottom of the chute with a thud.

Emily stood naked in the room and, turning away from the chute, spoke cheerfully into the all-white space, "Emily's Pop Jams Playlist, please."

A smooth blend of pop music poured out from a speaker in the upper corner of the room. Emily danced across the room and stepped over a raised curb and into the shower. A burst of warm soap and water washed over her, as she continued to dance and sing along with the inviting melodies of the music. She ran her fingers gently through her hair and massaged her scalp, calmingly reflecting on the day. It was good to be home. She began to retrace her trip to the pharmacy in her head, checking off the different essential vitamins and verifying Ted's medications through memory. She scrubbed at her body, as she made her way through the checklist. The comforts of the shower brought on a clean sense of renewal.

The water slowed and Emily stepped over the curbing of the shower. A set of four, cubby-style lockers were positioned neatly next to the shower. She reached into the third locker from the left and began to dry off with a fluffy white towel, the letter "E" embroidered at each end. She tossed her hair intensely in the towel, drying herself to the rhythm of the music. She bobbed and bounced until she stood completely dry before her locker. Turning back to the chute in the corner, she lofted the towel toward the opening.

Kobe, she thought, chuckling to herself as the towel flew through the air.

The towel thudded against the front of the chute, hanging half in and half out on the edge. Emily sighed and walked toward the hanging towel. From a distance, Emily reached out her arms and, extending her pointer finger its entire length, flicked the towel free from the edge of the chute with one finger. The towel tumbled down and Emily danced back to her locker, wiping her pointer finger on her thigh.

She reached into her locker and removed a clean outfit, wrapped in a light, plastic covering, from the top shelf. She unwrapped and unfolded the clothes neatly. Examining her home wear, Emily stepped into a white bodysuit. She pulled the sleeves comfortably over her arms and shoulders and hoisted a pair of loose white sweatpants up over her legs.

Dressed for comfort, Emily picked up the light, plastic covering and dropped it down the chute for sanitizing and reuse. She scooped up her tablet bag and the yellow, mesh bag of pharmaceuticals and stepped into her housing unit through a solid, sliding door.

"Hey, Em! How did the first day go?" her father asked cheerfully, as she stood in the housing unit doorway.

"It was really good. It was good to see Fae!" she replied, placing the yellow, mesh bag on the entryway table next to a decorative ceramic pineapple, sanitary wipes protruding from its leafy green top. Emily pulled a sanitary wipe from the pineapple and began removing and cleaning the bottles of vitamins from the bag.

Her father rushed over, interrupting sharply, "I've got it, Em. Go ahead and put your things down."

"Thanks, Dad," Emily replied. "I'm pretty tired. I think I'm going to go lie down for a bit if that is alright?"

"Of course!" he assured her. "Join us in the living room whenever you're ready."

Her father cleaned the items thoroughly, picking them up one by one, wiping them down, and placing them neatly into a cabinet in the corner of the kitchen. Emily's mother was seated quietly at the kitchen counter, staring intensely at her tablet and muttering a series of numbers under her breath. Emily knew that posture and intense gaze well. She was working late again.

Emily's mother worked incredibly hard and, although their housing unit had an office space, the work often followed her mother wherever she went. Her parents didn't argue often, but the few arguments that Emily could recall were usually related to her mother's work habits.

"Hey, Mom," Emily said softly, alerting her mother of her presence but taking care to not disturb her concentration.

"Hey, Em," her mother replied, eyes still fixated on the screen. "School okay?"

Emily replied, in an even softer tone that of her salutation, "Yeah, all fit."

Emily hurried away and started up the stairs toward her bedroom. She leapt the steps, four at a time, racing her own athleticism to the top. As she crossed the plane of the final step, Emily reached out her hands to brace herself against the wall opposite the stairwell. Colliding into it, she let herself bounce off it playfully and regained her balance.

Alerted by the sound, her younger brother leaned out into the hallway from his bedroom door. Large, over-ear headphones framed his face, accentuating its round shape. He stepped out into the hallway and turned toward Emily. The boy placed his arms neatly at his side, in a military-like pose. Emily mirrored his militaristic stance and stood staring at the boy.

After a long pause, the boy began to tap his foot. *Tap. Tap. Tap.* Upon the third tap, Emily and the boy stretched their arms wide and performed a dance routine in perfect unison. Their arms loosened in a wobbly, waving motion that mirrored the movement of the ocean. The boy froze, ceasing his movement like the stillness of a statue. Emily, feigning concern and stifling laughter, rushed over to him and began to mime the turning of a crank in the boy's back. After several mimed cranks, the boy exploded into a freestyle routine that finished with him pointing two fingers at Emily. Taking cue, Emily began to freestyle dance in response.

The two of them continued this back and forth of dancing, pointing, and playing until exhaustion took hold of them. Emily bent over, letting the weight of her body drop into her hands as she placed them on her knees. The boy leaned over, laughing. His laughter was quickly interrupted as he began to cough gently into his elbow, shaking his head side to side and closing his eyes tightly.

In between coughs, the boy muttered sharply, "I'm fine, Em … I'm fine."

"I know you are, Ted," she replied. "Where's your inhaler, though?"

Ted pointed toward the open door behind him and leaned up against the wall. Emily shot past him and entered his bedroom. She scanned the surfaces of the room, in search of a small, black inhaler with silver markings on it. Her eyes darted across the unmade bed, the dresser, and Ted's art supply-covered desk. She finally spotted the device on his nightstand. In a lunge, she snatched the object and hurried back into the hall.

Ted reached out and took two large puffs of his inhaler. He stood up straight and stretched his arms toward the ceiling, breathing deep and filling his lungs with air.

"Still my favorite game, though," he said, regaining his composure and smiling up at Emily.

Emily chuckled in reply, "Mine too, buddy."

Ted braced himself on the wall for a moment before he walked back into his room. Emily followed closely behind him to make sure that he was okay. She stopped in his doorway, watching as he lay down in his bed with his inhaler in hand. Confirming his safety, Emily continued down the hallway to her bedroom. She took deep breaths as she walked, testing her lung capacity with the length of her inhale and exhale. She took in quiet moments of gratitude in her head, thanking the universe for her health and for the ability to take deep breaths.

Not everyone is this fortunate, she reminded herself as she approached her bedroom door.

Stepping inside, Emily set her tablet bag down on her nightstand and laid down in bed. She rested her hands neatly across her chest and stared up at the ceiling. Emily traced the arrangement of stars and constellations that adorned her bedroom ceiling in delight. She settled on the Gemini twins, her favorite constellation.

Emily loved the permanence of the constellations. A few years prior, when Emily was eleven years old, Ted had had a major episode and had to be hospitalized because of his breathing. He was put on a respirator for three days and given heavy doses of medication to help stabilize his breathing. Emily recalled sitting in front of her tablet, keeping Ted company in the hospital through Vid.

The primary function of Vid was chatting with one's peers.

However, because of Emily's parent's work with EduView, Emily always downloaded the latest in educational software, apps, and games.

During those difficult times in the hospital, when their dance parties were not an option, Emily and Ted passed the time by playing educational games over Vid. Ted's favorite was identifying the different constellations and, although Ted now insisted that he was too old for childish things like looking at the stars, Emily always reminded him that the constellations got him through those long days in the hospital.

Emily traced the outlines of the Gemini constellation on her ceiling slowly and meticulously. As she rounded the final curve of the stellar array, a soft buzzing interrupted her concentration. She sat up in her bed and reached for her tablet.

New Message – Fae Dotterman, Emily read, as she straightened her posture.

She ran her finger slowly across the screen, from left to right, and the tablet unlocked to reveal Fae's message.

"*Em. R U watching the VAX????*" the message read.

Fae doesn't like video games, Emily thought. *I wonder why she's watching the Vax tonight.*

"*No... Why?*" Emily texted back.

Three dots appeared on her screen, indicating that Fae was typing, followed by the abrupt appearance of Fae's three word response, "*Just do it!*"

Emily stood up and made her way downstairs to the living room. Descending the stairs with curiosity, Emily wondered how she might raise the idea of changing the channel and watching the Eden Vax to her family. Upon reaching the main floor, she looked over to see her mother still pouring over her work in the kitchen. Her father and

Ted were seated comfortably in their chairs in the living room. Emily wandered over to her usual chair, neatly positioned to her father's left. She sat down, slowly lowering herself into the soft, curved back of the leather and looked up at the television. A man in thick-framed glasses was walking through an archive of old military equipment, explaining the differences between different drones and computer programs. Emily's father stared intensely at the program, soaking in the history lesson.

"What are you guys watching?" Emily inquired, feigning interest with her tone.

"A documentary about the 2030's," her father explained. "They're talking about drone warfare and the 2032 global engagement treaty."

Emily paused for a moment, politely taking in the program as a courtesy to her father and brother. After a few minutes, Emily interrupted the program, "Would you guys want to watch the Vax game?" she asked.

Her father shot her a suspicious, sideways glance. Her brother's face lit up.

"Sure, Em," her father agreed, half-heartedly. "Any particular reason why?"

"No reason," she casually replied.

Her father changed the channel, still perplexed by her request. The bellowing voice of the game's announcer erupted from the screen, filling the room with a tone and intensity far greater than the monotone ramblings of the drone documentary.

As she looked up at the television screen, the confusing arrangement of the program gave her a slight headache. The screen was divided into six different boxes, like squares on a chess board. Each box featured the perspective of a different player. Across the top of the screen, three green boxes identified the players' perspectives on the Eden Vax. Across the bottom, three blue boxes identified the perspectives of the players on the Tri-City Valor. Each box had a label, noting the player's name, position, and statistics.

Emily heard a flutter of footsteps coming from the kitchen behind her. She turned to see her mother standing in the living room, tablet in hand with a curious, but excited, look on her face.

"3 v. 3!" her mother exclaimed! "Why are you guys watching the Vax?"

"Emily's request," her father explained, shooting an inquisitive glance in Emily's direction.

Her mother eagerly maneuvered through the chairs and sat in the open seat between Ted and Emily's father. The four of them sat together and watched as a bright red "X" fell over one of the green boxes, indicating the elimination of that player. Shortly after, a red "X" fell over one the blue boxes. Both Tri-City and the Vax had lost a player each. Emily's mother looked over, noting the confused look on Emily's face.

"There are three players on each team," her mother explained, without prompting. "Once a player gets eliminated from competition, a red 'X' drops over their screen and the remaining players continue to play. They play until the one team has been eliminated entirely.

"So, what is the point of the game?" Emily followed up, turning toward her mother's chair.

A gleeful expression fell over her mother's face as she educated the group, "They have to finish the objectives." Her mother continued, "Right now, the Vax are on offense and have to cross the river. Tri-City is trying to stop them from going across either the bridge or wading below through the trench."

Emily looked up at the display, as the green boxed perspectives were all staring at a bridge and the blue boxed perspectives were all staring back at them from across the river.

"Think of it like a big puzzle," she continued. "Each player has a role to play. When all the pieces fit, the team is successful."

Her mother looked at Emily with a quizzical look, silently searching her face for the source of this newfound curiosity. Emily's father stood up and wandered into the kitchen. He arranged four forks and four water glasses on a tray, neatly wiping them each down with a sanitary wipe. He proceeded to fill the glasses beneath a motion sensor on the sink and retrieved four individual bowls from the refrigerator. He returned to the living room and, starting with Ted, walked in front of each person with the tray extended. Emily reached out and took the bowl, fork, and water in hand.

"Thanks, Dad," she said, setting the bowl on her lap and placing the glass in her chair's cup holder.

Gathering two carrots on her fork, Emily ate quietly and tried to follow the chaotic, six-box display in front of her. Her eyes settled on the green box in the top right and widened as she took note of the name on the label. "C. McDaniels – Striker." Emily's face lit up at the sight. She quickly picked up her tablet and texted Fae.

Does Cayden play for the Vax!? she wrote. Fae responded immediately with a winking smiley face emoji.

Emily stared intensely at the green label, repeating *C. McDaniels,* in her head. Without fully understanding the patterns or the movements of the gameplay, Emily found herself completely caught up in the spectacle and the movements of the green box in the top right corner. As red "X"s fell, one by one, on the other screens, only Cayden and one player on Tri-City remained in the game.

"Last chance to cross the bridge," her mother said, anxiously leaning forward in her chair toward the television.

A nervous energy fell over Emily as she found herself wrapped up in the intensity of the game. She rubbed her thumb against her pointer and middle fingers as sweat began to build in her palms. The sensation and thrill of the game suddenly made sense to her. While Emily didn't quite understand the content of what she was watching, she reveled in the shared excitement and passion of the living room. Tension built all around them.

As she watched Cayden's gameplay closely, his character drifted toward a covering in the middle of the bridge. He crept slowly and placed a small black box in the corner. After setting the black box down, he doubled back and descended into the water in the trench below.

"He has no idea," Ted said in disbelief. "The Tri-City player is heading up on the bridge."

Emily's mother and Ted exchanged looks, as they stood up from their chairs and stepped toward the television excitedly.

"Who has no idea?" Emily asked sharply, attempting to further participate in whatever development that she had missed.

"The Tri-City player. Did you see McDaniels put down that box?" Her mother asked.

"The black thing?" Emily asked. "Yeah, I saw it!"

Her mother explained, "It makes a pattering noise that sounds like footsteps, to distract the other team. It's quiet, but if a player gets distracted and steps onto the box they get eliminated. McDaniels set the box down and doubled back into the trench. He is crossing the river below, while the Tri-City player is still up on the bridge."

Emily's attention lowered to the blue box in the bottom row. The Tri-City player was walking toward the sound of the pattering footsteps. As the player approached the sound, a loud crack sounded and a bright red "X" fell over the display. The last Tri-City player had been eliminated.

The announcer called out, "And it's all over folks! The Vax have done it! A brilliant play by the newcomer, Cayden McDaniels, late in the game to flip the script! Tell us Cayden, why a footsteps box?"

The six boxes and red "X"s faded and the screen cut to a video display of Cayden, smiling. Across the front of his green T-shirt, the words "Eden Vax," were written in bold silver lettering. Cayden adjusted his large, over-ear headphones and pushed his dark brown hair back out of his face.

He responded confidently, "Man, so much respect for Tri-City. They play super aggressive on defense and you have to give them credit for a great game." Cayden paused to think and catch his breath. "Ummm, we hadn't used noise decoys or footsteps all game, so I wanted to mix it up. Couldn't have done it without my teammates and we're just happy to get the win."

Emily smiled at his respectful confidence as the announcer continued, "There you have it folks. The newcomer, Cayden McDaniels, has a dream debut in his first game for the Eden Vax. Keep an eye on this sixteen-year-old. He's on his way up!"

An ear-to-ear grin adorned Emily's face, as she melted back into her chair. Ted and her mother cheered excitedly at the Vax's win, pointing and recounting the events of the victory to one another. Their beaming turned to faint echoes in the background of Emily's mind as she stared up at the dark-haired boy on the television. She felt a warm, tingling sensation swell in her chest as she watched him smile and toss his dark brown hair in his hands.

Emily's father stood up slowly and collected the empty glasses and bowls from the living room. He approached Emily with a soft smile on his face and held out the tray. Snapping from her fixation, she placed her half-eaten dinner back on the tray and took a large, final swig of water before handing over the empty glass.

Her father took an extended pause beside her and waited patiently for her attention. She felt his presence and glanced up to make eye contact with him, as he held the tray at his side.

"He seems like a nice boy," her father said. "Don't you think?"

Emily blushed and, taking a deep breath, replied with a whisper, "Yes. Yes, he does."

GEMINI

Sunshine parted the beige, flowing curtains of Sam's bedroom. The bright light warmed his face as he lay in bed and he began to stir, slowly waking from a deep sleep. He rolled onto his side to hide his face from the sun and a chemistry book rolled with him, falling off of his chest and landing softly on the mattress. Sam had fallen asleep studying again, for the fourth night in a row.

Three weeks had passed since he returned for the spring semester, and the coursework of senior year had already started to pile up. Graduation was fast approaching and he wasn't sure that he was ready to leave all of this behind. Sam opened one eye slowly and peered over at the clock beside him. *8:13 AM.*

He groaned, realizing that he had woken up two minutes before his *8:15 AM* alarm. Every ounce of sleep seemed to count these days, as the long nights of studying were beginning to take a toll on him. He reached out to the nightstand and clumsily turned the alarm off, still half asleep and contemplating sleeping through the morning.

Sam rose from his bed slowly and placed both feet on the rough carpeting of his bedroom floor. He picked up yesterday's towel from the floor and made his way out into the living room. Unwashed dishes lay stacked in the kitchen sink and a disheveled array of books sat on the couch, marking the difficult week of preparing for their upcoming exams. He crossed the messy living room of their college apartment to the bathroom. Sam knocked courteously on the door, despite his confident assumption that Robbie was still fast asleep in his bedroom. Hearing nothing, he pushed open the door and stepped onto the dark-blue bath mat that lay outside of the shower.

He peeled back the once-white shower curtain and turned the handle in the direction of the dark blue, "C". Cold water rushed from the shower head and slapped against the back wall ferociously. A light spray of cold water misted Sam as he reached up to reposition the shower head to properly address his height and frame. He undressed and tossed his pajamas atop a pile of dirty clothes that sat in the corner of the bathroom floor.

Sam stepped in slowly onto the cold tiling of the floor and pulled the shower curtain closed behind him. His passive state quickly turned as the cold water poured over him. Sam picked up a bottle of a two-in-one shampoo and body wash from the shower floor and began to lather his body with the soapy gel. In a hastened fury, Sam scrubbed his body and rinsed off in one, fluid motion. In and out, he stepped onto the bathmat and picked his towel up from the ground. As he dried himself off, he noticed a large swath of suds still lingering on his leg. He wiped up the soapy remains with the towel, as he continued to half dry himself.

Sam neatly wrapped the towel around his waist and, hugging the pile of dirty clothes from the corner of the bathroom, walked back out into the living room. A trail of water droplets and dirty socks fell behind him across the way, as he struggled to maintain a hold of every article of dirty clothing in the pile.

As he entered his room, Sam dropped the clothes and towel in his closet hamper and proceeded to get dressed for the day. Sam's closet looked a chaotic mess of loosely scattered denim, T-shirts, and a wrinkled suit hanging on the far reaches of the leftmost hanging rod. He settled on a pair of dark-wash, skinny jeans and a light gray

T-shirt that read, "St. Agatha Lacrosse," across the front. He glanced over at the clock. *8:31 AM.*

The crash of a closing door sounded from the living room. Robbie was awake. Sam quickly gathered his things and headed out into the common area, where Robbie stood in front of the open refrigerator holding a half gallon jug of milk.

"Hrrmph?" Robbie grunted in Sam's direction, holding up the half-gallon as his glossy eyes met Sam's.

"Yeah, sure," Sam replied, translating Robbie's oafish grunt as an offer to make breakfast.

Robbie grabbed two bowls from the cupboard and filled them with a colorful, sugary cereal. He carelessly set the bowls down on the dining table and placed the half-gallon jug between them. Sam prepared their breakfast as Robbie returned to the table with two spoons. Sam took a spoon and set it between the fabric of his T-shirt, wiping it clean before beginning to eat. The two sat in silence and enjoyed their breakfast, occasionally exchanging morning pleasantries. After some small talk, Robbie brought his cereal bowl near his chin and slurped the remaining milk in the bowl obnoxiously. He exhaled in satisfaction, and slapped the bowl down on the table.

He looked up at Sam, a single stream of milk running down his chin, and asked, "So, Mouse's party tonight …. What time are we going?"

Sam responded by performing a wiping motion across his chin, attempting to alert Robbie to the remaining milk on his face.

Recognizing the gesture with an embarrassed look on his face, Robbie quickly addressed the stream of milk trickling down his chin. His hand rushed to his mouth. Taking a grip of his sweatshirt sleeve, he wiped his face excessively on the scratchy fabric. Robbie proceeded to make a spectacle of the event by wiping his nose, cheeks, and forehead, making absolutely certain that there was no remaining milk on his face.

Sam laughed at Robbie's self-deprecating performance. "Yeah, I'm not sure what time we're supposed to go," he admitted. "I think they're all starting at the twins' house at eight and then going to The Rue at midnight."

"Sounds like my kind of birthday party!" Robbie exclaimed, standing up and placing his empty cereal bowl in the sink.

Sam nodded and followed Robbie's lead, placing the bowl neatly in the sink beside its companion. Sam ran water generously over the dirty dishes and, with a small dollop of soap, called them clean and set them in the drying rack.

Sam meandered over to a hook on the wall near the door, and quickly tossed on his recently thrifted, light-gray peacoat. He pulled his backpack over his shoulders and headed out the door.

"See you later, bud!" Robbie called out.

Sam waved back over his shoulder, as the door shut behind him.

As Sam walked through the building, down the elevator, and out into campus, he pondered intensely, *What should I get Mouse for his birthday?... I still can't believe I don't have a gift....*

He racked his brain, wrought with guilt over the late timing of the decision. It's not as though Sam hadn't put any thought into the gift. If anything, he had over-thought it. Night after night, he had considered a number of different gifts, but one question persisted in his mind. *"What do you get someone who has everything?"*

Sam had never known Mouse to lust after things or express a desire for tangibles. Occasionally, he would purchase a designer sweater or brand name watch, but those things all stood well outside of Sam's means and he wouldn't know what to buy even if he could afford it.

Sam's stresses and anxieties over Mouse's birthday led him off campus and straight into the St. Agatha neighborhood shopping district. Monroe Street was lined with every store imaginable and, on most days, the packed sidewalks were nearly impossible to maneuver without being bumped into or spilled on. Sam stared down the length of Monroe Street, noting the early time of day and the unusual emptiness of the sidewalks. He scanned the store fronts for inspiration, as he strolled leisurely from side to side embracing the freedom of movement offered by the wide-open sidewalk.

Sam looked up to see a figure in the distance, waving and running toward him. It was Maisie. Maisie was dressed in athletic wear, black yoga pants and a black zip-up, running hoodie. In true Maisie fashion, she accessorized with a black bandana, covered in skulls, tied around her head and covering the tops of her ears.

"I can't tell if you're running or going to a punk rock concert," Sam hollered, teasing her as she approached.

Maisie caught her breath, "Ha. Ha ... very funny!" She slowed down and placed her hands on her knees as she stopped in front of Sam. "I couldn't find my headband!"

"How was your run?" Sam inquired, kindly.

Maisie stood up straight and gestured for the two of them to walk together. "It was good. What are you doing down here before noon?" she asked, accusingly smiling and raising an eyebrow.

Sam turned his face away from Maisie, staring off and avoiding eye contact. "I ... ummm ... don't have a birthday gift for Mouse," he said in an embarrassed whisper.

"Sam! Isn't Mouse's birthday party tonight?" she pressed, judgmentally. "Let's walk, they're just opening up down here."

"Are you sure? I don't want to interrupt your run," Sam replied, resisting her offer to join him.

Maisie shook her head and rolled her eyes. She grabbed Sam by the hand and dragged him down the sidewalk, in the direction of an upscale, menswear store. The store had a large white awning with fancy, cursive black lettering that read, "Paddington's." They stepped inside and were immediately greeted by a smiley, well-dressed attendant in his early forties.

Sam carefully scanned the racks of clothing, overwhelmed by the array of jackets and sweaters in front of him. He ran his fingers delicately along the sleeve of a soft, green plaid sweater, pinching the fabric between his pointer finger and thumb. He turned to Maisie with a curious smile.

"I don't know, Maisie. Do you think Mouse will wear this stuff?" he asked, looking down at the price tag on the sweater.

Sam's curious smile quickly faded, as he read the numbers on the price tag. His hand slowly drifted to the tattered, brown wallet in his back pocket, as the quiet shame of poverty set in. Sam had worked incredibly hard to get into St. Agatha University, earning every scholarship and applying to every grant program that he could find. There was a reason that he didn't go into stores like this. He could never afford anything.

When he was young, his parents had done well to hide their financial situation from him. Growing up in the Pacific Northwest, he never made much of the fact that they went hiking every weekend and spent most evenings at the public park. Pretty much all of Sam's childhood recreation took place in public spaces, where there was no admission fee. Sam learned to make a lot out of a little. Always.

Despite their financial shortcomings, Sam's childhood was filled with love and he never felt the weight of their lower-class status. His mother held a steady job as a kindergarten teacher. She loved her job and was amazing with young children. Sam's father, on the other hand, bounced from job to job. He was a hard worker, and a skilled auto mechanic, but his complicated past often limited the availability of secure, full-time work.

Maisie whispered to Sam with a kind, comforting tone, "We're nearing spring. A lot of the winter stuff is going to be on sale now. Let's look back here!"

Pulling him by the hand, she guided him to the back of the store. They arrived at a disorganized rack of winter jackets and sweaters labeled, "SALE." Sam picked up a hunter green jacket and tried it on over his shoulders. He was much taller and leaner than Mouse, but he attempted to guess Mouse's size nonetheless. The jacket, too short in length but baggy in the shoulders, seemed to be an appropriate size. Sam looked down at the price tag dangling from the jacket sleeve.

40% OFF, $218, Sam read to himself, perplexed by the labeling.

"Excuse me, sir," Sam asked the nearby attendant, as he held out the jacket nervously. "Is this 40% off of $218?"

"No, I'm sorry young man," the man apologized. "$218 is the final sale price,"

Sam nodded, "Okay, thanks. I was hoping to spend under $100. It's a gift for my boyfriend."

The attendant smiled and guided Sam toward a glass case, near the front cash register. The case housed a variety of wallets, belt buckles, jewelry, and other accessories. While it was all a bit trinkety, Sam felt confident that he would be able to afford something in this part of the store. He peered into the case and scanned the assortment of goods. As he reached the right side of the case, he pointed to a light-gray cushion that held a row of eleven small metal coins.

"What are these?" Sam asked, as he curiously examined the unique markings on each of the coins.

The attendant removed the cushion from the case. "We just got these in," the attendant explained. "They're just coins really, not a worn accessory, but they have different astrological signs on them. What is your boyfriend's birth sign?"

"Aquarius," Sam stated, searching the cushion desperately for the Aquarius sign.

"I'm so sorry," the attendant disappointedly replied. "That is the only one I don't have. As you can imagine, we sold out of this month's birth sign pretty quickly when they arrived in the store."

Sam nodded his head in understanding and turned toward the door with a somber look on his face. Maisie reached out and placed her hand gently on his back.

"Wait, Sam. Isn't there a month that is special to you guys? Something sentimental?" Maisie asked, hoping to inspire him and liberate him from his defeated posture.

Sam paused for a moment and thought back to the first day that he saw Mouse. After finishing his finals exams sophomore year, Sam signed up to stay on campus and work as an usher at the graduation ceremonies. St. Agatha University was beautiful in late May, and Sam certainly needed the extra money. Tasked as an usher, he was handing out programs at the entrance when a handsome, blond-haired boy wandered into the ceremony. His hair was the first thing that Sam noticed, its gentle waves glowing in the sunlight as the boy strolled through the campus gardens and toward Sam. His confident stride was intoxicating, as Sam found himself staring. The boy reached out to take a program and curiously held onto the folded paper for a second too long, making prolonged eye contact with Sam. As the boy walked away, Sam followed his flowing blond hair all the way down the aisle. He stood distracted as the boy walked to his seat, aimlessly holding programs out into the air to be taken by the passing attendees.

As the graduation ceremonies came to a close, Sam waited impatiently by the doors and hoped that the boy would walk again in his direction. He stared into the thinning crowds, but the boy never showed. They didn't start dating until the following year, but they often discussed this particular memory. Sam was relieved to know that Mouse recalled that moment just as vividly as he did. Some moments, like this one, leave an undeniable and unforgettable impression on a person's soul.

"Gemini," Sam spoke up, turning back to face the glass case. "Do you still have the Gemini coin?"

The attendant smiled and lifted the Gemini coin from the pillow. He wrapped it neatly in dark green tissue paper and placed it in a small box. He placed the box gently on the counter and pushed it in Sam's direction.

"How much are they?" Sam asked, pulling his tattered, leather wallet from his pocket.

"Go ahead," the attendant replied, ushering toward the door with a soft smile. "Your boyfriend seems like a wonderful person."

Sam paused and exchanged a curious look with the attendant. He took the box and placed it in his backpack. Sam wasn't one to take charity from anyone, let alone a stranger, and he prided himself on his work ethic and his ability to make it on his own, but this felt different. The look in the attendant's eyes was that of a deep empathy, a smile that evoked solidarity. Hope.

"Thank you," said Sam. "Thank you very much."

Sam and Maisie walked out the door, linking arms and reflecting on the kindness of the store attendant. They stepped out onto the Monroe Street sidewalk, which had quickly returned to its usual, crowded form. They started up the street toward campus excitedly. Sam was proud of the gift he had found for Mouse and breathed a long sigh of relief, as he zipped his backpack closed and pulled it up over his shoulders.

They sifted through the masses of people shopping and shuffling along the Monroe Street sidewalks. The crowds closed in on them and swinging shopping bags banged clumsily against Sam's legs. As they approached the crosswalk, groups of inattentive pedestrians ignored the opportunity to cross and halted in the middle of the walkway.

"Excuse us!" Maisie yelled into the crowd, her frustration boiling over.

The sea of people parted at the shrill sound of Maisie's voice and the two marched onward toward campus. Shocked glances followed Maisie and Sam, through the separated crowds. Maisie didn't seem to notice, as she charged forward down the street. As they crossed the threshold of the campus front gates, Maisie bid Sam farewell, remarking that she still needed to shower and finish a philosophy paper if she wanted to go out tonight. Sam checked his phone and, realizing he had plenty of time before the party to study, headed off to the library.

A remnant of the 1970s, the library's concrete columns stood out like a sore thumb on the St. Agatha University grounds. In contrast to the old East Coast aesthetics that defined the rest of campus, the library was a dark-gray, concrete monument to the experimental architecture of its construction date. Sam usually delighted in the historic red bricks of St. Agatha University, but he held a quiet place of aesthetic disdain in his heart for the look of the library.

As he approached the protruding, concrete shapes of the library's entryway, he took note of a strange contrast in student behavior near its front door. As news of the virus continued to spread, world leaders were calling on people to take extra precautions in public spaces. One particularly strong cry came from Denmark, where one of their health officials had insisted that all people wear facemasks in public and urged people to stop shaking hands.

This type of political consciousness hadn't taken sway in the United States, as the sitting President remained particularly calm about the rising death rates in East Asia and France. Despite little action from the U.S. President, some prominent actors and business people in the United States had started to raise alarms about the potential for the virus to reach American soil. In light of this, Sam was simultaneously surprised and unsurprised by the number of students wearing masks around campus. This, set in contrast to the crowds of students smoking cigarettes outside of the library, sparked a strange, social curiosity in Sam.

There's a paper to be written about this, he thought, as he passed by one student wearing a facemask and another smoking a cigarette in front of the library.

Sam stopped to flash his student ID to a security guard at the library's entrance and looked up in search of a familiar face. As the guard waved him on, he saw Mouse and the twins sitting at a round table near the library cafe.

Ignoring any sense of social courtesy on the quiet floor of the library, Jay stood up on his chair and yelled across the library, "SAM, WE'RE OVER HERE!"

All at once, each of the one-hundred students on the first floor of the library looked in Sam's direction, and then back at Jay, in disgust. Sam lowered his head and walked past the judgmental eyes of the studying students. Marvin and Jay burst into laughter as Sam drew nearer to their table and Mouse reached across and punched Jay in the arm.

"Hey guys," Sam whispered, bending down and hugging Mouse over the shoulders. "Jay, you're a dick."

Jay fancily turned his palm up and bowed, like an actor on stage thanking the audience for attending his performance. Sam took a seat in the hard-wooden chair next to Mouse and opened his chemistry book to a folded corner page in the book's fourth chapter.

Mouse pushed a battered blue, spiral notebook towards Sam. *General Chemistry 101*, was etched in sloppy handwriting across the top.

"Look at us. Just a couple of chemistry nerds," Mouse teased, flipping quickly through the pages of the notebook with a single roll of his thumb.

Sam chuckled. While Sam had decidedly been a biology major since he first arrived on campus, Mouse had bounced around from degree program to degree program. He had enrolled at St. Agatha as a political science major, originally thinking that he wanted to pursue a career in politics. He certainly had the charisma and charm to make a compelling and captivating candidate, but he abandoned that pursuit after a single semester. He tried his hand at business marketing for a year and then briefly considered communications, but neither stuck. He finally settled on majoring in art and design during the last semester of his sophomore year. He loved to draw and, during his family's extensive travels through Western Europe, he had developed an interest in old museums and French art.

A natural consequence of this academic trajectory was that Mouse had hardly completed any of his general education requirements for graduation. While each student declared a major, the university still required one general course in science, math, English literature, religion, history, and language before a student could be eligible for graduation. Mouse had long postponed his baseline science course. He hoped that Sam, in all of his expertise, would help him make sense of *General Chemistry 101*.

"Are your exams this week, Birthday Boy?" Sam asked, playfully.

"Yeah," Mouse said softly, "I'll be fine." He intertwined his fingers with Sam's and tried to hide his stress behind a smile.

Marvin slammed his fist on the table, "You know what, it's your birthday dude. Let's get out of here. Party today. Study tomorrow."

Jay packed up his things before anyone could respond and the twins stood up. They looked down at Mouse, waiting for a response. Mouse shifted in his chair and pulled gently at the edges of his chemistry notebook. He considered leaving. He had been studying for a few hours and it was his birthday, after all. Mouse looked over at Sam and, tracing the gentle outlines of his cheekbones, leaned back in his chair.

"You guys go ahead, I'm going to put in some more time," he replied. "Sam just got here."

The twins shrugged their shoulders in disappointment and headed toward the library's front doors, leaving the studious couple behind. Sam and Mouse sat quietly at the table for the next few hours. Occasionally, Mouse would ask Sam for clarification or help with a particular concept but, for the most part, they just enjoyed the opportunity to sit together.

"You look cute," Mouse said, his mind straying from his studies.

"Oh yeah?" Sam asked. "You think so?"

"Yes," Mouse replied, taking Sam's hand and kissing it.

While Mouse was committed to learning the material for his exam, he eventually grew tired of studying and stood up from his chair. His study habits weren't nearly as disciplined as Sam's, but no one on campus rivaled Sam's commitment to his education. Mouse kissed Sam gently on the cheek and exited the library en route to his birthday party.

After another hour of studying alone, Sam returned to his

apartment to drop off his backpack and change clothes. As he inserted his key into the heavy wooden door of his apartment, he overheard the sound of an angry, frustrated Robbie on the phone.

"Yeah, Mom. I know. I've got it," Robbie declared curtly, as he paced from his room to the kitchen and back again. "It's fine. I understand. Really."

Sensing something was wrong, Sam hesitated and then opened the door slowly. As he stepped inside, he looked at Robbie and tried to make sense of the distraught expression on his face. Robbie's footsteps became heavier and heavier as he marched around the apartment and argued with his mother in a deadly serious tone.

Sam set his backpack down on the floor slowly and wandered over to the refrigerator. He turned back to Robbie and waved to get his attention. Robbie, still pacing, glanced back in confusion.

"All good?" Sam whispered, as he opened the refrigerator, politely asking for permission to make dinner in the apartment's common area.

Robbie replied with a simple thumbs up and stomped into his bedroom, closing the door behind him. The muffled sounds of the verbal altercation could still be heard through the thin walls of the apartment. Sam tried hard not to eavesdrop, as he pulled a package of deli ham and a loaf of nine-grain wheat bread from the back of the refrigerator and fixed a simple sandwich. Scanning the pantry, he settled on a handful of pretzels and, arranging them hurriedly on his plate, sat down at the dining table to eat.

The first bite of Sam's sandwich was interrupted by the slamming of Robbie's bedroom door. Robbie emerged from his bedroom, visibly enraged.

"That woman!" Robbie said, as he clenched his fists at his side. "She keeps telling me that she wants to pull me out of school for the rest of the year because of this stupid virus."

He stomped furiously toward the fridge and grabbed a beer. He collapsed into the chair next to Sam and pulled back the aluminum top of the can, taking a big gulp. He continued, "If her President doesn't think the virus is a big deal, why is she harping on me about it?"

"Well, she voted for him. Tell her to trust his judgment," Sam joked. "What is she going to do? Drive down here and make you leave?"

"I wouldn't put it past her, dude!" Robbie replied. "She's really worried and, to be honest, I am too. I read that there were, like, fifty confirmed cases in Canada this week, but I'll be damned if I'm going to let that ruin my senior year."

Sam nodded, as Robbie raised his beer in celebration. Robbie's mother had a reputation for being dramatic and she loved telling Robbie what to do, but Sam found it odd that she would ask him to suspend his senior year and come home. St. Agatha University had one of the top university hospitals in the country and, of all places, Sam assumed they were safe on campus. Even though the student population was fairly international, the United States was yet to have a confirmed case inside of its borders and everything still felt pretty safe.

Robbie quickly washed down his frustration with a big, final gulp. With the tightening of his fist, he crumpled the can and tossed it into the recycling bin in the corner.

"So, are we going to this party, or what? I thought it started at *8:00 PM*," Robbie asked, forcing a cheery disposition in place of his lingering anger.

Sam looked over at the clock on the kitchen stove, ignoring the bread crumbs and stains on the uncleaned surface of the electric burners. *9:45 PM*, he gasped. *Mouse is going to be so mad.*

Sam stood up, still finishing his sandwich, and pulled on his coat. Robbie followed excitedly behind him, as they headed out the door. Sam, quickly remembering the Gemini coin in his backpack, bolted back inside, just as the door swung closed. He reached into his backpack on the floor and pulled out the small box, tucking it into his jacket pocket.

The twins lived just north of campus, renting a privately owned row house in an old neighborhood. Their house was within walking distance from campus, according to those accustomed to city living. However, for students who grew up in the suburbs, the trek up the street always seemed excessive.

As they approached the twins' house, the blaring party music could be heard from the street. Masses of students were scattered about the twins' lawn and front porch with red solo cups in hand. Sam scanned the different groups of people, huddled together in the February cold like sardines in a can, desperately searching for Mouse. Sam spotted Maisie up on the front porch, seated casually on the rustic, white handrail with her back against one of the porch's support columns. She was deeply engaged in conversation with Jay and a petite black-haired girl wearing a long winter parka. Sam and Robbie approached the group slowly, recognizing the intensity of their conversation as they got close.

"I just don't understand how the President could decline foreign medical assistance. The death rate is 13%. Do we want people to be safe or not?!" Maisie asked, fighting back the rising anger in her voice.

"Sorry we're late. Blame Robbie," Sam said jokingly, as they walked up to the group and interrupted Maisie's tirade.

"My sincerest apologies," Robbie explained, as he curtsied and bowed his head. "None of my outfits seemed to fit right."

The black-haired girl in the winter parka let out a soft chuckle and a loud snort, covering her face in embarrassment.

"No worries," Jay explained, gesturing over his shoulder toward the house. "Mouse is just inside. Did you guys hear that a Swiss company thinks they have a new way to track the virus? It sounds good, but the President came out today and said that he would be prioritizing American businesses ... sorry. It's a party. Let's talk about something else."

Standing up, Maisie introduced the black-haired girl standing next to her, "This is my friend Jenny Li. She's a transfer from Buffalo. We're taking McMann's 'History of Asian Philosophy' together."

The girl greeted Sam and Robbie with a kind, half smile and shook their hands. She straightened her parka awkwardly, as the quick introduction devolved into silence.

Maisie continued, in a mischievously flirtatious tone, "Jenny ... Did I mention that Robbie is also from New York?"

Maisie was a hopeless romantic and loved playing matchmaker. To her credit, she was incredibly good at it. Many different couples on campus owed their first introduction to Maisie Marks; however, it was a courtesy that she never lent herself. She and Jay had been casually dating for two years, but Maisie never took ownership of it. She didn't use words like boyfriend or girlfriend and she rarely talked to Jay, or about him, in public, but there was an undeniable chemistry between the two of them that she didn't feel the need to avoid.

"You mean Long Island," Robbie corrected, challenging the authenticity of Jenny's New York credentials.

"Queens," Jenny replied, nodding her head as a challenge to Robbie.

"Brooklyn," he challenged back.

Robbie and Jenny quickly disappeared in a playful debate about which iconic New York food, pizza or bagels, they could live without. Sam knew better than to argue with Robbie about New York things, but Jenny appeared to rival his intimate knowledge of the city.

Has Robbie finally met his match? Sam thought to himself, grinning as he left the group and entered the party. *Maisie Marks does it again.*

Sam sifted through the crowds toward the back porch. With his destination in mind, Sam walked the entire length of the party and scanned the different faces looking for Mouse. The sweaty crowd of drunk college students swayed from side to side, bumping Sam as he attempted to navigate the space. Suddenly, he felt two hands wrap around his waist from behind. He turned and looked down at a beaming Mouse, wearing bright red sneakers and light-wash, designer jeans. A tight, gray V-neck shirt accentuated the muscles on his chest and arms. Sam placed his arms gently around Mouse's shoulders.

"What took you so long?" Mouse asked, wide eyed and smiling from ear to ear.

"I was studying and lost track of time. I'm sorry," Sam explained. "But I have a gift for you. Can we go out on the porch?"

"At my own birthday party? Now, what would that say about me?" Mouse teased, as he pushed Sam in the direction of the porch.

Sam took a deep breath of the cold air as they stepped outside. He pulled his jacket collar up to cover his neck and sat down on a rickety piece of patio furniture. Mouse gracefully drifted behind him, running his fingers along Sam's shoulders as he passed. He took a seat beside Sam on an old bar stool. They sat for a moment, looking up at the stars, and took in the stillness of the February night. Despite the cold, it was gorgeous out. There wasn't a cloud to be seen, and the stars danced and glimmered across the night sky.

"You didn't have to get me anything, Sam," Mouse said, sitting up straight on the stool.

"I wanted to," Sam replied, as he pointed at a high point in the eastern sky. "Do you know what that is?"

"The Big Dipper?" Mouse responded, with a sarcastic grin.

Sam laughed and shook his head. "It's the Gemini constellation," he explained, still pointing. "Castor and Pollux were twins ... which actually makes this a little weird now that I'm saying it out loud."

Mouse laughed. "Go on," he insisted reassuringly.

"Well, they get separated by death. But Pollux asks Zeus if he would grant Castor immortality. Moved by the request, Zeus immortalizes them side by side in the stars ... forever," Sam continued.

Lowering his finger, Sam turned from the sky toward Mouse. "I don't know if we'll be together forever." He paused for a moment and took a deep breath, "But, if you were to ask me what my forever looks like, I would say that it was standing next to you."

Mouse looked at Sam for what felt like an eternity. He said nothing, but the gentle formation of a tear in his eyes spoke volumes. Sam reached down and pulled the gift box from his pocket, his hand shaking as he held it out toward Mouse.

Mouse closed his hand around the box, letting the warmth of his palm rest gently on Sam's for a moment. He opened the box slowly and carefully peeled back the folds of the dark green tissue paper to expose the Gemini coin. Taking the coin in his hand, he turned it over in his palm and examined it closely.

"It's great, Sam," Mouse said, fighting back tears. "But you know I'm an Aquarius, right?"

The two laughed and wiped their eyes. "Yeah, I know. They were sold out," Sam explained. "But Gemini is early summer. May and June. I just thought it would be nice to remember ...."

"The graduation ceremony," Mouse interrupted, setting aside his laughter. He stared intensely at the coin as he ran his finger along its edges. "Gemini."

THE MOUNTAINS

The delicate sound of wind chimes and chirping birds played softly in the background, as Emily opened her eyes and stretched her arms up over her head. The smell of fresh flowers and springtime filled her bedroom, and the sweet aroma woke her from her slumber. She rolled over and swung her feet over the edge of her bed, shifting into a seated position.

She spoke out into the emptiness of her bedroom, "Alarm off. Enhance springtime smell."

A burst of scented spray erupted from her ceiling fan and the morning's sound of chimes and chirping birds faded away slowly. Emily picked up a sanitary wipe from her nightstand and wiped down her tablet thoroughly. Continuing the morning ritual, she removed a small, cylindrical rod from her nightstand drawer and cleaned it robustly from top to bottom. She inserted one end of the rod into a small port in the tablet's face and raised the other end to her mouth. Placing it under her tongue, a shrill beeping sound and a flashing blue light emanated from the tablet and counted sequentially up to thirty.

"Beep. Beep. Beep. Beep… 98.2, Vitals normal. Good morning, Emily," called out the tablet, in its monotonous, robotic tone.

The flashing blue light turned green, and Emily removed the rod from her mouth. She wiped it down again and returned it to its resting place in her nightstand drawer. A pair of white, furry slippers sat neatly at her bedside. She stood up slowly from her bed and stepped into them. The soft, white slippers warmed her feet, as she walked across the spotless, hardwood floor to the wash station in the corner of her room.

Emily stepped up to the sink near the door and stared at herself in the mirror. She waved her hand over the sink's leftmost motion sensor and began to wash her hands and face. The warm water resurrected her from her tired state. Face still dripping wet, Emily stared blankly into the mirror and wrestled herself into focus. She reached out and picked up a green bottle labeled, "Oral Disinfectant," and took a large swig. The sharp sting of the green liquid filled her mouth. She swished it around her mouth reluctantly, and fought through the burning sensation by running her tongue over her front teeth.

"Blah," Emily groaned, as she spit the liquid out into the sink. She inhaled through her tightly gritted teeth and attempted to alleviate the burning sensation left behind by the morning ritual.

Turning from the sink, Emily found a set of clean house clothes wrapped tightly in her wardrobe. She unwrapped the outfit slowly and stepped into her usual white bodysuit and sweatpants. Checking herself one last time in the mirror, she adjusted her hair and headed downstairs to begin her day.

"Good morning, Dad!" she shouted cheerfully as she leapt the last two stairs of the staircase and landed gracefully in the living room. Emily's father was engaged in an intense workout on the stationary bike near the window. Panting excessively with sweat running down his face, he managed a half smile and waved loosely in her direction.

"Good morning, Emily!" he called back, peddling and breathing hard as he rose into an aggressive, standing pose on the stationary bike. "Your mother is in her office on a call. Your pills are on the table!"

Emily nodded in response and strolled casually into the kitchen toward the refrigerator. She opened the metallic refrigerator door slowly and took out an individually packaged jar of plain yogurt. With the jar in hand, she turned to face the far wall of the kitchen. A series of six glass cases lined the wall in front of her, each filled with a variety of leafy greens and produce. The cases were illuminated by bright, white light bulbs that were set in each of the cases' high corners. Emily approached the second case from the left and pulled open the lid slowly. She reached down and plucked a handful of fresh blueberries. She eagerly stepped up to the kitchen sink and rinsed them off under a misting of water and apple cider vinegar. Declaring them fit to be eaten, she tossed the blueberries into the jar of yogurt and set it down on the kitchen counter.

A clean spoon was set out for her at her place setting, near a small, ceramic dish filled with pills. She held the spoon up in the light and examined it carefully. Returning to the sink, she washed it once more before sitting down at her place at the kitchen counter. Emily looked down and counted the pills.

1, 2, 3, 4, 5….6? Emily counted to herself, surprised by the presence of a new, sixth pill.

"Dad, what is this last one?" Emily asked, yelling over her shoulder at the stationary bike.

"New Council mandate," her father explained. "Everyone over sixteen was issued an additional immunizer this week."

Emily sighed in frustration as she tossed the handful of pills into her mouth. She swallowed, twice, to ensure their successful consumption. A sharp pain shot down her throat and she grimaced as she choked down the colorful medley of vitamins, immunizers, and medications. Her eyes watered and she washed down the dosage with a spoonful of yogurt.

The hefty intake of pills was mandatory every day, seemingly growing in size as Emily got older. Most people adjusted over time to the routine, but Emily had always struggled with taking her pills. Ted had always seemed unfazed by the size and volume of his daily intake, often unflinchingly gulping the pills down without the assistance of water. He had been taking medication for his respiratory problems his whole life and, compared to the size of those, the standard daily intake was nothing. Still, no matter how hard she tried, Emily always reeled back when she took her morning medications. The appearance of a sixth pill wasn't just annoying, it was wildly unpleasant.

Enjoying her yogurt and blueberries, Emily stared blankly into the kitchen and began to plan her day in peace. She outlined her schedule and carefully went over her homework assignments in her head. A loud thud interrupted Emily's breakfast as Ted trounced down the stairs, jumping with two feet down each individual step.

"Woah, buddy. Slow down there," Emily's father hollered, cautioning Ted from the seat of the stationary bike. "Take a breath."

Slowing the rate of his work out, Emily's father dismounted the stationary bike and intensely cleaned the workout equipment with a sanitary wipe. He wiped his forehead with a small, blue athletic towel and marched triumphantly into Emily's parents' bedroom on the far side of the kitchen.

Ted scurried across the living area and stood next to Emily at the kitchen counter. Standing on his tiptoes, he tossed his pills into his mouth and effortlessly swallowed.

He looked up at Emily and asked, "Emily, will you make me a yogurt?"

She scoffed at him, "You can do it. You're old enough to fix your own breakfast."

Ted sighed in frustration as he stormed angrily to the fridge and removed a jar of yogurt. He stomped his feet as he walked toward the wall of glass cases and opened the case on the far right. The strawberry case.

"Hey, Genius!" Emily shouted. "Look at the chart. Blueberries are in rotation today."

Ted rolled his eyes and chirped back at her, "It's not like it matters. No one cares if I eat the strawberries a week early."

"Look. At. The. Chart," Emily hollered back at him, rising from her chair.

"Mind. Your. Business," Ted yelled back, matching her tone and volume.

The violent shouting match carried on, as Ted continued to justify his craving for strawberries and Emily insistently directed him to the rules. The bickering grew louder and their echoing voices carried through the house. A door swung open beyond the kitchen and the room went still. Emily and Ted shrank, as their mother emerged from her office with an enraged look on her face and fire in her eyes. She stared intensely at Emily, refusing to break eye contact.

"You know better," she said sternly at Emily, the harsh judgement of her look piercing Emily to her core.

Emily paused for a moment in fear, but quickly snapped back, "Ted is trying to eat produce out of rotation. Are you okay with that?"

Her chilling gaze shifted over to Ted, who immediately took three giant steps toward the blueberry case and began plucking the day's fruit in rotation.

"The actions of one," she barked at Ted, in a stern, lecturing tone.

"Carry the safety of us all," he said softly, staring at the floor to avoid eye contact with his mother.

The door slammed shut, as Emily's mother returned to her office. The loud bang of the door sent chills down their spines, as they stood like statues in the kitchen. Breaking loose of her stillness, Emily gathered her dishes in silence and placed them in a metal dishwasher next to the sink. She washed her hands quickly while Ted ate his breakfast in a defeated and angry fuss. Emily's tablet chimed to signify the hour, *9:00 AM*, and Emily started upstairs to begin her school day.

"Snitch," Ted muttered bitterly, as Emily walked past. "Do you ever break the rules?"

"Finish your breakfast and go to class, Bleach-Brain," she snapped, before ascending the stairs to her bedroom.

Shaken from the encounter, Emily trudged somberly into her bedroom and over to her work area. A bright-blue tablet stand was situated in the middle of Emily's desk. As she sat down, she logged onto her tablet, and the display timer counted down to the start of class. Emily looked nervously at the screen and adjusted her hair. An anxious feeling came over her as the timer closed in on zero and the other students began logging in for the day. A flurry of video chat windows appeared on the screen and the students waved as their video feeds came into view. Emily examined the familiar faces, greeting her peers as they came into view. Then, just before the timer disappeared, Cayden signed on and an overwhelming sea of waving students welcomed him to class.

Last week's victory over Tri-City had been a bigger deal than Emily had realized. The Eden Vax had underperformed for as long as Emily could remember. They consistently ranked near the bottom of the league, but the team's winning history carried the fanbase. The 2050s were the Golden Era of the Eden Vax, and the fans were much more interested in their former glory than on the team's current losing streak; however, this year was different.

"Eden Vax Welcomes New Era," read the week's news headlines. *"Is Cayden McDaniels the Answer?"*

Following the big win over Tri-City, Cayden had quickly become the talk of the town, and everyone at Walter Reed High School was competing for his attention. Emily pulled her hair gently out of her face and tucked it behind her ear, hoping that he was watching. She sat up straight, as Professor Haystead's video came on in the middle of Emily's tablet to begin class.

"Good morning, students," Professor Haystead said, sipping his morning coffee.

Professor Haystead sat at a large wooden desk, lined with old books, and held an antique, brown coffee mug in his hand. His wardrobe was as predictable as ever, brown slacks and a white button-down shirt. His thin, wire-framed glasses rested low on his nose as he awaited the students' response. Ignoring his salutation, the twenty other video chat windows sat in silence. They surrounded the central video chat window that displayed Professor Haystead, but no one responded to his morning greeting.

"Good morning, Professor," Emily finally chirped through the silence, searching the bordering windows for Cayden.

Professor Haystead smiled and leaned forward, "I'm glad someone is awake this morning. What about the rest of you?"

A chorus of mumbled greetings resounded at the Professor's request. As the morning salutations subsided, a private chat notification appeared in the upper right corner of Emily's tablet.

New Message – Cayden McDaniels. Emily smiled and clicked on the notification. A small chat window opened beneath the collage of video feeds.

A playful smiley face preceded Cayden's message, *"Suck up!"* he wrote.

Emily grinned and wrote in reply, *"You've gotta stay on your toes."*

The past three mornings had begun with her and Cayden's playful banter. They never exchanged more than just a few messages, but the first few minutes of class had quickly become Emily's favorite part of the day. Emily waited patiently for a response. Ellipsis appeared, then disappeared quickly. She sat up and stared intensely at the tablet screen, curiously searching for his response. After a long ten seconds, ellipsis reappeared as Cayden authored his reply.

"Walk home with me next week," Cayden responded brazenly.

Emily blushed at the boldness of his text. No question mark, no inquiry about her plans after in-school. Simply a command, *"Walk home with me next week."* She slid back in her chair, unsure what to make of the request. Emily was under no illusions that she was not the only person at school who was interested in Cayden. She would hesitate to call it a crush, but there was an intriguing *something* about him. 'Something' was the only word that she could use to describe the way that she felt.

She replayed their first interaction in her head. *Kobe*, she thought to herself. *Who says that?*

She straightened up in her chair and began to type a response. A sly smile slid across her face as she located Cayden's video chat window on the screen. He slowly ran his hands through his dark-hair and tossed his flow lightly. The waves of hair bounced atop his head and caught the natural light from his window.

"Maybe," she wrote, hitting send with an unprecedented amount of confidence and questioning where this bold, mysterious persona was emanating from, taking pride in her calm, cool response. She hid her quivering hands beneath the table and tried hard to hide her emotions from her face.

"Emily, what do you think?" Professor Haystead asked, calling her back to attention.

"What do I think? Sir?" she asked sharply, attempting to wrestle the last minute of lecture from her momentary lapse in concentration.

"Yes, Emily," he pressed further. "What do you think about section 1.6?"

Another private chat notification appeared. *New Message – Fae Dotterman*. Emily quickly clicked open the notification and read the message aloud with a false confidence, "Past participle?"

Professor Haystead rolled his eyes and responded, "Thank you very much, I'm guessing that message came from Miss Dotterman. If I wanted her answer, I would have called on her."

Disappointed, Professor Haystead moved on with the rest of the lesson. An embarrassed shame overcame Emily like a hurricane. It was very out of character for her to lose focus like that, and she partially blamed Cayden. She leaned into class intensely for the remainder of the morning's lessons. She spoke up multiple times to answer questions, in a desperate attempt to redeem herself from her slipup.

This was an important year for Emily, as the Aptitude Exams were only a few weeks away and she hardly felt like she was prepared. The two-part exam was the most important part of Year 11. While there was a distinct personality section, that would identify character traits and personal values, the academic portion was the more important of the two. The academic portion decided what industry you could work in, with politics and government, medicine, and computer science being of the highest pedigree. The personality portion, on the other hand, determined which career track you were placed on within that industry. These tracks became the focus of a student's education for Year 12 and into college.

Emily didn't have a particular career in mind. It was encouraged that the students be open to many different possibilities, as it was quite rare that someone's personal interests lined up with their exam results. There was an appeals process if someone could justify a different career placement, but Emily had never heard of anyone being successful in that endeavor. "The test is rarely wrong," insisted the Council.

Regaining her focus, Emily worked hard to earn back her reputation for the rest of class. As Professor Haystead bid the class farewell for the day, another chat notification sprang up on Emily's screen. *New Message – Cayden McDaniels.*

"*See you tomorrow.*" Cayden wrote.

Emily picked up her tablet and wiped it down with a sanitary wipe. As she cleaned the tablet's surface, a flutter of butterflies filled her stomach. She clutched her tablet with two hands across her chest and walked downstairs to the living room. She floated down the stairs. The simplicity of Cayden's message lingered in her mind as she wrestled with the realities of her changing mood. Just as quickly as she had blamed him for her absentminded start to class, she found herself now smiling ear to ear at the thought of them walking home together.

"That's a big smile," her father said from his chair as she entered the living room. "Did you have a good morning at school?'

Startled, Emily replied in a quick and skittish manner, "Yeah, it was fine. I mean, it was good. I'm just excited about the Aptitude Exams."

"That's great, Emily. Excitement is good and we've talked about how important they are. Do your best!" her father encouraged as he leaned back in his chair and examined his tablet.

As he swiped from left to right across the tablet's face, a pensive smile stretched across his face. Pausing occasionally, he looked down at the device with a loving fondness. Emily approached slowly and sat down in the chair beside him. She glanced over his shoulder at the tablet and furled her brow at an old, still photograph.

Intrigued, Emily asked, "Dad, what are you looking at?"

"Oh, these are old family photos," he explained. He adjusted the settings on his tablet and his screen was quickly projected onto the television. "Your great aunt sent them to me this morning. They're from a trip that your grandparents took to Yosemite National Park when they were in college."

Emily looked up at the television in confusion. The still photograph showed four people standing on the edge of a cliff, with a dome-shaped mountain prominently in the background. Emily recognized the two people standing on the left as her grandparents. Although she had never met her grandfather, she recognized her father's distinctive facial features in the man in the photograph.

"Wait. Dad, are they actually up in the mountains?" Emily asked, eyes wide.

She scanned their clothing carefully, taking in the vibrant medley of colors and patterns. Her grandmother was dressed in tight, black leggings and a neon-green, zebra-printed tank top. Her grandfather wore bright-red pants and a black T-shirt with a mountain graphic on the front. Emily was so accustomed to the monochromatic, modern styles that had defined her upbringing that she giggled at the sight of their attire.

"Yeah, before the 2020 Outbreak, people used to go up into the mountains all the time," her father explained. "But that was before we knew about the health risks associated with public spaces. They used to have common-use bathrooms, visitor centers, and common lodging. People used to go out for weeks at a time and hardly washed themselves."

"How did they shower? How did they sanitize everything?" Emily inquired.

"I'm not sure, Emily," he said. "I don't think they did. I wouldn't be surprised if your grandfather hadn't showered for days in this still photo."

Emily was perplexed by the features of the still photograph. She stood up and stared deeply at the television, tracing the lines on her grandparents' faces and examining their proximity to the cliff's edge and the mountains on the screen.

They look so happy, she thought. *Weren't they worried about their health and safety?*

She turned and walked toward the living room window. Looking out in the distance, the faint outline of the Cascade Mountains could be made through the wisp of the clouds. On particularly clear days, Emily could see the mountain peaks on her walk to school, but she never dreamed of actually going up into them. The mountains had always been somewhat of a mystery to her, more terrifying than intriguing.

Once, when she and Ted were little, her family had taken their car out to the city limits. They stopped at a high point near the last vital health check, on the edge of Eden on the way to Seattle. Her family didn't cross out of Eden, as this would have required special permission from the Council and a rigorous analysis of their health records. Instead, they sat in their car at the high point and looked down at the large concrete barricade that bordered the city.

"The city limits protect us," her mother explained, as she pointed to a red truck coming into town and the group of armor-clad officers that surrounded it. "When travelers or new people come to town, the checkpoints make sure they aren't bringing anything bad with them. Travel is one of the easiest ways that disease can spread."

Emily recalled looking out in that moment, half-listening to her mother's lecture, and seeing the mountains in full view for the first time. She didn't think much of it then, but, as she looked at this photo of her grandparents and then back out the living room window at the Cascades, that particular memory became all the more vivid. Her first memory of the mountains.

She replayed her mother's words in her head, *"The city limits protect us … Travel is one of the easiest ways for disease to spread."*

"Come take a look at this one, Emily!" her father called out, interrupting her contemplative recollection.

Emily brought her attention back to the photo on the television. Her grandparents were suspended on the cliffside by ropes and were grabbing the coarse, dirty rock with their bare hands. Emily stood, enamored at the sight. The primitive nature of the activity astounded her. She gawked as her father flipped through photos of her grandparents camping, fishing, hiking, and rock climbing through the mountains, covered in dirt, unshowered, and disheveled.

"Can you believe people used to do that stuff?" her mother groaned from the kitchen, announcing her sudden presence. "You know, you're a lot like him, Emily. Your grandfather."

"He was very smart, disciplined," her father continued, with a smile on his face as he scrolled through still photos. "You have the same wit and sense of humor."

"Me?" she asked in disbelief, looking up at the dirt-covered, mountain man on the screen.

Emily paused to share in the memories and the quiet joy that her father was feeling through the still photos. "Did he ever take you into the mountains?" she asked, curiously.

"No, unfortunately not. Most of the national parks were closed after the 2020 Outbreak, before I was born," her father explained. "But, it was very strange."

He choked back tears and paused to collect himself. "Your grandfather never talked about his life before the 2020 Outbreak. That is, until he caught the virus during the second big wave," he said. "I was twenty-two when he got sick. Your mother and I had just finished at Seattle State University. Toward the end, all he wanted to talk about was life before 2020. He told stories about climbing in the mountains and his adventures with his friends. He talked about seeing concerts in person and football games. It was like I was meeting him for the first time."

A somber fog came over the room as her father stopped on a final, still photo. Her grandfather was standing on top of a large boulder, two hands in the air in a triumphant pose. Emily's mother came from the kitchen with a glass of water on a tray. She walked up from behind her husband's chair and placed one hand on his shoulder. She rubbed his shoulders, gently offering comfort, and his hand reached for hers.

There were few moments in Emily's life that she had seen her mother and father break norms and engage in physical touch. She knew that they shared a bed, but they never touched one another in a common area or out in public. Somehow, in this moment, it seemed strangely appropriate, and the bond of their shared intimacy brought a smile to Emily's face.

Emily's mother turned to her and spoke softly, "Emily dear, would you mind running down to the front desk and asking Tommy if the building has more sanitary wipes in storage? We're running low."

"Sure, Mom," Emily replied, recognizing that her mother was asking for privacy.

Emily quickly tucked her tablet into her tablet bag and headed out the front door. The bright lights of the housing unit entryway gave her pause. Emily peeled off her house clothes and tossed them gently into the chute in the corner of the room. Reaching into her locker she unwrapped a package of outside clothing, gray pants and a gray hooded sweatshirt.

As she got dressed, she pondered the era before the 2020 Outbreak. The high peaks and snowcaps of the mountains had always seemed so far and off-limits. Emily could barely fathom going out into the wilderness, let alone living there.

That's so crazy. Emily thought, washing her hands at the entry-way sink before heading down the elevator to Tommy's desk. *How can you live outside? What else did they do?*

Her thoughts carried her down the elevator, as she lost herself to her imagination and traversed the mountainous landscape with her grandparents in her head. She stepped off the elevator and approached Tommy slowly, noticing that he was already engaged in conversation with an elderly man. His back was turned toward the elevator and, as Emily approached within ten feet, she came to a halt to provide a more-than-appropriate amount of social distancing.

Recognizing her standing there, Tommy held up a single finger in her direction and called out, "Just one moment, Miss Emily."

Emily nodded and the elderly man turned toward her, removing his facemask. It was Doc Abrams. Doc smiled and proceeded to hand Tommy a white, plastic package that was sealed at the top with a button. Tommy wiped the package down thoroughly and placed it on his desk. He lathered his hands with sanitizing gel and turned to address Emily.

"What can I do for you, Miss Emily?" he asked, rising from his chair with a soft smile.

"My mother was hoping you could grab us two rounds of sanitary wipes from storage, if that's at all possible," Emily inquired politely.

Tommy nodded confidently and left his desk through a sliding glass door behind him. Emily had never been down to the storage area. Few people other than Tommy had a need to go down there, but Emily knew that the building kept cleaning supplies, groceries, clothing, and other household necessities on hand. The supplies were inspected and cleaned thoroughly by the building staff, and they were made available for residents via pre-order; however, on occasion, Tommy was kind enough to grab things on the fly if the residents asked nicely.

As Tommy disappeared, Emily turned to address Doc Abrams. "Doc Abrams, I didn't know you lived in HC-F5," Emily said, attempting to make small talk while waiting for Tommy to return.

Doc Abrams limped in her direction and replied with a warm smile, "Miss Chang! How good to see you," he said, coughing lightly as he tempered his excitement. "I live over in HC-A3, actually. I'm just here on pharmacy business. Some of the older residents aren't able to come weekly, so I try to drop things off for them."

Emily was taken aback. The A-clusters were usually reserved for the senior Council members and the most important members of the community. She had never met anyone who lived there. Even the most wealthy and prominent of her classmates lived in the B or C-clusters. While she knew that Doc Abrams and the pharmacy were a vital part of the community, HC-A3 still seemed well above his station.

Maybe he just got lucky in the lottery system, she thought.

"Well, that is very kind," Emily stated. "Do you visit all of the clusters?"

"Every single one," Doc Abrams said, clearing his throat and taking a puff of his inhaler. "It's a lot of outside time, but I like getting outdoors. The fresh air is good on my lungs."

Emily's ears perked up at the mention of the outdoors. She looked closely at Doc Abrams' hands, curious about his past. They were aged and dry from washing, worn and calloused from use. She scanned his tattered, leather boots, taking in the creases and folds of their use.

"Excuse me, Sir. If I may be so bold, did you live through the 2020 Outbreak? I've heard that you're a survivor?" she asked curiously, immediately regretting her impoliteness and shrinking back into her posture.

A surprised look came across Doc Abrams' face, as he stiffened his posture and nodded to confirm. "Sure did. Those were difficult times," he responded with a saddened disposition. "Are you learning about the Outbreak in school? I'm not sure that a young person has ever asked me about that before."

Emily lowered her head apologetically and avoided Doc Abrams eyes. She folded her hands neatly across her waist and spoke up, "I'm sorry. I didn't mean to be rude …. We don't really learn about the Outbreak in school, only that it was very serious. I was actually more interested in your life before. Have you ever been rock climbing?"

Doc Abrams laughed and, startled by his own laughter, coughed harshly. He quelled the coughing fit with his inhaler.

"Rock climbing?" he said, taking a puff of his inhaler once more. "I haven't heard anyone talk about rock climbing in a long time. Sure, I've been once or twice. We used to spend a lot of time in the mountains."

Tommy emerged through the sliding glass doors and set two rounds of sanitary wipes on his desk. He thoroughly cleaned them and handed them over to Emily.

Arms full, she called out to Doc Abrams as he limped toward

the door, "Doc Abrams? Would you mind telling me about them sometime? The mountains, that is."

A renewed joy filled his eyes as he turned back to her. He smiled and answered softly, "Sure, Miss Chang. Come by the pharmacy any time."

Emily nodded excitedly and walked down the corridor to the elevators. As she stepped inside, she considered the open air of the mountains. The cold, steel walls of the elevator closed in on her in a new way. For the first time, this familiar space of comfort and home felt like a cage. She took a moment to look at each of the corners that made up the borders of the elevator and a sudden claustrophobia swelled in her chest. It suddenly felt so small compared to the wide, open spaces that she had seen in the photos of her grandparents.

The box came to a halt and the doors opened, seemingly slower than usual. Emily stepped out of the elevator hastily and took a deep breath, as she entered the entryway to her housing unit.

Her momentary anxiety subsided and the entryway bench invited her to sit down to collect herself. She lowered herself onto the bench carefully and began to clean the rounds of sanitary wipes thoroughly. She set them down neatly when she was finished and, in her usual fashion, discarded her clothes down the chute and changed into a new set of house wear.

Pulling on her white sweatpants, she stood for a moment in front of the entryway sink and stared down at her hands. Her fingertips were soft and delicate. She turned her hands over and over to examine her palms, knuckles, and cuticles. They weren't coarse or worn like Doc Abrams'. She wondered what it felt like to grab the sharp edges of the rock that made up a cliff's face. She wondered what it felt like to not shower for a week and live in the mountains.

As she approached the sink, the motion sensor clicked on and a rush of warm soap and water came pouring out of the spout. Emily stared at the flowing stream, but left her hands still at her side. The usual comforts and securities of the sanitizing ritual were nowhere to be found and she tilted her head slightly to one side, considering the stream in a new way. The rushing water ran its course and the swirling suds of soap spun down the drain.

She took a deep breath and, with dry unwashed hands, picked up the rounds of sanitary wipes and walked inside.

ANYTHING ELSE?

"That'll be $10.04," said the woman warmly, setting two coffees down on the counter. "Did you need anything else?"

Sam shook his head and proceeded to insert his credit card into the card reader on the counter. The barista reached across the counter and kindly held the machine secure for him, as he proceeded with the transaction. A signature box appeared on the scratched surface of the machine's display and Sam squiggled a line, loosely resembling his signature, within its borders.

"That's nice of you to buy coffee for your buddy," the barista said, gesturing to Mouse, who was standing behind Sam.

"Boyfriend," Sam corrected sternly. "I'm buying coffee for my boyfriend."

Mouse turned up a smile as the barista nodded in confusion. "Well, thanks for coming in," she said quickly.

She tapped her finger on the register anxiously, as she waited for the receipt to emerge. Ripping the paper receipt out sharply, she held out the receipt nervously toward him. Sam took the receipt in his bare hand and shoved it in his back pocket. Looking back at Mouse, he picked up both coffees and turned away from the register. Steam billowed over the rim of the paper cups and Sam felt the deep burn of the hot coffee on his palms. A row of cardboard sleeves were sitting just to the left of the cash register, next to the cream and sugar, and Sam breathed a sigh of relief as he spotted them.

He and Mouse wandered over and began to doctor their morning doses of caffeine. The surface of the condiment station was decorated with spilled cream and a spattering of loose grains of sugar. Taking a napkin in hand, Mouse wiped a clean space through the artistic array of coffee, sugar, cream, and wrappers on the countertop.

Mouse dressed his coffee in his usual way, with a splash of cream and a hefty pouring of sugar. Sam, on the other hand, took his coffee black. As the boys took their time, a few people began to file in behind them, pressing closely and impatiently waiting to access the mess of a station. The boys noticed the crowding line and quickly slipped cardboard sleeves over their paper cups and wandered out onto Monroe Street.

The streets were oddly thin. The Friday lunch hour usually packed Monroe Street with people, but the sidewalks looked different that day. Sam took note of the gaps and spaces between pedestrians where people should have been. He sipped his coffee slowly as they walked back toward campus, enjoying the emptiness and sunshine that marked the first day that truly felt like spring.

Tiny bulbs had appeared on the tulips lining the boutiques and restaurants of the St. Agatha University neighborhood. The warm array of colors would soon be a defining feature of their mornings, as the last week of March would become April, which would become May. Graduation was just around the corner, and a blend of anticipatory fear and excitement stirred inside of Sam.

As they approached the campus front gates, a lanky man walked toward them wearing a tweed sportscoat and a black cloth facemask. His stride and pace, accentuated by his height, indicated that he was in a hurry. A tattered messenger bag hung over his shoulder and he carried a brown, leather-bound notebook in his left hand. Looking up, he pulled down his facemask to greet Sam and Mouse.

"Samuel and Mouse! Two of my favorite students," the man called out. "What are you boys doing on campus? Shouldn't you be heading home for spring break?"

"Hey, Professor Bueller! Sam replied excitedly. "We're staying around here actually. Will you be around campus this week?"

"Sharp folks. It's probably best that we limit our travel with all of this virus stuff going on," Professor Bueller replied, with a firm, lecturing tone. "I will be around this week and I could use some company. Let's all get coffee; maybe I can convince Mouse to come back to the political science department."

Mouse laughed and held up his sketchbook, "Thanks Professor, but it's all art for me these days."

"That's a shame. You were awfully bright in my Political Ideologies class. Don't think that I've forgotten," Professor Bueller replied, looking down at his watch. "I'm terribly sorry boys, I'm late for an appointment. Come by my office on Tuesday and we'll chat."

The boys nodded as Professor Bueller pulled up his facemask and darted off toward Monroe Street. Professor Bueller was one of Sam's favorite teachers at St. Agatha University. He was in his mid-thirties, young for a professor, in both age and personality. Despite his age, he had been teaching at the university for over a decade. His classes were always full and the waitlist was a mile long. Students of every major jumped at the opportunity to study political science with him, but not solely because of his professional accomplishments. He was very well published and had advised on the previous President's 2012 campaign, but the students loved working with Professor Bueller because, quite simply, he cared about them and their interests. It wasn't more complicated than that.

Sam and Mouse had each taken Political Ideologies, at different times, and the class had had a lasting impact on them. It allowed students the opportunity to think about different political systems and forms of governance, and Professor Bueller always made it relatable. Sam imagined that now, more than ever, the class was exploring questions of governance and global health. The virus was all anyone seemed to talk about these days, and Sam was curious what Professor Bueller had to say about it.

As Professor Bueller made his way down to his appointment, Sam and Mouse enjoyed their coffees as they passed through the university front gates. The boys sat down on a park bench near the statue of St. Agatha and began the time-honored tradition of people watching. They drank deep the smell of springtime and fresh flowers and gawked at the passerby students dragging their suitcases toward the front gates. A line of cars stretched around the block, waiting to pick up students and take them to the airport.

"Just pick it up, dude," a thunderous voice yelled from behind them.

Sam and Mouse turned to see the twins, Jay and Marvin, lugging large, overstuffed bags alongside them. The twins were wearing bright-blue, Hawaiian shirts and excessively short, cutoff jeans. Ignoring the cold breeze of the early spring day, their summer attire let all of campus know that they were heading south for spring break.

"I've got it, Jay. Just worry about your own bags," hollered Marvin in response, as he wrapped two hands around the overstuffed bag dragging behind him.

With a single motion, he thrust the giant bag over his shoulder and stood up straight. It would be difficult to overstate the twins' strength and chiseled physique. Beyond being captains of the lacrosse team and spending a considerable amount of time at the school gym, the twins grew up on a dairy farm in northern Wisconsin and were raised doing manual labor. Sam had always imagined a caricature of them hoisting bales of hay on a farm in denim overalls, and it wasn't far from the truth.

"Do you guys need a hand?" Mouse called out to them, standing up and waving in their direction.

Jay hauled his overstuffed bag over to the bench and tossed it down on the pavement. "Hey fellas! Mouse, are you sure you're not coming with us? It's not too late to change your mind," Jay asked.

Jay was referring to the lacrosse team's annual spring break trip. They had been planning their vacation to Miami since last year, with Jay and Marvin renting a beach house that housed sixteen people. The trip mostly consisted of graduating seniors, but Mouse was one of the few juniors to receive an invitation. Sam was always welcome to join, along with the other significant others.

With that in mind, Sam had little interest in spending a week with the lacrosse team and their girlfriends on the beach. Playing gay best friend to a group of sorority girls wasn't his idea of a vacation. He would much rather return to Seattle to hike the Cascades with his parents than spend an entire week drunk on the beach. Mouse, on the other hand, had been looking forward to the trip for some time. He had his flight booked and bags packed up until three days ago.

On the previous Tuesday night, Sam's parents had called and asked him to cancel his trip home. He and Mouse were sitting on the couch watching reruns of an old teen drama, when Sam's phone had rung. His parents called once a week, on Friday, to check on him and update him on their life in Seattle. It was odd that they would be calling on a Tuesday, and the suddenness of the call was reason enough to be concerned. Mouse sat up slowly on the couch, realizing the severity of the call as Sam spoke.

"Yeah … No, that makes sense … If you're sure …." Sam said, anxiously tugging at the collar of his shirt. Sam hung up the phone and a nervous upset look came across his face.

"Is everything okay?" Mouse asked, inching closer to him on the couch.

"Yeah, I think so." Sam replied calmly. He paused and ran his hands through his hair, exhaling audibly. "They don't want me to get on a plane because of the virus. They're worried about all the people in the airport and all of the exposure. What am I supposed to do? Stay here on campus and …."

Without hesitation, Mouse interrupted him, "I'll stay." Sam looked up at him, stunned, as Mouse repeated, "I'll stay here for spring break."

"You can't do that," Sam responded sharply. "You've been looking forward to this trip for months."

"Nah," Mouse said with a grin. "I hate the beach."

They leaned back on the couch and Sam adjusted the volume on the television. He laid his head on Mouse's shoulder and reflected on the immense gratitude he felt for having met someone so kind and considerate.

The loud thud of another duffle bag shook the pavement, as Marvin chimed in after his brother, "Come on, Mouse. You're going to miss out on a hell of a spring break. You should come with us!"

"I'm all good here, fellas. Have fun with the team!" Mouse insisted. He hugged the twins goodbye, their muscular arms wrapping around him tightly. "Are you sure you guys don't need any help with these bags?"

The twins looked down at their bags and, in unison, struck bodybuilder poses and flexed their muscles. A group of girls walked by and giggled at the sight. Jay responded by kissing his flexed bicep and nodding his head in their direction. Laughter erupted, and the twins scooped up their luggage in a single, muscular movement.

With one more goodbye, they were off to the front gates. Miami awaited them.

The busyness of campus faded as the rest of the day went on. Sam and Mouse sat there on the bench, watching students load into car after car, until the rows of red-brick buildings became a ghost town. The wind picked up, and the sun began to set over St. Agatha University.

"Well," Mouse said, slapping a hand down on Sam's thigh. "Pizza?"

Sam chuckled and nodded. He paused for a moment and looked over at Mouse. His blonde hair was glowing in the sunset, as they sat together on the park bench. "I'm glad you stayed," Sam said with a soft smile.

"Yeah, me too," Mouse replied, taking Sam's hands in his own. "But, we're definitely getting pepperoni and mushroom."

The next few days went by in a blur, as the empty campus gave way to a variety of activities that would have otherwise been unavailable to Sam and Mouse. Mouse even stole a set of keys from the lacrosse coach's office and snuck them onto the stadium field. Running around, Mouse taught Sam how to properly pass a lacrosse ball and explained the nuances of the game to him. Sam had seen him play before, but, admittedly, he hardly understood the rules.

On another evening, they took a tent and a bottle of wine to the top of the student center and spent the night on the roof. They slept beneath the stars and traced the outlines of the constellations, pausing to take in the beauty of the Gemini constellation. Mouse playfully rolled the Gemini coin between his fingers and rested his head on Sam's shoulder.

Apart from a few other students and some stray faculty members, the campus was theirs and they made the most out of its vacancy.

Despite the circumstances, it was turning out to be the best spring break either of them had ever had.

Tuesday arrived quickly and Sam awoke, eager to meet with Professor Bueller and discuss the virus. He rolled out of bed excitedly and got dressed for the day. The warm welcome of springtime had grown over the past few days and the sun was shining brightly over campus. Sam pulled on a pair of khaki shorts for the first time that year, embracing the shift in weather, and buttoned up a light-blue dress shirt. Dawning a more casual look, he rolled up the sleeves neatly and opted to leave the shirt untucked. He stepped out in the quiet of the living room. It was strange not having Robbie around. The place was certainly cleaner, but the absence of his warm presence made the whole apartment feel less like home.

Sam pulled an apple from a wicker basket on the kitchen counter and wiped it clean on his shirt. The red skin began to shine under the kitchen lighting. A round sticker from the apple had rubbed off onto Sam's shirt. Tossing the sticker in the garbage, he examined the clean polish of the apple skin and headed out the door.

By the time Sam reached the heavy wooden doors of Main Hall, his apple had been reduced to a core. Main Hall was the original campus building. When St. Agatha University first opened, the entire college was housed within this old, red-brick structure. Its exterior was mostly original, but the clock tower had been restored in 1955 after it was struck by lightning during a storm. Main Hall housed the university's original four academic disciplines—theology, philosophy, mathematics, and, because of its relationship to D.C., political science. For Sam, it was the ultimate symbol of St. Agatha University.

That being said, Sam hadn't spent much time in the building. The rigors of his biology degree usually placed him on the other side of campus, but he loved what the building represented. He pulled open the doors and stepped inside, wondering when he had last been inside the building.

Like much of the campus, Sam found a refreshing newness about the space. With graduation approaching, he was committed to noticing the little details everywhere he went. A grand, imperial staircase towered over the lobby of Main Hall. Ornate wooden carvings lined the railings all the way up the diverging flights of stairs. A bold, red carpet rolled down the stairway tiers and filled the room all the way up to the doors.

Sam followed the crimson pathway up to the third floor, the political science department, and walked the route to Professor Bueller's office. As he walked down the long corridor, he saw a short, middle-aged man carrying a spray bottle coming toward him. A maroon, short-sleeve T-shirt identified him as a member of the university's maintenance staff; an assumption supported by the man's paint-splattered jeans and tan work boots.

"Good morning," greeted Sam cheerfully, as he approached the man.

The man looked up and nodded his head, "Morning!"

The man stopped in front of the next office door with the spray bottle in hand. The *tsst* of the spray bottle sounded against the office's doorknob. Blue liquid dripped from the brass and onto the hallway carpeting. The man took a tattered rag from his pocket and polished the knob and locking mechanism, before continuing in Sam's direction. Sam sidestepped the man, as they passed one another. Just beyond Sam, the man stopped to spray and polish the next doorknob and the one after that.

Eyeing the length of the hallway, Sam took note of the line of shiny, freshly polished door knobs that marked the man's pathway through the hall, like breadcrumbs on a trail.

Is he going to do the whole building? thought Sam.

Sam wandered further until arriving at his destination. He looked down at the shine and glimmer of the brass doorknob on the door of Professor Bueller's office, reached out, and began to turn it slowly. The cold chill of the brass doorknob gave him pause as he started to open the door. He stepped back and knocked, waiting for permission to enter. Silence.

Just then, the sound of footsteps and heavy breathing filled the hallway from behind Sam. Professor Bueller was jogging toward him, stuffing his facemask into his messenger bag and waving apologetically.

"Ah, Sam. I'm terribly sorry that I'm late for our meeting. I was on the phone with my parents all morning," Professor Bueller explained.

"Not a problem, Professor," Sam replied kindly. "I hope everything is okay."

"Thank you, Sam. You see, my parents are getting older now," Professor Bueller explained, as he stepped up to his office. He pushed open the door and politely turned open his hand, "Please, come inside."

Sam followed Professor Bueller's lead and took a seat in one of the empty wooden chairs across from Professor Bueller's desk. The office was a mess of organized chaos. Two full bookshelves lined the entire right wall, with volumes of political theory and U.S. history spilling over their edges. A messy stack of student essays sat in the middle of the desk under a half-full mug of days old coffee. A single, heavy black book lay next to the stack, *The Life and Works of Albert Camus*.

Sam noticed a framed undergraduate diploma from St. Agatha University, Class of 2002, hanging prominently on the open wall opposite bookshelves. Alongside of it, there was another diploma awarded from St. Agatha University for a PhD in political science.

Professor Bueller pulled the strap of his messenger bag over his head and sat down. He leaned back in a black, leather chair, and adjusted his disheveled hair.

He began again, "You see, my parents are getting older now. I'm afraid they're not taking this virus very seriously. With the death rate in Canada reaching 17% this week, I'm rather concerned for their well-being.

"I'm very sorry, Professor," Sam offered. He leaned forward in his chair and continued, "I was actually hoping that we could talk about the virus. I'm sure you have thoughts, especially about the politics of all of this."

"Thoughts I do, Sam!" Professor Bueller chirped back. His eyes darted to the empty chair next to Sam as he realized they were one shy of their proposed meeting. "Will Mouse be joining us today?"

"Mouse actually went back to Bethesda to spend a few days with his parents, but he sends his apologies," Sam replied. "I think I'm going up there on Saturday for dinner."

"Ah, we will have to schedule another chat for after the break. He was a lovely student, that Mouse!" Professor Bueller exclaimed. "Smarter than he gave himself credit for."

Professor Bueller's voice quickly transitioned into the Socratic tones of his classroom demeanor, "Since you brought up the subject, maybe you can help me understand what you mean by, 'the politics of all of this.'"

Sam smiled at the oh-so-familiar prompting of his former political science professor. He had missed the philosophical back and forth of these discussions. While Sam certainly enjoyed the scientific method of his biology classroom, he had always been intrigued by the practice of philosophical inquiry and discourse.

"Well," Sam said, clearing his throat nervously, "the virus is definitely a political event. Global health is political, or politicized, I guess. I think that we have a unique opportunity with the virus to observe how different political philosophies are handling similar crises. The virus makes people sick everywhere, but we are witnessing how politicians of different cultures, creeds, and philosophies are responding."

"I think you're right, Sam. The President of the United States and the President of China have very different political backgrounds and ideologies. With everyone dealing with the same global health crisis, we can think about how their differences play out in real life," Professor Bueller pressed further, "How are politicians responding?"

Sam paused for a moment and looked out the office window at the flowing tree branches on the campus lawn. He began to think back to his political ideologies class. Science and biology had dominated his academic headspace for most of the past two years. He talked about politics with his peers, but this conversation felt like he was flexing unused muscles. He searched desperately for the right words.

"Well, in the United States, the response has been limited," Sam said with a hint of uncertainty. "Our current President hasn't done anything to address the virus, and it is only a matter of time before it spreads in the United States, whether the President wants to admit it or not. While other countries are shutting down public gatherings and forcing businesses to close, he hasn't used his federal powers to intervene."

Professor Bueller sat up and, in his professorial manner, asked, "Limited is an interesting word choice. What makes that limited?"

Sam shuddered inwardly, unsure if Professor Bueller's use of the word, "interesting," was an endorsement or condemnation.

"Strictly speaking from their political ideologies, the President ran with a party platform that promises limited government," Sam said slowly, still forming his thoughts as he spoke. "That means that the federal government won't intervene in issues that the states should be handling. So, if California has a bunch of people who get sick, then it's California that decides how to handle it. The other states can do whatever they want."

Professor Bueller sat up, now pressing Sam further on his statement, "Okay. What does the other side look like?"

Sam replied, excitedly. "The other side is different. I think the federal government could just say that everything was shut down and they could just force everyone, everywhere, to stay inside and stop spreading the virus."

"I think you've painted both ends of the spectrum," Professor Bueller continued, "On one hand, you have absolute freedom; freedom of movement and freedom of enterprise. On the other hand, you have the government restricting those freedoms. What would it be like if the government shut down everything tomorrow? Every restaurant would close. Every store would shut its doors. People would be out of work and no one would be allowed to leave their home. How does that sound?"

The room got quiet. Certainly, fewer people would get sick. Fewer people would die. Concerts would be cancelled. Restaurants would close. Everyone would be forced to stay inside, and the country would dig in and get through the virus, however long it took.

What would that world be like? Sam thought nervously, as he folded his hands in his lap. *So many things would be different.*

"I'm not sure," Sam replied, lost in his own imagination.

That thought lingered with Sam for the rest of spring break. It followed him through campus, down to Monroe Street, and everywhere that he went. He imagined each of the stores empty, closed, and boarded up. He imagined staying at home on the couch for weeks or months at a time. The uncertainty of the road ahead made him anxious, but he held out hope that the United States was yet to have a confirmed case within its borders.

Rain fell hard on the last Saturday of spring break. The first April shower of the year soaked the budding flowers in the campus gardens. The warm sunshine that had been brought by springtime quickly turned into a wet and dreary mess.

The pitter-patter of rain on Sam's umbrella intensified as he walked out to his car, en route to Mouse's for dinner. He kicked the rain off his boots as he stepped inside the car. An array of fast-food wrappers covered the front seat and passenger-side floor mat. Sam tossed his umbrella on top of the mess and gripped the steering wheel with his cold, wet hands.

Turning the ignition, he placed his hands over the warm air pouring out of the vents. Feeling returning to his fingertips, he pulled out and drove off. The windshield wipers on the car struggled to maintain pace with the downfall of rain as he drove off. Replacement wipers were overdue months ago, but Sam had neither the time nor the money to address the issue properly. He swore under his breath as he tilted his head to see through the rain-covered windshield.

D.C. traffic was bustling and backed up, as usual. Sam had grown so accustomed to the emptiness of the campus that he had forgotten that D.C. was still conducting business as usual. There was no spring break for the working adults of the city. A chorus of car horns and sirens played symphonies as he drove up the long road to Bethesda. The tightly grouped row houses gradually grew in size and the spaces between them grew wider, marking the end of the city and the beginning of the D.C. suburbs.

By the time Sam crossed into Bethesda, tiny patches of grass had appeared in front of the houses and, eventually, some of them had full yards. The edge-to-edge row homes of D.C. had always felt foreign to Sam, despite having lived there for four years. In this regard, Bethesda felt much more like home to him. His parents' house in Seattle, albeit small, had all the charm of a small American suburb. There was no white picket fence out in front, but there might as well have been. Sam loved D.C., but Seattle would always be home.

Sam pulled up to the long driveway that led up to Mouse's house. The open front gate was adorned with two beautiful brick pillars. Bronze lion statues stood atop the pillars, marking the entrance to the property. Sam drove the winding driveway and looped into a circle at the front door of the two-story, white mansion. A large magnolia tree, in full bloom, stood tall in the yard. Sam pulled up beneath the tree, and hid beneath the swaying branches to protect himself from the pouring rain.

The large, navy doors swung open and Mouse stepped out onto the front step. He stood, smiling, in his black sweatpants and black hooded sweatshirt. Bright-white sneakers completed his look, as if he was plucked straight from an advertisement. His hair was messy, but stylistically so.

"Traffic?" Mouse asked smartly, tilting his head slightly to the side as Sam emerged from the parked car.

"I know. I'm sorry I'm late," Sam replied, jogging through the rain to the front step. "Again."

Mouse chuckled and greeted Sam with a kiss, before heading inside. The grand entryway and spotless marble flooring always made Sam uneasy. He wiped off his boots before stepping inside, and then once again on the entryway carpet. His squeaking rain boots echoed through the openness of the house, as they walked toward the kitchen.

Built for entertaining, the kitchen was Sam's favorite room. A long marble island separated the stovetop area from the rest of the room. A row of high-back barstools sat along the island, inviting guests to mingle and observe the kitchen activities. He pulled out a barstool and sat down, as Mouse poured two glasses of water and set them on the counter.

"Thanks for coming up here today," Mouse said. "When my parents travel, it's just me and Carol in this big house."

"Yeah, where are your parents off to this time?" Sam asked. "Hopefully not Paris."

He half-chuckled at Sam's dark humor. Mouse's mother had a taste for high fashion, which had certainly rubbed off on Mouse. Between New York, Paris, and Milan, she usually took one big trip every year that was dedicated solely to shopping. Paris was one her favorites, but there was no international travel in or out of France because of the dire nature of the virus there. Shortly following China, France had seen a massive uprising in diagnosed cases over the previous weeks. The government was also performing mandatory testing on all French citizens and working hard to identify and isolate all known cases.

"No, thank God," Mouse responded. "They're going to our vacation house in Argentina for two weeks. It's just me and Carol until lacrosse picks up again on Monday."

"Are you worried about the game on Friday?" Sam asked. "Isn't Marsten College supposed to be really good this year?"

Mouse took a big drink of water and tapped his fingers on the marble countertop nervously. "Yeah, a little bit," he replied. "They're tied with us for first place, right now. It's a big game and Coach wants me to start."

A heavy-set, elderly woman came bursting into the kitchen,

unannounced. "Well, of course he wants you to start! You're the best one on the team, Mousey!" the woman hollered as she waved a dusting rag in the air.

Mouse rolled his eyes and smiled. "What are you doing in here, Carol? Don't you have something to do in the other room," he teased.

Carol danced as she made her way down the console table, dusting the picture frames and glass orbs that decorated its surface. She hummed hit songs from the 1980s as her rickety dance moves made Mouse blush.

"What? Are you worried that I'm going to embarrass you in front of your boooyfriend?" Carol said with a sly smile, as she shook her booty in their direction.

Carol was Mouse's nanny, and his oldest friend. She came highly recommended to their family as a housekeeper many years ago, when Mouse was maybe one or two years old. When Mouse's parents saw how well she did with babysitting and housekeeping, they completely renovated the east wing of the house and asked Carol to move in. It was actually Carol who gave Mouse his nickname—after a character in his favorite children's book.

A single, reclusive woman, Carol mostly kept to herself in her living quarters, and even more so since Mouse had left for college. She had no children of her own and had never been married. Mouse was the closest thing she had to family. These days, she emerged for only two reasons, to clean and to aggravate Mouse when he was home.

"Hey Carol!" Sam greeted, interrupting her booty-shaking dance.

Carol laughed, "I'm sorry Sam. I'm sorry that Mouse is ashamed of his dear ol' Carol." Carol balled her hands in fists and rubbed them under her eyes, wiping away fake tears in a 'boo hoo' motion.

"So boys, what do we make of this here virus?" Carol asked, setting her cleaning rag down on the kitchen counter. "They're sayin' on the news that we haven't had any cases in the United States because we're not testing anybody. How are we supposed to know who's got it if we're not testing folks!?"

"I guess it could already be here and we wouldn't even know, Carol," Sam replied.

Carol picked up her rag and proceeded to wipe down the cabinets above the stove. She turned to Sam and said with a wink, "Well, thank goodness you're going to be a doctor. We need smart people like you to make sure this whole thing doesn't go to shit!"

Sam laughed, "Thanks, Carol! I'll do my best."

She kissed Mouse on the top of the head and proceeded onto the next room, with her dusting rag in hand. The issue of testing hadn't really been on Sam's mind. If anything, he took great comfort in the fact that there hadn't been a confirmed case in the United States. For most people, it was the last security blanket between them and total panic.

Later that evening, as the boys sat in front of the television in Mouse's living room, reports flooded the news that doctors all over the country were being denied testing kits. Despite their patients displaying all of the respiratory symptoms related to the virus, they couldn't get federal approval for testing. This was particularly true in major metropolitan areas, like New York, Los Angeles, Chicago, Miami, and D.C.

Fed up with the recurring cycle of news related to the virus, Mouse quickly rose from the couch and turned on a movie. They sat there, feigning interest in the comedic film, attempting to distract themselves from the monotony of every major news outlet, social media platform, and conversation. Everywhere they turned, there was more to learn about and hear about the virus. It was all anyone wanted to talk about.

As Sam drove away from the Bethesda mansion that night, the rain slowed. He nervously gripped the steering wheel with both hands, assuming a focused posture akin to his first days behind the wheel. The constant talk about the virus had his stomach twisted in knots. A red light flicked on the dashboard as Sam pulled across the D.C. border, and the bright letter "E" glared back at him.

I just filled up, Sam thought, considering the light weight of his wallet.

He scanned the city streets for a nearby gas station. The St. Agatha University neighborhood had no shortage of coffee shops, row houses, and bars, but the nearest gas station was deeper into D.C. and away from campus. He took a sharp right turn and headed into the buzz of the city nightlife.

Saturday night in downtown Washington, D.C. was bustling with people. Crowds poured out of the bars and restaurants as Sam drove through the crowded streets and into Dupont Circle. He pulled up to a stop sign and scanned the lines of people waiting to get into the city nightclubs. People pressed up against one another, breathing and coughing on each other in long lines around the block. The thought of entering the close quarters of a bar made Sam uneasy, as he watched a bouncer wave a group inside of a club called the Cheshire Cat.

Sam pulled into the gas station slowly, and began to turn into the parking lot. He briefly stopped to allow a group of club goers to cross the way in front of him. Three young women, holding hands, stumbled their way across the gas station parking lot toward the nightclub lines. Recognizing his politely halted vehicle, the nearest of the women waved a kind, 'Thank you,' at him as the group passed.

He pulled up to the pump and stepped out into the chilly breeze of the night. Pulling the nozzle from the machine, he inserted it into his gas tank and locked the handle gently in place. The gas pumped slowly as the numbers on the screen increased at a snail's pace. Sam hoisted his jacket tightly around himself, attempting to quell the cold of the nighttime air. Urging the pump to speed up, Sam began to tap his foot impatiently and his eyes wandered toward the sky. He had hoped for a cloudless night, but had no such luck. The rain had subsided, but the cloud cover remained. He searched the night sky for a glimpse of the stars, but the bright city lights and cloudy haze was far too dense. Sam sighed and stared back at the slow ticking of the pump.

After a few minutes, the gentle click of the gas pump sounded in completion. Sam removed the heavy nozzle from his gas tank, gripping the cold metal handle with his bare hands. As Sam scanned the numbered keypad of the machine, he reached back for his tattered, brown leather wallet. The keypad was worn. The number five had been completely rubbed off from years of being pressed. Its location was only discernible through memory and by the presence of the numbers four and six. Sam considered the years of daily gas station patrons in his mind. He considered all of the people who had pressed that number five, even just that day. A disgusted quiver ran down his spine and he looked down at his own now-dirty hands.

His eyes shifted to the gas station doors as he entertained paying inside instead of paying at the pump and having to touch the keypad again with his bare fingers. Two men in suits stood outside, laughing and smoking cigarettes. The glass doors were a short walk away and the nighttime cold was growing stronger. Heading inside, Sam held his breath as he stepped through the cloud of cigarette smoke and into the bright lighting of the gas station. The white walls and fluorescent bulbs were startling as he approached the front counter.

Thick, glass paneling separated the store's patrons from the cash register and the distracted gas station attendant, fiddling with his phone behind the counter.

"I've got the gas on pump 3," Sam said to the gas station clerk.

The clerk looked out into the parking lot and pointed to pump three with his rubber-gloved finger. A blue facemask covered the lower half of his face. He turned back to Sam and spoke through the muffled protection, "White sedan? That'll be $28.55. Did you need anything else?"

Sam turned away from the clerk. His eyes scanned the aisles of the gas station carefully. The rows of potato chips, candy, and soda provided him little comfort. With a concerned and nervous tone, Sam asked, "Yeah. Do you guys have any hand sanitizer?"

GOLDEN

In the several weeks since returning from their winter break, Year 11 had entirely shifted focus to the Aptitude Exams. The rest of her world had faded into the background. Every lesson, tutoring session, and conversation seemed to somehow loop back to this defining moment. It seemed strange to Emily that all of her hard work would culminate in one, six-hour test, but the day was finally here.

Emily sat down anxiously in her classroom booth and, with quivering hands, rested her tablet neatly into the tablet stand in the middle of her desk. As the digital display presented a timer, each passing number ticked more slowly than the last. The heavy weight of the fives, turning to fours, turning to threes pounded sequentially with the pulsing of Emily's heartbeat.

She glanced up and looked through the tinted paneling of her booth toward Cayden. His familiar tuft of dark hair sat beneath a backwards cap, flowing out the back and down his neck. In committing herself to her studies over the past few weeks, they were yet to spend time together. Cayden had reached out multiple times asking her to walk home with him. The budding of early spring provided an enticing atmosphere for a walk together, but the Aptitude Exams were her priority. She couldn't afford to get distracted and, given Cayden's rise in stardom, he had his own busy schedule to tend to. Emily was perhaps the only person at school who wasn't desperately trying to get his attention.

The timer ticked down to *0:00* and a prompt appeared on the screen, instructing Emily to enter her full name and family ID number. Emily shook her hands loose and, finding her composure, typed, *"Emily June Chang - 662123."*

The first exam question appeared and Emily took a deep breath. The moment had finally arrived. The exam was a strange medley of analytical questions and philosophical inquiries. While Emily had assumed that the academic and personality sections would be separated, there was no distinction between the two. The exam questions would rapidly switch between math, science, logic, reading comprehension, philosophy, and personality questions. This format prevented Emily from developing a rhythm, driving frustration and fatigue deeper into the process.

Silence had descended on the room. Every ten minutes or so, a frustrated sigh or groan would cut through the tension and reveal the onslaught of exhaustion that the exam was raining down on the room. As the fifth hour passed, Emily's fingers and wrists had begun to ache. She swiped, typed, and crossed the answers on the exam, fighting through each painful movement. She struggled to maintain focus, as a trance-like state fell over her and her efforts were reduced to zombie-like thought processes and half-hearted analyses.

She replayed Professor Haystead's words in her head, *"Endurance is probably the most difficult part of the experience. All of the academic preparation in the world won't prepare you for the exhaustion of the last part of the exam. Try and stay focused through the last few hours, and remember that you're almost there."*

Emily sat up straight, squeezed her eyes closed, and shook her head. Pressing her feet into the floor, she found a second wind and powered through the final section of the exam with just fifteen minutes to spare. The frustrated sighs and groans were quickly replaced by a chorus of students exhaling in relief as they leaned back in their chairs. The silent fog transitioned to the sound of tablet bags opening up and sanitary wipes being used to wipe down the student's tablets and desks, as students began to finish the exam.

As the clock counted down the final ten seconds, Fae stood up in her booth and yelled out, "Wow, fuck that! Thank goodness that is over."

Students stifled their laughter until the timer officially reached *0:00.* Cheers erupted when the final tone sounded. Exhausted, the students hurried out of the room and headed toward the departure scanners. Emily made her way slowly down the hall to the scanners, her mind completely drained from the exam. Standing patiently in line for the departure scanners, Emily searched the spaced queues of students for Cayden, in an attempt to quell her guilt over avoiding him over the past few weeks.

A voice spoke up behind her, "So, that sucked."

Emily turned to see Cayden a few feet behind her, standing casually in line. Startled, she fumbled clumsily through a reply, "Yeah. It was. It sucked. Totally."

Cayden shifted his weight to his left leg and smiled. He pulled open a white tablet bag and removed an "Eden Vax," branded face-mask. "Well, I'll see you around, Emily Chang," he said, nodding his head at the open departure scanner in front of her.

"Hey, I'm sorry if I've been distant," Emily started saying, as she took a step toward the departure scanner.

Cayden chuckled and shook his head. "Don't worry about it," he assured her. "I'll be here."

Emily nodded her head and smiled, pulling her tablet bag around her front. His words put her at ease. Now that the exams were over, she hoped that they could finally spend time together. The sliding doors of the departure scanner slid open and she stepped inside. She tapped her foot impatiently as the scanner passed over her. The monotony of the ritual and the tight confines of the scanners were growing irksome. Emily wiggled in place, exhausted from the day and having no patience for having her temperature taken again. The scanner passed over her twice, failing the first time as a result of her fidgeting and movement.

"98.2, Vitals normal," the machine finally announced.

Emily sighed and pulled on her facemask. The sleek contours of the light-blue facemask pressed hard into her cheeks as she stepped into the open air. A sheen of gray clouds covered the sky, fighting to open up and let through the sunshine. Emily flicked open the ventilator on her mask's right side and walked down to the sidewalk, the usual meeting spot for their friend group after in-school.

At least they're over, Emily thought, as she brushed away the stress of the marathon Aptitude Exam. *There's nothing that you can do about them now.*

"Can you believe that?!" Fae yelled into the air as she exited the scanner, releasing the frustration of the day onto the universe. "What were those personality questions even supposed to be about? Imagine yourself as a fish? Consider there are two diverging sidewalks? What a bunch of crap!"

Emily turned to see a group of students gawking, as Fae marched down the steps of Walter Reed obnoxiously. Stomping her feet the whole way, Fae pulled on a white facemask with gold trim as she approached Emily. Fae flung her tablet bag from one hip to the other with a loud groan.

"Yeah, some of those questions were really strange," Emily said, offering comfort and sympathy. "How did the rest of it go?"

Fae smiled at Emily's kind words and perked up with a chuckle.

"Oh Em, I have no idea," she explained. "It was a six-hour exam. I think it went well. We'll say that it went, 'okay.'"

The girls chuckled and looked back at Marshall, who was emerging excitedly from the departure scanner. He floated down the staircase toward them, with an enthusiastic glow. "My two favorite people in the world!" Marshall greeted with a wide smile on his face. "Tell me that you don't have any plans after dinner tonight?"

Emily and Fae looked at one another, curious about Marshall's cheery demeanor and shrugged their shoulders. "We're going over to Fae's for dinner, but I've got nothing after that," Emily explained. "I'll probably just go home and try not to think about the Aptitude Exams."

Fae inquired skeptically, "Why? What did you have in mind?"

"Well, to celebrate the exams being over, my mom bought us tickets to the Eden Vax Fan Experience tonight," Marshall explained. "Can you meet me at 20:00 and we can all check it out together?"

"Sounds like fun!" Fae hollered. "Anything to take my mind off that stupid exam." She proceeded with a hint of sarcasm, "That's when you know that we're desperate for a distraction. Emily and I are attending the Eden Vax Fan Experience."

The group laughed and started down the sidewalk on their way home, recounting the ridiculousness of the exam questions and discussing the sections that gave them the most difficulty. No one was particularly confident in their exam performance, but they took comfort in their shared fears and anxieties. The mutuality of their insecurity occupied their conversation all the way back to HC-F5.

They removed their masks as they entered the HC-F5 lobby and set a distance between themselves. Emily walked straight down the hallway toward Tommy's desk, stuffing her mask into her tablet bag carelessly.

"Em!" Fae called out in confusion, as Emily walked right past the entryway sinks. "Your hands."

Emily turned to see Marshall and Fae already washing their hands in the entryway and rolled her eyes at herself. Two women on the other side of the lobby eyed Emily with a concerned suspicion, their piercing gaze tracking her every movement across the lobby and back toward the sinks.

"Whoops!" Emily called out, loud enough for the entire lobby to hear. "My brain is still totally fried from the Aptitude Exams."

A mild satisfaction filled the lobby, as the women came to the realization that the group had all just completed their Year 11 Aptitude Exams. Everyone in the community understood this process and the enormous pressure that accompanied it. The previous generation were among the first to sit for the Aptitude system and the women knew well the rigors of the exam period. On any other day, chastisement would have been in order, but today was different. Emily washed her hands with extra diligence and care, as Marshall and Fae watched her closely with caution and curiosity. It was unlike Emily to accidentally miss the sinks, even on a day like today. It felt almost intentional.

The group arrived at the elevator and each of them stood in front of the scanner, announcing their Family IDs and having their vitals scanned. With a thud, Marshall's family elevator arrived on the far side of the right bank.

"Awesome! I'll see you guys at 20:00," Marshall said as he headed through the opening doors that led to his family's unit. "Have fun at family dinner!"

The girls nodded and waited patiently for the elevators to arrive. This dinner had been marked on their calendars for many months, not only for the Aptitude Exams but also for a visitation day. Within the housing clusters, each family was permitted one night a month that they could visit another housing unit. Families would apply as a pair and, after submitting their health records, they were permitted to visit either's housing units. The occasion usually fell in the middle of the month and, more often than not, the Changs and Dottermans paired up together.

"What are the chances that we talk about anything other than the Aptitude Exams tonight?" Emily asked, in anticipatory dread of the coming dinner conversation.

Fae chuckled as her elevator arrived and, strolling casually in its direction, joked, "If you thought you got grilled by that test, wait until my dad gets cooking."

Emily shook her head and rolled her eyes, pleasantly dismissing Fae's wordplay. Heading toward her own elevator, Emily called back, "I'll see you in a bit!"

The elevator ride felt longer than usual. The steel box clamored through the elevator shaft, inch by inch, all the way to Emily's housing unit. A barrage of questions undoubtedly awaited Emily in the living room and she was in no mood to entertain them.

The doors opened slowly to the entryway and Emily dragged her feet over to the shower. She undressed and stepped into the shower slowly, letting the water wash over her. With two hands on the wall, Emily stared down at the water swirling down the shower drain. The soap and suds spiraled around Emily's toes, making their way to the drain in unpredictable patterns. She soaked under the soothing heat and closed her eyes. Too soon for Emily's liking, the hot water timed out. Emily dried herself off with a fresh towel and sat down at her locker. The cold plastic of the bench felt harsh against her skin as she sat down. She wasn't ready to go inside. A deep breath quelled her nerves and brought confidence and energy back into her body.

You did your best, she thought. *It's just the rest of your life, no big deal.*

Finally rising from the bench, Emily changed into a set of clean house clothes and worked up the courage to go inside. Her parents were standing in the kitchen, pouring over their latest EduView curriculum. They looked up from their work and briefly greeted her with a smile, quickly returning to the curriculum. Ted was sitting in the living room, deeply engaged in a video game on his tablet.

The room felt strangely occupied; a stark contrast to the interrogation that Emily anticipated. Rather than waiting to hear about her exams, her parents were both busy with work and intentionally avoiding making eye contact with her. Ted didn't greet her in his usual way. Something was up and Emily could feel it.

After a long minute, her parents stepped back from their tablet and finally spoke. "Hey Emily! Can you be ready to leave for the Dottermans' in fifteen minutes?"

Emily nodded and headed upstairs, befuddled at her family's disinterest in her day. She took each stair slowly, one at a time, fully expecting someone to call out to her from the living room and inquire about her day. A mild frustration set in as she reached the top of the stairs and wandered down the hall, stopping to listen for any conversation in the kitchen. Confused, Emily set her tablet bag on her nightstand and laid down on her bed.

Did they forget that my exams were today? Emily wondered.

The soft plush of the blankets calmed her. She hugged her pillow to her chest and closed her eyes, taking in the warm comforts of her bed. She was exhausted, not only from the day, but from the past few weeks of preparation and anxiety over the exam. Only in this moment did the full weight of the exam really overcome her. With a sigh of relief and a tightening grip on her pillow, Emily sank deep into her bed and drifted off to a half sleep.

After fifteen minutes, her mother called concerned up the stairs, "Em, are you ready to go?"

Emily opened her eyes slowly and sat up in bed. "Coming!" she called back down the stairs as she stood up and walked over to her wardrobe.

She scanned the shelves for a clean outfit to bring to Fae's housing unit. Her eyes settled on a pair of black jeans and a tight black shirt in a plastic package on the top shelf. Before her mother could call out again, Emily grabbed the plastic package of clothing and bolted downstairs.

Ted and Emily's parents were gathered in the kitchen around a tray of water glasses, casually chatting as they waited for her. The same, curious avoidance stretched across the room. They greeted her warmly and, without mentioning the Aptitude Exams, began to examine their belongings. Emily's mother checked that everyone had their visitation necessities. Each person held up a sealed package of day clothes and a pack of sanitary wipes. Four pairs of plastic-wrapped socks lay on the kitchen counter and Emily's mother distributed them accordingly.

"All good?" Emily asked, tucking the socks and wipes under her arm and turning toward the door.

"Just the immune boost!" her father reminded her as he gestured to the tray of water glasses on the kitchen counter. He held up an eyedropper filled with blue liquid and squeezed three drops into each glass.

The droplets swirled and danced through the water, misting as they sank into the water. Emily took the glass in her hand and stared intensely at the spinning wisps of color. They drifted and danced like the blue skies of Yosemite Valley.

"Bottoms up," she said and chugged down the tasteless, blue-tinted drink.

They set their empty glasses down on the tray and her mother proceeded to place their dirty dishes in the dishwasher. Satisfied with their preparedness, Emily's parents led the way out into the entryway and into the elevator.

Appropriate spacing separated them, even inside the confines of the elevator box. Ted bounced up and down as they descended to the main lobby. With each bounce, the elevator shook slightly.

Finally reaching a point of frustration, Emily's mother scolded him sternly, "Theodore, please be on your best behavior tonight."

Ted went quiet and brought his bouncing to a halt. Embarrassed, he pulled hard on his inhaler and filled his lungs deep with the rush of medicinal spray. The elevator came to a halt, bringing a rising sensation to their knees as it arrived. Everyone gave space as they exited through the elevator doors, one at a time in perfect distanced harmony.

Bright, fluorescent lights illuminated the empty lobby, casting a sparkling shine onto the white floor. Emily's mother glided gracefully across the shimmering surface and approached the facial scanner. After wiping it down with a sanitary wipe, she announced herself.

"Samantha Chang, 662123. Visiting," she called out, prompting the facial scanner to run over her face.

The machine called back to her as the scan completed, "98.2. Vitals normal. Guest one of four approved."

They all stepped up individually and replicated the procedure, each time having their visitor status and vitals approved. The elevator to the Dottermans' arrived and they rode up, again in distanced harmony.

The Dottermans' entryway was nearly identical to the Chang's unit. Same sink. Same shower. Same clothes chute. Same row of lockers. Apart from some specific amenities, the housing units were relatively the same. Residents had some say in the room layouts and arrangement of the kitchen, but the furnishings and mandated washing locations were all issued by the Council. The uniformity made the visits comforting, as they prepared to enter the Dottermans' housing unit.

They each undressed and carefully opened their individual packages of day clothes. After washing their hands at the sink, they got dressed and packed their used clothes away in Emily's father's duffle bag. They left their shoes in the entryway corner and slid the clean pairs of socks over their feet.

"Everyone good?" her father asked, as they stood in the entryway. A series of half-nods prompted him to speak up, "Patrick Chang, Visitor."

After a few moments, the door to the Dottermans' housing unit opened and they were greeted by Fae and her parents.

"Hey you guys! Thanks for coming over!" Fae's mother said warmly.

Fae's mother shared Fae's looks and body type, much more so than Fae's father. She was tall and lanky, with curly brown hair. They were generational mirror images of one another.

"Come in, come in," Fae's father continued. "We have the dining room all set up."

They followed the portly man to the dining room, where two square tables were set up with a foot of separation between them. The Changs sat down in the usual way, at the table with four chairs and place settings. The Dottermans quickly sat down at the other table. The harsh back of the chairs dug into Emily's back. A family of three, the Dottermans didn't usually set their dining room in this way. The extra chairs were cleaned and brought up from storage for the occasion.

"Well, we're all really excited to be here," Emily's father said, as he removed four sets of silverware from his bag. "I'm glad we've been able to do this so frequently. We've been approved for home visits each of the past six months."

Fae's mother spoke up cheerfully, "Well, let us celebrate our health and good fortune tonight then! The actions of one..."

"Carry the safety of us all," Emily responded half-heartedly with the group, as she distractedly glanced around the room.

Fae's housing unit had one of the bigger kitchens in HC-F5. Her mother worked as an advisor to the Council, focusing on produce and food distribution. Early in her career, Fae's mother had actually designed the hydroponic systems that allowed individual housing units to grow their own produce. Every housing unit had a system that was derived from Dr. Dotterman's original hydroponic design. Eventually, she left her job as an engineer to focus on consulting and policy. While not nearly as lucrative of a career, Fae's mother felt like she could do more good when she was informing the Council on issues related to food security and sustainability.

Large glass cases of produce extended from the kitchen through the dining room, each filled with fruits and vegetables that Emily had never seen before. Scanning the cases, she caught Fae's reflection in the glass. She turned to see Fae mouthing a phrase from across the gap in the tables.

"Aptitude Exams?" Fae mouthed silently at her.

Emily shook her head and inconspicuously shrugged her shoulders in Fae's direction, careful not to interrupt the families' conversation. Fae's family had also been avoiding the topic of the exams, leaving both of the girls confused. It was the biggest event of Year 11 and no one had even asked about it.

After some chatter, Fae's mother returned with two dishes filled with vegetables and set them in the middle of the Chang's table. A shiny serving spoon wrapped in plastic sat between the dishes. She left again and set the Dottermans' table the same way. Everyone proceeded to unwrap their serving spoons and serve themselves. An array of small talk ensued, covering every topic about their family lives with one exception. There was still no mention of the Aptitude Exams.

Finally, Fae spoke up in a brazen, annoyed tone, "I'm sorry, but did you guys forget that Em and I just had the most grueling exam of our lives today?"

An awkward silence came over the room. They looked blankly at one another, until Ted spoke up, "I thought we weren't allowed to mention it."

The group laughed at Ted's comment and a quiet ease came over the room. "We can talk about it if you girls want, or we don't have to," Emily's father explained. "It's up to you."

Emily smiled at their thoughtfulness and tears began to form in her eyes. These past few weeks had been so stressful. She took a moment to be grateful for her family and the space that they were giving her. There are moments in life where you just want to be held, and there are moments where you need space, and love is so often about standing right where someone needs you to be. She wiped her eyes and smiled at her parents.

"Thank you all, but I think I'd just like to enjoy dinner tonight," Emily said, as she took the opportunity to set the Aptitude Exams to the side for the first time in weeks.

"Did we tell you that we're going to the Eden Vax Fan Experience?" Fae asked excitedly. "Marshall's mom got us tickets and I guess we get to meet the players or something."

Emily's mother and Fae's father both perked up. "You are?!" they asked, nearly in unison.

Wide-eyed, their parents went on and on like true Vax fans. They went into great detail about the history of the International Gaming League and the legendary Eden Vax squads of the 2050s. Emily paid close attention, desperately trying to soak up the wealth of knowledge being offered to her by two Eden Vax superfans. She felt somewhat guilty about attending the event while there were the true generational fans missing the opportunity to chat with members of the squad. Still, Marshall and Fae were her best friends and she was excited to spend the evening with them. With that in mind, she took it upon herself to ask questions and prepare well for the night ahead.

It wasn't long before the conversation quickly turned to Eden's new Golden Boy, Cayden McDaniels. The table recycled headlines about the resurgence of the Eden Vax and about Cayden's natural instincts for the game.

Fae's mother went on about Cayden's past, knowledge she derived from watching an interview with Cayden's parents about his recruitment to the team. Cayden's parents were both entry-level programmers at a gaming company. While they couldn't afford to send Cayden to any of the premiere gaming academies or expensive camps, the interview discussed the McDaniels' obsession with old video game systems. Their house was filled with video games dating back to the early 2000s, and Cayden had been raised on old sports games. Fae's mother quickly rattled off the names of old gaming systems and games, none of which sounded familiar to Emily. Cayden had certainly inherited his passion for video games from his parents.

"Cayden and Emily are good friends at school," chirped Fae,

raising her eyebrows snarkily.

"Are you really?" Emily's mother asked, at first shocked and curious. Her mood quickly shifted, as she pressed on with suspicion, "Wait. What kind of friends?"

"Just friends, Mom," Emily assured, ignoring a series of teasing gestures and kissing noises from Ted.

"Well, that's great," Emily's father chimed in. "You'll have to say something during the question and answer portion. I'm sure he'll be glad that you guys were there!"

The kind pleasantries of the evening carried on as the Fan Experience approached. Checking the time, Emily and Fae were given permission to leave the table for the night. They said their farewells and Fae headed upstairs to her room. Emily, bidding a final farewell to the Dottermans and thanking them for their hospitality, darted through their entryway and headed down the elevator. She tapped her foot impatiently as she rode the elevator down. She nearly sprinted across the lobby to the face scanner and rode the elevator on the other side back up to the Chang's housing unit. The elevator doors could barely contain her enthusiasm, as she sprang into the entryway. Autopilot flicked on and she quickly performed her entrance cleaning ritual.

Emily discarded her used outfit down the chute and dove into a fresh set of house clothes. A nervous excitement swelled in her chest. Each stair brought her closer to the event, and her bounding, ascending leaps up the stairwell reflected her anticipation.

Her tablet flicked on and a notification appeared in the middle of the screen. *"Private Event Invitation - Marshall Kunitz,"* displayed in bold, Eden Vax green, lettering. Emily clicked on the notification and her screen divided into two sections. On the left, Emily entered Vid, where she would conference with Marshall and Fae. They were already deeply engaged in conversation, recounting the happenings at dinner and Fae's parents' fascination with the one and the only, Cayden McDaniels. On the right side of her screen, a white timer counted down on an all-green background. Emily adjusted her audio settings to distinguish between the video conference with Marshall and Fae and the Eden Vax Fan Experience—one playing through her speakers and the other through her headphones.

"Hey Em!" Marshall greeted through the tablet speakers, as Emily entered the video conference. "I hear that you're an expert on all things Eden Vax now."

Emily laughed and quipped, "Oh yeah! You're looking at the Eden Vax's number one fan!"

"Or at least Cayden's," Fae replied, with a wink.

Laughter erupted among the group, and Emily chastised Fae for her incessant teasing as she adjusted her headphones, "Fae, you're ridiculous!"

Just then, the timer on the right side of her screen reached *0:00* and intense, inspirational music came blaring into her ears. The familiar melodies of the Eden Vax theme song introduced a giant, "Eden Vax" logo that filled the right side of the screen. Big, green explosions framed the logo boldly. Marshall's face lit up in anticipation and even Fae seemed to be captivated by the moment.

"Welcome, Vax Fans!" an announcer yelled, as the theme music faded into the background. His booming voice filled Emily's ears.

"Are you ready to get fit, Eden?! Are you ready to get Vax-inated!?" The announcer hollered. "Let's meet your Eden Vax!"

One by one, the announcer introduced the Eden Vax players. While 3 v. 3 was undoubtedly the most prestigious game within the IGL, there were many other players who filled different, less-marketable gaming roles for the team. Eddie Boom was the captain of the 8 v. 8 team, Lorraine Fritz was an elite 1 v. 1 player, and Colby Wellems was an up and coming player on the technical team. With each new introduction, another video window came onto the screen that displayed the individual players. They were all dressed in Eden Vax apparel, and the team was ready to talk with the fans.

These were all names that Emily recognized from the conversation at dinner, but seeing their faces appear on the screen helped Emily put the game into perspective. Cayden was significantly younger than the other players on the Eden Vax and the rest of the league. Most of the players in the league had been recruited at a young age and had been immediately enrolled into gaming academies around the country. They would spend half of their day playing video games, coached by former professional players and programmers, and the other half of their day would be spent in a traditional, albeit less rigorous, learning environment.

On rare occasions, a player would be brought onto a professional team before graduating high school. Even then, they were usually well into Year 12 and came from one of the elite gaming academies.

Cayden was a unique talent. Unlike many of his older teammates, he was recruited to play for the Eden Vax at the conclusion of his Year 10. Further, he wasn't a product of any major gaming academy. Even now, after going pro, he still attended public school.

The announcer made his way through the entire roster and finally arrived at Cayden's name. "And last, but not least, Eden's Golden Boy, Cayden McDaniels!" he yelled.

An ornate gold frame surrounded Cayden's video feed, as his face appeared in the middle of Emily's screen. A nervous, slightly embarrassed look came across his face as he casually waved at the audience and pushed his hair out of his face. The whole experience was very new to him.

Cayden's video feed descended to the bottom of the screen, and all fifteen of the Eden Vax players and one elderly woman were now on display. The rows and columns of their individual windows filled the screen like squares on a checkerboard.

A small chat function appeared at the bottom of the screen, with a general chat line and a button that read, *"Submit Question."*

"They're going to do question and answer now," Marshall said, excitedly. "I'm totally going to ask something."

"Thank you all for coming," the elderly woman announced. "It's great to have so many people in attendance for this year's Eden Vax Fan Experience! I'm Coach Crumpler and I've been coaching the Vax for twenty years now."

The general chat function flooded with applause and positivity in bold, black font. Sporadically, a line of the chat would contain a profanity or espouse support for another team in the league. These lines would immediately turn red, as moderators flagged trolling and muted attendees that were violating the terms of participation in the event.

"Now, it's been a long time since our last championship," Coach Crumpler admitted somberly. "But I see a lot of winning qualities in this team right here. So, come on Eden! Let's bring a championship back home! Who has questions?"

A flurry of questions ensued, mostly directed at the 3 v. 3 team and the coaching staff. Emily followed the conversation closely and tried to make sense of the nuanced and detailed discussion. Some questions were about strategy and technique, and others were about the players' everyday lives.

Emily perked up whenever a question was directed at Cayden, who had loosened up as the event went on. His nervousness had quickly returned to the quiet confidence with which he carried himself at school. Emily smiled as his casual swagger came on display, responding with an unrivaled expertise when asked about the nuances of 3 v. 3 play. She didn't understand everything about the game, but she recognized the depth of knowledge in his responses.

"It's really about thinking four moves ahead, at all times," Cayden explained. "Before I do anything, I've usually calculated a number of different outcomes. From there, it's just about execution."

Coach Crumpler nodded confidently and followed up, "Okay Cayden, I think we've got time for one last question. Marshall Kunitz from Eden wants to know, "What is it like playing on the Eden Vax and still being in high school?"

Emily's eyes opened wide and she looked down at Marshall on her screen. He and Fae chuckled, quickly quieting as Cayden began to respond.

With a sly, confident smile, Cayden began, "Marshall is actually a classmate of mine and a friend. Thanks for coming tonight. I hope you convinced Fae and Emily to tune in."

Emily blushed and Fae's jaw dropped on the tablet screen. "Are you kidding me, Marshall?" Fae shouted, hardly making an attempt to control the volume of her voice. "Cayden McDaniels just said our names in front of thousands of people."

Cayden continued, "I'm trying really hard to have a normal high school experience. We actually had our Aptitude Exams today, so I'm pretty excited to get my results." He paused for a second and collected himself, "But, before anything else, I'm focused on bringing a championship back to Eden. I came here to win."

Applause and cheers filled the chat function, not a single red font to be seen. Emily leaned back in her chair and her heartbeat intensified. Butterflies filled her stomach, as she listened to the Fae and Marshall's muffled celebrations.

"Thanks Cayden," Coach Crumpler said proudly. "And, thank you Vax Fans! That's all the time we have for tonight. Make sure you catch our game on Saturday against the Scottsdale Sirens. Go Vax!"

The Fan Experience window closed, leaving just Marshall, Fae, and Emily in Vid together. While Fae and Marshall went on and on about the night, Emily remained quiet—still stunned by the mention of her name and overwhelmed by the event.

"Marshall. That was amazing. Thanks for inviting us!" Emily finally spoke up, radiating with happiness. "Make sure you tell your mom that we said thank you."

The group said their goodbyes and Emily removed her tablet from the stand. She crawled into bed and held her tablet tight across her chest. Laying on her back, her toes and fingertips tingled with a mixture of happiness and nervous energy. She bit her lip and closed her eyes, attempting to settle down her excitement and fall asleep. She curled deeper into her sheets and pillows. The comforts of her bed failed to bring her racing mind and pulsing heartbeat to a calm.

Her tablet vibrated on her chest and she held it up over her face. *New Message - Cayden McDaniels.*

Emily opened the message and fought back a giddy smile.

"Thanks for coming tonight."

RED

A tiny drop of blood fell onto the carpet of the student lounge, and the pool cue crashed to the ground with a loud clatter. A group of students turned, alarmed at the noise, to see Maisie pinching her pointer finger to quell the pain of the wooden splinter. She raised her find to her lips and sucked hard on the wound, making a puckering sound with her lips.

"Can you believe these things?" she called out through gritted teeth, wrestling the splinter free from her finger pad. "You'd think they could afford some decent pool sticks around here with all the tuition money we're paying."

Sam nodded and bent down. With a slight hesitation, he pulled the sleeve of his sweatshirt down over his hand and picked the stick up off the ground.

"I totally agree. Who needs statues and new sports facilities when we could have state-of-the-art pool cues in the student lounge?" Sam asked sarcastically, as he tossed the pool stick back in Maisie's direction.

Pulling her finger from her mouth, Maisie caught the stick in her wounded hand and looked down at the pool table. "Very funny, Sam," Maisie replied.

The colorful arrangement of balls was evenly laid out across the table, equal amounts of stripes and solids on display. She leaned over to line up her next shot. With a careful and calculated movement, she slammed the cue ball with a firm precision and knocked in two striped balls with one shot. Maisie circled the table and began to chalk up the splintering pool stick. She turned the corner of the table like a tiger stalking her prey, eyeing the wealth of possibilities with which she could finish off the game.

"So, what time are we heading over to the game today?" Maisie asked, casually glancing the cue ball off a railing and knocking in another striped ball. "Did Mouse say anything about Marsten College? Are they good?"

Sam rolled his eyes as the ball fell gracefully into the pocket. He had lost to Maisie three games in a row and was growing tired of the casual nature with which she continued to beat him. Realizing that his turn to shoot would not be coming soon, he shifted his weight to one side and leaned against the wall in quiet defeat.

"Yeah, they're supposed to be good," Sam responded. "Mouse said it's a big game, so maybe we should get there a little early, like, *2:00* or *2:30*."

"Eight ball, far corner," Maisie called out. With a swift stroke, she cracked the cue ball across the table and slammed the eight ball into the corner pocket with a hard thump. The cue ball rolled casually to the middle of the table, a perfectly executed shot. Maisie smiled and looked up at Sam, "*2:00* works!"

A group of boys wandered to the table and asked if they could play next. The wooden pool stick, over five feet in length, reached across the room, as Sam held it lengthwise in their direction. The distance between them felt far and impersonal, but Sam had made a point to distance himself from other people since spring break. Maisie politely handed over her pool stick, and she and Sam turned to exit the student lounge.

Maisie glared intensely at the splinter in her finger, pinching and pulling at it as they walked down the hall toward the elevators. As they stepped into the lobby of the building, Sam noticed that the front desk remained empty. The girl who usually worked the day shift had been absent all week. The ghost of her warm salutations and pleasant smile lingered in the emptiness of the lobby front desk. Despite having barely known her, Sam was surprised how much he missed her daily greetings.

"It's weird without Bailey, huh?" Maisie said, noticing Sam's lingering gaze on the empty front desk.

Startled, Sam turned and replied, "Yeah, sort of. She's just so nice all of the time. 'Hey Sam! How was your day?' or 'Nice shirt!' It's the little things, I guess."

"I heard that both her parents got tested for the virus over break and that's why she didn't come back," Maisie informed. "Jack's little brother called her and I guess she's staying in Arizona for the rest of the semester."

Sam shook his head in disbelief. He looked back at the empty front desk one more time, before turning to face the elevators. The slight discoloration of the elevator buttons stared up at Sam; the scratched surface of the once-clear plastic waiting to be pressed. He curled his finger and pushed against it, knuckle first, and the button lit up in a burnt orange haze.

The doors opened and Sam followed Maisie into the elevator. She pressed her finger against the button and they rode up to Sam's room on the fourth floor. As they exited the elevator into the hallway, the stinging smell of bleach filled their nostrils. The sharp scent hung in the air of the hallway, furiously stinging the nose of anyone who walked by. They passed a short senior boy named Danny, who was scrubbing furiously at his apartment doorknob with a rag.

"Sorry," Danny muttered. "My roommate woke up with a runny

nose this morning and I'm freaking out."

Maisie rolled her eyes, pinching her nose between her fingers as she sidestepped Danny and his bleach-soaked wrists. Following Maisie's path, Sam stepped around the boy and continued down the hallway toward his room. The sharp smell lingered in the hallway, tracking the entire length of the hallway to Sam's apartment.

The apartment keys clattered noisily in Sam's hands, as he unlocked the door and pushed it open into his apartment. In a hurried, awkward shuffle, Robbie and Jenny separated immediately from each other on the couch and nearly knocked over a lamp on the far side of the living room. The lamp wobbled and shook through the silence of Sam's embarrassed, wide-eyed expression.

"Woah!" Maisie called out, chuckling as she entered the room. "Excuse us."

Jenny adjusted her shirt and sat up straight, staring blankly at the television. "Hey you guys!" she replied, quelling the awkwardness of their intrusion. "We were just about to start a movie."

"Sorry for barging in. We just came back to study before the lacrosse game," Sam explained, as he tossed his keys onto the kitchen table next to a stack of books.

The loud thud of the keys on the stained, wooden surface was Sam's way of announcing that they wouldn't be leaving. In acknowledgement, Robbie pressed play on the remote and started the movie. A recognizable symphony poured out into the living room and introduced a romantic comedy set in New York City; the perfect movie for a budding romance between two native New Yorkers.

Sam and Maisie sat down at the kitchen table and began to flip through the pages of their *Advanced Chemistry* textbook. Sam paid particular attention to the scribbled, handwritten notes in the page margins. These notes often identified key parts of the class lecture and tipped off potential exam questions. Having to pay for any of his schooling that wasn't covered by scholarships, Sam was unable to purchase new textbooks. However, he had perhaps stumbled upon one of the most useful college hacks. Used textbooks always had tips written in them from the previous semester's owner. The margins of a good used textbook were often more useful than the book itself. They warned of nuances of a teacher's lecture style and gave insights that were otherwise lost to the financially fortunate.

The movie played on, as familiar scenes of Central Park, the crowded New York subway, and an acceptable replica of Robbie's favorite bodega in the East Village played softly in the background. A radiance emanated from Robbie's smile as Jenny curled up next to him on the couch and rested her head on his shoulder.

"What's this?" Maisie asked, holding up a large book titled, *General Chemistry 101.* "Are you brushing up on your periodic table?"

Sam smiled and took the book in his hand. "Mouse left it here last night. He's still finishing his general science credits, but I think he's actually enjoying it."

"I think he just likes spending time with you," Maisie teased.

"Well, maybe that too," Sam said, flipping through the pages of the book and reminiscing about his first semester chemistry class at St. Agatha University.

The coarse, tattered pages brushed against his fingertips as he turned page over page and recalled those early lessons. The passage of time felt simultaneously fast and slow. So much had happened over that past four years, but they had all gone by so quickly. The volume of memories, good and bad, was overwhelming.

How did it go by so fast? he thought, as he turned the last page of Mouse's textbook.

A shiver ran down Sam's spine and goosebumps formed on his arms. Chilled by the trip down memory lane, Sam rose from his chair and grabbed a St. Agatha University pullover hanging near the front door. The number 11 was stitched into the right chest, beneath the university coat of arms. The faint scent of Mouse's hair gel lingered on the fabric as Sam pulled it over his head. The short fit hugged his body tightly, cradling him in the comforts of the familiar smell of his boyfriend.

The next ninety minutes passed quickly, as Sam and Maisie poured over their notes in preparation for their coming exams. Flashcard after flashcard fell hard on the kitchen table, building a graveyard of learned key terms and formulas. Sam committed every piece of information to memory. Chemistry, in particular, came easy to him. His aptitude, in this regard, was part of what inspired him to become a biology major. Despite his affection and prowess for deciphering chemical formulas, he embraced the challenge and reward of excelling in biology. The movie came to a close, as credits began to fall over a passionate kiss in New York City's DUMBO neighborhood. The movie faded to black and Robbie wiped a single tear from his eye. With a sniffle, he stood up and walked to the bathroom. Jenny, Maisie, and Sam exchanged curious glances, investigating the abrupt nature of Robbie's departure.

"Great movie," said Sam sarcastically, as Robbie emerged from the bathroom wiping his eyes.

Maisie began to organize her books and notes in neat stacks on the table. She playfully added her opinion to the room, "Very moving. What did you think Robbie?"

Robbie smirked and looked over at the kitchen stove. "First, I think it's time to go down to the lacrosse fields," he announced. "And, second, it's 2020. Are we still shaming men for tearing up during a rom-coms?"

A round of chuckles brought the group to their feet and they headed out the door.

The crisp, springtime air felt soothing on Sam's face, as the group walked through campus toward the stadium field. Crowds of spectators were gathered down by the field entrance. A sea of navy sweaters and shirts swayed from side to side, shifting through the gates and into the stadium like the tide returning to the shore.

Amidst the crowd, a few scatterings of red could be seen in the shuffle. As Sam scanned the groups, he was surprised by how many Marsten College students had made the trip to D.C. Their crimson colors were bold and stood out in contrast to the sea of navy. As the group drew closer to the stadium entrance, the number of red shirts in attendance seemed to grow in size. The game didn't begin for another thirty minutes, but the crowds were already overwhelming.

Sam tussled with his jeans pocket and searched for his lanyard and student ID. The hard edges of the plastic card rubbed against his fingers, as he gripped the ID and approached the entrance.

"Sam, Sam," sang a voice from behind the group, in an odd melody. "Sam, I am, Sam, I am."

Before Sam could turn around, he already knew. It was Carol. Carol was dressed head to toe in St. Agatha colors, a bushy pom-pom in one hand and a foam finger on the other. In full, superfan mode, all that Carol was missing was face paint to complete her look.

"Hey Carol," greeted Sam. "You look awesome!"

Carol smiled and waved her pom-pom in the air, the white, gray, and navy ribbons rustling in the brisk chill of the early spring day.

The group shuffled anxiously through the crowd, now just a few feet from the entrance. Shoulder to shoulder, discomfort and unease began to set in as they stood in line. Sam cringed with each hip bump and brush against his arm, longing for the liberation of the entrance and the freedom of his own seat in the stands. Tight, claustrophobic spaces had never bothered him, but the virus suddenly made every day feel unsafe and unclean.

Feeling the discomfort radiating from Sam, Maisie spoke up in an attempt to shift his attention, "Carol, it's really great to finally meet you. I'm Mouse's friend, Maisie."

"Maisie." Carol said quietly. "Maisie Marks! Mouse has told me about you. Which means that you're Robbie and you must be …"

"Jenny Li, ma'am," Jenny offered. "I'm pretty new to the friend group, but I'm a big fan of your son."

Carol chuckled and corrected her, "Oh, Jenny Li. I'm not Mouse's mother. Heavens no. I'm his sitter."

Carol hated the word nanny or housekeeper, but was also hesitant to call herself family. As long as Sam had known her, she had insisted that she was Mouse's "babysitter." It undoubtedly added to her efforts to embarrass Mouse, as he endured playful teasing from the boys on the lacrosse team about the superfan babysitter who yelled his name at every home game.

"Oh, I'm sorry," Jenny replied. "I didn't know Mouse still had a … sitter?"

"Well, who's going to wipe his bum?" Carol replied jokingly, as she paid for her ticket and passed into the stadium.

The group chuckled and filed through the entrance one at a time, student ID cards in hand. Carol smiled wide as she waved goodbye to the group. She marched down the metal of the stadium seating and took her place in the front row of the St. Agatha family section. Sam watched as Mouse immediately left the huddle and sprinted over to her. Mouse reached his hand over the railing to bump fists with Carol, tucking his lacrosse glove under his armpit. His blonde hair flowed out from beneath his helmet and onto his collar, ornately crowning the number 11 on his back.

The coaching staff watched reluctantly while Mouse performed this pregame ritual, which had become a condition of his participation in the team. He left the huddle before every home game to bump fists with Carol. The coaches hated it, but his talent and performance always justified the interruption.

Jenny led the way up into the stands and toward the student section at the far end of the bleachers. The warm embrace of navy quickly devolved into an adversarial tension. The abundance of navy sweatshirts and fanwear turned to crimson red, as they walked past the visiting fans. Marsten College was a four-hour drive away, just outside of Pittsburgh. St. Agatha certainly had its historic rivalries, mostly built around the basketball program's success in the late 1990s and early 2000s. In this case, the rivalry with Marsten College had bled over into lacrosse.

Jenny waded between the visiting fans carefully and politely, offering quiet pleasantries in abundance. A tall man in a Marsten College button-down shirt stepped to the side in front of them. He parted the crowd, placing a hand on the shoulder of a blonde woman next to him and steering her to one side. The path widened at the man's efforts, as he stared intensely at Jenny.

"Thank you," Jenny said with a smile, as she stepped through the gap that he had created for her.

The man nodded at her with a nervous expression, as he eyed Jenny from head to toe. His gaze traveled from her jet-black hair, down to her feet, and then back up again, taking in the makeup of her facial features. He parted the way further as Jenny passed, sternly pressing the tall, blonde woman closer to the walkways edge.

"Careful," the man said to the blonde woman next to him, as he stared at Jenny. "The Chinese Virus."

Sam's eyes grew wide as he overheard the man's remarks, hoping dearly that Jenny hadn't heard him. A short hesitation in Jenny's stride indicated otherwise, but the briefness of her pause couldn't confirm her reaction. She marched on through the crowd and toward the student section, refusing to be slowed down by his words.

"Wow. Fuck you," Maisie said to the man in disgust. "Do you feel cool?"

Sam and Robbie shot dirty looks at the man as they passed, and headed on toward the student section. Incidents of anti-Asian racism were popping up around the world, as world leaders pointed to Asian immigrant communities as the source and cause of the virus.

Putting the man behind them, the familiar faces of their peers brought them comfort. St. Agatha students filled the stands all the way up to the railing. They spotted four open seats near the middle of the student section and made their way up the stairs. Their heavy footsteps banged against the metal as they climbed the bleachers to their seats. They carefully danced across the students in their row, stepping over and between the tight obstacle course of knees and shoes. The rows were narrow and the seats stacked on top of one another. St. Agatha University's stadium field, like many in the country, prioritized volume over comfort when installing the new rows of stadium seating last season. Sam's long legs had him awkwardly eschewed in the seat as he sat down, knees spread and still almost touching the person in front of him.

"Welcome to St. Agatha University!" the announcer boomed through the PA system. "Home of your St. Agatha Serpents!"

Hissing noises erupted from the student section and everyone stood up, hands raised in a serpent gesture.

The announcer continued, "Today's matchup features the St.

Agatha Serpents hosting the Marsten Bears! The visiting Bears are undefeated in the E-10 Conference, sharing first place with your undefeated Serpents!"

The starters stepped out onto the field and took their positions, as the announcer began to cycle through the players on the Marsten College team. Their red jerseys streaked across the field in a furious vigor, bringing their fans to a thunderous roar. If not for the giant navy serpent decal painted in the middle of the field, the noise from their fans might have convinced everyone that they were the home team.

"And now, your St. Agatha Serpents!" the announcer called out, as a rumbling of stamping feet shook the metal of the stands.

Each player ran out to grand applause, touching the grass as they took their position. Mouse looked up at the student section, searching the crowd for Sam. A confident smile came across his face as his eyes settled on their group. Sam smiled back and Mouse, adjusting his knee brace, took a crouched position and prepared for the face-off.

The sharp sound of the whistle initiated a fierce, faceoff tussle between Mouse and the Marsten midfielder. With a drop of his shoulder, Mouse managed to knock the Marsten player back and Mouse scooped the ball off to his teammate. Securing the ball, the Serpents took control on offense. The whizzing ball flew around the field with grace, as the navy-blue attack formation circled the Marsten goal.

The players danced with one another through a series of picks and transitions, red chasing navy in a diligent fervor. Mouse whipped the ball over to Marvin and, with a hesitation and body fake, Marvin found himself free from his defender. He hurled the ball with perfect accuracy into the top right corner, just beyond the Marsten goalie's outstretched stick.

In a matter of seconds, the Serpents had scored the first goal, and the crowd exploded with enthusiasm. Marvin ran over to the student section and ripped his fist through the air, feeding off of their raucous energy.

The duel intensified as Marsten College matched every goal that St. Agatha could score. One to one, two to two, three to three, the score rose, without a lead exceeding one goal. The physicality of the game also intensified. Defenders on both sides battered the attacking team, smacking and whacking at their opponents. Given the intense nature of the rivalry, a brutally physical game was anticipated. The team and fans knew to expect a few cheap shots, especially from the twins.

Jay and Marvin welcomed the physicality of the sport and took pride in dishing out big hits. At one of the first lacrosse games that Sam attended, Jay had body checked a player on the other team and dislocated his shoulder in the process. Jay immediately stood up in a triumphant glory and popped his shoulder back into place. Despite protests from the coaching staff, Jay yelled back to his coach that he didn't need a substitute and that he wanted to keep playing. A few days later, after a visit to the hospital, Sam found out that Jay had actually broken his collarbone in two places.

With just a minute left in the game, Marsten College led by one. Mouse stood patiently on the sidelines and gulped down a swig of water. He had perhaps taken the most hits of anyone on the field. He had three goals to his name, and the Marsten defense was targeting him every time he touched the ball. The coach waved him over and, after giving clear instructions, sent Mouse back into the game. Mouse ran out onto the field and quickly took control.

"Mismatch! Mismatch!" he called out, after switching defenders onto a slower, less capable opponent.

Bouncing off of a Marsten player, Marvin hucked the ball

awkwardly in Mouse's direction. An off-balance pass, Mouse collected the ball with difficulty and found his footing in front of his defender. His footsteps intensified. He faked right and darted off to the left side of the defender.

A barrage of swinging lacrosse sticks rained on his arms, shoulders, and helmet as he weaved through the collapsing Marsten defense. A defender came crashing into him and, as he fell, Mouse whipped the ball between the goalie's legs.

He tumbled head over heels as the ball hit the back of the net, tying the game, with just twenty-five seconds to go. A sharp pain shot through his knee, as he stood up and pulled his gear back into alignment. Mouse's knee brace had completely turned around and his helmet had shifted out of place as he rolled.

With a hard thump, Jay smacked the top of Mouse's helmet and screamed in his face, "Hell yeah, Mouse! Let's go get another one!"

They quickly celebrated the goal and ran back to the face-off circle. Mouse looked down at his turf-burned knees. The red scratches and black turf beads blended in a colorful array on his legs. He touched his lacrosse glove to the bloody surface and gritted his teeth. He bit hard through the stinging sensation and crouched down for another faceoff.

With twenty-five seconds left, the game boiled down to this faceoff and one final attacking play. Sam rose to his feet with the audience and cheered loudly.

"Come on, Mouse," Sam whispered, as the referee brought the whistle to his mouth.

Exhausted and bleeding, Mouse found one last burst of energy in the roar of the crowd. He dug deep into the turf and locked eyes with his opponent. The whistle sounded and their sticks immediately smacked against one another. Feeling his legs give way, Mouse took a half-step back and let the Marsten player fall into him. The ball sprang loose, as the Marsten player fell, and Mouse scrambled to the loose ball. He knocked it back toward Jay, who picked it up and ran into the offensive zone. The crowd erupted as the navy attack surrounded the goal. St. Agatha would get one last possession to try and win the game.

Tension rose and Sam held his breath. He finally exhaled as he looked over at Carol, who was screaming Mouse's name at the top of her lungs in the family section. Her giant foam finger waved vigorously through the air, inspiring the audience of parents behind her. Sam chuckled at Carol's theatrics and the spectacle brought him comfort.

The ball came whizzing over to Mouse on the far side of the field and two defenders immediately swarmed him. He faked once to his right and executed a perfect spin move, rolling off of the defender and into space near the goal. Mouse leaned back and loaded up to shoot, noticing the clock quickly approaching zero. Sweat dripped down his face, as he scanned the goal for gaps in the goalie's positioning. The defense closed in on him hard and the goalie set both feet sternly into the turf in a perfect defensive stance. No gaps.

Instinct took over and Mouse quickly passed the ball away, into what appeared to be empty space on the far side of the goal. The ball floated into the absent nothingness of neither navy nor red—just empty green turf. It hung in the air for what seemed like minutes, as the Marsten defenders turned their heads to follow the ball toward the far side of the goal.

Just then, out of nowhere, a flash of navy came flying in from the backside. In a single motion, Jay collected the pass and ripped the ball into the open net as the clock reached zero, winning the game in a single, heroic moment. Jay immediately dropped his stick and took off running toward the bleachers. The stands shook as the students poured up to the railing and pulled Jay hard into their embrace. They were followed shortly by Marvin and the rest of the team, jumping and leaping against the metal stands in celebration.

As Maisie, Robbie, and Jenny joined the mob in excitement, Sam looked down on the field to find Mouse. Beyond the raging students, Sam spotted him wandering slowly toward the students. He pulled his helmet off and shook loose the sweat from his golden hair. A proud look came across his face as he watched the team in passionate, triumphant celebration with their fellow St. Agatha University students. Mouse took a knee and leaned painfully on his helmet. After a grueling battle, they had won.

The adrenaline slowly subsided and the rioting crowds began to disperse. Fans headed toward the exit, players returned to the huddle, and Sam waited patiently with Carol to be allowed onto the field with the players.

"Hell of a game," Carol said, clutching her pom-poms tightly as she looked over at Sam. "Our Mouse is just so quick out there!"

Sam smiled and nodded his head. He was fairly certain that Mouse could do anything and Carol would be proud. She could watch him tie his shoes and she would still remark to everyone about how wonderful his bows looked. After about ten minutes of waiting, the gates opened and the team concluded with a unified, "1, 2, 3, SERPENTS!"

The black turf beads bounced uncontrollably as Sam and Carol's feet wandered onto the field. With each step, the beads sprang up into Sam's brand-new, all-white shoes and laces.

"Game ball for you, my number one fan," Mouse said with a sly grin, as he tossed the ball to Carol.

Carol snatched it out of the air with incredible athleticism and grace. "I'll add it to my collection, Mouse!" she replied with a smile. "Great game. I'm proud of you."

"Thanks for coming," Mouse said. He turned to Sam and his smile widened, "Both of you."

The twins trotted by, en route to the locker rooms, and Jay called out, "Looking good, Carol! When are you going to let me take you out to dinner?"

Carol let out a loud belly laugh, "In your dreams, boy. I'm too much woman for you!"

The twins laughed and continued on their way toward the gates. The air began to chill as the sun dipped nearer to the horizon and the evening approached. Sam, Mouse, and Carol followed behind the twins and waltzed slowly across the field. Waves of parents, students, and coaches shrouded Mouse in praise and congratulations, as they drew near the stadium gates. In Mouse's quiet fashion, he replied with calm gratitude and nods of appreciation, but his pace began to slow as exhaustion set in. He came to a full stop and braced himself on Sam's shoulder.

"Everything okay?" Sam asked. "You got beat up pretty bad out there."

Mouse took a deep breath and straightened his posture. "Yeah, I'm good. Rivalry games are brutal," he replied with a painful, half-smile.

As they reached the stadium gates, a short, freshman boy approached them nervously. He stood awkwardly in front of them for a moment and finally muttered his way through an introduction, "Mouse, can I get a word for *The Hiss*? My name is Marcus Froll and I'm working on the sports column."

The Hiss was the student-run newspaper. It was widely circulated on campus and covered everything from prominent alumni, student profiles, academics, major donations, and, of course, sports.

"Sure, man," Mouse said quietly, still catching his breath. "Any chance we can sit down, though?"

The boy nodded in agreement and they wandered over to a campus bench nearby. Mouse lowered himself to a seated position slowly, tending to his sore muscles and pressing hard on a muscle cramp in his right calf.

The first half hour after a game was always the worst. Mouse had a bad history with muscle cramps and lived on home remedies of bananas, honey tea, and, of course, the occasional professional massage.

"I'll just wait over here," Sam said.

He politely wandered a few feet away and started to scroll on his phone. The usual headlines about the virus abounded, covering everything from new cases in Europe to new research about community spread in China.

"So, can you walk me through that last play?" Marcus asked. "An amazing assist. How did you know Jay Bantz was going to be there?"

Mouse leaned back and cleared his throat harshly. "Yeah, I shook two defenders and I thought I had a good look at the goal," Mouse explained. "Jay and I have been playing together for a long time. I saw the pass early and he executed perfectly. You should really get an interview with him. He won the game for us."

Sam listened as Mouse eloquently detailed the events of the game through the interview. Mouse was quietly humble, descriptive, and his passion came out in every response. He had no aspirations of playing professional lacrosse, but Sam listened carefully as Mouse conducted the interview with a high degree of sophistication and professionalism.

"One last question," Marcus continued. "You've been on the team since you were a freshman. With the Bantz twins graduating, do you see yourself taking the role of team captain?"

Mouse curiously raised his brow and took a harsh breath. He started his response, "Wow. I guess I hadn't really considered it." Mouse took an awkward pause and swallowed hard, fighting against a rising pain in his chest. "I'm not sure. I love the team and I love the game. But I have to think there are other guys who ...."

A concerned look came across Marcus' face as Mouse put both hands on his knees and leaned over. With a pained look, Mouse took another deep breath.

"Mouse, are you okay?" Marcus asked.

Sam's ears perked up and he turned back toward the interview. Marcus placed a hand on Mouse's back.

"Mouse, are you okay?' he repeated.

With a loud wretch, Mouse cleared his throat and spit hard onto the sidewalk beneath the bench. Marcus stood up immediately and stepped back. A large pool of blood and mucus stained the concrete surface.

"Oh man. I'm sorry," Mouse said, spit and blood dripping from his chin. "I don't know what that ...."

Mouse coughed hard twice, covering his face with his hand. His eyes lowered and a terrified look overcame him. Blood covered his hand and forearm. In a panic, Mouse rose to his feet. Too weak to stand, he immediately fell back onto the bench. The blood dripped down his wrist and he looked up at Sam with terrified eyes.

"Sam?" he called out. "Sam, I'm not .... Get Carol."

Sam rushed over in a hurried panic and sat down next to Mouse. He yelled out to Carol, "Carol, get the car! Please hurry!"

Sam sat there for what felt like an eternity, as Carol darted off and brought the car around to the field. She drove them up the street to the university hospital and helped Mouse into the empty hospital lobby.

The sterile white lights of the waiting room were blinding. The discomfort of the plastic seats dug into Sam's back. Carol paced frantically back and forth in the lobby, rubbing her hands together nervously. The hospital staff wouldn't allow her to accompany Mouse into the examination room because she wasn't technically family. She didn't care to argue and Mouse was too weak to insist. She simply marched around the lobby, occasionally stopping to ask Sam a medical question.

Sam looked down at his new, white shoes and a deep fear set in. He scanned the bright-white laces and all-white logo, tracing the lines of the white stitching. He stopped, as his eyes honed in on a single red drop of Mouse's blood on his right toe.

He was terrified for Mouse. Terrified for himself. Terrified for the community. If this was the virus, then it was only the beginning. What was once bright and beautiful, was forever changed.

PLACED

"Emily, wait up!" Cayden called down the long hallway, drawing turned heads and curious glances.

The sound echoed off the walls and a group of students watched Cayden accelerate his pace down the bright lighting of Walter Reed High School. They stared and whispered among themselves, as Cayden trotted down the hallway. A few weeks had passed since the Eden Vax Fan Experience and word had spread of the famous shoutout that Cayden had given to Marshall, Fae, and Emily. Emily looked back and smiled at the sight of Cayden coming toward her. Butterflies rose in her stomach, as she tried to hide her enthusiasm behind a calm, collected demeanor.

Emily had been eager to speak to him during in-school every week since the Fan Experience. They had exchanged messages nearly every day and she had been considering asking him to walk home together, but she had held off out of nervousness. The anticipation of her Aptitude Exam results and a general fear of rejection kept her at bay. She was worried that she missed her window of opportunity, but she found renewed hope at the sight of him running toward her.

"Cayden McDaniels, Eden Vax Golden Boy," she replied. "To what do I owe the pleasure?"

Cayden chuckled casually and stepped inside her four-foot social perimeter, with a confident disregard for the rules. "The pleasure is all mine," he chimed back.

Emily blushed and instinctively rocked back a half step to a more comfortable distance. Catching her balance, she quickly swayed back inside his radius and smiled flirtatiously.

"Are you nervous about getting your Aptitude Exam results back today?" Cayden asked, staring intensely into Emily's eyes.

She turned and, reluctantly breaking eye contact with Cayden's intense and intoxicating stare, replied, "I'm very nervous!"

Taking a few steps in the direction of Professor Haystead's class, Emily listened carefully for the sound of Cayden's footsteps behind her. Her gaze locked on the far end of the hallway, refusing to look back to check if he was following behind her.

"Yeah, totally," Cayden remarked, pulling his tablet bag onto his shoulder and hurrying after her. "I'm pretty excited to see our results. I'd be fit with pretty much any placement, but I think it would be cool to work in health care or engineering."

She looked back at Cayden with a surprised look. "Health care?" she asked. "Cayden, I'm sure that you can apply for an appeal and keep gaming. You're the best player on the Vax," she said reassuringly, as she searched his face for a response.

"Really?" Cayden called back, eyes wide and a sly smile stretched across his face. "You think I'm the best player on the Vax?"

Emily scoffed playfully. "Is that the only thing you heard me say?"

Cayden laughed and assured her, "No, I get it. I could probably do that." He hesitated for a pensive moment and stared longingly at the ground beneath his feet. "Gaming is great. I've been doing it forever. I just wonder if I could be good at anything else."

With a surprised expression, Emily replied, "I'm sure there are lots of things that you're good at .... Like walking me home today." Emily watched, as her words inspired a smile on Cayden's face.

"Yeah. I'd like that," he said confidently.

They continued down the hall and the walls were lined with the watchful eyes of Emily's peers. The haunting sound of salacious whispers filled her ears. Their quiet words, perhaps about anything, felt targeted and rose in volume in her imagination. She nervously increased her pace through the halls and Cayden followed closely behind her. While Emily was certainly interested in Cayden, she had no interest in being at the center of the latest string of gossip at school.

As they approached the classroom, the bustling ruckus of the students' conversation could be heard well outside of the room. The sound of the Year 11s, eager to see the results of their Aptitude Exams, spilled over the doorway and into the hallway. Emily approached the room, and a tinge of excitement came over her. She eagerly joined her fellow Year 11s in their anticipatory disquietude. Their communal hard work and shared anxieties had all worked up to this moment. The tension filled the classroom. Groups of students were gathered around their booths, guessing and stressing at where they would be placed.

"Engineering, I think," speculated a petite girl named Rae.

"That'd be cool. I'd love to work in health care, like at the pharmacy or in one of the research labs," replied Josh, a red-haired boy seated in the booth beside her.

Rae looked back at him excitedly and replied, "Health care would be cool!"

Emily sifted through the sea of anticipatory conversations and arrived calmly at her booth. She watched, as Cayden wiped down his booth and placed both hands on the back of his chair. With a deep breath, Emily casually tossed her tablet bag into her booth. Her knees began to shake and she lowered herself into her chair. For a brief moment, the surrounding conversations faded and Emily found herself alone with her thoughts.

Aptitude Exams. No big deal, she thought. *It's just the rest of your life.*

Over her shoulder, she heard the sound of footsteps approaching and a pack of sanitary wipes fell onto the desk in front of her. Startled, she turned to see Patrice smiling at her from behind her thick, red glasses.

"One time, I got a day-kit without wipes and I was freaking out all day," Patrice explained, politely. Patrice gestured to the pack of wipes, "Go ahead. You can use my extra pack of wipes, but I'm surprised that Emily Chang doesn't keep extra wipes in her tablet bag."

Irritated, Emily looked down at the pack of wipes that Patrice had tossed onto the desk surface and opened them slowly. She rolled her eyes and started to wipe down her booth, in line with the techniques required by in-school policy.

Emily quickly scolded herself and found her manners, "Thank you, Patrice. I was so nervous when I opened my day-kit and these weren't there. You're a lifesaver!"

Patrice chuckled with a smug grin, "Oh honey, it's totally fit. I couldn't just let you sit in that dirty booth."

Before Emily could respond, Patrice turned and walked back to her booth. A judgmental fog lingered in the air. Emily scoffed and pulled open her tablet bag, tucking Patrice's extra package of wipes next to the pack of wipes that had been included in Emily's day-kit.

Mind your own business, Patrice, Emily thought, uncharacteristically frustrated by the intrusion of Patrice's help.

She rustled her tablet free from her bag and set it down in the tablet stand. The room grew quiet as the timer ticked down to the start of class. Emily's fists clenched tightly on the desk's edge and she closed her eyes tightly. The uncertainty of the exam results crept deep into her chest with a tight, narrowing sensation. *0:04, 0:03, 0:02, 0:01.*

The timer reached zero and Professor Haystead appeared on the tablet screen. His normal vintage clothing was nowhere to be found. The stack of books on his desk had been replaced with a silver tablet stand and he was strangely dressed, in a slick, white suit and a black cravat tied that ran halfway down his chest. There was a curious professionalism about him. Even his posture reflected the seriousness of the day and the coming of the students' Aptitude Exam results.

"Hello everyone," Professor Haystead announced. "I'm sure you're all anxiously waiting for your exam results, but you'll have to bear with us for a few minutes longer. In upholding tradition, Dean Blackwell will be joining us in person to say a few words before your results are unlocked on your screens."

Resounding groans of disapproval filled the room and Emily added her voice to the chorus. As quickly as they started, the groans came to an abrupt halt. Dean Blackwell entered the room with the booming presence of an all-black, formal jumpsuit. Her look was flawless, as she matched the occasion's formal aesthetic. Although, for Dean Blackwell, formality was the norm in her everyday appearance.

An elderly man in a white robe, recognized as the official Council uniform, wandered in behind her. He was short and portly in stature and his presence felt oddly familiar. Emily studied his face carefully. With each step, she traced his wrinkled brow and the strands of long white hair that flowed from his head and into a neatly tied braid.

He and Dean Blackwell arrived at the front of the room and Emily took note of a pin on the man's chest. She knew that these pins indicated Council rank and the member's years of service, but she had never seen this particular pin design before. Most of her exposure to the Council came from the annual visit that the F-Block Council Housing Authority paid to HC-F5. A relatively low-ranking Council member, the housing authority's pin was a simple gold stripe with three decorative houses above it.

She studied the elderly man's pin closely. A ring of golden stars surrounded a gavel and weighted scale, adorned by two olive branches. While the intricacies of the Council ranking system were a mystery to her, she knew well enough to associate the complexity of this design with a high rank. This was clearly someone important and her classmates seemed to recognize the man, as the volume of their whispers grew around her.

That's a lot of stars, Emily thought, as she quickly tried to count them clockwise. She reached twenty-two, about three quarters of the way around the pin, when she was brought to attention by the sound of Dean Blackwell's voice.

"Good morning, Year 11s," Dean Blackwell said sternly, bringing the whispers to a quiet murmur. She repeated herself, even more sternly this time, "Good morning, Year 11s!" The quiet murmur came to an absolute silence.

With a pleased smile, she continued, "We have the extremely rare privilege to be joined by Council Justice Evans today, who has never been inside the walls of Walter Reed High School before. Please give him a warm welcome. The actions of one."

"Carry the safety of us all," the students called back, with firm attention and respect.

Emily recalled where she had seen this man before. He was the face of all of the public service announcements that she had seen on television. They mostly covered security topics: curfew, city borders, emergency action, and quarantine.

"Thank you, students, and thank you Elizabeth," Council Justice Evans greeted them, looking over and nodding at Dean Blackwell.

Elizabeth? Did he just call Dean Blackwell, 'Elizabeth'? thought Emily, sharing in the startled expressions of her peers as she glanced around the room.

"It is an honor to be here," he continued, boldly addressing the students. "It's quite rare that the Aptitude Exams reveal the unique range of results and talents like your class and you should all be very proud of your hard work." He paused for a second and shifted his gaze in Emily's direction, almost settling on her. "The results from this year are particularly special, and it is an occasion that I wanted to be here for in person. Professor Haystead, if you would."

In near unison, the students turned to face their tablets, and Professor Haystead unlocked their results with the push of button. Large envelopes appeared on the digital display and the front fold opened before them. Emily placed both hands, palms down, on the desk surface and took a deep breath. A wave of anxiety came over her, as she heard a combination of students cheering, groaning, sighing, and questioning their results all around her. She curled her fingers and balled her hands into tight fists in anticipation. As the audible responses of her peers filled the room, her envelope finally opened to reveal her placement.

"Politics and Government - Council Justice," appeared in bold, golden writing across the screen. Stars surrounded the writing, in an array that mirrored the design of the Council pins.

Emily exhaled audibly at the sight. Uncertain how to feel about her results, she had them now and that was enough to briefly quell her anxiety. Politics and government was the highest academic tier achievable and many of the high-ranking Council officials enjoyed the luxuries of the HC-A and HC-B lifestyles; however, the Council also held the weight of the community's safety on their shoulders. Council membership was undoubtedly the most stressful and demanding position in the community, and there were only three active Council Justices in Eden. She scanned over the bold, golden lettering of her results; once, twice, three times over. A strange mix of relief, excitement, and fear swelled in Emily's chest.

The chattering excitement of the room grew quiet and a wide shadow cast over Emily's booth. She looked up to see the stern face of Council Justice Evans hovering over her. His bright, golden pin on full display.

"Ms. Chang, it is a pleasure to meet you," he said loudly, simultaneously addressing Emily and the entire room. "It has been ten years since a student posted the unique scores required for the Camillus Program and, when I heard the news, I wanted to be here in person to congratulate you. It has been a long time since we've had a candidate for Council Justice."

Emily again felt the gaze of her peers and she rose from her chair to a slouching, nervous pose. She muttered quickly, "Thank you, sir. The actions of one."

"Carry the safety of us all," Council Justice Evans replied, with an approving smile. "I look forward to seeing you at the Council, and congratulations on your placement."

Council Justice Evans turned and walked out the door, followed closely by Dean Blackwell. The students continued to chatter among themselves, as Professor Haystead attempted to put together a meaningful lesson about reading comprehension. Despite his best efforts to teach, he fully anticipated the students' distraction and was lenient with their lack of attention. The class went by slowly, as the students exchanged messages about their results. In an effort to regain her focus, Emily disabled incoming messages and tried to participate in the half-lecture fumbling out of Professor Haystead's mouth.

She glanced forward at Cayden, eager to hear about his placement. He had been surprisingly quiet and focused throughout class, in stark contrast to the rest of the students. He curiously toyed with the corners of his tablet and ran his hands through his dark hair, staring intensely at his screen and never once turning around. Emily curiously peered over his shoulder to see his results, but could only make out Professor Haystead's face in the center of the screen.

"Well, thank you all for your work and enjoy the day. I'll see you next week," Professor Haystead said, sharing in the students' relief that the distracted session of class was now over.

Emily rose from her desk and began to wipe it down, carefully covering the edges of her tablet stand and the intricate corners where the paneling met the desk. She removed a second wipe slowly and wiped her chair thoroughly. Flurries of congratulations were thrust upon her, as her classmates passed by her booth. They exchanged pleasantries as Emily reciprocated their praise and, in return, asked to hear about their results. Oddly, the quietest and briefest congratulations came from Cayden.

"Council Justice Chang," he teased, slinging his tablet bag over his shoulder as he headed out the classroom door. "It's got a nice ring to it."

"Thanks, what did you ...." Emily called out, but Cayden had already left the room.

She turned and scanned the room for Fae, spotting her and Patrice talking near the back row of booths. She waved for Fae's attention and waited patiently for her to finish her conversation. Eyes wide and mouth gaping, Fae crouched down in a low, attack pose and prowled in Emily's direction.

"Are. You. Kidding. Me?" Fae said, in a low whisper that rose in excitement as she grew closer. "People are saying you had the highest academic score in Year 11. You must be thrilled!"

Emily chuckled and awkwardly rubbed her hands together, "I'm pretty nervous, to be honest. What about you? Where did you place?"

Fae straightened her posture and gripped her tablet bag under her arm. "Fae Dotterman. Education – Secondary School," she replied in a low tone, attempting to sound preposterously professional.

Emily burst with excitement, momentarily forgetting her personal stresses in the shared celebration, "Oh my goodness, Fae. You're going to be an amazing Professor. I can totally see it! You should talk to my parents about their work with EduView!"

Fae nodded excitedly, and the girls headed out into the hallway, cheerfully bouncing out the door and into the chattering glee of the halls. As they parted ways for their next classes, Emily paused and leaned against the wall around the corner from Professor Haystead's room. The chill of the cold, white brick soothed her back as she gave her weight over to the wall and pressed against it.

Passerby students chatted amongst themselves about their placements. Their wandering eyes rested for a second-too-long, searching Emily's expression for a grain of truth in the rumors of her exam results. Whether they were gossiping about her or not, every pair of eyes felt like it was searching her for information. The cool, relaxing comforts of the cold brick wall quickly became stressful, as Emily attempted to shrink from their gaze. She composed herself quickly and rose from the wall. As she turned the corner, she was startled by a tall, towering figure standing there waiting for her.

"Hello Emily," Dean Blackwell greeted. "I was hoping that we might have a moment to chat today. Would you mind accompanying me to my office?"

Emily paused, shocked by the invitation, and mustered a response, "Yes, of course, Dean Blackwell. But, I have Coding and Languages this period …."

"I'll take care of it, Emily," she replied. "We can certainly make an exception on placement day. I insist."

With a nervous nod, Emily followed Dean Blackwell into a large, high-ceilinged office near the school's front entrance. Wide, heavy glass doors parted in front of them and Emily stepped inside slowly. Dean Blackwell stepped around a sparkling marble desk and sat down in a domineering, black armchair. A silver tablet stand was situated in front of her, sleek in fashion and two towering bookshelves framed the desk on both sides. Emily examined the abundance of medical textbooks that filled the shelves and the numerous accolades from the Seattle Medical Society.

The career path that led to Dr. Elizabeth Blackwell's appointment as dean often sparked curiosity among the students. As Emily understood, Dean Blackwell was an accomplished medical doctor, who had made several major scientific discoveries at a medical research facility in Seattle. After meteoric success in her early thirties and a vast accumulation of wealth, Dean Blackwell grew tired of the minimum, sixty-hour work week. She petitioned for early retirement and accepted a position as a science teacher at Walter Reed High School. Fast forward fifteen years, and she was now, Dean Blackwell, M.D. Ph.D.

Emily removed a sanitary wipe from her tablet bag and wiped down the chair positioned across from Dean Blackwell's desk. A low, backless chair, the seat brought Emily oddly close to the floor as she lowered herself onto it. Dean Blackwell crossed her hands neatly on her desk and sat up straight, her intense gaze descending on Emily.

"First, let me say congratulations," Dean Blackwell began. "The

Camillus Program is very prestigious, and it is very rare that a student be placed in Council Justice candidacy. It is an honor to have one of our students place so well; although, I'm not surprised that it was you."

Emily felt a warm ease in Dean Blackwell's kind words. Her stiff, rigid posture relaxed back onto the stool as she replied, "Thank you, Dean. It's been a pleasure to learn here and I have to especially thank Professor Haystead for his guidance."

Dean Blackwell nodded approvingly and stood up carefully from her chair. Her formal attire shimmered in the streaming sunlight coming through the window. She wandered slowly over to the window and stared outside at the campus front steps pensively.

"You've been an impressive student, Emily," Dean Blackwell explained. "Beyond your academic achievements, which are noteworthy on their own, I've also followed your behavioral record very closely since you arrived here." With a concerned tone, Dean Blackwell carried on, "I was worried at first, given the unique flair of your close company. But your conduct has been a model for the other students, and I think you'll make an exceptional Council Justice. We're all very proud of you."

A strange silence filled the room, as Dean Blackwell waited for Emily to respond. At first feeling complimented, Emily raised her brow in confusion and attempted to make sense of the nuanced undertones of Dean Blackwell's remarks. Emily was certainly grateful for the praise, but she pondered the backhandedness with which Dean Blackwell went about complimenting her.

A model for my peers? Is that what people think of me? she asked herself, staring at her hands, folded neatly in her lap. *The unique flair of my close company? What does that mean? Is she talking about my friends?*

Dean Blackwell broke the silence sharply, "Well, Emily. Thank you for your time and congratulations. You can return to Coding and Languages class."

Emily nodded and rose slowly from the chair. A fog of confusion and curiosity hung over her, as she walked to her next class. Still shell-shocked from the thrill of receiving her exam results, Emily was now neither enthused or disappointed. With each step, she continued to process her placement, wavering between excitement and worry. Despite her internal demand for clarity, her frantic thought processes brought her little comfort.

The rest of the day went by in a blur. Class after class, the Year 11 students discussed their results and an outpouring of congratulations and gossip fell upon Emily. Shock and awe echoed throughout the halls, as tales ran wild of a senior member of the Council personally presenting Emily with her placement.

"Well, at least they're not talking about you and Cayden anymore," Fae joked playfully, as they met outside of the departure scanners.

All of Emily's concern about students' gossiping about her and Cayden seemed so irrelevant now. She regretted the morning, where she had hoped that her peers would move on from talking about her and Cayden's budding relationship. She never anticipated that the next bit of gossip would be about her Aptitude Exam results.

Emily clutched her tablet bag tightly and, looking back at the departure scanner, responded to Fae's teasing in a serious tone, "I guess. I'd rather they not talk about me at all. Can we just go back to when no one noticed us?"

Fae smirked as she followed Emily's eyes, which were fixed longingly on the departure scanner. She chirped accusingly, "Are you looking for someone?"

Just then, Marshall emerged from the departure scanner and came stomping toward them.

Emily laughed, turning back to Fae with a smart grin, "Yeah. Marshall. I was looking for Marshall."

Emily winked and stepped to the side, making room for Marshall on the sidewalk as he sauntered up to them. Today was a day of emotions for the Year 11s. While some students would walk home from school feeling inspired and roaring to pursue their career training in Year 12, other students would be forced to wrestle with the disappointment of their placements. As she traced the somber look on Marshall's face, Emily feared that he was in the latter category.

Fae spoke up first, blunt and to the point, "Where did you place?"

Marshall started to speak but fought to choke out the words, "I just …. I know we're not supposed to expect anything …."

Fae looked at Emily, urging her to offer a wise word of sympathy or compassion. Emily searched frantically for something to offer him, but only managed to reply in platitudes and insincerities.

"It will work out. Whatever it is," she said. "Maybe you'll grow to like it."

Marshall opened the strap on his tablet bag and slowly pulled out his tablet. The tablet display flicked on and he scrolled through to his exam results. A worried suspense set in, as sharp, bold blue lettering ran across the screen.

"*Security - Patrol Officer*," was written above the bold watermark of a shield.

Emily sighed and looked out at two looming patrol officers standing across the way. Their all-white body armor glistened in the sunshine and shimmering light reflected off of the assault rifles held across their chests. The two officers hollered at passing students, commanding and reprimanding them for violating even the slightest infraction or breach of social distancing.

The group watched together, as one of the officers forced a student to stand at attention outside of the departure scanner. Pressing the butt of his rifle sharply into the student's chest, the officer backed him up against the wall and forced him to open his tablet bag. The officer examined the bag's contents carefully before waving the student on his way dismissively, providing no explanation for the stoppage. Reminded of their forceful presence, Emily quickly pulled on her facemask and turned back to Marshall. She felt his concern deeply and she stared into his worried eyes.

"You'll be great Marshall," Emily assured him, enthusiastically. "You don't have to be like them. I know you. I know that you'll have the courage to be different."

Marshall raised his chin, revealing a half-smile, and replied, "Thanks, Emily …. Or, should I say …."

Fae giggled and Emily shook her head. "Don't say it, Marshall," she lectured, pointing a finger at him.

"Thanks …." he blurted out, before saluting her at attention. "Council Justice Chang."

Marshall ran off, in fear of retaliation. Fae laughed and started jogging after him. She turned to see Emily looking back at the departure scanners, longingly.

"Are you coming, Em?" Fae asked.

Emily stared at the departure scanners, hoping to see Cayden's familiar dark hair emerge from the parting doors. "You guys go ahead," Emily replied. "I'm going to wait a little longer."

With a kind nod of understanding and appreciation, Fae turned and chased after Marshall. The two of them laughed down the sidewalk, as Marshall returned to his usual playful and joyous demeanor.

Emily smiled as she watched them. *The unique flair of my close company,* she thought proudly. *I wouldn't have it any other way.*

After a few minutes, Emily settled against the sidewalk curbing and tried to find some sense of comfort. The sun lowered and the rate at which students exited the scanners began to slow. The sun dipped behind a cloud and a cold chill set in. She looked down at her shoes, as she came to accept a reality that she already knew. Cayden wasn't coming and they weren't walking home together.

She toyed with her tablet bag for a few moments as she stared back at the scanners. She removed her tablet slowly. Taking it in her hand, she began to draft a message to Cayden. Writing, erasing, rewriting, as she searched for the words. Was she disappointed? Angry? Concerned? Maybe all of the above. He had left their classroom so abruptly after receiving their exam results.

"How was your day!?" she drafted and erased.

"Did you still wanna walk home together?"

"I'm outside the departure scanners, if you're around."

"Are you still at school?"

She stared down at the tablet for what felt like an eternity, wavering back and forth on if she should hit send. She looked back at the scanners with one last hopeful glance, before she reluctantly turned toward home. As she took her first steps toward HC-F5, she erased the message drafts entirely and began to write again.

"Hey Kobe, give me a call later." she wrote. Pressing send, she lifted her face to the sun and continued down the sidewalk toward home.

HOME

A dull pain swelled in Sam's tailbone. An hour had passed since he had sat down on his bedroom floor and started packing away his belongings. A scattering of half-packed boxes surrounded him, as he sifted through a removed desk drawer set out on the floor. He leaned up against the foot of his bed, shifting his weight to relieve the pain shooting up his back.

He flipped through crumpled-up notes, old pictures, and little trinkets in the drawer—keepsakes and things collected from his years at St. Agatha University. He began organizing them into two piles—keep and throw away. To his left, a cardboard box sat open, marked for the things he would take with him back to Seattle. To his right, a small trash can. Sam made a conscious effort to throw things away. He had already anticipated that his car would be full for the drive back, and he gave careful consideration to those things that would bring him joy and those things that he could throw away.

The university had announced the official closure of campus during the previous week, the morning after Mouse had tested positive for the virus. With the virus on campus, St. Agatha University would be closed for the remainder of the semester and classes would be moved online entirely. All of the students in on-campus housing had to be fully moved out by the fifteenth.

In the days since the lacrosse game, Mouse's parents had paid over $100,000 to have the entire lacrosse team tested for the virus.

Despite a plethora of media coverage detailing a national shortage of accurate testing, the almighty dollar and familial connections seemed to find no difficulty in securing tests on short notice.

Mouse's parents were still in Argentina, wrestling with the idea of leaving their vacation home and returning to Maryland. As the virus continued to spread, South America had remained relatively untouched. On their most recent video chat, Mouse's father had remarked that it might be better for them to stay there until all of this blows over.

Of the forty-four active players on the lacrosse team, fourteen tested positive for the virus. While Mouse was the first on the team to actively show symptoms, many others had since spoken up about experiencing shortness of breath during the game and they were all being held in strict isolation at the hospital. Fortunately, Sam felt fine, but a quiet resentment brewed inside of him at the fact that Mouse's parents hadn't thought to extend the testing outside of the lacrosse team. Without Mouse to advocate on his behalf or money of his own, Sam knew that the possibility of securing a test for himself at this point was a long shot.

Similar outbreaks had happened in Los Angeles, New York, and, notably, Miami, where the lacrosse team had spent their spring break partying on the beach. The virus was officially in the United States and, as many scientists were arguing, it had probably been circulating within the U.S. borders for a while.

Sam lifted a composite notebook labeled, "Chemistry Lab," from the drawer and a rubber lacrosse ball rolled out toward him. Surprised at the sight, Sam tossed the notebook into the cardboard box and took the ball in his hand. The scuffed surface was cold to the touch, as Sam rolled it around in his palm and tossed it gently in the air. It had been awhile since Sam had looked at it, but the memory attached to this particular lacrosse ball came back to him vividly. It had been one of their best days together this past summer.

"Keep it," Mouse had said with a grin, as the ball rolled in Sam's direction on the patio. Mouse flipped his hair out of his face with a smile. "I've got loads of them."

Sam had picked up the ball from beneath the patio chair and stared back at Mouse. Mouse was drenched in sweat in front of the lacrosse goal in his parents' backyard, a scattering of practice balls around him. A stack of papers was splayed out on the patio table, as Sam looked over the syllabi for his upcoming classes and Mouse hurled practice shots at the net. His flowing, blonde hair glistened in the August heat. It was a simple day, filled with the defining features of their lives at the time.

Sam teared up thinking about how simple life seemed just eight months ago. His biggest worries were school and Mouse's biggest worries were the coming lacrosse season. A single tear ran down his face, as he considered how quickly things had changed. Mouse was now laying in the hospital, hooked up to oxygen, fighting for every breath between coughing fits and the agonizing consumption of chicken broth and hospital jello. Sam was packing up and moving home to Seattle.

Their interactions had been reduced to the occasional video chat, if Mouse could find the strength to hold the phone with his frail hands. The conversations between them were brief. Sam would recap his day and fill Mouse in on what was going on in the world. Mouse barely spoke and coughed frequently, but the sight of Sam's face brought him a much-needed comfort. With everything going on, talking to Sam brought him a sense of normalcy. Thankfully, Carol had been permitted to see him and she rarely left the hospital. A rustling sound in the doorway caught Sam's attention and he glanced up from his packing and the sentiment of the lacrosse ball in his hand.

"You need a hand?" Robbie asked, as he entered the room and sat down next to Sam on the floor.

Startled by his presence, Sam's eyes met Robbie's sympathetic gaze. "Yeah, that'd be really … that'd be really …" he said, fighting to get the words out.

Sam felt the rising tide of emotion in his chest. The feeling of absolute helplessness, the feeling of responsibility and regret, the feeling of worry and concern. At this moment, it all began to boil over and Sam broke down on the floor. A streaming flood of tears hit the carpeting. The crushing weight of the week sat heavily on his back, as he sobbed and collapsed beneath it.

As he buried his face in the carpet, the comforting embrace of Robbie's arms wrapped around him tightly. Sam leaned into it, fighting for breath between sobs.

"Hey, it's going to be okay," Robbie said, softly caressing Sam's back. "He's going to be okay."

He pulled Sam into his chest, providing a comfort and camaraderie that summed up their years together. Sam composed himself slowly and wiped his cheeks dry with the sleeves of his shirt.

"I know," Sam replied. "Thanks, man. For everything." He pulled free of Robbie's grip and pointed at a box in the far corner of the room. "Can you just pack up my books over there?"

"Totally," Robbie replied.

They packed boxes for the next few hours of the morning. Robbie lightened the mood with his usual jokes and they laughed over fond memories of their time together on campus. A flurry of remember-whens and impersonations of their peers filled the room and Sam found himself at ease for the first time all week. The cathartic release of emotions and Robbie's comforting friendship brought a soothing ease to Sam's mood.

A few boxes at a time, they emptied Sam's apartment and loaded up his car near the campus front gates. With the last box in hand, Sam swung the apartment door closed one last time and locked it behind him. He pulled a white, surgical mask over his face and scratched gently at the strap running around his ears. The annoying discomfort of the strap pressed hard against Sam's cheeks, irritating his skin.

Well, I'll have to get used to this if I'm going to shadow at the hospital this summer, Sam thought, as he adjusted the facemask and considered his future in health care.

The events of this week, and the surge of media coverage about the virus, only amplified Sam's desire to become a doctor. He fully intended on securing a job in Seattle at the hospital or doing something health care–related.

With his mask secured and both hands beneath his last moving box, Sam walked down the hallway toward the elevator. Open doors and a few scattered suitcases lined the halls, as the mandatory move-out time had quickly approached. Students had been moving out sporadically throughout the week. Most underclassmen moved out immediately at the beginning of the week, in an effort to escape the dangers of the virus. Others waited until the end of the week.

Many of the graduating seniors chose to maximize their time on campus and were packing up on that day. They were in no rush to leave the place that they had called home for the past four years. While maximizing his time on campus was certainly a motivation, Sam also wanted to be close to Mouse. He was nervous for Mouse and Carol, and he wanted to be there in case anything happened or Carol needed help with the house.

Despite his desire to stay longer, it was time for him to leave and return to Seattle. His parents had been begging him to come back all week and, although Carol had offered him a room at Mouse's parents' house, he thought that he should return to Seattle in case the government put travel restrictions in place. So many other countries had done so, in response to the spread of the virus, and Sam wanted to be in Seattle if a nationwide lockdown occurred.

Sam stepped over a box and weaved around a suitcase, the sharp sting of bleach penetrating his nostrils down the hallway. Danny was still busily spraying down his apartment with bleach spray, door wide open and smell wafting across the threshold. With a polite nod, Sam passed by Danny's apartment and held his breath. Danny, standing in the near-empty apartment, wiped the sweat from his brow and continued to spray down his kitchen table.

Sam approached the elevator and hoisted the box under one arm. He initially reached out with his hand, but hesitated and nervously flared out his elbow instead. Awkwardly bent over, he pressed his elbow against the elevator button and nearly fell over. He secured his grip under the box and regained his balance.

The arriving chime of the elevator put Sam at ease. The smell of bleach followed him into the elevator, as he repeated his now signature elbow-wiggle-button-push. He rode the descending elevator from the fifth floor.

The elevator halted at the second floor and the doors opened in front of Sam. A girl and a woman, presumably her mother, stood there waiting with armfuls of boxes. Sam took a casual step to his left, reluctantly making room for them in the tight quarters of the elevator, but the girl's mother spoke up.

"Oh, I'm sorry. We'll get the next one," she said, politely avoiding the close proximity of the space.

Sam nodded approvingly from behind the closing elevator doors and proceeded to ride down to the first floor. As he exited the elevator, he wandered past Bailey's empty front desk and strolled back onto campus. The emptiness and lack of crowds, reminiscent of spring break, felt different now. Where he and Mouse had once found an enjoyable comfort in the emptiness of the university buildings, lawns, and park benches, he found a tragic emptiness overcoming the university grounds. Fear quelled any sense of comfort to be found in the budding tulips of the campus gardens. It was as if the buildings themselves were saddened by the news of the closing school year, wearing red, brick frowns on their facades.

As he crossed the quad in front of the statue of St. Agatha, a light misting of spring rain began to fall. Sam hurried up to the front gates and searched frantically in the rain for his car keys. Fumbling, with a box in one hand and the other in his pants pocket, he wrestled for the unlock button on the car keys. With two clicks of the button under his thumb and the flicker of red lights up ahead, Sam quickly approached the dry comforts of his trusted white sedan.

Boxes and blankets filled the back seat, pressed up against the windows. The entirety of his life at St. Agatha University was packed away, stacked and crammed in his car. This was it. Everything he owned was right here.

He had reserved a spot for his backpack and this last box in the front passenger seat, next to a bag of salt and vinegar chips and a family-pack of gummy worms. He quickly set the box down and, swinging it shut, scurried around the car to avoid the rain. He pulled open the driver-side door, as the wet metal of the door handle chilled his pruning fingertips. Placing one hand on the door and another on top of the car, Sam looked up at the St. Agatha clock tower one last time as the misting of rain dampened his brow.

The heavy hands of the clock tower ticked slowly and the falling rain seemed to stand still at attention. He stared, feeling regret and gratitude in the same instant. He considered everything that he might have done differently over the past four years but, standing where he was now, maybe he wouldn't change a thing. It's easy to look back at the past and wish to change things. It's much harder to feel gratitude for the little things that made life so special. In that moment, Sam simultaneously embraced and revolted against both emotions and smiled proudly. *One must imagine Sam happy.*

He nodded confidently at the clock tower, silently thanking it for watching over him for the past four years. *Thanks for everything,* he thought.

Sam wiped the rain from his face and stepped inside the car. Without allowing hesitation to permit him another glance back at campus, he pulled away and headed for the highway.

The rain picked up and slapped hard against the windshield for the first few hours of the drive. The trip proceeded as most multiday road trips go—miserably. Typically, Sam would have built a national park visit into the trip, but this hardly seemed the time. He would drive as far and as long as he could, minimizing his stops along the way.

The only saving grace was that there were far fewer cars on the road than usual. With the news of the virus spreading, people had started staying home more frequently and traveling less. The roads were mostly occupied by necessary travelers, like Sam, heading to the destination where they would stay for the upcoming isolation period. The other travelers were a strange scattering of foolishly defiant vacationers. Their ignorant commitments to previously planned trips to Nashville or New Orleans would lay the groundwork for the horrific tragedies that would follow.

After about fourteen hours on the road, Sam had driven to

his limit and pulled off the highway to a motel and diner. Rows of semitrucks, RVs, and family vans lined the parking lot, as small gatherings of truck drivers smoked cigarettes and chatted among themselves. Having completely lost himself in the monotony of the drive, Sam had little sense of exactly where and when he was. He sleepily stepped out of the car into the darkness of the night and searched for the motel's signage to orient himself to his location.

"Minnesota Star Motel and Diner," was written in neon green lettering across the front entryway. Sam yawned fiercely and stretched his arms high above his head. He pulled his backpack over his shoulder, packed loosely with a change of clothes, his laptop, and a few toiletries. Sam wandered across the parking lot beneath the starless night and walked past a group of mingling truck drivers in the parking lot. He nodded kindly toward their suspicious looks and continued up to the motel front desk.

"How much for the night?" Sam asked politely, fighting the strain in his sleepy eyes.

A youngish man stood behind the desk, half watching a battered television in the corner and half working through a stack of old, paper invoices. The man looked up slowly at Sam and spoke through a wad of chewing tobacco, packed tightly into his lower lip, "$54 for the night, $22 for the hour." The man raised a paper cup to his lip slowly and spit into it, eyeing Sam's slim-fitted jeans and gray, Henley shirt. A trickle of brown spit lingered on his lip, as he set the cup of dip-spit down on the front desk.

Sam looked down at his wallet and carefully calculated his budget for the road trip. Considering gas, food, and another two nights in motels, $54 was right at the limit of his budget.

Sam nodded reluctantly and handed over his bottom-tier, student credit card. "Just one night," Sam said, softly.

The man took the card and swiped it through the card reader. "Where you coming from?" he asked, punching away at the keyboard of a heavy, dated box computer.

"Washington, D.C.," Sam replied. "On my way to Seattle."

"East Coast, eh?" the man said, with a curious tone. He tapped his fingers impatiently, as the dial tones of an aged internet connection processed the payment. He spoke over the dial-up connection, "I heard on the news that they're shutting down all the schools out east. Heard they're putting entire cities on lockdown and trapping folks in their homes."

"I hadn't heard that," Sam replied, calmly. "But, I'm glad to be going home."

With an agreeable smile, the man returned Sam's credit card and handed over a key ring. "114," he said bluntly. "Ice machine is at the far end."

Avoiding any offense to the man, Sam turned away from the desk and covertly wiped his credit card and the key ring down with a sanitary wipe. "Thanks," Sam hollered over his shoulder, discarding the used-wipes in a trash bin by the door.

As Sam exited the lobby and stepped back out onto the parking lot, a low grumble rose in his stomach. The exhaustion from the long, fourteen-hour drive was only rivaled by his hunger. He glanced to his right, down the dimly lit walkway toward room 114. He glanced to his left, at the truck stop diner at the far end of the parking lot. Hunger took way and his feet carried him toward the enticing smell of grease and breakfast food that filled the night air.

As he pulled open the diner door, a loud bell announced his arrival. The few scattered trucker drivers seated at the countertop glanced toward the door and, with a nod, returned to their meals.

"Anywhere you like, sweetie," an elderly waitress wearing a

maroon apron hollered across the room, as she refilled one of the driver's coffees.

Sam smiled politely from behind tired eyes, and sat down on a tattered stool at the countertop. Removing a pack of sanitary wipes, he thoroughly wiped down the diner countertop and plastic menu in front of him. A burly man, wearing tattered jeans, a bright red shirt, and a flannel button down scoffed in Sam's direction dismissively.

Ignoring the man's disregard, Sam set the now-dirty wipes next to a pile of straw wrappers and single-use coffee creamers on the counter. Feeling his stomach rumble again, even louder than before, he peeled open the plastic menu in front of him. The Minnesota Star Diner served all of the diner classics. An extensive breakfast selection, served twenty-four hours, took up the entire left side of the menu. The right side was an odd scattering of burgers and forgotten entrees of yesteryear.

Sam passed over the large header that read, "Best Fish Fry in Minnesota," and arrived excitedly at the breakfast selection. He loved diners for just this reason. There were no places in D.C. that offered two eggs, two strips of bacon, two pieces of toast, and a short stack of pancakes for $6.99. In comparison, Sam had ordered lattes that cost more than that on Monroe Street.

The waitress, whose name tag read, "Dolores," approached with a kind smile and asked in a strong Midwestern accent, "Hey der, what can I getcha?" Her voice reminded Sam of the Bantz twins and the long way that they carried their vowels.

"I'll do the breakfast combo," he replied. "Eggs over easy and sourdough toast, please."

"Oh-ver easy and sour-doh-gh, coming right up. Any coffee?" Dolores followed, scribbling indecipherably on a notepad.

Sam shook his head in reply. With great confidence, she ripped the paper from the pad and seamlessly clipped it to the ticket line behind her. A few minutes later, a tall line cook emerged from the back and stepped up to the griddle

Dolores returned with a glass of water and set it down in front of Sam. "Taking a trip out west?" she asked, with a surprising level of cheer for the late hour.

Sam glanced up and replied, politely correcting her, "Heading home, actually. Back to Seattle."

"Safer there, I hope, with all this virus stuff going on," she remarked, her Midwestern accent now featuring more prominently. "I worry with all the travelers passing thro-ough here. I wouldn't be surprised if one of the drivers was carrying the virus with them. These f-oh-lks rely on the public restrooms, rest stops, and diners for their livelihoods. I appreciate you wiping everything down." She gathered the pile of dirty wipes in her hand and tossed them in a trash bin behind her, with a smile.

Sam nodded his head and replied, "It's the least I can do. I think everyone just has to be a little more cautious these days."

Dolores kindly agreed. "Well, your food should be right up," she assured him and returned to her responsibilities at the far end of the diner counter.

When his food arrived, Sam ate quickly and in silence. The hearty meal brought welcome nourishment to his grumbling stomach. His diet had thus far consisted of potato chips and gummy worms, and he enjoyed the savory taste of a cooked meal.

Uncomfortably full, Sam took one last sip from his glass of water and stood up from the diner stool. He twisted from side to side to aid his digestion and set $13.00 on the counter next to his place setting. Dolores nodded in affirmation, as she took another customer's order down the way. Sam turned, slowly nursing his full belly, and walked out the door.

He crossed the darkness of the parking lot in a tiresome haze. His heavy eyes fixed on room 114 and he trudged, full and exhausted, up to the heavy, red door. Sam turned the key and stepped inside. The stale smell of the musty motel carpeting filled his nostrils, but Sam hardly noticed at this point. After a long and emotionally draining week, he didn't have the energy to brush his teeth or wipe down another surface. He stumbled inside and nearly collapsed onto the bed, shuffling his legs free from his jeans. Sam slipped under the covers and collapsed into the bristly, cheap fabric of the pillowcase. In a matter of seconds, he fell into a deep sleep and found rest for the long day of driving that awaited him in the morning.

What felt like minutes later, Sam woke the next morning to the risen sun and sprawled out, stretching across the bed. The sunlight against the red curtains of the motel room cast a pink illumination across the room. The light warmed the room, as Sam emerged from beneath the covers.

He dragged his feet across the rough carpeted floor to the bathroom and jumped in the beige tub shower. The water fluctuated in temperature uncomfortably, prompting Sam to rush through his daily shower routine. He ran his hands gently through his hair and washed the grime and sweat of the previous day's drive and the motel bed off of his body.

He emerged quickly from the rushing water with a renewed sense of self and began to dry off. He peered out the bathroom door at the digital clock display at the motel bedside.

7:48AM, he thought. *I've gotta get on the road.*

Sam quickly dried himself off and tossed on the change of clothes that was stored away in his backpack. Wearing black sweatpants and a black, crew neck sweatshirt, Sam prioritized comfort for the day's drive. He gathered the rest of his things and, with a sanitizing wipe in hand, opened the motel room door and stepped out into the parking lot.

The bright morning sun was blinding as the sunshine ripped through the clear blue sky. Still waking up slowly, Sam cupped his hand across his forehead to block the sun from his eyes. He slowly strolled across the warming asphalt and entered the motel lobby.

"Good mornin', East Coast," the attendant greeted. "Everything good with your room?"

"All good," Sam replied, wiping down the set of keys with a sanitary wipe and handing them over to the youngish man.

"Well, travel safe and stay healthy," the man replied, setting the keys down on the desk.

"Yeah, you too," Sam replied, turning and heading back out on the open road.

The next few legs of the road trip went by in a haze. Sam continued to drive long, exhausting hours through to Seattle. His eagerness to reach home was demonstrated by his commitment to his driving plan; minimize stops, eat on the road, and listen to 80's rock when your eyes get tired. He played through audiobooks, podcasts, and a scattering of playlists that Maisie had put together for him. Their musical tastes were not even remotely in sync, but he appreciated the gesture and the diversity it brought to the drive. After a few days on the road, Sam finally emerged from the trance of highway driving, and the beauty of the mountains came into full view.

Just a bit further, he thought, checking the GPS on his phone for confirmation.

The sight of the mountains welcomed him home as he approached the greater Seattle area. He scanned the horizon and identified the familiar mountain peaks, naming them as he drew nearer to his parents' home. Sam was surprised at the distinct features of the mountains. The cloudless day gave way to an unprecedented line of sight in all directions. Sam felt the familiar embrace of the Seattle landscape and scanned the horizon to his left and right; this was home. He opened his windows and let the chill of the springtime air fill his car.

There it is, he thought, as he set eyes on the exit to his parents' house.

He pressed on the accelerator and sped up in anticipation, changing lanes to pull off of the highway. The looping exit brought him to his parents' street. Sam pulled up into the driveway and slowly traced the outlines of his childhood home. He looked over the beige siding, the red front door, the young oak tree growing in the front yard, the brick walkway that he and his father had laid three summers prior. He was deeply comforted by the sight and breathed a hard sigh of relief. Putting the car in park, he sank back into his seat and turned off the ignition.

Sam's eyes settled on the open garage. His father was hunched over, carefully inspecting the engine of an old, battered camper van. Sam stepped out of the car casually and called out, "Might be time to retire that hunk of junk, Pop."

Sam's father stood up tall, emerging from under the hood of the van. Sam had inherited his father's height, but his lean frame was undoubtedly his mother's. His father was a densely built mountain man, in the most stereotypical fashion.

The burly mountain man wiped the grease from his calloused hands on a once-white towel draped over his shoulder. With a proud smile, he replied, "I think the van has got a few more trips in it, don't you?"

Sam shrugged his shoulders and gave his father a warm hug,

pulling him in closely and burying his face in his shoulder. He felt the muscular arms wrap around him tightly and a serene comfort came over him.

"Welcome home, Sammy," his father said, still smiling as the two separated. "How was the drive?"

Sam straightened his shirt and responded, "It was good. I could use a bite to eat."

"Still growing, huh?" his father chuckled. "Toss me that crescent wrench and go hug your mother. She's been baking all morning. We should have enough muffins for two winters."

"Thanks, Pop," Sam called out, as he started walking back to his car. "I'll be back to help with the van. Just let me unload my stuff."

Starting in the back seat, Sam took two heavy boxes in his arms and headed inside. The warm smell of banana muffins filled the house. Sam's favorite. Intoxicated, he followed his nose through the living room, past a green recliner chair, and toward the small galley kitchen that divided the house in two. He set the boxes down slowly and peered around the corner. His mother, back turned, was carefully washing dishes at the kitchen sink. Three trays of muffins were set out on the small work space beside her, begging Sam to enter the kitchen.

From left to right, the trays were arranged in order of ingredients: banana chocolate chip, banana walnut, and plain banana muffins. Sam's mother was an exceptional baker and always welcomed Sam home with some type, or types, of muffins. A bubbly, petite woman, Sam's mother brought all the charms of her Southern roots with her to the Pacific Northwest.

Many years ago, she had taken a year to tour the United States after completing college. Her travels brought her to the Seattle area, where Sam's father was working that summer as a hiking and climbing guide. Committed to a year of adventure, she signed up for a guided climbing trip on a whim and fell in love. She fell in love with climbing, hiking, rafting, biking, and the handsome guide who was leading her excursions through the mountains. Despite leaving the South, she never left her roots behind. Sam's mother insisted that her son grow up with three things: a kind heart, a proper ethic of hospitality, and a taste for sweet tea.

She turned slowly from the sink to see Sam standing in the doorway. Eyes wide she tossed her drying towel onto the counter and took two giant steps toward him. She took his face in her hands and smiled lovingly, with a look of calm and relief.

"I was so worried about you, Sam," she said softly, still holding his cheeks in her hand. "They're saying all sorts of things on the news about the virus. How's Mouse?"

Placing his hands on top of his mother's, Sam lowered her hands from his face. He held his mother's hands softly. "Hi, Mom," he said, matching her kind smile. "Mouse is okay. He's fighting. I called him from the gas station and he sounded a little stronger. It's hard to tell."

"You picked a strong one, Sam," she said, reassuringly. "He's strong and kind and has a good heart. We've been praying for him." Sam's mother paused for a moment and squeezed Sam's hands. She frantically turned back to the galley kitchen and a fast flurry of words poured out of her mouth, "You must be hungry. I made muffins. Do you want a sandwich?"

Sam chuckled at her fondly. He had missed his mother's thoughtfulness and over-consideration, particularly around the practice of eating. She was always insisting that he take a banana or a sandwich with him out the door, even if he was already on his way to meet friends for lunch or their family had just eaten at home.

"Just a muffin, Mom. It smells great in here," he replied with a chuckle.

She smiled and handed him a banana chocolate chip muffin. "Is your father still out there fumbling over that van? He wants us to drive up into the mountains this weekend," she asked.

Sam bit into the muffin and savored the warm taste. The combination of banana and chocolate chip brought him to a blissful state and he savored the sweet taste of home. He closed his eyes in ecstasy and spoke through a mouthful, "Mom, you've really outdone yourself."

She smiled and shrugged her shoulders, "You're sweet. Take a muffin to your father. He needs all the help he can get out there."

With a wink, she tossed him another muffin and returned to doing the dishes. As Sam wandered back through the living room toward the garage, he stopped to take in the familiar comforts of the room. He slowly scanned the odd collection of throw pillows on the couch, the bookshelf filled with old DVDs, the ceramic chicken in the corner, and all of the quiet idiosyncrasies of the place where he grew up.

A wooden oar sat comfortably on the wall behind the couch. It was from one of their first rafting trips together, on the White Salmon River, and it was one of his mother's favorite keepsakes. Sam breathed a sigh of relief and read the wood-carved writing on the oar blade silently to himself, as he had so many times before.

"Home isn't a place, it's a feeling."

SETTING

A gust of wind brushed the hair out of Emily's face. She secured her tablet bag at her side and tightened the wrap of her spring jacket around her shoulders. Glancing up at the sky, she urged the single cloud covering the sun to move. With a glimmer of hope, a tiny sliver of sunlight began to clear the cloud.

Foxx Avenue was relatively quiet for a Monday afternoon, scarcely populated by a few pedestrians and essential workers. The downtown area was almost entirely made up of Eden's essential services. Apart from the pharmacy, a small grocery depot, and a few specialty manufacturers lining the sidewalks, there was little to be found in the area.

As she walked by the specialty manufacturers, she carefully took in the unique smells of each boutique. She inhaled deeply through her mask, as she wandered toward the pharmacy. As she passed the first storefront, the smell of chocolate and cocoa beans filled her nostrils. Then, the smell of freshly roasted coffee crept in. A few storefronts later, the overwhelming smell of laundry detergent flooded her senses. Each manufacturer delighted in its own way, and Emily embraced each fresh scent as she walked.

She stared through the big glass windows that bordered the sidewalk, carefully examining the heavily geared workers inside. Peering in, she watched as they honed their craft. Through protective gear and heavy facemasks, they poured chocolate, sorted through coffee beans, and provided cleaning supplies for the grocery depot with focused expertise. The artists of craft worked beneath a heavily painted City of Eden crest, towering boldly behind each work area. Its watchful eye hung over the specialty production that fueled the city of Eden. Pretty much anything that couldn't be produced through the home hydroponic systems was produced through essential industries downtown.

The sea of fragrance fell behind her as Emily trotted excitedly toward the pharmacy. Her stride gave way to a light, involuntary skip, as the lone cloud covering the sun finally moved and let the sunlight shine down on the cold concrete of the sidewalk. Emily grinned from behind her facemask, welcoming the warmth of the sun and taking in the fresh air of the sunlit spring afternoon.

Her upbeat mood carried her all the way to the pharmacy entrance and, as the doors parted in front of her, a friendly and familiar voice welcomed her to the space.

"Emily Chang," Doc Abrams wheezed from inside his glass booth, excitement in his raspy voice. "I've got your family's essentials all prepped."

Emily waved kindly from the pharmacy's entryway and began washing her hands at the sink. The rush of warm soap and water felt good on her cold hands. She pulled them slowly from the warmth of the water and flicked the remaining droplets of water back into the sink.

"Thank you, sir," Emily replied with cheerful surprise, turning to face Doc Abrams. "That's incredibly kind of you."

Doc Abrams rose from his seat and began to sort through the essentials. "And, don't think that I forgot about Ted, either," he continued. "His respiratory aids are right here and I've included some eucalyptus ointment. It doesn't get prescribed all that often anymore, but I think it might help with his breathing."

Doc Abrams began to sanitize the essentials carefully and placed them on the counter in front of Emily. The plastic bottles glistened under the fluorescent lighting, coated with the wet sheen left behind by the sanitary wipes. Emily wrestled a yellow mesh bag from her tablet bag and picked up the bottles one at a time. She dropped them carefully into the mesh bag and she mentally checked them off of her list, confirming the accuracy of Doc Abrams' already prepared assortment. The essentials were all there.

"Our family ID is 662123," Emily spoke up, the mesh bag now full and resting comfortably at her side.

Doc Abrams casually typed from inside of his booth and processed her family ID. He nodded warmly and replied, "You're all set, Miss Chang. It's good seeing you again."

Emily nodded politely back at him and turned for the door. After a few steps, she called nervously back to him. "Excuse me, Doc Abrams?" she asked. "If you're not too busy, I'd still love to hear about your time in the mountains."

Doc Abrams sat up, surprised by the inquiry, and straightened his medical white coat. "Well," he replied, looking seriously around the pharmacy. "As you can see, I'm very busy with customers right now."

Emily scanned the empty aisles of the pharmacy. She peered around the corner to check the back section, by the respiratory aids, to see if there were people waiting for Doc Abrams' attention from a distance away. There was no one else in the store. Feeling oddly dismissed, she glanced back at Doc Abrams and lowered her head in a quiet defeat.

"I understand," she replied. "Thank you, sir."

"I'm kidding, Emily," he said, shocked at her lack of wit and social awareness. "Is sarcasm still a thing? There's a chair around that corner. Give it a quick wipe down and have a seat."

Emily smiled and chuckled at herself. She was certainly familiar with the concept of sarcasm. The joke would have landed coming from any other source, but there was something odd about Doc Abrams' friendly disposition. Most of the community elders carried themselves with a serious and quiet demeanor. This was especially true of the survivors. In Emily's experience, survivors didn't speak very often. If they did, it was usually with a soft sadness in their voices. It felt impolite to joke and tease someone of his age, but Doc Abram's sarcasm seemed to invite a playfulness that put her off balance.

Around the corner, Emily found a plastic chair. She began to wipe it down and carried it back to the front of the store, discarding the dirty sanitary wipes in the entryway trash can as she passed.

Doc Abrams cleared his throat as Emily sat down. "So, what do you want to know about the mountains?" he asked.

Emily paused to collect herself. *Is 'everything' an appropriate response?* she wondered.

After a few moments, she spoke up, "Well, a few weeks ago, I was sitting with my father in our living room and we were looking at old pictures of my grandparents. A few of them were taken during a hiking trip that they took to the Yosemite Valley and … well, I'm not sure."

"Yosemite is quite beautiful," he replied, quietly. Doc Abrams took a puff of his inhaler and continued, "I've only been out that way a few times, but once was enough to make an impression. We also used to hike in the Cascades all the time."

Emily sat up, her curiosity holding her at attention. Her eyes widened and she inched onto the edge of the plastic chair. Captivated, she inquired nervously, "Did you ever camp in a tent?"

Doc Abrams chuckled, but quickly apologized, "I'm sorry, dear. I forget that you've never been .... Yes, Emily. We camped in tents. We slept under the stars. We ate wild berries. The whole deal."

As he spoke, his tone revealed the vivid return of fond memories, and a quiet joy lit up his face. Emily prepared a reply, but she paused to observe the transformation of his facial expression. She watched intensely as Doc Abrams lost himself to the memory and stared blankly at the clear, glass front doors of the pharmacy. His eyes wandered through the doorway and out to the subtle peaks of the Cascade Mountain Range that could be made out in the distance. Emily had never seen someone get lost in something so fondly. His old, wrinkly cheeks puffed up and his eyes shimmered with joy, revealing an emotional excitement beyond anything that Emily had ever experienced.

When I'm old, she thought, *I hope I can look back on my life with joy like that.*

"Wild berries, sir?" she asked, calling Doc Abrams back from the trance of his own memory. "From, just anywhere? How did you clean them?"

Doc Abrams turned his eyes back to Emily and grinned. He closed his eyes for a moment, growing tired from the conversation but not wanting it to end. Clearing his throat, he prepared a response. "Well, we just ate them," he said bluntly.

The next thirty minutes went by quickly, as Doc Abrams entertained Emily with tales of hiking, camping, and rock climbing. She hung on his every word, asking questions and requesting clarifying details. Her intrigue seemed to breathe new life into his tired and damaged lungs. Doc Abrams fought through his fatigue, fueled by fond memories and an eagerness to share his life with her.

Emily was particularly enthralled by the stories of him hiking and climbing in the Cascade Mountains. Just a short drive away, Emily was well acquainted with the high peaks that made up the Cascades. On the rare clear day, she could see them on her walk to school. As she sat before him, soaking in the wisdom and joy of his stories, she imagined herself summiting the mountain tops that had stood quietly in the background of every major moment in her life. It felt as if she were breathing for the very first time.

After thirty minutes of stories and laughter, Emily checked the time on her tablet. Not wanting the stories to come to an end, she accepted the sad realization that she should be getting on her way. With curfew approaching, she knew that she had to go. She stood up slowly from her chair. She opened her tablet bag and began to search for her sanitary wipes.

"Ah, I'll take care of that, Emily," Doc Abrams said, rising from his seat in the booth. "Thank you for allowing an old man to reminisce."

Emily's eyes lit up as she spoke, "Doc Abrams. Thank you. This was so wonderful." Stepping away from the chair and toward the pharmacy exit, she continued, "I have so many questions. Can we do this again?"

Doc Abrams brought his inhaler up to his mouth and pulled hard, breathing the medicinal spray in deeply. As he finished, he nodded confidently and he replied, "I would like that."

Emily nodded back and headed to the departure sink. She hurried through her hand-washing routine. Still captured by Doc Abram's stories, she stepped triumphantly through the sliding doors and back onto the sidewalk in a daze. Beyond the storefronts and streetlights, the faint outline of the Cascades stood tall in the distance. Before she knew it, the sight of their snowcapped peaks took hold of her.

Still staring, her feet led her in the direction of the mountains and she found herself wandering down Foxx Avenue. The smells and essential workers of downtown no longer held her interest. Instead, her eyes set on the small gaps of snow between the evergreens in the mountains. As much as Emily was enjoying the view of the mountain range in the distance, she found herself craving the view from the other side. She yearned for the view from the summit. The mountains let out a gentle inviting call on the wind. They whispered softly to her, *"Emily."*

She stepped in their direction. *"Emily,"* they called to her again, louder this time. She continued walking toward the mountains, following the soft call on the wind in a trance.

"Emily?" the voice said, more clearly and deeply. "Are you okay?"

Snapping from her daydream, Emily turned to see Cayden standing beside her. Captivated by her own thoughts, she had walked right past him. Her eyes rose to meet his, as he tossed his hair in his hands and adjusted his facemask.

He gave her a curious look and, waving his hand in front of her, he repeated himself, "Emily? Is everything alright?"

"Cayden!" Emily chirped, more loudly and aggressively than the situation called for. She spoke again quickly to compensate for the awkward volume of her salutation. "Yes. Sorry. I'm fine. What are you doing down here?"

Cayden started walking down the sidewalk, nearer to Emily, and gestured for her to lead the way. "I was just picking up a few things at the grocery depot before heading home," he explained. "I'm happy we bumped into each other though. Do you want to walk together for a bit?"

Uncertainty set in. Emily was still feeling burned from when

Cayden stood her up after school. She flashed back to standing outside of Walter Reed High School on their placement day, waiting for Cayden to walk home with her. She felt a bitter agitation with him. While she had played cool and they had been texting in the days since, she still felt slighted. For the first time, she was guarded with him.

"Sure," she replied, apathetically. "I'm heading this way."

They walked the sidewalk together as the sun began to dip and the air chilled. Spring was Cayden's favorite season and he enjoyed the cool breeze of the springtime air. Most of his day was spent pouring over video games and training with the team. On the rare occasion that his family needed something from the grocery depot, he eagerly volunteered to make the trip. With his tablet bag slung over his shoulder, he casually stuffed his hands in his pockets and embraced the crisp air of the late afternoon.

"So, you're going to be Council Justice," Cayden remarked. "That's kind of a huge deal. Your folks must be really proud of you."

Emily shrugged her shoulders in reply. "I guess," she said, warming to his inquiry. "Honestly, my family hasn't talked about it much. I think they're trying to give me space. I'm still not even sure how I feel about the whole thing."

"That makes sense," he replied, with understanding in his tone. "Your parents sound really cool. With everyone at in-school making such a big deal about it, it's probably cool to go home and not have to worry."

Emily turned toward him, curiously searching his face for the source of his concern. "Yeah, the whole thing is a bit overwhelming," she chuckled to herself. "Not everyone had a stranger from the Council come in and announce their exam results, and I sort of hate being the center of attention. What about you? You bolted out of class pretty quick that day."

Cayden chuckled, tiny fractures forming in his cool, confident persona. "Yeah, the exam ..." he began, slowly. "I was ... umm ... surprised?"

Cayden jumped up onto the sidewalk curbing. Placing one foot in front of the other, he balanced playfully along the narrow platform. With surprising grace and poise, his stride carried them down to the corner without offering further explanation about his Aptitude Exams. Emily matched him stride for stride, wondering if she should press him for details or if she should back off from the subject.

"Surprised, huh?" Emily asked, deciding to probe once more as they arrived at the corner.

After a brief pause, Cayden looked out into the crosswalk and looked off in the direction of his housing cluster. Emily glanced at the sidewalk to her left. A left turn would lead her home, to HC-F5, and she wondered if she should just abandon their conversation and head home. The streetlights took on a light pink hue and Emily's tablet began to feel heavy in her tablet bag, begging her to check the time.

"Well, I'm this way," Cayden said, deflecting Emily's curiosities. "It was good to see you, Emily. Thanks for walking with me."

Emily chirped up, before he could finish his goodbye, "I'm actually heading that way, too. I've got one last stop down this way."

Cayden skeptically checked his tablet for the time. New to town, he assumed that Emily knew the streets better than he did. He was certain that she could successfully manage curfew. After all, she grew up in Eden. Setting his skepticism aside, Cayden shrugged his shoulders and made room for her in the crosswalk.

A stiff tension started to wash over her and her chest tightened. The streetlights drifted into a deeper shade of pink and approached a curfew color red that would demand she race home. Still, she fought through the tension and swallowed her nerves.

"Your exam results must have been pretty surprising, then" she teased, half seriously demanding an explanation for his standing her up. "You were supposed to walk me home. Or, did you forget?"

The tension brought on by the curfew was quickly replaced by the awkward tension between them. Cayden gripped the back of his neck, anxiously searching for something to say. He nervously swayed from side to side and, after a few long seconds, spoke up.

"I'm sorry, Emily," he said, bluntly. "I should've sent you a message."

Emily nodded sternly and replied, "Thanks. You should have."

They walked in silence for the next block, drawing nearer to the edge of downtown. The row of essential storefronts devolved into a scarce spattering of empty buildings. The buildings grew further and further apart from one another, revealing unused alleyways and corridors.

"Cayden," Emily said softly. "If you want to talk about your exam results, we can. I wasn't super thrilled with mine either."

Cayden chuckled through a soft sadness. "You know," he started. "My folks didn't ask about the results. I'm not even sure they know that we've already been placed." Cayden straightened his posture and fought back against the fractures forming in his confidence and poise. "My exam results and placement were inconclusive."

Confused, Emily slowed her pace. "Inconclusive?" she asked, certain that she misheard him. "What does that mean?"

Cayden laughed and shrugged his shoulders, "I know, right? Everyone at in-school spent the whole day talking about their results, and I didn't know what to say." His tone grew more frustrated and irritation stepped in where Cayden usually projected calm. "But I guess it happens in gaming," he explained. "Coach says that it's the

Council's way of telling you to keep your hands on the controller."

Emily looked down at the ground, surprised and not surprised. The Eden Vax were the pride of the city and Cayden was their star. It made sense that the Council would want to keep his results from him. He could have his high school experience, if he must, but only so much of it. Cayden was now a famous gamer. The better that he performed, the less his life belonged to him. It belonged to the team and the team belonged to the Council.

The streetlights took on a deep, red glow as Emily and Cayden reached the edge of downtown. Beyond the last storefront, the road led out to the city limits.

"I'm sorry, Cayden," Emily said, wishing she had something more comforting to say.

"Thanks, Emily," he replied. He quickly regained his cool and confident posture and, checking the streetlights, leaned away from her. "Well, I should get going. Curfew is coming up."

"Yeah," Emily replied with a smile. "Get home safe."

She watched intensely as he darted off toward his housing cluster, shrinking from view as he trotted one block, two blocks, three blocks into the distance. The Aptitude Exams had decided so much for Emily over the past few weeks. She had spent her nights imagining her life as a Council Justice.

What would it be like? Would she be successful? Would she lose touch with Marshall and Fae?

Emily had spent hours considering the ways that her life would be different when she moved forward with her exam results in Year 12 and onto college. Year 12 would be an intensive study of the Council. She would learn the careful nuances of the different positions and get a first-hand look at the governing structures behind the City of Eden. While the prospect of her life changing was scary, the Aptitude

Exams brought her future into focus. Her exam results gave her a roadmap for the rest of her life. She would follow the path, closely and carefully, and she would be the next Council Justice. Council Justice Chang.

For Cayden, however, there was no exciting roadmap. The anxious buildup to their exam results was fruitless. There was no scary intrigue to look forward to on the horizon. There was no possibility of life changing. The Aptitude Exams basically told him that he was already living his exam results. They had already been decided for him.

He would've been good at a lot of things, she thought. *I'm sure of it.*

As Cayden faded out of sight, Emily checked the streetlights and scoffed at their reddening color. The bright hue of red taunted her, pressing her to turn toward home and abandon the fresh air and sight of the mountains. She removed her tablet from her bag to check the time. *16:06.* With heavy, disappointed footsteps, she turned left and reluctantly hastened her stride toward the concrete columns of HC-F5.

She stomped in a straight line down the middle of the sidewalk as she headed home, drawing the attention of two patrol officers heading in her direction. They stared at her with harsh, disapproving looks, as they stepped around her on the sidewalk. They tightly clutched their rifles and grunted at her through their facemasks.

Emily would have normally matched their efforts to create space on the walkway, but she held her ground. She didn't know whether their disapproving looks were because she was pushing curfew or because she didn't politely make room for them on the sidewalk. Either way, she didn't care.

In proud defiance, Emily puffed out her chest as she marched down the street. Her pace began to slow, despite the red color of the streetlights and her eyes slowly returned to the sight of the Cascades on the horizon.

The sun had cut across the blue sky and was beginning its descent. The late afternoon light brought the mountains to a delightful glow, slightly illuminated in orange, pink, and red. Some magnetic force pulled Emily off balance. All of her instincts told her to keep walking home, but her feet carried her across the street toward the mountains.

When she reached the corner, Emily turned right to face the mountain and gave into the draw of the magnetic pull. She looked hard at the red streetlight and, for the first time in her life, she taunted back at it. Heading in the opposite direction of home, Emily drifted off in ecstasy toward the city limits in search of a better view of the setting sun over the Cascades.

There were no housing clusters down this way. The northwest edge of Eden was just an empty warehouse and a vital health checkpoint that marked the edge of the city. Staffed by three officers and one medical professional, the checkpoint consisted of a single-lane road that ran in and out of Eden. Cars would stop, register with the Council, and travelers would have their health records reviewed. If everything seemed fit, they were allowed through the guard gate and into the city.

A few blocks away from the checkpoint and officers, Emily attempted to shrink from their view along the edge of the sidewalk. To her right, a grassy hill created some elevation. Her eyes locked on the hilltop, maybe one seventy feet high overlooking the city's border. She scanned the hillside for a winding road, sidewalk, or stairway that led up to the top of the hill, but she found nothing. The steep route to the top was marked by a few scattered boulders and trees amidst the grass and dirt.

Emily took a deep breath and clutched her tablet bag close to her side. She looked down at her white sneakers and closed her eyes, searching for common sense and the urge to return home. Finding no desire to turn back, she raised her foot onto the sidewalk curbing and scampered into the grass. As the route became steeper, she placed two hands in the dirt and began to scramble up the hill. She felt the earth beneath her fingers and delighted in the grit under her nails.

On the occasional Saturday, Emily's family would go to the F-block park and enjoy the outdoors for a few hours. However, it was always a very sanitized experience. They would clean a set of chairs that sat in storage and take in the fresh air through their facemasks. To avoid overcrowding, housing units had to apply in advance and were given a specific Saturday during the month and a time slot that they could visit the park.

Once, when Emily was young, she had rubbed her hands in the dirt during one of their park visits and received a harsh scolding from her mother, who promptly wiped her hands with sanitary wipes. Emily's mother explained that there were germs and bacteria in the dirt that would make her sick. It wasn't the first time that Emily had heard that word, "sick." Without requiring further explanation, the young Emily knew that the word was serious, and she asked her mother to wipe her hands down again.

Despite all of this, Emily embraced the feeling of danger and rebellion as she scrambled toward the top of the hill. Dismissing her mother's scolding, the patrol officers' dirty looks, and the Council's expectations, Emily gripped a small rock protruding from the dirt and pulled herself up by the natural features of the hillside. Sweaty and dirty, she arrived at the top of the hill and settled against a large boulder.

She leaned against the hard surface of the rock face in exhaustion. Feeling the jagged bumps in her back, she turned and pressed her hands against the cold surface of the granite. The divots and ripples in the rock invited her to climb. Emily placed her fingers in a small crack in the rock and pressed her feet against a small protrusion at the boulder's base. Placing a hand here and foot there, Emily felt for inconsistencies in the otherwise smooth surface of the rock face. Securing her footing with each move, she climbed her way to the top of the eight-foot-tall boulder. Triumphantly, she sat down and turned to face the mountains. She watched as the sun continued to dip nearer to the horizon, losing herself completely in its beauty.

Her tablet buzzed furiously in her tablet bag, but she refused to reach for it. Instead, she set the bag behind her and stared out at the setting sun. Tiny scuff marks colored the soles of her shoes. Her hands were covered in dirt and grime. Emily pinched her thumb against her middle and pointer fingers and rubbed them together, remarking at the gristle of the dirt flakes falling off of her fingertips.

She sat there for some time, watching the sky light up in a furious blaze of orange and pink majesty as the sun fell slowly behind the mountain range. The snowcapped mountain peaks danced in the sunset, celebrating the day's end beneath the whirlwind of contrasting colors. Inspired, Emily began to dance with them. Swaying from side to side in her seat, she embraced the chill of the evening and praised the view.

She had watched the sunset before, usually with her parents from her living room window. But, this was different. Alone, sitting on the cold granite with dirt under her fingernails, she thought to herself, *When I'm old, this is a memory that I can look back on with joy.*

The sun finally disappeared behind the peaks and Emily stood up tall in the darkness. She pulled her tablet bag over her head and laughed. *I'm totally fucked,* she thought, still refusing to take out her tablet.

She gleefully descended the boulder and the hillside through the darkness and found her way back to the sidewalk. The streetlights were full on, crimson red, but she already knew that she had stayed out past curfew. She turned toward home and started walking, scanning the streets for officers on patrol. She scurried across the street and hopped up onto the sidewalk, but, after a few steps, a flashlight beam shined brightly in her face.

"HANDS UP!" a voice commanded, angrily.

Emily smirked dismissively and put her hands in the air, slowly. The armor-gloved hand of an officer on patrol gripped her arm tightly. The officer's booming voice demanded an explanation, but Emily could barely hear him yelling. Instead, she turned to steal one last glance at the mountains through the darkness. In the faintest of ways, she swore that she could make out their snowcapped peaks in the distance among the stars.

ORDER

"Can everyone hear me?" Professor Lewis shouted into the computer. The camera was fixed on his wrinkled forehead, as he leaned forward into the computer's microphone. "Can you all see my screen? Is the slideshow up?"

Sam sighed and clicked the "raise hand" button on his screen. St. Agatha had institutionalized the use of a new software, called EduView, for distanced learning. The virus had many schools scrambling for a way to keep classes moving forward remotely, and EduView, a Seattle-based tech startup, had quickly become a household name. Sam had used the platform once previously. His high school had been selected for an initial pilot, back when the company first started to attract investors. EduView had made some significant changes since then, but Sam was familiar with the different functions and uses. Professor Lewis approved Sam's request and unmuted him.

"Professor, there should be a 'share screen' button in the lower left corner. The icon looks like two overlapping boxes," Sam explained, guiding Professor Lewis through the complicated steps of sharing his screen with their class.

Professor Lewis was an elderly gentleman, who had taught at St. Agatha for forty years. His lecture style was dated and, of all of Sam's professors, Professor Lewis was the least suited to make the transition to online classes. At the same time, however, Professor Lewis was a brilliant scholar and it was hard to graduate from St. Agatha's biology department without taking one of his classes.

"Thank you, Sam," Professor Lewis said, finding the button and sharing his screen. "Now, as you can see, the hemoglobin proteins are ...."

This was their class's third attempt at distanced learning. St. Agatha had given an extended week of vacation after closing campus, allowing students time to move home and settle in before resuming classes. Everyone was required to download EduView and complete a three-hour tutorial on how to use the platform. While the students seemed to make the adjustment well, the professors were struggling with the transition. Their first two class attempts consisted mostly of Professor Lewis lecturing through a spotty internet connection, with half his body off-screen. In a bold and daring move, this third lecture included the dynamic addition of a screen share and slide show.

With a loud knock, Sam's mother entered his room with a basket of laundry. Sam quickly adjusted his chair and gestured for her to leave the room. She ignored his waving hands and proceeded to walk to his bed, in full view of his class. She began to lay out the stacks of clean, folded laundry onto his bed.

"Sam, did you have a question?' Professor Lewis asked, mistaking Sam's hand-waving as him offering a comment. Professor Lewis unmuted Sam again.

"Mom, I'm in cla ... No, sir. I don't have a question. I was just talking to my mother," Sam explained, as his face began to turn red in embarrassment.

Sam's mother stepped up behind him and placed two hands on his shoulders. She crouched down into the camera view. "Hey everyone!" she hollered, planting three quick, consecutive kisses on Sam's cheek.

Sam squirmed away, brushing off his embarrassment, "I'm sorry. Please continue, Professor Lewis."

Class resumed, as a chorus of silent chuckles rang across the muted faces on the screen. Professor Lewis continued through his slideshow presentation, covering the nuances of oxygen-carrying proteins and the differential diagnoses associated with low red blood cell counts.

Sam had started class by diligently taking notes, but his mind quickly drifted. His family had plans to drive into the mountains for the afternoon and hike. Washington State had tightened its restrictions last week, as the number of virus cases continued to rise across the country. Sam had hoped to return to some sense of normalcy in Seattle, but quickly found that normal had become a distant memory. The virus' reach had become inescapable, and the fractures of life before the virus began to scatter.

In the weeks since the lacrosse game, Seattle had fought hard for early testing and had already identified eight thousand cases in the city. Relative to the other major metropolitan areas, this number was actually pretty low. The virus was highly contagious and deadly, and it had ripped through the country with a furious rage. Businesses closed, stadiums emptied, concert venues shut down. This had quickly become their new normal.

With everything closed, Sam's father suggested that they escape to the quiet comforts of the mountains for the afternoon and Sam had agreed. He could use the refreshing familiarities of the mountains, especially given all the stress that he was under and his constant worrying about Mouse. His notetaking faded and Sam daydreamed his way through the next twenty minutes of lecture, shifting between an anticipatory excitement for the mountains and imagining worst-case scenarios for Mouse. It was exhausting.

"Well, thank you all for your focus today," Professor Lewis said, ending his lecture right on time. "I know these are unprecedented times and I appreciate everyone's patience as we adjust. Have a good rest of the day."

Sam closed his laptop slowly and yawned. The time change back to the West Coast had not been kind to him. His classes were still being conducted during their usual times. That meant that his *10:00 AM* class with Professor Lewis actually began at *7:00 AM* in Seattle. The early mornings had proven difficult. As Sam adjusted to his new schedule, he had spent the past few days in a strange, tired fatigue.

Sam stood up slowly from his desk and went over to his bedroom closet. He sifted through his neatly arranged hangers for a lightweight hiking shirt from his trip to Yosemite National Park. He and Mouse had taken a long weekend there last summer, over the fourth of July. Sam spent most of the weekend teaching Mouse how to set up a tent, build a fire, and the basics of outdoor survival. Mouse had never been camping before and he was nervous about the whole ordeal.

As they had driven out of the park, Mouse had insisted that they stop for a souvenir. They had the time of their lives and he couldn't leave the trip without memorializing it with something. As Sam waited patiently in the car, Mouse emerged from the gift shop with a Yosemite-branded hiking shirt and gave it to Sam as a gift. Commemorating their trip together, the shirt had quickly become one of Sam's favorites.

He found the shirt hanging on the far side of the closet and, pulling it over his head, he walked out to the living room to find his parents eating breakfast at a small kitchen table in the corner. His parents made room for him at the breakfast table. They scooted their chairs to opposite edges of the round table, revealing a place setting between them that invited Sam to sit down. His mother had prepared him a plate of scrambled eggs. Two, triangle cut pieces of wheat toast neatly adorned the upper left and right corners of the plate.

"Your breakfast is getting cold, Sammy," his father said, through a mouthful of eggs. "Fuel up! I've got plans for fifteen miles in Mount Rainier today!"

"Fifteen miles?! What's the elevation gain?" Sam asked nervously, as he pulled out his chair and sat down.

"You bet," his father confirmed. "Maybe, three thousand feet. You think you're up to it?"

Sam had grown ravenously hungry during class, without even knowing it. Scooping a portion of eggs onto his toast, he took a bite and began chewing. Sam's father stood up, stacking his fork and knife neatly in the middle of his plate. Sam's father stepped around and into the galley kitchen and started doing the dishes.

"Up for it?" Sam's mother asked, as he rounded the corner. "Connor, you barely made it back to the car the last time we went hiking."

Sam's father returned to the living room upon hearing her comment, a wet dish and drying cloth in hand. With the raise of his eyebrow and a smile, he responded, "I told you. I forgot my good hiking socks."

They all laughed. Sam finished his breakfast and they prepared to leave for their hike. Sam quickly packed a light day pack with two liters of water, a sandwich and granola, a baseball cap, and a small pack of sanitary wipes. He paced around his bedroom, running through a mental checklist of things that he needed for the hike. His father always carried a first-aid kit and he could rely on his mother if he needed any other snacks. The last thing left on his list were his shoes. Scanning the floor of his closet, he found his old hiking boots tucked behind a box of his childhood books and toys.

He laced up his hiking boots and met his parents outside. The dense cloud cover hinted at rain, but Sam had checked the weather forecast and things were supposed to hold out until the evening. Sam's father slammed the hood of the white van shut as Sam approached. The van shook lightly, dust flying from the rust spots near the passenger door. Sam walked around the van slowly, examining the dented sides and beat-up hubcaps. His father had rescued it from a junkyard and restored most of the vehicle. Their "retirement vehicle," he called it. Sam's parents had long talked about selling their house and living out of the van for the rest of their years, and Sam's father was working hard to make it possible.

An old cargo van, the back section was a blank canvas. His father had built a bed frame in the back, installed a sink and a stove top through the middle, and set up a water system and a detachable shower head that hung from the back doors. They were a few thousand dollars away from installing solar panels and they could be on their way. One day at a time, they saved and labored in the hope of a life fueled by their love for one another, their love of the mountains, and about twenty-two gallons of diesel in the tank.

Sam opened up the back doors of the van and tossed his day pack on top of a stack of fixed ropes and climbing gear. He walked around the side of the van and loaded in a cooler packed full of snacks and cold beer. It was tradition that they celebrated the end of every hike with a cold beer in the parking lot. After the van was loaded up, Sam got in the back and flipped down a jumper seat. He pulled the seatbelt across his lap. His parents settled comfortably in front and they were on their way.

"How was class this morning?" Sam's father asked, as they pulled out of the driveway. "Are you guys learning about viruses and all that? There were more cases today."

Sam leaned forward, directing his voice at the gap between the front seats, "The virus comes up a little bit, but we're still covering a lot of the basics. I'll get to some more of that stuff in medical school."

"I'm learning so much about the virus on the news," his father explained. "I haven't had this much science since high school. They were talking about viruses mutating and changing. Can they do that?"

"Yeah," Sam chimed in. "Viruses certainly can, but the mutations can be slow and they don't necessarily mean it's worse or more deadly. Just different."

"Well, you've got your mother's big brain," Sam's father joked, reaching for his wife's hand.

Sam's mother took her husband's coarse, calloused hand in her own and laced their fingers together. Their route took them briefly through downtown, on their way to the highway. Sam stared curiously out the window, eyeing the empty storefronts and "closed indefinitely" signs that decorated the once-vibrant streets of downtown Seattle. Earlier that week, the governor had issued a "Stay-at-Home Order" to slow the spread of the virus. The order required that everyone self-isolate with the members of their household and avoid gatherings of ten people or more. All nonessential industries were also required to close business, including most of the bars, retailers, and restaurants downtown. If they could slow down the spread, maybe more people could survive and recover from the virus.

"Eerie, isn't it?" Sam's mother said, noticing Sam staring out the windows at the ghost town. "I don't think I've ever seen downtown so quiet."

Washington's governor was ahead of most of the rest of the country in this regard. While governors around the country had issued similar orders for their states, the reception of the new policy was split. Some people were compliant and hoped to stop the spread of the virus. Others tried to maintain their normal lives, going on about their day as if nothing else was going on. Some people even denied that the virus was real, chalking it up to some strange conspiracy.

Photos and videos had emerged from around the country of protestors, deniers, and virus-truthers who all insisted that the virus wasn't actually happening. They gathered at state buildings and congregated in public, defiantly hugging and shaking hands. As they mocked the virus, more and more people were testing positive for the virus every day. More and more people were dying.

Sam thought about the handful of blood that covered Mouse's wrist as he keeled over on the park bench after the lacrosse game. He recalled how frail and weak Mouse had looked as they carried him into the hospital. He replayed the raspy sound of his voice on video chat from the hospital bed. A strange combination of emotions swelled in his chest. Sam was grateful for how proactive Washington was being about the spread of the virus but, simultaneously, a deep anger filled him at how foolish and ignorant other parts of the country were being. If only these protesters had been there to see Mouse in the hospital, then they would understand. This was one of those moments where, until it happens to someone that you love, you might live your whole life without caring or knowing any better.

"Sam," his mother said softly. "Are you okay? You're awfully quiet back there, honey."

Sam smirked, burying his rage and shaking free of his rambling thoughts. "Yeah, Mom," he replied. "I'm great. I'm just tired." Sam unclenched his fists, not realizing that he had balled them up tightly with his fingernails digging into his palms.

"Why don't you try to get some rest?" she encouraged him,

concern and compassion in her voice. "We're still a ways away."

With a soft grin, Sam leaned up against the window and rested his forehead against the cold glass. His eyes grew heavy and, as they continued down the highway, the gentle sway of the van rocked him to sleep.

Sam slept the whole way to Mt. Rainier and awoke to the blaring of car horns, as his father scoffed and slapped the steering wheel violently in the parking lot near the trailhead. Sam slowly opened his eyes and gawked at the unanticipated scene in the parking lot. His father was waving angrily at a luxury sports car blocking traffic. The parking area was overflowing with cars, as crowds of people fled the city and into the mountains. Sam should have seen it coming. With everything closing for business, the national parks offered the last beacon of recreation and opportunity for people to get out of their homes. Spring was well underway and summer was quickly approaching. The urge to rebuke the stay-at-home order was only intensified by the pleasant change of weather.

Sam's father navigated the narrow spaces between the double-parked cars and masses of pedestrians with delayed success. They inched their way through the parking lot at a snail's pace, frantically searching the lot for a place to park.

A veteran of the area, Sam's father pulled through the lot and into a hidden group of grass parking spaces behind the public bathrooms. Typically reserved for private hiking guides who were registered with the park service, a few hidden spaces were left empty because of the closing of private guide companies due to the Stay-at-Home Order. A single, beat-up car was parked in the space next to them that Sam recognized immediately. It belonged to their old family friends, the Garcias.

Sam clumsily emerged from the backseat. As his feet hit the

ground, he stretched his arms high over his head. His back and neck ached from the discomfort of the jump seat. As much as he needed to catch up on sleep on the ride down, it was hardly worth the soreness he experienced as he stepped onto the grass. Twisting and stretching, he made his way around the back of the van and pulled open the backdoors. He pulled his day pack over his shoulders and bent down to retie the laces of his hiking boots.

Sam waited patiently for his parents to gather their things, watching the masses of people waltz in and out of the public bathrooms near the trailhead. The crowds entered the bathrooms in small groups, struggling to pass one another through the narrowness of the small doorway.

"There's no soap left," called out a well-dressed man, as he exited the men's restroom. Sam stared suspiciously at the man's outfit. *I would not hike in those shoes*, Sam thought to himself, curious if the man knew what he was getting into, as the man walked toward the trail.

Prepped and ready for their hike, Sam's mother led the way. She sprinted ahead, excitedly darting toward the trailhead. Despite her petite and quiet stature, Sam's mother hiked with a furious passion. She loved the mountains and she spent most of her free time planning outdoor excursions with her husband, girlfriends, and really anyone she could convince to spend time with her outside.

As they approached the trail map and bulletin board, Sam stood in awe of the gathering crowd. There must have been thirty people standing around the trail map. Sam's mother walked around the large group, cautiously keeping her distance from the collective of hikers bunching up near the trailhead. She paused in the early part of the trail and waited anxiously for Sam and her husband to catch up with her. Looking back at them, she placed her hands on her hips and tapped her foot theatrically. Sam's father chuckled and, jogging past Sam, ran ahead to catch up with her.

"Does everyone have water?" Sam's mother asked, as Sam arrived at the beginning of their planned hike.

"Yup," Sam's father said, as Sam nodded in agreement.

The group started on their way, nervously sidestepping the other hikers on the trail. Sam was accustomed to enjoying the quiet solitude of his family's hiking trips, but this was different. The hiking experience was nearly unrecognizable, as a constant flow of two-way traffic defined the winding dirt pathways. Sam weaved through the crowded groups of hikers and attempted to quell the rising discomfort in his chest. The path grew claustrophobic and Sam anxiously sought a clearing or less densely populated part of the trail. He increased his pace and tried to liberate himself from the suffocating masses of first-time hikers that surrounded him. People were generally polite, sidestepping and attempting to abide by the state guidelines for distancing yourself from other people. The recommended distance was six feet, but the pathway proved too narrow to maintain as the walls of trees closed in on the trail.

The crowds finally began to thin, when Sam's family reached mile five and the dirt pathways became snow. The casual day hikers had all turned back and abandoned the fifteen-mile trek that looped into the higher elevation before rounding back to the parking lot.

At the first sight of an empty opening, Sam took a deep breath of the fresh mountain air and embraced the quiet calm of the snow-covered trail. His eyes followed the winding lines of animal tracks through the snow, as the trail finally began to feel normal again. The playful pairs of animal prints darted between the trees and weaved through small gaps between boulders.

Sam wandered into a steep section of the trail and his eyes drifted down to the trail, focused on the rough terrain. Leaping over a boulder, he found himself fatigued and out of shape. Despite having grown up in these mountains, Sam was struggling to keep pace with his parents. He had grown soft in D.C., where the short hikes of northern Virginia offered little elevation gain and looped only three or four miles in total. Sam paused for a moment and leaned against a tree. Running his hands through his sweaty hair, Sam pulled his day pack off and set it down in the snow. He unzipped the top pouch and tossed a handful of granola into his mouth.

Catching his breath, Sam heard a chattering of voices up ahead on the trail. He washed the granola down with a swig of water and pressed on. He hopped over a fallen tree across the trail and landed softly on the scattering mix of dirt and snow. The chattering of voices grew louder and, as he turned the corner and pulled himself up the rocks, Sam saw two familiar faces laughing in conversation with his parents.

"Well, look who it is," Elena called out, as Sam approached. "Are you really gonna let these old geezers beat you on the trail?"

Sam smiled and scrambled to his feet. "I'm just giving them a head start," he joked in reply. "How have you been, Elena? Hey, Meg! I missed you guys!"

Elena and Meg Garcia were his parents' best friends. Sam's father had guided hikes with Elena in Mt. Rainier in their early twenties, and, when Sam's mother first moved to Seattle, Meg helped her find a job at an elementary school. Meg was a high school teacher in the Seattle public school system and helped set up her first interview.

"We've been good, Sam!" Elena replied. "We've been busy with the coffee shop. We're still living in Capitol Hill."

"She's being modest," Meg interrupted. "The coffee shop is busy all the time ... or it was busy, I guess. What about you? We were sorry to hear about Mouse. Is he okay?"

Elena and Meg had met Mouse when he had come out to Seattle to visit the previous summer. Sam had arranged for them all to go out to dinner, where Elena had grilled Mouse with questions. She prodded and probed him about his intentions, taking teasing jabs at his fancy wallet and perfectly styled hair. A good sport, Mouse passed the test with flying colors and was quickly welcomed into the fold.

Sam shifted his weight nervously to his left side and cleared his throat. He gathered the words slowly, but replied, "Thanks. Mouse is doing a little better every day. He'll be happy to hear that you guys asked about him."

The Garcias smiled and nodded. Sam wanted nothing more than to hug them, but held back. It felt strange to see two people who had been such a big part of his life and not be able to greet them with a hug. As he smiled back, the warmth and love between them floated in the air. In this new way of existing in the world, affection would have to be understood rather than physically expressed.

Sam's family joined Elena and Meg for the remaining ten miles of the hike, as Sam detailed his acceptance into St. Agatha's Medical School and his plans to come back to Seattle after his residency. Like most of Sam's recent conversations, they talked about the virus. Elena sought Sam's advice regarding her business. With most of her savings tied up in her coffee shop, she probed about the health and safety concerns of reopening.

"My staff are all people from the neighborhood," Elena explained. "Mostly LGBT folks and people of color. Don't get me wrong, I think the Stay-at-Home Order is totally necessary. But it's going to be hard on my staff. They've got rent, student loans, bills."

"Being out of work is hard," Sam's father chimed in. "If not for all of Sam's scholarships, there's no way we would've been able to send him to St. Agatha and make the payments on our house."

"I just don't know how we'll serve food and coffee," Elena said, boldly. "Does my whole staff wear masks? Do we let people sit inside?"

The group went back and forth; the conversation carrying them through the rest of their hike and back to the trailhead. Litter abounded as they rounded the trail back to the parking lot. Sam's father bent down and picked up a handful of wrappers and empty, plastic water bottles lying on the ground. He tossed them in the trash as they passed the public bathrooms on their way to the car. Visibly frustrated, he recited one of his favorite adages.

"Leave the trail better than you found it," he said, shaking his head in disappointment at the state of the parking lot.

As they approached the van, Sam felt a deep muscle ache settle into his lower back and thighs. He leaned up against the van and stretched. Taking the toe of his right foot in his left hand, he pulled hard and relieved the tension and lactic acid building up in his quads. He repeated the motion with his other foot and sighed in relief.

"Not as spry as you used to be?" Meg asked, teasing him.

Sam cleared his throat with a smile and replied, "I guess not. You guys really took it out of me!" Taking a beer from his father, Sam cracked open the can and took a long sip.

Meg tossed her backpack in the backseat of their car and looked lovingly at Sam. "It's great to have you back, Sam."

"Thanks," he replied with a smile. "Honestly, there's no place that I'd rather be."

The group laughed and continued to catch up over their beers. Seeing the Garcias and sharing a beer in the parking lot, Sam momentarily forgot about everything else going on in his life. The Garcias had been such a huge part of his childhood, as friends, mentors. They were family. With a distanced farewell, they promised to meet up again for another hike the following week and Sam crawled slowly into the backseat of the van. Exhausted, he plopped down into the jump seat with a loud thud. He extended his legs across the van floor as far as they could reach and leaned back, settling in for the long drive.

The trip home went by quickly. Sam's mother insisted that they play road trip games for the duration of the drive. They searched intensely for different state license plates and played word games for the first thirty minutes, but their games faded as the sun began to dip behind the mountains. Sam looked out at the horizon and soaked in the beautiful colored hues of orange and pink that skirted along the snowcapped mountain peaks. He missed sunsets like this when he was at school but, despite being captivated, part of him felt like he should be watching the sun set over the St. Agatha clock tower instead.

It should be him, Mouse, Maisie, Robbie, and Jenny coming home from dinner on Monroe Street and watching the sun come down over campus. They should be talking about final exams, the big end-of-year concert, the NCAA lacrosse championships, and, of course, graduation. Instead, Sam wriggled uncomfortably in the jump seat of his parents' van and looked out at the setting sun with disappointment and longing. Sam's sadness took full hold as they pulled into the driveway and began to unload the van. He missed school and he missed his friends.

"How about pizza?" Sam's father asked, slugging him casually in the shoulder as they walked back into the garage. "I think Sparky's is still open for delivery."

There were few things in this world that cheered Sam up like Sparky's Pizza. The thought of their sweet sauce and thick, cornmeal-dusted crust immediately shifted his mood. He smiled with enthusiasm and nodded his head.

"Can we do pepperoni and mushroom?" Sam asked, already salivating.

"Whatever you want," his father replied. "I'll call in the order right now."

Sam took off his boots in the garage and hobbled inside, stiff and sore from the day's hike. He wandered through the living room, past the kitchen, and straight into the shower. After slapping the shower head a few times, the sputtering stream of cold water finally steadied and became warm.

Sweat and dirt ran off of his skin and swirled around the shower drain. He took his time washing his hair and body, enjoying the embrace of the warm water on his aching bones. Knowing his childhood home well, Sam recognized the limited availability of hot water in the tank. Preferring to avoid a lecture from his parents when they went to take showers of their own, he quickened his shower routine. He dried off and scampered to his bedroom, wearing only a towel.

Finding his most comfortable pair of sweatpants and an old shirt from high school, Sam shuffled out into the living room. He took a seat on the couch next to his father's green recliner. The scratchy fabric of the tattered couch cushions was by no means comfortable, but it was home.

"What are you sewing?" Sam asked, noticing his mother working her way through a sewing pattern at the kitchen table.

She curled her fingers and guided a floral, green piece of cloth through her sewing machine. Adjusting her reading glasses, she replied, "Facemasks! The folks at the homeless shelter don't have any. So, I signed up to make some with the ladies at church."

"That's great, Mom. Let me know if there's anything that I

can do," Sam volunteered, half-hoping that she would turn down his offer.

Sam checked his phone for the time, hoping that Mouse might call him soon. They had made arrangements to talk at some point, but he knew that Mouse's days were difficult. His recovery had hardly been linear, with some days being more difficult than others, but the doctors seemed to think that he was getting better.

That's more than most folks could say, as the death rate continued to rise across the country and the virus took more and more lives every day. With the large number of new cases, hospitals were operating at capacity and working with limited resources. Every hospital bed was full. Even the doctors and nurses were getting sick.

"If you're trying to stay busy until Mouse calls, then you're welcome to cut some elastic straps for me," his mother teased, catching him staring intensely at his phone.

Sam chuckled and rose from the couch. He picked up a pair of scissors out from his mother's sewing kit on the table and began measuring out twelve-inch lengths of elastic.

"Like this?" he asked, holding up his first attempt.

Sam's mother nodded in approval and straightened her glasses on her face. After cutting twenty straps, two per mask, Sam flexed the fingers of his sore right hand and switched the pair of scissors to his left. His mother looked down at the pile of elastic straps and smiled, waving him back to the couch and liberating him from his responsibilities.

"Thank you, Sam," she said, politely.

A firm knock on the door gathered the attention of Sam's father, who came barreling out of his bedroom like cannonball. "Sparky's, Sparky's, Sparky's," he sang, as he pulled open the door.

The Sparky's delivery boy removed two large pizza boxes from an insulated heat sleeve and handed them kindly over to Sam's father. Sam recognized the boy immediately as Ron Sparkman Jr., his former high school classmate. Sam and Lil' Sparky, as he was known, weren't particularly close in high school. They had a few overlapping friends, but hadn't really kept in touch since Sam had left town. Sam sat awkwardly on the couch. Their relationship probably warranted a hello, but it would have been totally acceptable for Sam not to say anything. Lil' Sparky was right on the cusp of being a friend and just some guy who Sam went to high school with.

"Thank you, Ron," Sam's father said, handing the boy a cash tip. "Have you guys been pretty busy this week?

"Appreciate it," Lil' Sparky said, stuffing the cash in his back pocket. "Yeah, I'd say so. Folks still gotta eat, but we're a little short-staffed. It's just me and one other driver."

Sam's mother stood up from the kitchen and wandered over to the front door with two facemasks in hand. With a kind smile, she handed them over to Lil' Sparky. "Well, if you're going to be going door to door all night, please be safe," she encouraged him.

Lil' Sparky pulled one of the masks over his head and nodded kindly. "You guys are too nice. Thank you," he replied. "Welcome home, Sam! I'd say that we should grab a drink while you're back, but we might have to put that on hold for a while."

Sam chuckled and waved back from the couch. "As soon as all of this is over, we'll get some of the crew back together for a party at Monica's. Just like the old days," Sam joked.

"Just like the old days?" Sam's mother asked, accusingly.

Lil' Sparky replied nervously and started walking back to his car, "Well, thanks again and you guys have a good evening."

Sam's mother raised an eyebrow at Sam and shook her head disapprovingly. She walked to the kitchen and grabbed a stack of plates and set the table. The sweet smell of tomato sauce and melted mozzarella cheese filled the living room, as Sam's father opened the pizza box and released the delicious fragrance from its cardboard prison. The scent surrounded Sam and lifted him from the couch and over to the kitchen table. He quickly served himself three slices and asked to be excused with his plate full of pizza.

Sam's patience had reached its limit and he wanted to call Mouse. With his parents' approval, he scurried back to his bedroom with dinner and sat down on his bed. Sam held up his phone and opened his video call app. He dialed Mouse, waiting on edge for him to pick up. Sam breathed a sigh of relief as the video call went through and he waited for Mouse's video to load.

"Thanks, Doctor Carter," Mouse muttered in a raspy tone, raising his phone to his face. He coughed and cleared his throat. "Sam! I was just about to call you."

His excitement clearly overworked his vocal cords, but he looked surprisingly strong. The color in his cheeks had returned and he seemed more upbeat than usual.

Shocked, Sam leaned forward in his bed and replied, "Mouse, you look great! How are you feeling?"

Mouse laughed painfully and ran his hands through his hair. "Why, thank you. I think these hospital gowns really bring out my eyes." Mouse stifled another cough before continuing. "My last chest x-ray was pretty bad and they think my lungs will probably be damaged for a while, but I'm not contagious anymore. They think I can go home tomorrow."

"Mouse, that's amazing!" Sam exclaimed. "I was so worried."

"Yeah, the both of you," Mouse replied with a faint smirk.

Flipping his camera around, Carol was fast asleep in an armchair in the corner of the room. Her mouth wide open, drool trickled down her cheek and gathered in a small wet spot on the shoulder of her gray shirt. Sam could hear the sound of her snoring through the phone and tried hard not to laugh. He stifled a giggle, still staring at the video screen as it turned back to Mouse. He traced the outlines of Mouse's face and delighted in the news that he might be going home soon. Sam desperately wished that he could be by Mouse's bedside to celebrate in person.

Sam felt so far away, but these calls had been the highlight of his days all week long. He longed to hold Mouse and lay next to him, but this would have to suffice for now. The impersonal nature of video chat had become their new normal and Sam would definitely take this over nothing at all.

"Well, I should get some sleep," Mouse said, his eyes growing heavy. "I miss you."

"I miss you too," Sam replied. "Thanks for chatting!"

As the call ended, Sam leaned back against his headboard and picked up his plate of pizza. He savored the warm taste of Mouse's favorite toppings, pepperoni and mushrooms, with each bite. Eating too quickly, Sam cleared his throat and washed the pizza down with a drink of water. When he finished, Sam wandered back to the kitchen and set his dishes in the sink.

His mother was still busily sewing masks and his father was sitting in his green armchair, enjoying a second or third helping of Sparky's in front of the television. Not wanting to bother them, Sam rinsed his plate in the sink and tiptoed back to his bedroom. Exhaustion set in and, full of pizza and exhausted from the hike, Sam got into bed. Feeling the warmth of the room, he pulled the covers below his chest and tried to find a comfortable sleeping position. Turning on his side, he brought one leg out from under the sheets and exposed it to the room. Before long, he was fast asleep.

After just a few hours, an aching pain swelled up in Sam's back and stirred him from slumber. His hair and shirt were dripping with sweat and he looked over at the clock on his nightstand. *4:23 AM* stared boldly back at him.

His feet touched down on the floor of his bedroom slowly. His body ached furiously, starting in his back and working its way through his limbs. The cold ground felt soothing on the soles of his feet, but a chilling shiver shot down his spine.

He made his way slowly to the bathroom and stared blankly in the mirror. His face was pale and his palms were clammy. His forehead felt like it was on fire and sweat continued to form on his temples. As Sam cleared his throat again, he felt the faint taste of iron in his mouth. Fearfully, he leaned over the sink and closed his eyes.

Sam slowly brought his saliva and the taste of iron to the front of his tongue. Time stood still as he pursed his lips and let the spit fall from his mouth onto the white porcelain sink. It landed with a hard splatter and Sam opened his eyes. He stared intensely down at the droplet of spit, as a heavy streak of blood swirled through the droplet, confirming his deepest fear.

CURFEW

Tall pillars of white marble stood on either side of the heavy wooden doors. The door's dark stain looked of an aged sophistication that suited the Eden Council. Decorative wood carvings, depicting a ring of stars arranged around a gavel and weighted scale, ornately dressed the doorway.

Emily tapped her foot nervously on the floor while she sat on a bench in the large, open lobby. She straightened her dress pants and folded her hands neatly in her lap. The hard discomforts of the bench intensified the waiting experience. She stared down intensely at her manicured hands. The short trim of her nails and glossy polish finish glistened in the lights of the chandelier hanging high above her head, as she anxiously rubbed her fingertips together.

"Emily Chang?" asked a tall woman, blonde hair running down her white Council robes.

Startled, Emily's eyes shot up to meet her gaze. "Yes, I'm Emily Chang," she replied, quickly rising to her feet and bowing.

"They'll see you now," the woman stated bluntly, as her hand turned open toward the wooden doors.

Projecting false confidence, Emily nodded at her parents and followed the woman across the lobby toward the towering pillars of white marble. The woman waved her hand in front of a motion sensor and the wooden doors opened, slowly revealing a white room with twenty-foot-high ceilings. The scale and size of the room shook Emily to her core, as she shrank beneath the severity of the space. At the far end of the room, the tile flooring transitioned seamlessly into a set of stairs leading up to a raised stage. Three people wearing white Council robes sat at a long table at the top of the stairs, as Emily's fate hung in the balance.

Emily walked toward them slowly, her feet weighing heavier with each step. The trio of faces stared down at her from the height of their platform, eyes locked intensely on Emily's face as she marched toward them. Emily recognized Council Justice Evans immediately. Disappointment filled his eyes and Emily felt it more strongly with each stride. The woman on his left examined Emily with an equally disappointed look, scanning her from head to toe. The woman adjusted her dark hair from beneath her robe collar and leaned forward. To Council Justice Evans' right, a young man with red hair looked curiously down at Emily. He attempted to match the intense glares of his fellow Council Justices, but his youth rendered him much less intimidating.

Emily arrived at a small painted circle on the floor beneath the stage. She stepped inside the designated area and stood patiently in front of the jury of Council Justices.

"Ms. Chang," Council Justice Evans called out, his booming voice filling the room. "You are here to face judgement for a violation of city curfew. These are my colleagues, Council Justice Sara Steward and Council Justice Garreth Merr."

Council Justice Steward spoke with an even more thunderous tone than Council Justice Evans, "Ms. Chang, we have had very high expectations for you, given your admittance to the Camillus Program. I'm sure that someone with your potential would have an explanation prepared for us."

Emily's stomach began to turn and her anxiety quickly devolved into nausea. The taste of shame filled her mouth, as she searched frantically for the words that she had rehearsed. She had stood in front of the mirror all week, going over the right things to say and carefully curating her explanation, but it was all lost now. She was crumbling under the weight of their judgment and a bead of sweat began to form on her forehead.

"Ms. Chang? Your explanation, please," encouraged Council Justice Merr, with an unexpected softness in his voice.

"Council Justices," Emily began, with a quiver. "I … I was out past curfew. I cannot offer an explanation beyond that, because there are no excuses that would justify my being near the city limits at that hour. I can only offer my apologies and a promise that it won't happen again."

Council Justice Steward turned and spoke softly to her colleagues. The Council Justices congregated briefly, rotating in their chairs to prevent Emily from hearing their discussion. Emily turned her head slightly to the side and leaned toward them, hoping to hear a murmur or a word of their debate.

Turning back, Council Justice Merr inquired, "Ms. Chang, what do you expect of us, given that you have offered no explanation for your behavior? No line of reasoning?"

Emily looked up at the Council Justices and found her confidence. She had prepared for this question and line of inquiry, and her nerves settled as her morning preparations came back to her. She straightened her posture and spoke with a renewed sense of self, "I welcome the standard punishments for a violation of city curfew, but I would remind the Council that this is my first offense and that my record in this community has been spotless up until this incident."

Council Justice Evans looked down at her, unimpressed and further disappointed. "In our line of work, Ms. Chang, you will learn that a third offense is always preceded by a second. And, before that, a first," he lectured. "Your strong track record will offer you no favor in this court."

Council Justice Steward quickly followed, "Your Camillus candidacy makes this exceptionally difficult. We expect more of you as a future Council Justice. The law is the foundation of Eden, as you will learn in time in the Camillus Program."

The three Council Justices rose from their seats and retired to a room behind the stage. As they walked away from her, Council Justice Merr looked back and nodded reassuringly. Emily found a strange kindness in him. The soft look on his face was gentler than that on the faces of the other two Council Justices. She took comfort in his simple gesture and relaxed her shoulders. As they exited the room, Emily looked up at the empty stage and imagined a fourth seat at the table. Her seat. The seat of Council Justice Chang.

She found the thought appealing, even if just for a brief moment. The Council Justices were in charge of keeping the law and, from those chairs, they kept people safe and healthy. Wrongdoers were punished, and the community was more fit for it. The Justices served a very important function and Emily understood the need for law and order, even as she stood trial for a violation of city curfew.

The Council Justices emerged from the back room in a single-file line. Walking in order of seniority, Council Justice Evans, Steward, and Merr approached the table slowly. One by one, they took their respective seats and looked down at Emily. In near unison, they each removed a pack of sanitary wipes from their robe sleeves and wiped down the table's surface.

Normally, Emily would have been unfazed by this behavior, but she couldn't help but consider the practicality of their effort. Certainly, it was always practical to clean a surface before using it, but the action seemed to be more performative than anything else.

She stood there for what felt like ages, as they finished wiping the table, discarded their wipes into a trash bin below the table, and brought their heavy gaze back onto her. Council Justice Evans removed a small tablet from the sleeve of his robes and opened Emily's file.

"Emily Chang," he began. "Given the evidence and the lack of appropriate reasoning, we, the Council Justices of Eden, find you guilty and in violation of the citywide curfew."

As Council Justice Evans sat back in his chair, Council Justice Merr followed, "As such, we have reached a decision on your punishment by a vote of 2 to 1."

Emily's knees began to shake. She stood on pins and needles, waiting for the heavy hand of justice to come crashing down on her. No amount of rehearsal could have prepared her for the anxiety of waiting, as she looked to Council Justice Steward for the final word. Council Justice Steward adjusted her robes slowly, almost delighting in the suspense. Emily continued to shake, as Council Justice Steward began to speak.

"You will be denied in-school privileges for four weeks," she declared. "As this is your first offense, we will waive the three-day isolation sentence that accompanies the length of time by which you missed curfew. You are, even if barely, above the Age of Responsibility. Therefore, you will also complete a twelve-week course on the different city violations. You will learn about order, Ms. Chang."

Emily swallowed the bitter, embarrassing taste of punishment. *Four weeks of no in-school and a twelve-week course on city violations, on top of her Year 11 course load?* she thought.

As she reflected on her punishment and new schedule, she breathed a sigh of relief at the pardoning of her three-day isolation sentence. The previous summer, when Marshall had just turned sixteen, he had been stopped for questioning by an officer on patrol. The officer's lengthy interrogation had caused Marshall to be three minutes late for curfew. Despite Marshall's insistence that he needed to be on his way, the officer held him deep into the redness of the streetlights and sent him on his way with little time to spare before curfew.

The officer conveniently left that detail out during Marshall's online hearing and Marshall was sentenced to a single, twenty-four-hour period of isolation. He was brought to the Eden Council and placed in a small, white room with a single plastic bed and toilet. The twenty-four-hour sentence allotted him three meals and thirty minutes of time with his tablet. Otherwise, Marshall stared blankly at the wall and counted the minutes as they ticked by. One thousand four hundred and forty minutes.

"Ms. Chang," Council Justice Evans called out. "If there is no confusion around your sentencing, you are free to leave. I hope that the next time we see you in this chamber will be on your first day of training in Year 12."

"Yes, sir," Emily replied. "Thank you all for your time and this won't happen again."

In unison, the Council Justices called out to her, "The actions of one,"

"Carry the safety of us all," Emily shouted back to them.

She took two steps backward out of the circle on the floor, before turning and heading out the wooden double doors. She held her breath nervously as she trudged down the long walkway, waiting for the thunderous voice of a Council Justice to call her back for more punishment. Each step brought her closer to freedom. As she crossed the wooden threshold and wandered back out into the lobby, a wave of relief washed over her and she finally allowed herself to exhale. The weight of this hearing had hung over her all week, and she was glad that it was finally over.

Her comfort would be all too momentary. Emily emerged to the sight of her parents' disappointed faces, as they stood anxiously in the lobby. They had never looked like this before. Usually, their faces beamed with pride and hope for their daughter's future. Emily found none of that in their eyes. Instead, all of that had been replaced with sadness and tragic disappointment. Her father's eyes mourned the death of her innocence, as he bid farewell to the perfect image that he held of his oldest child.

"Well," Emily's mother spoke up. Her mother's tone shifted from disappointment to concern. "What did they say? Are you going into isolation?"

Emily shook her head and replied, "No, they waived it because this is my first offense. Four weeks without in-school and a twelve-week course on city violations."

Tears ran down her mother's face, but her concern was quickly interrupted by Emily's father. Standing tall and refusing to look Emily in the eyes, he snapped at them, "She got off easy. Let's go."

Emily and her parents walked past a series of offices on their way to the departure area: Council Agriculture, Council Works, Council Patrol, Council Housing. Emily looked curiously at each set of wooden doors and carefully examined the unique ornate wooden carvings that adorned them. Slowing her pace behind her parents, Emily distracted herself from the guilty pit in her stomach by taking in the intensity of the building. Busy-looking men and women darted between offices with serious purpose, the long fabric of their Council robes waving behind them. The atmosphere was sharp and sophisticated, and Emily felt the importance of the Council's work with every person that she saw.

Guilt and regret sat heavy in Emily's stomach like a brick, as she trudged slowly behind her parents toward the departure scanners of the Eden Council. Typically, a violation of city curfew would have been handled entirely online, but Council Justice Evans specifically requested that Emily appear in person because of her candidacy in the Camillus Program. Her candidacy was a once-in-a-decade occurrence and there was a strange curiosity around Emily among the entire Council. Having to appear in person to address a violation was not how Emily wanted to be introduced to the building, but here she was.

As they arrived at the departure sinks, Emily watched as her parents diligently washed their hands under the rushing water. Her father carefully turned his hands over and scrubbed at his wrists, palms, and fingers with specificity and focus. Her mother matched his attention to detail, lacing her fingers with bubbling soap and pressing beneath her finger nails.

Emily stepped up to the sink and watched as the timer started counting down from twenty. She stared down at the streaming soap and water and placed her hands in the warmth of their embrace. Her hands and wrists were consumed by suds, as she scrubbed with a strange fervor. She dug her nails deep into her hands and scratched hard. As guilt and shame continued to rise in her gut, Emily tried to scrub away more than just germs and bacteria.

The timer hit zero and Emily removed her hands slowly from the sink. Her palms were bright red. Tiny scratch marks colored the backs of her hands and the slight sting of lingering soap persisted in the scratch marks left behind by her nails. Her parents stood up ahead, lingering outside of the departure scanner and waiting for their turn to enter. Emily's father stepped inside first, giving her a moment alone with her mother.

"Emily," her mother said calmly. "Your father is taking this very hard. We're not sure where your behavior is coming from. I know that I've been busy with work and maybe we've missed a few things, but you know that you can talk to us about anything."

Emily swayed from side-to-side and nervously searched for a reply. She was shocked by her mother's compassionate interest. If anything, Emily had feared her mother's reaction far more than her father's. The stark contrast in their reactions, his coldness and her warmth, startled her.

"I know, Mom," Emily said softly. "It's not your fault. I don't really know what's going on with me. I've ... just been ... curious. When the streetlights turned red, I didn't want to go home. I wanted to watch the sunset over the mountains."

Emily's mother looked back at her, confused and intrigued. "The sunset?" she asked. "Honey, we can watch the sunset from our housing unit."

"This was different, Mom," Emily replied, wanting so badly for her mother to understand. She wanted so badly for anyone to understand and help her make sense of what she was feeling. "I was outside. The Cascades. I was sitting on a rock on the hillside. This sunset was different. I want ...."

Her mother's kind intrigue quickly faded. Any sense of understanding and compassion faded, as her tone became emotionless and Emily felt the emptiness in her next words.

"I know, Emily," her mother said. Sadly, she and Emily both knew that she didn't have a clue.

The scanner doors opened and Emily's mother turned away from her. Before Emily could say anything in reply, her mother turned and headed off to the departure scanner. Emily stared at her mother's back, watching silently as she walked away. Discouraged and alone, Emily's gaze fell to the floor. She released a deep, frustrated sigh and waited for her turn to enter the departure scanners.

The doors parted slowly in front of her and Emily stepped inside. Caught somewhere between gratitude and resentment, Emily stiffened up as the scanner ran over her. The voice announced into the room, as the light turned from blue to green, "98.2, Vitals normal." The doors parted before her and she stepped out onto the steps of the Eden Council, beneath the cloud cover and gray skies of another dreary afternoon.

An awkward fog fell over the Chang household for the rest of the week. Emily's father had hardly spoken a word to her, and the distance between them showed no sign of narrowing. At every turn, he avoided eye contact with her and barely acknowledged her presence in their housing unit. Their home was small and it was difficult to avoid anyone. Somehow, her father was making it look easy. In her father's absence, Emily leaned hard on Marshall and Fae for support, seeking guidance from Marshall and his previous experience with the Council.

"That's wild!" Marshall exclaimed during the gang's daily Vid call, as Emily recounted her Council appearance. "I still can't believe that they made you come in for a curfew violation," he said, with a shocked lock on his face.

Fae chimed in, similarly shocked by her story, "I've never heard of anyone having to appear in person. For anything .... Did they say why?"

Emily adjusted her tablet carefully on her desk and let out a hard sigh. While it was Marshall and Fae's first time hearing the story, Emily had no desire to recall the intricacies of the event. She would rather forget the whole ordeal, but, in seeking their support and guidance, she owed her friends the details.

"Yeah," Emily began, gathering her breath. "They wanted me to come in because of my Aptitude placement. I thought they were going to pull me from the Camillus Program. Maybe I was hoping they would pull me from the Camillus Program. I don't know."

Her friends looked back at her curiously, uncertain how to respond. Fae replied, concerned with Emily's depressed and confused state, "Emily, you're going to be a great Council Justice. This is just a little slipup. It happens. It happens."

Despite their best efforts to raise her spirits, Emily moped around the house in a quiet sadness. She wandered aimlessly from room to room, barely engaging with her family. Truthfully, she wasn't sure if she wanted to. If her father didn't want to talk to her, she had no problem retreating to her bedroom. At least that's what she told herself.

This sparked a strange curiosity in Ted, who knew nothing of her curfew violation, her Council appearance, or her punishments. Still, Ted could sense that something was wrong. It felt wrong to keep him out of the loop, but Emily's mother decided on not telling him any of the details. She insisted that it would be for his own good. After all, he wanted to be just like Emily when he grew up.

"Em, do you want to watch a movie?" Ted asked, urging her for the fourth night in a row to join him in the living room.

Emily lifted her head from her tablet and sat up in her bed. "I'm not really up for it tonight, buddy," Emily replied, and quickly sank back into her pillows.

"You said that last night," Ted called back in defeat, as he sauntered down the hallway toward the stairs.

Emily hadn't felt particularly motivated in the days since her hearing. She felt distant from her family and, more importantly, distant from herself. She bounced mindlessly between her school work and her conversations with Fae and Marshall. She buried herself in her old habits, working hard and doing extra reading for school; yet, she felt oddly removed from all the things that used to bring her satisfaction. Something had changed in her and she couldn't quite place or name it.

Emily rolled over onto her stomach and stared at her tablet. A bold news update came across her home screen, *"Eden Vax Falls Behind Again."* A thumbnail photo of Cayden, pulling at his hair in frustration, was paired alongside the headline. Emily clicked open the article and began to read a scathing article of Cayden and his recent string of performances. Once Eden's Golden Boy, Cayden had quickly become the scapegoat for the team's five-game losing streak. As the world seemed to be collapsing around her, Emily slammed her tablet down on the bed beside her and buried her face in her pillow. She screamed into the soft fabric and tears began to form in her eyes.

"Emily, are you okay?" her mother asked softly from the doorway. "Do you want to come down to the living room and watch a movie with the family?"

Emily glanced toward the door, without raising her head from the pillow. She wasn't okay. She sat in silence until her mother repeated her inquiry.

"Emily, please come down and watch a movie with the family," she pressed.

It was less of a question and more of a statement. Emily begrudgingly rose from her bed and dragged her feet across the room. She followed her mother down the stairs to the living room, where Ted and her father sat comfortably in their chairs. Emily took her seat and stared up at a blank television screen.

"Well, what are we watching?" Emily asked, curiously eyeing the room.

Emily's mother sat down slowly and announced, "I thought it would be nice if we watched a documentary about nature. You said you were curious about mountains and EduView has some great documentaries in the research archives. What do you say?"

Emily held back politely, fighting the urge to roll her eyes and head back upstairs to her bedroom. Forcing a kind, half-smile, she replied, "That sounds great, Mom."

Emily's mother smiled and started the movie. As the television came on, the lights dimmed and Emily settled in for a long hour of educational material about the mountains. The EduView logo appeared in the middle of the screen and a mountain landscape faded into view behind it.

Panning the summit of an undisclosed mountain top, the deep voice of the narrator began, "Tall and majestic, most of the mountain ranges in North America were formed by the bumping of tectonic plates. Below the ground, the Earth's tectonic plates shift and move creating the geological features of the land ...."

The narrator droned on, carefully detailing the science behind the mountain formations and the shifts in air current that result in changing weather patterns on either side of a mountain range.

As a courtesy to her parents, Emily tried hard to focus. Ted's efforts were nonexistent, as he pulled out his tablet within the first five minutes of the documentary. After thirty minutes, the atmosphere in the room became dull. However, Emily and her parents remained committed to the facade of interest. On a few occasions, Emily swore that she heard her father doze off and snore. As the documentary finally came to a close and the credits began to fall, Emily sat up in her chair and stretched. The Chang family sat in silence for a few moments before her mother spoke up.

"That was interesting. I think we all learned a lot," Emily's mother said, rising from her chair and walking over to the kitchen. "Does anyone want any dessert? Or we could play a game."

Emily rose from her chair and started walking toward the stairs. She called back to her mother, "I'm okay. I'm just going to go to bed. Thanks for the movie."

Her mother's efforts weren't lost on her. Emily realized that her mother had been more present this week. The old days of her long office hours and working from the kitchen counter were a remnant of the past and those moments felt distant and far away. These days, Emily felt suffocated by her mother's renewed interest in forming a bond. But she was still grateful for it.

As Emily reached the bottom of the stairs, she looked back at her mother sanitizing a spoon in the kitchen and smiled proudly. *She was trying*, thought Emily.

Emily's mother glanced up to meet Emily's eyes. She smiled back at Emily softly and mouthed the words, *"Thank you."*

Emily nodded and walked slowly up the stairs. With each step, Emily's anxiety faded and she felt a calm peace come over her. She climbed into bed and stared up at the stars on her ceiling. She traced the shapes of the constellations and, naming them, imagined the chill of the outside air on her skin. Her eyes settled on the Gemini constellation and Emily drifted off to sleep.

LANDED

The entire plane shook, as the wheels touched down at Seattle-Tacoma International Airport. A light mist of rain covered the pavement and the tires came to a screeching halt between the bright lights on the runway. Mouse toyed with the Gemini coin in his hand, turning it over and over in his palm anxiously. He had held it every day since he had gotten sick, and he was convinced it was the reason that he had survived the virus.

According to the latest numbers, the death rate in the United States was approaching 20% and the hospitals were overflowing with patients. In the off chance that someone could get a bed at the hospital, the staff had been working with such limited resources that it didn't make much of a difference. Doctors and nurses were working exhausting double shifts and providing the best care that they were capable of giving under brutal circumstances. Thankfully, the President had flown a fighter jet over the hospitals in New York as a thank you to healthcare workers.

A proper response to their desperate outcries for more protective equipment and medical supplies, thought Mouse sarcastically.

Mouse stared blankly out the window. He didn't know what to expect with his flight. The airport in D.C. was eerily quiet, like he had never seen before. The security lines were empty. Every TSA worker wore protective gear and ensured that social distancing guidelines were being observed all around the airport. The few travelers

245

wandered through the airport procedures with heightened caution and awareness, sanitizing everything and breathing through make-shift masks distilled from scarves, bandanas, cloth masks, and other creative half-solutions. As Mouse boarded the plane, he overheard a tall man wearing a suit and tie talking on his phone.

"They offered me a facemask at security," he shouted into his phone. "Can you believe that? Trying to make me wear a mask for some phony virus. I don't have to wear one if I don't want to. It's a free country."

Despite the overwhelming number of hospitalizations and deaths, the man's words expressed a common sentiment in the United States. People were hesitant to admit how bad things were getting. They were afraid, terrified even. Admitting the truth would make it real.

There were seven people on Mouse's flight from D.C. to Seattle, scattered systematically at a distance throughout the plane. Most people were wearing a facemask and the flight attendants diligently wiped down the chairs as passengers entered and exited the plane. As Mouse looked around at his fellow passengers, he felt their fear swelling in the air. A nervous tension had filled the recycled air of the plane and, now that the plane had landed, everyone was eager to escape the tight confines of the space. Mouse listened for the sound of the jet bridge connecting to the plane and, upon hearing it click in, he rose from his seat and gathered his things.

A week had gone by since Sam started showing symptoms and, although the virus was progressing slowly for Sam, he was getting worse. His symptoms mirrored Mouse's. They began with fatigue and shortness of breath, followed by coughing fits and a rising fever. For Mouse, the first few days had been the hardest. The virus hit him fast and he got the worst of it early. His coughing fits had slowed since leaving the hospital and he was slowly getting his strength back.

Thankfully, both of Sam's parents were asymptomatic carriers. They had managed to make it to a testing site, where they both tested positive for the virus. In an unlikely occurrence, neither of Sam's parents were displaying any symptoms. They had been cautioned to self-isolate to the best of their ability, as they could still spread the virus to other people, but they were otherwise unaffected by the virus. This was what made the virus so tricky. There were thousands of people walking around and not showing any symptoms, but they were still passing the virus to others. Anyone could be a carrier. Your best friend, your cousin, or even a kind woman trying to make ends meet at a truck stop diner. It didn't matter.

Mouse stepped out into the aisle of the plane and adjusted his facemask. He knew that he was in no danger of catching or spreading the virus. The doctors had made clear that he wasn't contagious and they had cleared him to travel out to Seattle. His lungs still burned if he took a deep breath and he still had a slight cough, but his condition had dramatically improved over the past week. Despite all of this, he chose to wear his mask as a courtesy to the people around him and to remind people that it was part of the new normal.

He exited the plane with his backpack and marched toward the arrivals pickup area. The empty atmosphere of the Seattle airport was just like D.C. Mouse walked down the wide, open corridors without seeing a single new traveler. The first people that he saw were the three people waiting for their luggage around the luggage carousel.

Mouse watched as a young woman removed her roller bag from the carousel and immediately wiped it down with a sanitary wipe. She pulled out the retractable handle and, also wiping the handle down, wheeled it toward the exit in a hurry. She and Mouse met awkwardly at the exit doors, both coming to a hard stop at the narrow opening between the automatic doors. In unison, they both stepped back and insisted the other party go first.

The woman chuckled and spoke through an all-black, cloth face-mask, "No, please. You go."

Neither party wanted to infringe on the other's space and they awkwardly hesitated to walk through first. Existing with heightened courtesy and politeness was the safest course of action, but it was socially awkward.

"After you," Mouse replied, stepping back excessively to give her room to pass through the doors.

The woman smiled from behind her mask and stepped through the doors. Mouse followed slowly behind the woman and stepped out onto the wet, rainy Seattle sidewalk. He stared out through the mist of rain and searched for a familiar face. Sam's father was supposed to pick him up and, with traffic limited and very few travelers, Mouse assumed that he would be waiting outside. He hadn't told Sam that he was coming out to be with their family, and he was eager to see everyone.

Mouse walked over to a covered park bench on the sidewalk and sat down. Foolishly, he didn't look at the seat and he felt the cold, damp bench on the butt of his jeans. He sighed in frustration, as he felt the dampness creep through his underwear and press on his bare skin. Refusing to stand up, he embraced the unfortunate circumstances and sat back. He placed his backpack in his lap and tried to take a deep breath of the early morning air. As he inhaled, he wheezed and coughed harshly into his facemask. The doctors weren't sure if his lungs would ever fully recover from the virus, but at least he wasn't contagious any more.

Looking out into the rain for a familiar car, Mouse rolled the Gemini coin between his fingers. He flipped and tossed the coin playfully from one finger to another, a skill that he had developed during the many hours that he lay in the hospital. On those lonely nights, he had nothing to entertain himself with except for Carol, the Gemini coin, and the memory of the night that Sam gave it to him beneath the stars.

Here, on the park bench, Mouse thought back to that night at his birthday party. Everything seemed so simple back then. The stark differences between the then and now stood out, as Mouse watched the scattering of masked travelers air-hug their loved ones and toss sanitized luggage into the back seats of their cars. He wondered how things might be different moving forward. Some things might just be temporary adjustments and other things might be permanent. No one knew how drastically things would change.

Honk! Honk! A loud car horn blared at him, as a small car pulled up to the sidewalk a few cars back from the covered park bench.

Mouse turned and searched through the rain for a familiar face. Expecting Sam's father, Mouse was surprised to see that it was Elena and Meg Garcia in the honking car. They honked again and waved excitedly at Mouse. He hoisted his backpack over his shoulders and walked toward their car. As he approached the curb, the sound of the car unlocking granted him permission to get inside and he climbed into the backseat.

"Hey! Thanks for picking me up," Mouse said, as he liberated his face from the sweaty prison of his facemask. "Is everything okay with Sam?"

Elena turned around in the passenger seat and replied, "Sam had a setback this morning, so Connor asked if we could pick you up while they try to get him in at the hospital. Didn't he text you?"

"No, I'm sure he's busy though," Mouse replied. "Hospital beds are pretty full, huh?"

He already knew the answer to his question, but Elena lied kindly. "They're optimistic that a bed might open up this week," she said, with confidence in her voice. "We're keeping our fingers crossed."

No one was optimistic about the prospect of a bed opening up. The hospitals were full and the staff worked tirelessly to free up space for the flood of new cases that were coming in every day.

The rain intensified, slapping hard against the windshield as they pulled away. The wiper blades screeched as they cut across the glass, and Mouse looked out at the Seattle landscape. He hadn't been out to visit since last summer, but the drive from the airport felt comforting and familiar. Seattle had become somewhat of a second home to him and, despite the circumstances, it felt right to be back and to be with Sam's friends and family.

Meg chimed in, attempting to change the topic from Sam's worsening condition, "How was your trip, Mouse? Have you eaten lunch?"

"Honestly, I haven't," Mouse admitted. His stomach began to rumble. "I haven't had much of an appetite lately, but I should eat and keep my strength up."

Mouse coughed hard into his elbow, as the conversation began to take a toll on his throat. He took a sip from his water bottle and settled back into his seat, inhaling slowly to ensure that he got a full breath of air.

"Well, there are a few burger places that still have their drive-through open," Meg explained. "If you want to stop, they should be serving lunch now."

"That sounds great," Mouse said excitedly. "Is the rest of town pretty much shut down?"

Meg changed lanes to the right, and Mouse's weight shifted abruptly in the backseat. She swerved skillfully around a slow car and took the next exit in a flash. She took a sharp right and a fast-food burger joint came into view down the way. The bright red awning could be seen through the mist and rain from miles away and the smell of grease filled Mouse's nostrils as they grew closer. The delicious aroma overwhelmed him and he quickly realized the severity of his hunger. Meg pulled into the parking lot and looped around the building into the drive-through, and Mouse felt his stomach rumble again.

"Welcome to Fancy Burger. Can I take your order?" a voice shouted through the drive-through speaker.

"Do you know what you want?" Meg asked kindly, as she turned around to make eye contact with Mouse.

He scanned the menu quickly and replied, "Just … one #6, extra pickles." Meg repeated his order loudly into the rusted speaker box, emphasizing the additional pickles with her tone and delivery.

Elena quickly followed, yelling across Meg's lap, "Two #4's and a medium onion rings."

Meg raised her eyebrows accusingly at Elena, who reacted by yelling again, "Make that a LARGE onion rings, for the lady." Meg rolled her eyes in response.

"Will that be all?" the voice called back. Meg confirmed their order confidently and pulled up to the cashier's window.

Mouse quickly pulled out his credit card and offered to pay. Handing the card firmly to Meg, he insisted, "Please. You guys came all the way out to the airport. Let me buy you lunch."

Meg parked the car and reluctantly took the credit card from Mouse. With the coffee shop closed, Elena had been struggling to find an alternative income. The Garcias were renting the coffee shop space and their landlord was holding firm to their contract. Elena and Meg were still expected to pay the rent on the building, even though they had been forced to close the coffee shop for business. While they were proud people and the prospect of a free meal wasn't entirely appealing, they recognized the difficult situation they were in.

"Thank you," Meg replied, sincerely. "That's very kind."

The cashier opened the drive-through window and wiped down the window sill with a sanitary wipe. A grease-stained facemask covered his mouth and nose, and he wore purple, medical-grade rubber gloves. His gloved hands took the credit card from Meg and he mumbled the price of their food into his facemask. His muffled voice was lost in the fabric, but Mouse had a fair sense of what their order would cost and nodded in approval.

As the cashier completed the transaction, the heavy smell of fat and grease wafted out of the drive-through window and into the backseat. Taking in the delicious scent, his stomach rumbled again and his mouth began to water.

The cashier disappeared into the kitchen, joining the busy line of fast-food workers assembling orders. Mouse looked back, as a line of cars began to stack up behind them. While everything was closed, the few restaurants that were allowed to open were flooded with patrons. People had been following the Stay-at-Home Order for weeks and they leapt at any excuse to leave the house.

The longer people stayed inside, the more entitled they felt to venture out of their homes, as if they had earned a break from the virus. All around the country, people's patience with their new stay-at-home lifestyles was wearing thin and they began to take risks. The solitude and isolation were taking a toll on people—physically, mentally, and emotionally. Everyone was having difficulty saying goodbye to their old lives and they desperately craved something normal.

As he watched the cars stack up behind them, Mouse thought,

What could be more normal than a drive-through cheeseburger?

The cashier returned quickly with their food and passed it over to Meg. As they pulled out of the drive-through, Elena sifted through the bag and began to divide their meals. Steam rose from the freshly fried onion rings and filled the car.

Elena's outstretched hand held a #6 sandwich, extra pickles, in front of Mouse. Yes, Mouse felt a little guilty about ordering a fried chicken sandwich from a place called Fancy Burger, but a craving was a craving. He carefully unwrapped the sandwich and smiled, as pickles overflowed from every side. Taking his first bite, the flaky, spicy breading made his tongue tingle and the thick white meat of the chicken breast melted in his mouth. He moaned in ecstasy and fell back into his seat in delight.

"Woah there, fella," Elena teased. "Keep it PG with that sandwich!"

Mouse chuckled; mouth still full of chicken. "Sorry," he mumbled, quickly chewing and swallowing. "I guess I was hungrier than I realized."

They all laughed and a gentle ease fell over the car. Laughter felt rarer these days. Stress and fear had consumed them, and Mouse welcomed the change in mood. The drive quickly brought them to Sam's neighborhood and a rush of memories came back to Mouse. He followed the familiar trees and houses that led to Sam's driveway, recalling their late-night walks around the neighborhood on their visits to Seattle. Mouse's nostalgia reached its peak as the car pulled up to Sam's house. Mouse stepped out onto the driveway and slowly approached Sam's white sedan. He placed his hand on the hood of the car and smiled. It was good to be back.

Elena rolled down her window and called out to him, "We'll see you soon, Mouse. Thanks for getting lunch!"

He had assumed that they were coming inside with him but, given Sam's condition, it made sense they would want to keep their distance. "Thanks for the ride!" he called back, as they pulled away and drove out of the quiet charms of Sam's neighborhood.

Mouse wandered slowly into the open garage, his eagerness to see Sam competing with his desire to soak in the familiarities of the setting. The white camper van was just as he had remembered it. He wandered past its dented sides and the scattering of tools that dressed the garage floor. He approached the door and considered knocking, but instead placed his hand on the door knob and turned it gently. With a soft push, the door swung open and Mouse stepped inside.

At the sound of the door, Sam's mother emerged from the kitchen holding a rubber spatula. "Mouse! Oh, my goodness!" she said excitedly. "Connor said that you were coming out to surprise us. Come in! Put your things down."

"Hi Mrs. ... I mean, Annie," Mouse replied. Sam's parents had insisted, time and time again, that Mouse call them by their first names. It always made him uncomfortable, but he was adjusting to the informality slowly. "Can I see him?" Mouse asked, getting straight to the point.

"Of course, Honey," She replied, her excitement fading as she recalled the purpose of his visit. She was so happy to see him that she had almost forgotten why he had flown out. "He's in his room."

Mouse set his backpack down next to the green recliner in the living room and walked slowly down the hall to Sam's room. He brought his footsteps to a quiet tip-toe, as he approached Sam's bedroom door. He opened the door slowly and peered into the dark room. The curtains were drawn shut over Sam's bedroom window and the musty smell of sweat filled the room. Through the darkness, Mouse could make out the outline of Sam's body rustling beneath the covers in bed.

"Mom?" Sam wheezed, painfully. "When can I take more medicine?" He groaned and rolled onto his side.

Mouse remembered that feeling all too well. Body aching like it had been hit by a truck. Drenched in sweat. Fever running hard and cold chills all over his body. Looking down at Sam, Mouse empathized with every ounce of his being. He winced at the painful memories of his own battle with the virus and took a step closer to Sam's bed.

"Hey there," Mouse called out into the room, closing the door behind him.

Sam sat up slowly, grunting through the pain as he propped his body up against the headboard. "Mouse? What are you doing here?" Sam coughed gently into his arm and squinted his eyes hard. Opening them, he spoke again, "Are hallucinations a symptom now?"

Mouse chuckled, "No hallucinations here. It's me, in the flesh."

Sitting down the foot of the bed and leaning over, Mouse reached out and took Sam's hand. Sam tugged gently and Mouse climbed up into bed beside him. They laid down slowly and Mouse wrapped his arms around Sam's sweaty, feverish body, holding him with a gentle tightness and kissing him softly on the back of the neck.

"I missed you so much," Sam whispered, taking care not to strain his vocal cords. He closed his eyes and leaned back into Mouse's embrace.

Without pause, Mouse whispered back, "I missed you too, Sam," and he held Sam until he felt him fall asleep.

Mouse cradled him in bed, gently caressing his arm and lacing their fingers together. Having spent so much time apart, it felt amazing to be back together. The past few weeks had felt like months, years even. Each day had been filled with so much stress and anxiety. He buried his face in Sam's hair and breathed in the familiar smell. This was home.

After about an hour, Sam was woken up by a harsh coughing fit. He pulled free of Mouse's embrace and leaned over the side of his bed. As his coughing subsided, Sam spat a mixture of mucus and blood into a trash can at his bedside.

Mouse grabbed the roll of toilet paper from the night stand and handed it over to Sam, who promptly wiped the trickle of blood from his lips and let out a low groan. Noticing the empty water glass on the nightstand, Mouse crawled out of bed and headed out to the kitchen to get Sam more water. He made his way to the galley kitchen and approached the sink in a hurry but, as he began to fill it up, a low voice startled him from the living room.

"Was it like this for you too?" Sam's father called out desperately from his green recliner chair.

After stabilizing the half-full water glass in his hand, Mouse stepped out of the galley kitchen and walked into the living room. He looked over at Sam's father, slowly scanning the heavy look on his face. Sadness swelled under his tired eyes. Any semblance of concern in his expression was quickly transforming into fear. He was beyond worried or nervous for his son. He was terrified.

"Yes, Sir," Mouse replied, with a reflective seriousness in his voice. Mouse cleared his drying throat and coughed gently into his elbow. "Mine came on a bit more quickly, but it looked a lot like this. The blood. The coughing fits. It's pretty much how it was for me."

Sam's father sighed and leaned forward, placing his elbows on his knees on folding his hands in front of him. He stared contemplatively at the floor for a long while before speaking again, "You're a good man, Mouse. Coming out here to be with us."

Sam's father paused again and looked up at Mouse. He spoke

again with a quiet tremble in his voice, "When you have kids, you spend a lot of time thinking about what their future will look like. I don't think I had any idea what Sam's future would look like, but I know one thing. Whatever dream girl or, dream guy, I guess, that I had imagined for him. You blow that guy out of the water."

"Thank you," Mouse replied, fighting back tears. "I'm glad that I could be here with you guys. This place has always felt like a second home for me."

A loud thud sounded behind him, from down the hallway toward Sam's room. Sam had emerged from his bedroom slowly and braced himself on the wall with one hand. His weak knees began to buckle and he gripped desperately at the tattered wallpaper for support. Mouse quickly set the water glass down and rushed to his side.

Pulling Sam's arm over his shoulder, Mouse hoisted him up and stabilized him. As Sam began to find his footing, Mouse walked him over to the couch. The scratchy, aged couch cushions braced Sam's fall, as he collapsed onto the couch and raised a weak finger to point at a patterned blanket on the far side of the room. Sam's father rose from his armchair and carried the patterned blanket over to Sam. He gently laid it across Sam's body and tucked the sides underneath him.

"Thanks, you guys," Sam wheezed. "I just thought that I'd come out and join the party. You know I hate to miss a good time."

Sam's father walked into the kitchen and shouted back, "You're just in time. We were just about to get the beer pong going!"

"I'm only doing shots these days," Sam insisted. He coughed hard, before collecting himself. "Double shot of cough syrup with a pickle back."

Mouse smiled. It was good to see that everyone still had their sense of humor. The comedic banter between Sam and his parents had always been one of Mouse's favorite parts of their trips to Seattle. Sam inherited his intelligence from his parents and it showed when they lovingly teased each other. It warmed Mouse to see them still joking but, as he found himself smiling, he realized that Sam's family didn't have much of a choice.

By now, enough information was out about that virus that they knew what Sam's odds were. The death toll was rising every day, the hospitals were full and short on supplies, and Sam's condition was only getting worse. With hope slowly going out the window, their comedic family banter was all that they had left. For them, their familial humor was the last standing piece of normal.

Sam's mother emerged from her bedroom, Sam's car keys in hand. "Does anyone need anything from the pharmacy?" she asked. "I placed an order for curbside pickup and I want to get there before they close. Curfew starts tonight."

"Curfew?" Mouse asked. "What curfew?"

"Seattle is starting a citywide curfew," Sam's mother explained. "The mayor's order came out this morning and they're talking about going statewide if things don't slow down."

"Wow," Mouse replied, mouth open. Maryland hadn't considered anything like that and the virus was tearing through Baltimore at an alarming rate. "I'm sure the stores will all be crazy. Do you need any help?"

"I'll be okay, Mouse. Thank you," she assured him. "But I'm getting more medicine and coconut water for Sammy. Do you need anything while I'm out?"

Mouse shook his head and leaned back on the couch. Without any additional list items from Sam, she pulled on her facemask and headed out the door.

Sam's father returned from the kitchen with two beers and a

carton of coconut water. He handed the coconut water to Sam and offered Mouse one of the beers. Mouse appreciated that Sam's father drank normal beer. Seattle had its fair share of craft breweries and fancy IPAs, and D.C. was quickly catching up. Sam's father, like Mouse, found the fuss and circumstance of craft beer to be unnecessary. Simple light beers were all that they needed. Sam's father opened his beer and sat back in his recliner. He quickly changed the channel on the television, as Mouse opened his beer and helped Sam open the carton of coconut water.

Sam's father settled on a trivia game show. It was clearly a rerun, but Mouse wasn't familiar with the show. He recognized the host, from one thing or another, but he watched with intrigue as the host went through the trivia categories. Question after question, Sam's father shouted out the correct answers at the television, proudly displaying his knowledge of the obscure categories. Sam would occasionally mutter a correct answer under his breath, but the struggle to speak exhausted him.

Eventually, Mouse found the courage to participate and began spouting out incorrect answers about history and geography. Sam smiled and chuckled, as Mouse continued to shout random guesses at the television and joined in the fun. Mouse cared less about being right and more about cheering up Sam at this point, but he found his rhythm in the fourth round.

"Another term for the body's acid–base balance is what?" the game show host asked.

"Ph balance," responded Mouse.

His eyes widened as he realized that he had actually answered a question correctly. The two contestants on the gameshow proceeded to get the question wrong, before the host confirmed Mouse's answer.

"Nice one, Mouse!" Sam's father congratulated him.

The host continued with the category, "Referred to as the building blocks of protein, what is the name of this compound?"

"Amino Acids," Mouse blurted out.

Sam gave Mouse a curious look out of the corner of his eye, shocked by Mouse's confidence. The host quickly confirmed Mouse's correct answer and Mouse took a sip of his beer to hide his excited smile.

"Big science nerd over here," Sam teased. "Someone has been studying for their Chemistry final. Are they going to let you do the makeup work?"

Mouse shrugged his shoulders and responded, half-confidently, "I think if I can catch up, then I won't have to retake the class in the fall. Thanks to my very handsome chemistry tutor."

The game show approached its final round and the group found themselves deeply invested in the show's end results. The final round consisted of a single question, yet to be announced. As the game show host approached his podium, everyone leaned forward in their seats. Sam's father lowered the extension on his recliner chair and placed both feet on the floor.

"What is the state dog of Massachusetts?" the host asked.

"Beagle," Sam's father said, with absolute certainty.

"Beagle?" Sam said softly, rolling his exhausted eyes at his father. "No way .... Bloodhound."

"Golden Retriever," followed Mouse.

They sat patiently in front of the television and waited for the host to announce the answer. The group hadn't even bothered to listen to the contestants' responses. The rights to the room boiled down to one final question, as they scooted to the edge of their seats. The game show host straightened his tie and revealed the answer, slowly building suspense with his delivery.

"The correct answer," he called out dramatically. "To the final question. The name of the state dog of Massachusetts. Is ... The Boston Terrier."

A chorus of boos erupted from the group. Even Sam managed to hiss a boo from his raspy, swollen vocal cords. Sam's father hucked his empty beer can across the room, bouncing off of the television screen and landing in the middle of the room.

"Boston Terrier?!" he yelled, rising to retrieve the empty can before Sam's mother returned home. "Can you believe that bullshit?"

He stormed off into the kitchen to retrieve another beer, slamming the fridge shut in frustration. Mouse smiled at the sight and curled up next to Sam on the couch. The circumstances were less than ideal but, for the first time in a long time, he felt like he was exactly where he needed to be.

RELEASE

The remainder of Emily's four-week suspension from in-school went by in a blur. Every day felt the same. She would get out of bed, attend her online classes, work out, message with Fae and Marshall, and go to sleep. On some days, she would work out twice just to pass the time. In addition to her punishments from the Council, Emily's parents had forbidden her from running family errands or leaving the housing unit for any reason. This included walks outside, visits with her friends, and her weekly trips to the pharmacy. Trapped in the housing unit, Emily tried to make the most of every day.

The Changs had applied for a monthly visitation day with the Dottermans, but their request was denied for the first time in months. While not formally announced in the message, everyone knew that the denial was linked to Emily's curfew violation. Instead, the Changs stayed home, and the Dottermans visited with the Kunitz family, venturing out to spend the evening with Marshall's family. Fae and Marshall made sure to update Emily about their dinner exchange over Vid, trying their best to include her in the festivities.

As the weeks trickled by, Emily missed the little day-to-day freedoms that she used to enjoy. She particularly missed her conversations with Doc Abrams and daydreamed about returning to the pharmacy. Her curiosity about the mountains had faded in the first few days after her Council hearing. She was left shook by the experience and her lapse in interest was a result of her fear, but her curiosity quickly returned. From the exercise bike in the living room, Emily could see the mountains through the window. Pedaling and covered in sweat, she prepared loads of questions for her first trip back to the pharmacy to pass the time. It was her curiosity that made her miss curfew in the first place but, as time passed, the intrigue of the mountains won out over her concern for getting in trouble.

After four long weeks, Emily was just a few days away from being allowed back to Walter Reed High School for in-school. On the Saturday before her return, she woke up giddy with excitement. Waking up before her *8:00 AM* alarm, Emily stretched her arms over her head and took her temperature to start the day.

"98.2," her tablet called out to her. "Vitals normal."

She bounced up from her bed excitedly and started getting ready for the day. She had nothing special planned for that particular Saturday, but the prospect of returning to in-school in two days was enough to carry her through the weekend. She went through her morning routine, rinsing her mouth with oral disinfectant and washing her face carefully. There was no explanation for the good mood that she found herself in, except for the fact that the worst of her Council punishments were behind her. She was almost free.

Emily cheerfully skipped down the hallway and pranced downstairs, her bubbly mood radiating down to the living room and kitchen. Her feet hit the floor of the living room with a loud thud, drawing the attention of her parents from the kitchen.

"Well, someone is wide awake this morning," Emily's mother said with a chuckle, as she stood up and walked toward their home garden to grab a handful of fresh berries for her yogurt.

"I guess I am!" Emily exclaimed, following her mother over to the hydroponic garden. "I'm just in a good mood I guess."

The lid on the glass casing creaked open slowly, as Emily lifted up on the strawberry case. Ted's ears perked up from the living room. He coughed gently into his elbow and rose slowly from his chair. Setting his tablet down on the chair, his eyes set upon Emily with suspicion. As indicated by the chart, blueberries were clearly in rotation this week. The strawberry rotation didn't start until Sunday.

In the subtlest of ways, she winked at Ted from across the room and plucked a handful of strawberries from the plant. She wandered into the kitchen slowly, washed the strawberries, and took a bite out of the biggest one. The fresh taste made her tongue tingle and berry juice burst out from the side of her mouth. She smiled and wiped her mouth off on her sleeve.

Savoring every bite, Emily ignored her daily intake of pills on the kitchen counter and meandered into the living room. Ted was sitting in his chair, intensely playing through an Eden Vax game simulation on his tablet. Emily stepped around the chairs to the far side of the room and sat down, careful not to disturb Ted's focus. She fiddled with her tablet and casually read through the morning news, but she secretly watched Ted's screen as he played as his favorite Eden Vax player, Cayden McDaniels. Emily knew the particular simulation that he was playing well. It was the same set of objectives from the game against Tri City, where Cayden made his debut for the team. The complexities of the game were still a bit of a mystery to her, but she smiled as she thought back to the first time that she watched Cayden play. As far as debut games go, that night was one to remember.

Leaning back in her chair, Emily opened up the video games application on her tablet and began to sift through the different gaming options that she had downloaded. Settling on a memory game, Emily began to sort and match the different signs and symbols. She loved puzzle and pattern games.

An arrangement of seven symbols would flash on the screen briefly, giving Emily a short amount of time to recreate the arrangement from memory. It was a simple game, but Emily found it incredibly challenging. The arrangements became more complicated as the rounds went on and the symbols eventually all started to blur together. Her favorite arrangements were constellations. The different arrangements of stars were all seemingly indistinguishable, but Emily knew the stars well. She always did well with the constellation rounds.

"That's a pretty cool game you're playing over there," Emily remarked, as she leaned toward her brother. "Any chance you can teach me how to play?"

Ted glanced up at her, his excitement quelled by his suspicion. "You want to learn how to play?" he asked.

"Sure!" Emily replied. "If you'll teach me. What are your favorite games?"

Ted smiled and turned his tablet in her direction, cheerfully showing Emily the different moves and characters that you could play with. His eyes lit up, as Emily nodded and asked clarifying questions about the different types of gameplay. It was the first time that they had played video games together in a long time, and Ted was set on making up for lost time.

They sat there playing video games for another hour, jumping between games and comparing scores. They laughed and challenged one another for more points or linked their tablets to play head-to-head in multiplayer games. Emily was particularly bad at racing games, but they were some of Ted's favorites. She happily obliged his requests to race cars or planes or helicopters, no matter how many times he beat her.

Ted's loud belly laugh turned quickly into a raspy cough, as

Emily's car spun out of control on the track for the third time in a row. He smiled through his inhaler, taking a puff to quell his cough. As they sat together, she fondly looked over at him while he taunted her with exuberant celebrations. She didn't care that she lost, because she was happy that he won. You couldn't put a price tag on his smile. As he raised his tablet over his head to celebrate his victory, Emily reflected on her Year 11 and the time that she had missed with Ted. She had probably neglected her younger brother the most through all of this.

Between her friends, the Aptitude Exams, and the stresses of her Council hearing ... she hadn't been there for him, she thought to herself.

"Here, hold your tablet like this," Ted explained, holding his arms out in front of him and demonstrating the proper way to grip and steer with the tablet. "I know it feels weird, but it will be way better for taking the sharp turns."

Emily followed Ted's instructions and adapted her playing style. With each of the following races, she found herself closing the gap between them. Working through the awkwardness of her extended arms, the tablet slowly felt more comfortable in her hand and she felt the game get a little bit easier as she adjusted.

Truthfully, Ted had relaxed his competitiveness and was letting her catch up to him, but he never eased up enough to let her win. Their cars would bump and swerve and, on a few occasions, Emily was right near the finish line with Ted. She found herself captivated by the game and she was finally getting into her groove, when the unexpected voice of her father called out to her from the kitchen.

"Emily, can you come here for a moment?" her father asked, breaking the four-week deadlock between them for the first time.

They had passed each other in the halls of their housing unit, but he hadn't spoken to her about anything of substance since before her Council hearing. Their interactions had been reduced to simple pleasantries and questions of necessity.

"Can you pass the salt?"

"Are there enough sanitary wipes in the dispenser?"

"Is your mother in her office?"

"Sure Dad. I'll be right there," Emily replied, setting her tablet down on her chair and walking over to the kitchen nervously. "Is everything okay?"

As their eyes met, Emily saw something different in his facial expression. It was kinder than it had been over the past four weeks. His blank, disappointed look had faded and his stern glare had softened. Emily sat down at the kitchen counter and glanced down at the daily intake of pills that she had forgotten. She reached for a glass of water on the tray and took the handful of pills in her mouth, grimacing as she washed down the colorful medley.

"Emily," her father began, stepping up to the opposite side of the kitchen counter. "Your mother and I have been talking, and we think that your punishment has gone on long enough. We applied for a park slot at 10:30 and, if you're up for it, I'd like it if we all went to the park today."

"The Dottermans are going as well," her mother followed up, quickly joining the conversation from across the room.

Emily's eyes opened wide, questioning whether or not she had heard her parents correctly. *Are they serious? Are we really going to the park?* Emily thought, eyes widening with excitement.

She stared back at them, rendered speechless by the surprise change in her father's tone and demeanor. Emily's mother looked sternly over at her husband and nodded her head, encouraging him to speak again.

He cleared his throat and spoke again, "We're very proud of you, Emily. I want you to know that. We were very surprised by the Council hearing, and we just want you to be safe and healthy. That's all."

A wave of relief washed over her and she leaned back in her chair. After a long pause, Emily nodded her head and replied, "Thanks. The park sounds great, Dad."

Her father smiled softly back at her and the tension between them faded away. Nearing 10:00, Emily rose from the kitchen counter and walked upstairs to her bedroom.

As she plopped down on her bed, she messaged Fae, *"I can't wait to see you today!!!"*

Fae quickly responded, *"You're coming!?!?!?! YES!"*

Emily tossed her tablet down on her bed and rushed to put on a new set of day clothes from her wardrobe. As the morning light came through her window, she felt a quiet peace and the weight of her father's disappointment began to fade away. She had an opportunity to start fresh. She pulled her tablet bag over her shoulders and made her way back downstairs. She waited anxiously by the door for the rest of her family, eager to feel the freedom of the outside air. The smile on her face refused to fade, as she imagined the grass beneath her feet and the cool breeze on her skin.

As her parents and Ted approached the door, Emily led the charge down to the lobby excitedly. Heading down the elevator and skipping across the shimmering floor of the lobby, Emily marched purposefully toward the HC-F5 storage area. Tommy laughed and waved from his front desk as she passed by.

"Hey there, Miss Emily. Good to see you again!" he called out.

She hollered back to him over her shoulder, too excited to stop, "Hey Tommy!"

Emily turned the corner on the other side of Tommy's desk and walked up to a large metal door. Like the elevator banks, a facial scanner was set up a few feet in front of the doorway. Emily stepped to the side of the scanner and waited for her father to catch up to her.

Wiping it down with a sanitary wipe, he leaned forward and let the scanner pass over his face. "Patrick Chang," the scanner announced, and a series of mechanical noises started churning from behind the doors. Each housing unit came with a personal storage locker. The size of a small room, the lockers were held underground and brought up when they were needed. Facial recognition told the computer which storage unit to bring up to the lobby.

Before long, the mechanical sounds ceased and the door opened to reveal the Chang family's storage unit. Emily's father walked up to the doors and, as they slid open, he stepped inside to gather their things. Dimly lit, the room was sparsely populated with a few storage bins, some EduView equipment, and four lightweight foldable chairs.

Emily opened her tablet bag and quickly removed a pack of sanitary wipes. One by one, her father passed each of them a chair and they wiped them down diligently. Pulling her freshly sanitized chair up under her arm, Emily turned and headed toward the HC-F5 front doors. The mechanical sounds of the storage unit system rumbled behind her, as she stepped outside.

"Have a great day, you guys!" Tommy hollered, laughing at the sight of Emily bursting out of the lobby doors and onto the sidewalk.

The delicate breeze washed over her and she took a deep breath of fresh air. Emily slowly pulled her facemask on over her head, embracing the first few moments outside without restriction. The F-block park was just up the way, near HC-F3. Each of the different housing blocks had their own park. The A, B, and C-block parks were certainly more spacious, but the F-block park had the most green space. Most of the parks were an equal combination of grass and pavement, giving a variance to the different designated seating areas. The F-block park, however, was mostly grass seating and trees.

As they headed up to the park, Ted jumped up onto the sidewalk curbing and danced with perfect balance toward the park. Emily chuckled as he stuck out his arms and leaned from side to side, playfully pretending that he was going to fall off.

"Ted, would you just …" Emily's mother called out after him. "Oh, never mind."

Shooting a sly glance in the direction of his wife, Emily's father jumped onto the curb and chased after Ted. With significantly less grace and balance, he stumbled his way across the curbing. Emily's mother shook her head disapprovingly, but she let the faintest smile crack as she watched their lively display.

As the park came into full view, Emily's eyes lit up with excitement. She sped up, trotting behind her father and Ted toward the park gates, but her excitement quickly faded. Her pace was brought back to a walk, as she spotted a patrol officer standing outside of the park gate next to the check-in counter. Uneasy, she sank back into her anxieties and a shiver shot down her spine. His all-white body armor glistening in the sun, the officer stood tall and his commanding presence loomed over the park entryway. Emily watched nervously, as her father approached the check-in counter and removed his tablet from his tablet bag.

"Chang - 662123," he announced, as he held out his tablet to the Council Official at the park desk. "We're permitted for 10:30."

The Council Official, a young woman with curly black hair, leaned over and examined the reservation carefully. The woman adjusted her facemask and looked back at the list of permits on her tablet, confirming their time slot.

"Everything looks good!" the woman replied cheerfully. "Head on down to #16. Wash up going in and out."

The patrol officer stared down at Emily intensely, safely behind the authority of the heavy rifle that rested across his chest. His stance and posture demanded her respect and conformity but, as Emily looked out at the open green grass in front of her, she felt empowered beyond her fears. A renewed sense of confidence set in, and she puffed out her chest at him as she walked through the park gate. In that moment, she swore that he flinched.

After washing their hands thoroughly at the entryway sinks, Emily walked with her family along the roped path to seating area #16. Each plot, a fifteen by fifteen–foot square, was reserved for a single housing unit with an hour gap between uses. Reservations for the F-block park could be made by only the families living in the F-block, limiting opportunities for interaction with the other blocks of housing clusters. As she walked by, Emily smiled at the familiar faces of her neighbors and carefully scanned the surrounding areas for the Dottermans.

Seating area #16 was an all-grass plot, half covered in shade by a nearby Norway tree. Stepping beyond the wooden sign and roped perimeter that marked #16, Emily planted her chair down directly in the sunshine. She carefully sanitized the back and arm rests of the chair and sat down comfortably in the midday sun. Emily turned her arms over, exposing her forearms to the light and her skin began to warm. She relaxed back in her chair and closed her eyes. A deep satisfaction came over her, as she basked in the loving embrace of the sunlight and fresh air. It felt good to be outside again.

The quiet peace of the park was quickly interrupted by the sound of Emily's tablet buzzing loudly in her tablet bag. With no sign of

Fae, Emily curiously pulled her bag into her lap and fished out her tablet.

Where was she? Emily thought, as she took her tablet in her hand.

The glare of the sunlight reflected harshly against the tablet screen and Emily quickly switched the tablet into its outdoor mode, dimming the screen to minimize the blinding reflection. She tilted her tablet out of the sun and checked to see if she had any new messages. She looked to the top right corner of the screen, at the notifications panel.

"New Message - Cayden McDaniels," she read to herself.

Surprised, Emily sat up in her chair and clicked open the notification. She hadn't messaged Cayden since they had walked together downtown on the night that she had broken curfew. Over the past few weeks, she had considered messaging him several times. His name had been all over her news updates, as the Eden Vax struggled to win a game and teetered on the cusp of playoff contention.

Cayden's gameplay had been heavily criticized by sports journalists and Eden Vax fans alike, and the moment never seemed right to reach out to him with a message. A lot had changed for them since his electric debut for the team, and Cayden was beginning to get a sense for what it meant to be a star in the IGL. When the team won, he was their Golden Boy. When the team lost, it was because he wasn't performing well enough. The weight of their expectations fell heavily on his sixteen-year-old shoulders.

As the message opened, Emily read silently to herself in her chair, *"Marshall tells me that you're coming back to in-school this week. I bet you're excited to be back!"*

Emily paused and thought for a moment. Staring down at her tablet, she began to draft a response. She looked over at Ted and asked, "When is the next Vax game?"

Ted curiously looked back at her, from across the grassy area, and replied, "Tonight. Against Boston. Why? Do you want to watch?"

Emily looked back down at her tablet and wrote her response to Cayden, *"Two more days! Good luck against Boston tonight. I'll be chereing for you!"*

As she hit send, she smacked herself in the forehead upon seeing her typo. She quickly drafted a correction. After typing the words, she erased the message and decided to leave it alone, before quickly returning to her original decision of sending the correction.

Ted looked back at her toying with her tablet, excited at the prospect of watching the Vax game as a family. Quickly realizing that she was messaging Cayden, Ted began to mutter a sly, teasing remark, but he was quickly cut off by Emily's mother. With a stern glance, Emily's mother silenced the coming flurry of jokes about Emily's new "boyfriend."

The Age of Responsibility was a curious thing for teenagers and adults alike. Emily's mother wasn't sure where this crush on Cayden was going. She wasn't even sure that she approved of Emily dating yet, but she recognized that Ted's teasing wouldn't contribute anything positive to the process.

"We should watch the game tonight," her mother said, kindly. "I think it'd be nice to watch as a family."

Emily tapped her fingers impatiently on the surface of her tablet, waiting for a response from Cayden. After a few moments, she returned her tablet to her tablet bag. She refused to let her attention linger on his pending response. It was their family's day at the park and she was going to enjoy it.

Emily stared out at the open greenery and scanned the gatherings of families and couples across the way. Everyone was seated neatly in their sanitized chairs, reading their tablets or playing games or just enjoying the midday sun. The layout of the park scenery was pleasantly simple.

A couple across the way, in seating area #17, carefully unpacked their individual lunches and sanitized their utensils. From a distance, Emily watched closely as they began to eat a colorful spring salad with an assortment of berries. Her mouth began to water and she turned toward her father.

"I know," he said, empathizing with the hungry look on Emily's face. "I saw them, too. I've got some berries from the garden. Hang on."

He reached down into his tablet bag and pulled out a small, tightly sealed container of blueberries from their home garden. The last day before the produce switched rotation was always tricky. Their meals were composed of the end-of-week produce, as the cyclical rotation of fresh fruits and vegetables looked forward to the next week.

Emily's father stood up and walked the container over to Emily, handing her a set of utensils from the kitchen. One by one, Emily proceeded to sanitize the utensils and the container. She pulled open the tightly sealed lid with the wedge of her fork. Removing her mask, Emily stabbed a forkful of blueberries and raised them up to her mouth. The sweet taste satisfied her craving, as she bit the first mouthful off of the prongs of the fork. She savored the flavor and shimmied her shoulders in delight. Still chewing, Emily stabbed aggressively at another forkful and shoveled more berries into her mouth.

"Girl, what did those poor berries ever do to you!?" Fae's familiar voice teased from the walkway.

Emily turned red with embarrassment, as she looked back to see the Fae and her parents approaching. Fae's brown, curly hair shined in the sunlight. She was wearing an all-white outfit with a matching white facemask and her parents were wearing matching beige shirts and beige facemasks. Their family was well dressed for a day at the park. They strolled in casually, smiling excitedly as they walked up to the Chang's seating area.

Chuckling through the wet mouthful of blueberries, Emily replied in a low, monstrous rumble, "Lay off me! I'm starving."

Fae laughed and stepped up to the roped barrier around the Chang family's assigned seating area. "Hey, Chang family!" she greeted the rest of the group. "Feeling more like Sun-Day out here with this weather, huh?"

Emily rolled her eyes, as her parents chuckled at Fae's cheesy wordplay. Her jokes always landed with parents.

"It's a pretty perfect day." Emily's father exclaimed, sitting up straight in his chair and smiling. "And, how are the Dottermans?"

Fae's parents stood casually at the edge of the seating area, next to their daughter. "We're doing better now that we're outside!" Fae's mother exclaimed, tightening her grip on her chair. "We had a bit of a rough start to the day. The lights in one of our gardens went out, so we've got to deal with that today."

The Dottermans' hydroponic garden setup was particularly complicated and replacement bulbs were one of the few household essentials that weren't kept in the lower storage rooms of HC-F5. Tommy had access to pretty much everything that the residents needed, but the bulbs went out so infrequently that it didn't make sense to keep them in stock. Instead, they were sold downtown at Eden Essential Electrical.

"Oh, I'm sorry to hear that," Emily's mother replied. "That's such a pain."

Fae quickly spoke up, seizing an opportunity to have some alone time with Emily, "I could run downtown and pick up new bulbs.

Maybe Emily could keep me company!"

With a concerned tone, Emily's father began, "I don't know if
…." But he was quickly interrupted by his wife.

"That sounds great," Emily's mother interrupted, raising an
eyebrow at her husband. "Emily, just make sure that you're back by
15:30, and not a minute later."

"15:30. Absolutely," Emily confirmed, as she began to gather her
things. "Mom, can you bring my chair back for me?"

Emily's mother nodded and Emily wiped down her chair thoroughly before stepping out of their seating area. She pulled her tablet
bag up over her shoulder, and she and Fae headed toward the exit
area.

A pair of sinks on either side of the exit, the girls parted near
the door and began washing their hands. Emily stepped down on a
pedal that initiated the steady flow of soap and water, and placed her
hands beneath the stream.

She counted down in her head from twenty. 9 … 8 … 7 … 6 … but
she pulled her hands as the countdown reached five.

Overwhelmed by the excitement of being reunited with her best
friend, she flicked her hands dry and after Fae through the exit gate.
The girls bounced down the sidewalk toward downtown, thrilled to
be back in one another's company. Catching up, their laughter and
jokes carried them out of the F-block neighborhood and toward the
edge of downtown.

"So, now that you're a total badass rebel," Fae started. "How does
it feel to be on the other side of your punishment?"

Emily smirked and shook her head. "I'm not a rebel, I just had a
slipup," she explained.

"Honestly, Emily," Fae replied, with growing concern in her
voice. "We never talked about what happened. Why were you so late

for curfew?"

They wandered down the sidewalks and Emily paused. She looked out at the Cascades, as they danced and sparkled in the sunlight. The sunlight rained down on them and she felt the lightest breeze on her skin. Like gravity, she crossed the street away from downtown.

"I don't know," Emily replied, honestly. "The streetlights turned red, like they always do, and I just didn't go home …. Can I show you something?"

"Always!" Fae replied, adjusting her facemask around her ears. "Where are we going?"

Emily led the way toward the edge of town, retracing her footsteps from the night that she missed curfew. Fae followed curiously behind her, loyally along for the ride. The vital health checkpoint at the edge of the city came into view and Emily pointed up ahead toward the small grassy hill.

"We're almost there!" Emily called out, excitedly raising her finger and pointing to the exact boulder that she sat on to watch the sunset.

"Almost where?" Fae asked, hoping against hope that Emily wasn't pointing to the top of the hill. "Emily. Have you seen my outfit? It's literally all white. ALL WHITE. There's no way that I'm climbing up that ridiculous, filthy hill."

Emily shrugged her shoulders. "At least one of us is a badass rebel," she called back, jumping up the sidewalk curbing and scrambling up the hillside.

Fae took a deep breath and said a silent prayer, before tiptoeing daintily up the steep hillside after her best friend. *You've got to be kidding me,* Fae thought, as she gripped a rock for support and tried to keep up with Emily. Her hands were getting dirtier with each move up the hillside and she winced at the grotesque sight of dirt collecting under her fingernails. *Urrgh. This is so gross.*

Her loyalty and love for Emily triumphed over her desire to turn back. She scrambled up the last segment of rocks and found herself at the foot of the final boulder. Fae's eyes opened wide, as she watched Emily climb hands and feet up the boulder and sit down on top. Shaking her head, she reluctantly climbed up after Emily. Hands and feet on the rock, Fae pulled herself up clumsily and cursed under her breath with each individual move.

She reached the top and sat down beside Emily, sighing in frustration. Fae immediately started to clean her hands with a sanitary wipe. She grunted and scoffed as the white wipe became tan with dirt. Fae stared intensely down at her hands, scrubbing at the dirt on the tips of her fingers.

"This is it," Emily whispered, as she pulled off her facemask and leaned back.

Furious and sweaty, Fae replied, "This is what? This is a dirty fucking ...."

Fae stopped halfway through her frustrated sentence and, for the first time since they left the comforts of the sidewalk, she stared out at the mountains. They sat together in silence and soaked in the majestic view and Fae leaned back.

"This is proper fit, Emily," she declared, with an appreciative smile. "It's so different than the view from home."

Emily looked over at Fae and replied, a sly grin coming across her face, "You should try watching the sunset from here."

Fae gasped. "You did not!" she exclaimed. "The whole sunset? Like after dark? Past curfew? Into the night?"

Emily nodded and the two girls laughed. They sat there and stared out at the mountains for an hour. Emily felt so relieved to share the hillside with her best friend. She had felt so alone in her curiosities over the past few months. Now, on top of the boulder, Emily finally felt heard. The empty feeling of screaming into the unheard void was gone. Instead, Fae was there.

Fae finally sat up on the boulder and sighed. "Thanks for sharing this place with me, Emily. It's really beautiful," she said softly. "But I've still got to pick up those bulbs and figure out how I'm going to get all of this dirt off my pants."

"For sure!" Emily responded, pulling her facemask back on. "Let's go downtown!"

"Can we come back here?" Fae asked. "Maybe with Marshall?"

Emily smiled and nodded, glad to hear that Fae wanted to return. The girls rose to their feet and Emily helped Fae down the backside of the boulder. They descended the hillside slowly, taking care to keep their clothes clean on the way down. As their feet hit the sidewalk, Fae removed her tablet from her tablet bag and checked the time. *13:17* stared blankly back at her, and they made their way toward downtown.

As they approached the stretch of stores on Foxx Avenue, the girls scanned the storefronts for Eden Essential Electric. Marked by the city crest and a bright-yellow awning, the storefront stood out. There were no pleasant smells or aromas emanating from the store, just a bright-yellow awning and minimal signage. Anxious to get home, Fae darted across the street and headed up the block.

As Fae headed in one direction, Emily stopped in her tracks and looked the other way. She had little interest in going with Fae to Eden Essential Electric, but there was one place that she wanted to visit before she went home. She had plenty of time before she had to be home. Looking across the street, Emily called out to Fae, "You go ahead. I'll catch up with you later tonight."

"Are you sure?" Fae hollered back, looking suspiciously at Emily.

Emily nodded and replied, "Yeah, I just have to make one quick stop."

STAR

Mouse flipped through his chemistry notes at the small kitchen table in preparation for his upcoming final exams. He tried hard to focus, but he was quickly distracted by the harsh sounds of another coughing fit coming from Sam's bedroom. He cringed at the sound of each painful cough, as Sam gasped for breath desperately. Recalling the agony of his own coughing fits in the hospital, Mouse stood up from his chair and slowly began to close his laptop.

"I've got it, Mouse," Sam's mother said, rising from her seat on the couch. "You've been doing so much around here."

She grabbed a clean dish towel from the kitchen and poured Sam a glass of water, before heading back to his bedroom. The routine had become second nature to them. Sam would take medicine every four hours, drink water regularly, and, if he had a coughing fit, he needed a towel to wipe his mouth and dab the sweat from his forehead. His diet had been reduced to bone broth and soft foods. Eating had become an even bigger challenge over the past few weeks, as Sam's throat was increasingly raw from coughing. It was a process, but Mouse and Sam's parents had become more adept at caring for him as the days went by.

On a good day, Sam would sleep for two or three hours before being thrown awake by another violent coughing fit. He had to sleep on his back, propped up slightly to help him breathe. Mouse and Sam's parents took turns getting up in the middle of the night, but

Mouse had taken more shifts than anyone.

Exhausted, the heavy weight of her footsteps echoed down the hall. Mouse listened closely for the sound of Sam's door closing, ready for any indication that Sam's mother needed help. Upon hearing the door close, he turned back to his laptop and carefully compared his notes to the lecture slides that were posted on EduView. Mouse was slowly adjusting to St. Agatha's remote learning format. Learning online was certainly difficult, and there was a lot to keep track of on the new platform, but he was getting the hang of it.

Over the past week, Mouse had used most of his free time to catch up on the work that he had missed while he was in the hospital. Because of the weeklong extension for students to move home, he was really only a few important lectures behind. Scanning the lecture slides, Mouse felt his phone buzz in his pocket. He reached down and, pulling out his phone, read the text message notification curiously.

New Message - Maisie Marks, he read on the display.

It was unlike Maisie to text him. He had always felt like she was more of Sam's friend than his own. They had developed their own friendship through Sam, but they never spent time together without him. He opened the message quickly, concerned and curious.

"Hey! How's Sam doing? Are you guys watching the Presidential Address tonight???" the message read.

Mouse attempted to decipher the message. *What address?* he thought.

Racking his brain, he quickly remembered that the President was giving an emergency address to talk about the virus later that night. He had been so distracted over the past few days. Meanwhile, the rest of the world was hanging in suspense around the cryptic announcement of an important Presidential Address. Speculative headlines ran wild, guessing at the reason for the emergency address.

Did they have a vaccine? Were they issuing a nationwide lockdown? Was there a mutation or variation of the virus? No one knew, and everyone had a guess.

Over the past few months, the President had been heavily criticized for his handling of the outbreak and many people blamed him for the rising death rate, which was nearing 24%. The virus was running rampant in the United States due to a lack of testing, late response time, and a massive shortage of medical supplies. Other countries had managed to hold the death rate to a still staggering 10%, but their leaders could hide behind the embarrassing display of leadership going on in the United States.

"He's doing okay." Mouse wrote back to Maisie, lying. No one wanted to admit it, but Sam was getting worse with each passing day. *"I'll try to be better about sending updates! Sorry! And, we're definitely going to watch the address. How are you? How's home?"*

Mouse reached over and grabbed the television remote. He flicked through the channels and quickly found the evening news broadcast. The President's Address would begin in fifteen minutes, according to the timer counting down on the bottom of the screen. Setting his phone down on the kitchen table, face up, Mouse returned to his studying and worked through the previous week's lectures. As he stared at his computer screen, the chemical formulas began to blend together and he felt his eyes grow tired. He insisted on finishing one more set of slides before giving up for the night.

"He's sleeping again," Sam's mother said, as she returned to the living room and fell onto the couch. Her body crashed down onto the couch cushions and she curled up into the arm rest. "Is this the President's Address?" she asked, pointing at the television.

Mouse nodded and handed her the remote. His phone buzzed again.

"I'm okay," Maisie wrote. "I'm going a little nuts at home. This house is way too small for me and my mom, but I'm hanging in there. We're safe and healthy, and we have each other! I miss you guys!"

Sitting back in his chair, Mouse closed his laptop and replied, "We miss you too!"

Sam's mother leaned forward on the couch, as the timer on the bottom of the screen approached zero and the President appeared on the screen. Wearing a suit and tie, he sat in the Oval Office with his hands folded professionally in front of him. Four advisors stood behind him, separated by six feet of social distancing, but only two of the four advisors were wearing facemasks. Competing information had been circulating about the importance and effectiveness of masks. The President was rarely seen wearing one, giving even more room for speculation around the practice.

Two large infographics were displayed to the left and right of his advisors. To the left, a large chart showed the dramatic uptick in new cases in the United States. To the right, the global trend in new cases. The comparison was stark, but it was an honest expression of how the virus was being handled in the United States. Other parts of the world had done relatively well containing the spread of the virus, but the same could not be said about the United States.

The appearance of the charts was startling, both because of how much worse the situation was in the United States and because it was maybe the first time that the President had elected to display how poorly his administration had responded to the situation. His approval ratings were at an all-time low and only his staunchest supporters were left standing by his side. The steep red line on the infographic revealed the dark truth about the virus. It was everywhere and it was spreading fast.

As the address began, the President leaned forward and

straightened his posture. He adjusted a small stack of papers in front of him and cleared his throat. Mouse noticed tiny fractures forming in his usually confident demeanor. Something was different about him. The President wriggled uncomfortably in his chair, shifting his posture again before speaking.

"Good evening, America," he began, struggling to get the words out. "Over the past few months, we have seen an unpredictable rise in the spread of the virus. Our health-care workers have been doing an amazing job with the resources available to them, but the virus is proving too difficult to contain. Maintaining this crisis has been an incredible challenge and I believe that the country needs to head in a different direction. While none of this could have been prevented and I have done as good a job as possible, it is with a heavy heart that I am announcing my formal resignation as President of the United States."

Sam's mother gasped audibly and sprang up from the couch. She rushed to the garage and whispered loudly, attempting to not wake Sam, "Connor! You have to come in here. I think the President just resigned!"

Wiping his oil-soaked hands off with a towel, Sam's father came in from the garage. "About fucking time," he said angrily, as he stepped into the living room and leaned against the side of his green recliner.

"I am leaving the country in the very capable hands of my Vice President," the President explained, as he stood up from his desk chair. "Serving this country has been a privilege."

Everyone sat completely still in the living room, shocked at the gravity of the announcement. Mouse's phone buzzed furiously with news notifications and text messages from his friends. The Vice President stepped into camera view and, shaking hands with the President, took his seat in the Oval Office. He turned to address the camera, staring intensely into the living rooms of the American public.

"Thank you, Mr. President. Your service to this country is an inspiration," the Vice President declared. Sam's father rolled his eyes, as the Vice President began again, "I have assembled a National Health Council, composed of experts from the Centers for Disease Control, the National Institutes of Health, the World Health Organization, and the Food and Drug Administration. This Council will help us to establish strict guidelines and laws to keep us safe moving forward. Under the guidance of this Council, we will beat the virus! I promise you that. And now, I'd like to give Dr. Eleanor Star, of the National Institutes of Health and the head of this new Council, the opportunity to speak."

The camera quickly panned over one of the advisors standing behind the President's desk. Dr. Eleanor Star wore a gray suit beneath a white medical coat. Her medical-grade facemask covered most of her face, but her piercing green eyes were deep and intense. Staring into the camera, she concisely explained the chart that demonstrated the rising number of cases in the United States. Her explanation was clear and digestible and she spoke with a bold confidence and authority. Her tone, while serious and deliberate, put Mouse at ease.

"... According to the tracking data in your cellular devices, we can identify the weeks where the virus was spreading the slowest," she explained. "We know that the virus spreads by human to human contact, so the best thing that we can do is STAY HOME. Only go outside if you have to and when you do, wear your facemasks. This is not a negotiation. Anyone caught outside without a mask will be arrested. It only takes one infected person to get a whole grocery store sick. The actions of one carry the safety of us all."

With that, the Presidential Address came to a close. Mouse repeated her last words to himself, *"The actions of one carry the safety of us all."* They sat awkwardly in silence, soaking in the severity of the President's announcement. He had resigned. Just like that.

A flurry of celebrations erupted across the country, as if the President's resignation would single-handedly end the virus. Certainly, his administration had mishandled the spread of the virus at every turn and caused countless unnecessary deaths in the process, but the road back would be long and hard. It would require an unprecedented amount of sacrifice from the American public. It would require things that no one had imagined, as the potential for a second wave of the virus or a mutation loomed in a countless future of unknowns.

"I'm glad that the Vice President is listening to this National Health Council. That guy is an idiot," Sam's father stated boldly. "But Dr. Star seems like she knows what she is talking about. I like her."

Sam's mother nodded and rose from the couch. Mouse turned back to his laptop and recommitted himself to his studies, but chemistry was hardly a good distraction from the mess of politics that was going on. His phone continued to buzz, but he refused to pick it up. It was too much. He needed a distraction from all of it—from the virus, from the politics, from his own anxieties.

After another half hour of studying, he gave up and searched desperately for something else to occupy his time. Throwing his headphones in, he settled on watching an old cartoon that had recently been made available online. With all of the stores, bars, restaurants, and parks closed and everyone on lockdown at home, most of the popular old television shows had been released online for free.

Mouse lost himself in the show, as a cartoon dog ran rampantly around town getting into mischief and disrupting the monotony of the town's daily routine. It was a simple show, but simple was what he wanted. Simple was what he needed.

Eventually, Sam's mother excused herself to her bedroom and Mouse made his bed on the couch. He fluffed out a single sheet, blanket, and pillow that Sam's parents had provided for him. He reached into his backpack, grabbed his toothbrush and toothpaste, and wandered over to the kitchen sink. He tried hard to keep his mind off of the President's resignation, but it was no use. As he brushed his teeth, he replayed the Presidential Address over and over again in his head, wondering what other new initiatives the National Health Council would implement. The virus would undoubtedly shape the political history of the country, but no one could have predicted this.

When he finished brushing his teeth, he spit into the sink and washed his face. The cold water felt good, as he cupped his hands together and splashed water up onto his cheeks. Looking down, he washed his hands thoroughly and dried them off on a kitchen towel before heading back to his bed on the couch.

Mouse settled in and pulled the blanket up over his legs. The living room was cold, but not cold enough to warrant full blanket coverage. He hadn't been able to adjust to the temperature since he arrived. It probably had more to do with stress and worry than the actual temperature of the room but, as time passed, he was slowly growing more comfortable there. He cuddled into the cushions and buried his feet below a throw pillow on the far end of the couch.

Another episode of the cartoon played through and eased his mind. The sounds distracted him from the worries of the day and, closing his eyes, he drifted off to deep sleep.

After a few hours, as he felt a gentle tug at his shirt, Mouse stirred from his slumber. He rolled onto his side to see Sam hovering over him, wrapped in a blanket. Sam's frail bone structure and thin face looked ghoulish in the dim lighting of the living room.

"Sam?" Mouse whispered, checking his phone for the time. It was *3:00 AM.* "What are you doing awake? Are you okay?"

Sam nodded and pulled again at Mouse's shirt. "Come on," he said, his voice raw and raspy. "I want to go for a walk."

Mouse rubbed his eyes and sat up. Looking at Sam, he traced the outlines of his face in the darkness. Mouse hadn't realized how much weight Sam had lost over the past few weeks. He raised his hands and held Sam's face softly.

"Sam, come on," he whispered softly. "You've got to get back in bed. It's the middle of the night."

Sam pulled away from Mouse and let out a gentle cough into his elbow, fighting to keep quiet so as not to wake his parents. He leaned back against his father's green recliner and cleared his throat, painfully.

"Please," Sam begged. "I just want to go outside for a little bit."

Mouse sighed, hearing in Sam's tone that a trip outside was happening no matter what. Mouse squinted his tired eyes and pulled himself free from the embrace of the couch. Rising to his feet, Mouse grabbed his sweatshirt from the back of the couch and pulled it over his head. A ghastly chill had come over the living room and he knew that the outside air would be even colder.

Sam placed a hand on Mouse's shoulder and shifted his weight from the green recliner onto him. Mouse slid beneath his weight and helped Sam hobble over to the front door. Sam fought with each step to keep his balance, but he had grown weak and his knees began to shake. The virus was slowly eating away at him and he was wearing thin, both physically and emotionally.

Reaching out, Mouse unlocked and opened the front door. A rush of cold air hit them in the face, giving Mouse even more pause about going outside. Before he could speak up, Sam had already taken the first step out the door and onto the front step. Sam's bare feet charged out into the night, as Mouse turned around to look for a pair of shoes. As Mouse scanned the front entryway and living room for any pair of shoes, Sam left him behind in the doorway and started walking himself toward the end of the driveway.

A few moments prior, Sam could barely stand on his own, but the night sky suddenly carried him down the driveway with perfect grace and balance. The cold air was bitter and every breath brought a stinging pain to Sam's throat, but he didn't care. He pulled his blanket tighter around his shoulders, as he breathed in the night air. His lungs and the bottom of his feet ached because of the cold. As he reached the end of the driveway, he slowly lowered himself onto the pavement and sat down.

Mouse followed quickly behind, closing the front door as he pursued Sam. He scurried down to the end of the driveway and sat down next to Sam, wrapping his arm around him. They pulled each other close and sat together for a few minutes, before Mouse spoke up.

"What are we doing out here, Sam?" Mouse asked. "It's freezing out."

Sam tilted his head back and looked up at the sky. It had rained nearly every day since Mouse had arrived but, on this particular night, the sky was clear. The rain had subsided and the clouds disappeared, just long enough to lend them a clear view of the stars. Far enough outside of the city, the shimmering array lit up the night sky.

Pressing his hand on Mouse's chest, Sam laid them down together on the driveway and rested his head on Mouse's chest. They lost themselves in the beauty of the stars. The bright lights danced and flickered across the sky. Outside of their trip to Yosemite, Mouse had never seen a night like this. He had rarely even seen a shooting star. On that night, they cut across the sky in abundance.

Sam shifted on Mouse's chest, as he carefully scanned the horizon. "There it is," he whispered, smiling as he raised his finger and pointed across Mouse's body. "Gemini."

Mouse turned and spotted the constellation in the distance. The stellar arrangement shined brighter than any of the stars around it, as Sam traced it with his finger.

"What's the story again?" Mouse asked. "They get to be together forever?"

"Forever," Sam replied, smiling up at Mouse.

Mouse smiled back, as he ran his hands through Sam's hair. Sam felt the gentle rising and falling of Mouse's chest, as Mouse inhaled and exhaled. Sam was exactly where he wanted to be and there was nothing that could move him from the comforts of Mouse's embrace. No cough, no amount of cold. Not even death could take this moment away from them.

He looked up at Mouse and whispered, "I love you," for the first and last time.

Mouse brought his hand under Sam's chin and softly whispered back, "I love you too," and kissed Sam beneath the starlit sky.

It was one of the last nights that they would spend together. Sam died two days later. His inability to breathe had reached its climax during the early hours of the morning. They rushed him to the hospital, but it was too late. He was gone.

Mouse didn't cry at first. He watched as Sam's parents sobbed on the floor of the waiting room at the hospital, but he was numb. He stood there, under the bright lights of the sterile, hospital waiting room and felt empty. He felt utterly and completely helpless, in a sea of people fighting for beds at the hospital. The frantic sounds of the hospital all faded into the background, as Mouse watched Sam's father cradle his sobbing wife in his arms. The tragic grief of losing their child was too much.

He held Sam's parents up over the next two weeks, as they filled out paperwork, looked through Sam's things, and arranged for a funeral ceremony. Because of the new regulations put in place by the National Health Council, group gatherings were limited to ten people. In place of a traditional funeral, Sam's parents held a virtual ceremony where Sam's friends and family could offer stories and memories of Sam over video chat. Of all of their stories, Maisie's was the hardest to watch.

Maisie appeared on the screen wearing a black dress, disheveled, and sitting next to her mother in their living room. She recounted the first time that she met Sam at St. Agatha University. She was on her way to class, during their first week on campus as freshmen. She was lost and Sam had helped her locate the science building. As she began to describe the kind details of Sam's personality, she broke down and wept. Maisie tried hard to fight through her tears and continue her story, apologizing between breaths and desperately trying to finish, but her mother pulled her back from the camera and rocked her gently in her arms. Giving into grief, Maisie cried hard into her mother's shoulder and clutched tightly at the fabric of her dress.

There was no good way to say goodbye, but they made the most of what they had.

A few days after the funeral ceremony, Mouse packed his backpack slowly in the living room. At his feet, a stack of his clean laundry sat folded next to the couch. He smiled at Sam's mother's kindness. A hand-sewn facemask sat on top of the pile of clothes, next to a plastic bag with two freshly baked banana muffins.

Mouse tucked the clothing, muffins, and facemask neatly in his bag, next to his laptop and toiletries. As he pulled his backpack over his shoulders, he breathed in the smell of Sam's house one last time. He wasn't sure when he would return to Seattle, but he knew that he would be back someday. Over the past few years, and even more so now, this place had become a second home for him.

"Are you guys really sure about this?" Mouse asked, turning to face Sam's parents in the living room. "It's really too much."

Sam's mother wrapped her arms tightly around Mouse's shoulders. "He would have wanted you to have it," she assured him.

"Just change the oil like I showed you and pay attention to the engine light," Sam's father added, handing the keys to Sam's car over to Mouse.

Mouse turned the car keys over in his hand and rubbed his thumb along the plastic key fob. He walked out the front door with a mound of uncertainty. Sam's parents followed closely behind him. His pace halted on the front step, and he stared out at the white car in the driveway. The navy, St. Agatha University lanyard still draped over the rearview mirror. Everything about the car was familiar, but the best part of it was now gone.

"Please come visit us, Mouse," Sam's mother begged, as she held back her tears. "You're family."

Mouse nodded and hugged her again. Sam's father joined their hug and held them both in his wide embrace. "Thank you," he said softly, before pulling away.

He wasn't sure that he was ready to leave, but it was time. Mouse walked slowly around the car and gripped the door handle. He felt Sam's hand slide under his own and open the door with him, assuring him that it was okay to leave and that his parents would be fine.

As Mouse sat down in the driver seat, he felt the warmth of Sam's fingers wrap around his own and turn the key. Before driving away, he looked back at Sam's parents. They waved to him, with a deep sense of gratitude and love, and he drove off.

The multiday road trip back home would be long, but he felt comforted by the thought of Sam having recently completed the reverse trip. Mouse was retracing Sam's drive mile by mile, as if he and Sam were driving back to school together for another year at St. Agatha University. He would be a senior and Sam would be starting medical school.

Mouse gripped the steering wheel tightly and began to cry. He pulled over to the side of the road and let himself sob into the dashboard, beneath the scenic beauty of the mountains. The weight of the loss came crashing down on him and he finally collapsed. He couldn't keep it together any longer.

He allowed himself to cry on the roadside for what felt like hours, until gathering himself and pulling out onto the highway. As he reached the city limits, his cruising speed was brought to a sudden halt. The highway had been blocked by an ad hoc toll booth, made up of a barricade of police cruisers and propped-up chain-link fencing. Near the front of the barricade, a group of police officers in protective gear were gathered by a single small opening between the police cruisers. The opening was just wide enough for a single car to pass through.

Mouse pulled into a line of cars, all being halted by the barricade and leaned out the window to see what was going on up ahead. The array of orange brake lights lit up in the early morning fog, as they inched toward the front of the barricade. Mouse watched as a police officer and a man wearing a full hazmat suit approached each of the cars that pulled up to them. They were checking something, but Mouse couldn't make out what they were looking for. With a slight shiver and a curious uncertainty, Mouse readied his wallet in his lap.

As his turn arrived and he pulled up to the checkpoint, a police officer approached his car and gripped the heavy rifle resting across his chest. The officer adjusted his facemask and spoke, "Where are you heading today?"

"I'm driving to Maryland," Mouse explained, fighting the scratchiness in his throat. "Is there something going on?"

The officer looked suspiciously at Mouse and waved for a man in the hazmat suit to come over. "Maryland? That's a long way to travel," the officer stated, looking suspiciously at Mouse. "We're just checking people's health, especially folks traveling in and out of the city. Can I see your ID?"

Irritated, Mouse cleared his throat and replied, "I'm a Maryland resident." He handed his driver's license over to the Officer, as the man in the hazmat suit stepped up to the car window.

"Matthew Abrams?" the officer read aloud, turning over Mouse's Maryland driver's license in his hand. "Mr. Abrams, do you have any reason to believe that you've been exposed to the virus?"

Mouse straightened up in his chair, as the man in the hazmat suit unwrapped a single-use thermometer and began to sanitize it. Mouse turned sharply and looked up at the officer. "Yes," he stated. "I'm a survivor. I was discharged from the hospital over a month ago and cleared for travel by my doctors."

The officer leaned back nervously and handed Mouse's ID back to him from a distance. "I'm sorry for the inconvenience. This gentleman is going to take your temperature and you'll be good to go. Stay safe."

The man in the hazmat suit stepped up to the car window and

held out the thermometer. His gloved hands quivered, as he placed the thermometer under Mouse's tongue. The cold, sanitized thermometer was uncomfortable in his mouth. The taste of sanitizing liquid still lingered on the end of the device. After about a minute, the man in the hazmat suit removed the thermometer and stared at the temperature display.

Discarding it into the trash, he announced through his muffled face covering, "98.2. Vitals normal."

GLIMPSE

Emily took a deep breath, as she stared down the street at the pharmacy. After her morning at the park and her trip with Fae up the hillside, she had one more stop that she wanted to make before heading home. So much of the past few weeks had been defined by her guilt. However, as the pharmacy came into view, she hardly felt weighed down by the pressure of her Council hearing or the disappointment at home. She felt free.

As she approached the pharmacy, she spotted Doc Abrams standing curiously outside. He was leaning against the building, staring out longingly at the horizon. He must have been on a break, enjoying the Saturday afternoon sunshine.

She walked faster, excited to see her dear friend again. Of all the things that she had missed during her time at home, she had perhaps missed her conversations with Doc Abrams the most. A facet of her weekly trips to the pharmacy, she swelled with eager anticipation. She was sure that he had missed their conversations as well.

"Doc Abrams!" Emily shouted through her mask, jogging toward him excitedly.

He turned and adjusted his posture, leaning hard on a walking cane. Emily knew that he walked around the pharmacy with a slight limp, favoring one knee over the other, but she had never seen him use a cane. He smiled his sweet smile and, pulling his mask briefly away from his face, took a puff of his inhaler.

"Ah, Emily," he wheezed cheerfully. "I was wondering when I would be seeing you again."

"I'm very sorry." she replied, shamefully. "I've been at home. I was suspended from in-school for a curfew violation and my parents were pretty upset."

"A curfew violation?" Doc Abrams said, inquisitively. "Curious. The Council must think very highly of themselves if they're suspending students for curfew violations these days." He scoffed and leaned on his cane. "Would you like to sit, Emily?"

Emily nodded and followed behind, as Doc Abrams hobbled over to a nearby park bench. His slow pace required Emily's patience, but she didn't seem to mind. He finally arrived and sat down on the near end of the bench, without wiping it down. As he settled in, he took another puff of his inhaler and leaned back. Emily stepped around him and set a distance between them. Instinctively, she removed her sanitary wipes and began to cleanse the bench surface.

"I imagine you had a good reason for missing curfew," Doc Abrams probed, his statement taking the shape of a question.

Emily chuckled, as she sat down. "Honestly, no. It's quite silly. I wanted to watch the sunset over the mountains," she admitted. "Did you ever miss curfew when you were my age?"

The question hung in the air for a fair moment. Doc Abrams chuckled, as he sat forward on the bench. "We actually didn't have a curfew when I was growing up in Maryland," he explained. "But I wasn't a well-behaved youth, if that is your question. No, we used to stay out all night when I was in college, socializing, partying, looking at the stars. The curfew didn't come around until the first wave of the virus hit."

Doc Abrams sighed and a deep sorrow filled his eyes. His normally cheery disposition and sarcastic attitude began to fade and he stared out at the mountains, lost in a memory.

"If it's not too bold, Doc Abrams, why did everything change?" Emily asked, increasingly curious about life before the outbreak.

Doc Abrams smiled through his sad eyes. The memories of the virus clearly haunted him, but he was excited to be sharing his life with someone. Anyone really. Most of his pharmacy patrons came and went without a word and nearly all of Eden's youth were nervous around him. He welcomed Emily's curiosity with open arms, as the stories flowed out of him.

"No Emily, that's not too bold at all," he assured her, his sorrow turning to contemplation. "I think that things changed because people lost track of what was important. We didn't know how to keep each other safe and healthy, or maybe we didn't want to. By the time the executive orders and nationwide lockdown came, it was too late. So many people had already died ...."

Emily shivered in her seat. She couldn't even imagine living through something like that. She considered her family. Mom, Dad, and Ted. Everyone back then probably watched a friend or family member die from the virus.

"I'm sorry, Doc Abrams," Emily offered. "That must have been terrible; having to say goodbye to so many people."

Doc Abrams took a deep breath. "Thank you, Emily," he replied. "It certainly wasn't easy. You know, I've been alive for a long time and I always imagined that things would go back to normal, but they're just different now. It's a strange concept, isn't it? Normal?"

Emily nodded, listening carefully to Doc Abrams' wisdom. He spoke with a quiet and subtle confidence, as if he understood something that no one else did.

As they sat together, Emily soaked in the sunshine beaming down on them and Doc Abrams relaxed back into the park bench. He stretched out his arms and they stared out at the mountains together for an hour, in total silence. The snowcapped peaks of the mountains stared back at them, offering her a glimpse at a lifestyle lost to time and offering him a glimpse of a future yet realized.

Doc Abrams reached into his pocket and took a small metal coin in his hand. He began turning it between his fingers, revealing its worn sides and faded markings.

"You remind me of someone," Doc Abrams said, as he tucked the coin back into his pocket. "He was smart and curious, just like you. And, he loved the mountains."

Emily smiled, looking up at him with all of her appreciation and curiosity. She reached out and took his aged hand in her own and a soft smile came across his face.

"Thank you," she replied. "He sounds wonderful."